I0687532

SIX HEADS, ONE CROWN

Volume 3-The Pearl of Wisdom Saga

Jason Paul Rice

SIX HEADS, ONE CROWN
Volume 3-The Pearl of Wisdom Saga
Written by Jason Paul Rice

Published by Jason Paul Rice

Cover Art by Nikola Avramavic
Formatting by Polgarus Studio

1st Edition(2017)

Special Thank You: Nandita, Nik, Mom, Scarlett Harrell-Koettel, Tara Woods, Bob Morrison

For a view of the full color map go to: http://jasonpaulricebooks.com

Prologue

Mim walked through the castle after a ride with Paul. The fresh-faced teen had a figurative golden glow surrounding her face when she smiled, and it gave her an angelic quality. She always smiled when thinking about Paul. They were cousins, although Aunt Telly had always indicated to Mim that they weren't related. Her aunt had never fully explained why, and Mim always got nervous and couldn't broach the subject when the two ladies were alone. The two teenagers were paired together for almost everything that required a partner. They were a great looking couple and looked perfect together. Mim thought about Paul's jet-black hair, brushed to the side and tucked behind his ear. He was a sturdy young man, yet lightning quick with a sword. Mim recalled last year's tourney when Paul finished fifth at only fourteen. He had won the swordplay event, defeating his uncle in the final match. He had a big nose, a longstanding trait in the Burke menfolk, but Mim had never noticed it. She usually focused on his haunting dark eyes. Mim got to her room and her guard opened the door for her. She immediately noticed the window was open. She went over and stuck her head out but didn't see anything amiss. She used the hand crank to wind the rosace window shut again and wondered how someone had got past her guards.

Nothing looked to be out of place and she sat down at her desk to start a new section for the stories of the fall season. Mim opened the book and the title page looked very different. Finely detailed family crests now occupied the previously blank areas. Mim recognized the Burkes' black bear, the Colberts' golden bull. The Wamhoffs' red fox, the Etburns' silver eagle and many more in brilliant color. She stared at the illustrations and knew this had to be Glenn Rosewell's work. Mim flipped through some more heraldic drawings and stopped at a glittering gold dragon. She turned the page and a silver dragon met her eyes. The castle bells struck three and Mim knew she had to get to the theater to hear her aunt's stories. She wanted to stay and inspect all the new pictures, but she needed to get the details of the books to write them. She closed the book and rushed to the theater.

Telly said, "So it should seem that six had their sights on the ultimate prize, felicity in the kingdom be damned. Internecine discord appeared inevitable. These strong-willed men and women would never back down. Blackbirds usually fly away as the year starts to get cold so they won't starve, but in this particular season, there would be plenty for them to eat. Some crows became so fat they couldn't even fly anymore. Can you imagine that? They waddled from battleground to battleground to enjoy their fill and the unfortunate citizens became a steady feeding supply, no matter which king or queen they backed. Fall brought a chill to the realm but the ultimate heat will be felt my many. This story is filled with violent action so get ready for a wild adventure with unexpected twists and turns. These words are not for the faint of heart. Be glad you've grown up in the time that you have. My upbringing wasn't as nice and early that season I remember watching that awful duel. Elisa didn't think I saw the brutal event, but I did. However, this story starts in the Pearl Islands and from what I remember…"

To see all the maps for The Pearl of Wisdom Saga, please see:
jasonpaulricebooks.com

RICEROS

The newly assembled squad walked along a narrow path in a sparse forest. Riceros didn't know what to make of his travel partners. He had heard stories about Dragon-Eyes ever since he could understand words, but the man was incapacitated almost all the time. The Imp Wizard only whispered into Russell or Shireez's ear when he needed to provide directions. Russell carried the half-man in a sling on his back and the two girls always trailed behind him. Dioneer, the Cyclops, probably outweighed the other five combined and only Russell didn't look like a child's ragdoll next to the giant. The Pearl Islands remained sultry year round, but today Riceros felt continuous rippling waves of boiling hot, stale air coming at him. He remained unaffected by the heat but noticed everyone else dripping with sweat as early morning, the coolest part of the day, slowly slipped away.

The noble dragons had advised Riceros that he could trust this group. He had instantly connected with Russell and could see that his new friend seemed to carry a heavy burden as well. Fire Mountain began to rumble again, causing Riceros to jerk his head to the left. He couldn't see the mountain through the overlapping tree branches but could feel the intense heat radiating from the giant mound. Ominous, black clouds spewed out of the vent, darkening the sunny sky.

"Does anyone have coin for ship fare?" Riceros asked.

"We still have two gold rounds and some silvers, plenty to get to where we need to go," Russell answered.

The wind picked up but the thick air seemed to stick to his skin instead of just blowing by. As they neared the edge of the woods, Riceros spotted a bright orange substance streaming down the mountain. It looked like smooth pumpkin soup with large chunks of burning embers mixed in. Fire Mountain appeared to be on fire. Smoke billowed out of the top of the mountain and the confused winds blew the black clouds in every direction. The dark brown dirt of the mountain had started taking on a reddish hue and Riceros knew they had to act fast.

"It sounds like the Gods are banging two boulders together inside the mountain," observed Shireez.

"That doesn't sound welcoming," said Russell.

Dioneer and Lizeria walked in silence. They didn't say much unless someone asked either of them a question.

"How far is the port?" Riceros asked.

"Shouldn't be too far from here," said Shireez, who knew the land better than the others did.

The angry mountain quieted down enough that Riceros could hear Dragon-Eyes snoring. He sniffed the briny smell of the sea and could hear the crashing of the waves from a distance.

Riceros' biggest worry was getting Dioneer onto a boat that was sturdy enough to bear his massive body. A sudden boom almost knocked everyone to the ground and Riceros felt the earth shake beneath him. He steadied himself and looked up in disbelief as flowing liquid fire shot high into the sky. The air became denser and hotter. He could hear the muffled growl of pressure building inside the earth. The sounds went back and forth between a whisper and a shout. Riceros rubbed the sweat away from his eyes to look at another eruption of condensed flames leaping from the gorge and landing on the opposite side of the mountain. However, this explosion was followed by thick pockets of air that felt like the flaming breath of a dragon. Riceros could handle extreme heat but the others were getting purple blood burns on their arms. They stopped watching the spectacle and sprinted for the boats. Dioneer picked up the girls and the group tried to beat the fleeing citizens of the island as the docks came into view. Their mad dash lasted only a few minutes before they reached a mob of confused people, all with quick evacuation on their minds. The smallish Riceros got pushed and shoved around by the raucous crowd. He tried to stay as close to Dioneer as possible.

Riceros heard a loud bang and looked back to see Fire Mountain launching another huge burst of liquid flames upward. This payload landed on their side of the mountain and slowly glided down toward the port. Another blast of heat followed and Russell had to shield Dragon-Eyes completely from the rippling warmth.

Dioneer turned around to the group and said, "Follow me. Stay close."

The giant held the two girls tight and began to plow his way through the crowd. They went down a narrow pier and Dioneer knocked several people into the water as he forged ahead through the frenzied crowd. Russell and Riceros stayed right behind as the Cyclops neared the end. Dioneer placed the girls on the Red Kraken, a small merchant vessel, and held back the oncoming horde of desperate people to allow the men to get on.

The Cyclops jumped on and landed with a thud as the ship owner came over screaming. "You cannot stay on this boat. It's for my family, and only my family."

The giant picked the man up and tossed him into a smaller boat being undocked about ten feet away. "Does anyone else have a problem with me and my friends?" yelled Dioneer.

Everyone stared in fear at the one-eyed behemoth but nobody objected. The thirty-foot boat was overfilled and as it left the harbor, people leaped off the end of the docks to try to grab onto the side and hoist themselves over. About forty men flung themselves hopelessly at the port side and no one succeeded. Riceros watched the horrific beach scene as they sailed away.

The glowing orange ooze had almost made it all the way down the mountain and the citizens tried to swim out to sea after all the boats had left. Some used planks of wood for support and others paddled with all their strength. A fiery hell washed over the beach, silencing all the screaming people and rushing out into the pearly green waters to cause more destruction. The glowing orange substance turned black as it crashed into the oncoming waves and plowed right through the raging saltwater with burning intensity. The early morning looked like late night as thick, ebony smoke rose from the ocean and clouded the sun.

Riceros turned away and began to think practically. He took all his new friends below deck to check for supplies. The boat twisted back and forth as the twisting waves were pushed back out to sea by the rolling fire, creating uneasy conditions. They found enough food and drink for about twenty people to make it to Gama Traka. However, there were at least one hundred people above them on deck.

A loud crash of violent water rocked the hull and violently knocked the vessel sideways. Riceros and his group fell to the floor. The boat started listing on its side, threatening to sink as they made it to their feet and up on deck. Almost all the passengers had been thrown overboard and the group scrambled to save the ship. Dioneer fought his way to the highest part of the ship to steady it with his weight. Riceros and Russell teamed up to use the heavy wind to help them. They fixed some of the sails to catch the breeze just right and an eerie sound of creaking wood followed. The boys got to two more sails and after a few perilous minutes, the boat was upright again. Only twelve remained after the scare and a close inspection proved the vessel to be completely seaworthy. There wasn't any structural damage to the boat and their biggest problem had sorted itself out. They had plenty of food to get to Gama Traka.

The seafarers did have one severe issue now. The only man who had ever captained a boat was lost in the monster wave. They had a captain's apprentice who claimed he was sixteen, but the boy looked as young as Riceros.

The Red Kraken, with its yellow masts and sails, flowed along the rolling waves at a decent clip. The ship was aptly named as the outside was painted a deep crimson with the black outline of a mighty kraken on both sides. The sharp color of the ship mingled nicely with the aqua green ocean despite the ring of sea filth and water weeds pasted around the hull, although Riceros didn't like that the ship was so bright and visible, making it an easy target for the pirateers.

They sat down to a supper of salted beef, stale bread and a tart red wine. Riceros could barely eat because the waves had become increasingly larger as they moved farther out to sea and were making him sick.

"Who would have thought a mountain could spit a mix of fire and water?" Russell asked.

"I thought demons were going to come from the under the earth to fly out of the gorge and attack us," Riceros said.

"It becomes queerer by the day. I cannot imagine what lies ahead in Gama Traka," added Shireez.

The ship fought through the treacherous green waters but Riceros didn't put much faith in the boy captain to get them to their destination.

Dioneer recognized a familiar-looking island and redirected the route. Riceros noticed Heldoor from afar before an increasingly odorous stench filled his nostrils. When they reached the side of the island where the Bigwuns lived, scorched black earth stretched as far as the eye could see. The offensive smells multiplied as the ship dropped anchor and docked. Dioneer jumped from the boat and the others climbed down the side ladder to get to land. The ground was strewn with charred, petrified bodies that looked like black statues, frozen forever in time. Dioneer dropped to his knees and wept. The Bigwuns had finally been freed by Riceros only to be captured and cooked alive. There were only a dozen bodies and Riceros wondered what had happened to the rest of the giants. He patted his friend on the back of his neck, but Dioneer probably barely felt the soothing taps.

Half of the island had been burned by dragon fire. Riceros noticed several gigantic footprints as evidence that dragons had been there. He felt extreme sympathy for his friend. He understood what it was like to have your family ripped away. *Why would dragons come here and kill the Bigwuns? I know this wasn't the Noble Dragons.*

No one in the group could console Dioneer as they got back on the ship. They also made it a rule not to discuss the trip around any of the other passengers or captain. They battled rising waves again despite the fact that there hadn't been a storm in days. The skies had been clear and blustery on the Sea of Green. None of the weather patterns seemed to make sense as the boat tossed and turned through the waves.

Riceros and Russell went to get some food for dinner and encountered a troubling sight. When they opened the door, about two dozen rats scattered from around a pile of food. The damage was already done as the rats had eaten more than their weight in cheese, bread and dried meats. They set the upturned table back upright and put the food on it but the rations had taken a serious hit. Riceros didn't want to think about the hard decisions that might become necessary if the food started to run out.

He went back up on deck and stood near Dioneer. After being tossed from the last boat he had been on, Riceros stayed as close to the giant as possible. The Cyclops was still mourning the death of his brethren. Riceros maintained a gentle attitude toward his broken friend but knew that time would heal much better than words.

Riceros looked over his travel companions. They were a unique bunch. Ranging in size from dwarves to a giant, they had skin ranging from pale white to deep ebony. There were girls and guys but Riceros couldn't see this undersized, unorthodox force taking on an army of demons. He assumed they must be together to deliver an important message to the real warriors, not to actually fight in battle. As the trip continued, the horrendous conditions intensified with lightning storms accompanying the uneven waves, and Riceros began to worry about the young captain's ability even more.

EMILIA

"GET BELOW DECK," screamed Ali-Steven as he followed Pariah into the hatch.

A sideways mixture of rain and salty seawater plastered Emilia and soaked her clothes. The weary invaders thought they might be in the clear until another epic storm had rolled in again. Ali-Samuel cursed as he watched two ships carrying siege weapons sinking in the dark distance. Frequent flashes of webbed lightning illuminated the scene and showed three more of their vessels being swallowed by the angry sea. Emilia hadn't seen a cerulean sky for the past three days and couldn't tell if it was day or night. The ship had been blown greatly off course and she hadn't seen a land mass in days. Thunder cracked simultaneously with a rogue wave that smashed the port side of the ship, knocking Emilia and Ali-Samuel to the deck. The ship tilted suddenly, causing her to slide across the slick deck and crash into the hard wood of the starboard side. Pain ran up and down her left leg and panic shot through the rest of her body. She noticed an upright support beam protruding from the flat wooden wall and dug her nails in. She held on with every last shred of strength to avoid a tempestuous death. The ship slowly righted itself before steadily climbing another enormous wave. Emilia felt a great queasiness as they reached the top and quickly dropped into the next valley of water. A firm grip on her arm proved to be Ali-Samuel and he dragged the small woman over to the hatch. Even below deck, the boat bobbed back and forth, making Emilia feel even worse.

JASON PAUL RICE

Ali-Samuel went straight to their cabin as Emilia finally gathered her bearings, shook off the pain and went to see how the Histoman were doing. They had gathered in a hold where the people could sit and talk. However, the terrified passengers sat in silence, praying to Rolog every time the ship conquered another wave. Pariah, Princess, Cobra and about a dozen Histoman all looked terrified.

Emilia walked over to her friends.

"SO LAT PO DON TEL AH SPE HO," Cobra said in a dismissive tone.

"What did he say?" Emilia asked Pariah.

The young woman responded, "You…no, he didn't say at all."

Emilia could easily tell Pariah was lying and said, "I won't get offended. Tell me what he said."

"He say you are liar. You never tell Histoman this is happen," Pariah told her with a lowered head.

Emilia defended herself immediately, "You can tell him that I've never been in a storm at sea so this is a shock to me too. Furthermore, none of the Histoman are following me to Donegal. They are following Ali-Steven like a flock of sheep. I don't control the weather and if they should die, so do I."

Pariah translated the message and Cobra scolded her and moved to the other side of the room. The dirty looks from around the room told Emilia to tread lightly with dismissing Ali-Steven as a son of their God. An elder man named Stag Horn jumped up and ran over to the metal barrel of overflowing vomit. He lost the contents of his stomach just as the boat shifted and dumped the dross all over his lower body. The repulsive smells attracted the tiny flying creatures which needed to be constantly swatted away. She scanned the room again and saw the blame on their faces and the judging eyes of her supposed friends.

What has become of me? Only months ago I could snap my fingers and have anything I wanted. I used to live in the King's Castle and now I travel in filth with barbarians. I can't believe they blame me. They need to realize they serve a false idol. We need Cleon to see us back to the civilized side of the world so we can cleanse the sins of the Histoman properly. My Gods will lead them to safety and they won't even thank me, I'll bet. I cannot wait to convert these people to The Faith of Eternal Light when we win.

With everything swirling in her head, Emilia had forgotten they were almost out of food. They had brought enough for an unexpected delay, but the unpredictable Sea of Green had already forced them to nearly exhaust the emergency supplies. Emilia left the nasty room and couldn't understand why the Histoman didn't use the plush cabins. This was a luxury vessel and the finest one in the shrinking fleet. The Histoman wanted to be together but they had chosen the worst possible area in which to congregate. Many areas of the interior of the ship were decorated with gold and precious gems, and Emilia thought about the irony of the situation. They had the money to purchase more food than they could ever eat anywhere in the world. The only exception was being lost at sea.

She entered her room and unknowingly complained to Ali-Samuel about the Histoman.

He stayed calm and said, "Those ungrateful barbarians. You are taking them to a place where they can become civilized citizens. Our first decree shall be to outlaw heart eating. Look, we can use them to serve our purpose and then we won't even have to see them again."

"That isn't what I meant. I want them to like me. I like them and would never lead them into danger. They just need to be polished up a bit but they are like a second family to me," Emilia said.

"Make up your damn mind. One moment you hate them and I sympathize and then you suddenly love them again," Ali-Samuel replied.

"Well, it's somewhat like you and me. I love you with all my heart but sometimes I get mad at you. That doesn't mean I've stopped loving you. I am just upset with them right now," Emilia said.

Two days later, the thunderstorms ceased but they still couldn't find dry land. Emilia slowly savored the last bite of smoked pig's ear. Emilia had been experiencing terrible dreams involving both of her sons. In the night terrors, an eighteen-year-old Ali-Ster and a redheaded newborn were always in the middle of the woods. Snarling woods foxes moved in and ate Ali-Ster as Emilia was forced to watch with her eyelids being held open by Ali-Stanley. After the beasts finished with her older son, they moved on to the baby but she woke up before they attacked her younger boy every time. Emilia didn't know what to make of all this because she had been informed that Ali-Ster had died from an arrow attack. She only took the nightmares as a sign that she would soon be joining Ali-Ster in the heavens. She made peace with death and constructed a final plan. Before she succumbed to starvation, Emilia was going to plunge into the emerald waters and put her fate in her Gods' hands. She hadn't seen the Histoman in the past few days, preferring to stay positive. She didn't need Pariah to translate the hateful words coming from the Histoman to understand they still blamed her. A pounding sound startled her. Ali-Samuel leaned over and opened the door.

His father greeted them with a wide smile on his face. "We've found land," Ali-Steven exclaimed.

"Hot damn," screamed Ali-Samuel as he jumped out of bed, clapping his hands. They went up on deck and were greeted by a gorgeous sight. They had not only hit land but a booming port to boot.

At least we can land in a civilized kingdom.

As they got closer, Ali-Samuel said, "Interesting. We're landing in Elkridge."

"Bullswaggle," his father retorted. "Look at the flags. A black field with a gold sword."

"I do have eyes, father, and they work much better than yours. This is the standard of the bastard warrior I told you about. He is quite dangerous. Perchance we should reroute down to Lightview," Ali-Samuel suggested.

"No. We need to land here. We won't be welcome anywhere in Donegal but let's see if gold can erase some of those concerns. I would hate to have to use force," Ali-Steven said.

Emilia looked around at the incoming ships. Only a small fraction of the hundreds of boats that had left Histoman Bay floated into the Elkridge Harbor. The harbormaster permitted all the boats to dock in exchange for an exorbitant portage and cranage fee. Most of the passengers leaped from the vessels to kiss the dry earth and thank their respective God or Gods. The ships carrying gold and precious metals arrived along with a few other stragglers. The Wamhoff men found a watchman who agreed to talk to them for two pieces of silver.

The watchman, who was a thin man with scraggly black hair and a triangular, bristly patch under his lip, stuffed the coins into his belt pouch. He said, "From what I knows, The Man with the Golden Sword left 'bout yesterday or two days ago now. They says he's headed for either hell or the King's Castle. He got everyone callin' him King a Donegal, but The Man wears no crown. Far is I know, the only gold is on his sword. He left a few men to protect Elkridge, but not many. Sorry, but that's 'bout all I know 'bout it." The man slunk off with his hand covering the leather pouch of silver.

A few hours passed and the leaders decided that they needed to formulate a quick plan. The Histoman consoled each other over losing several thousand brethren to the seemingly starving Sea of Green. Emilia felt empathy but didn't believe she was in any way responsible for their tragic losses.

They apotheosize Ali-Steven and do anything he says. He told them to get on the ships, not me.

"Alright, let's take stock of the losses," Ali-Steven hollered at the men.

Most of the men hustled off to count the inventory as the Wamhoffs and their top advisors huddled up to devise a strategy.

They had lost all the siege weapons and horses. Several thousand Histoman now permanently rested at the bottom of the briny deep along with two ships carrying combat weapons and armor. After the ships were almost completely unloaded, Ali-Steven yelled for everyone to hurry up.

"What's the plan?" Emilia asked Ali-Samuel.

"We need to get completely unloaded and up that hill to Elkridge posthaste. If we should beat The Man with the Golden Sword to that stronghold, we could have them trapped between the Blue Caps and Elkridge. We know he will get word of our landing so we must act quickly. Gather your things."

He rushed off and Emilia went to collect her meager belongings. She only had a few dresses and her castle cards. She thought about the extravagant gowns she had worn in the King's Castle. Comparing them to these poorly made coverings again made her question her decision of going with Ali-Samuel as she plodded through the sand with only an armful of belongings and a fading memory of the life of luxury.

Her distant lover specialized in this type of warfare and his concentration would now be totally devoted to taking the crown. She assumed Pariah and Princess would be her closest companions until the fighting was over. After everyone collected their possessions, Ali-Samuel instructed the men to go down shore to the south. Two of the smaller boats were beached and the Histoman dragged them onto land and moved them up the hill. Some of the men shoved the massive structures up the steep hill while others pulled the ropes from above. Most of the Histoman carried heavy loads as well. The only men not to carry anything of substance were Ali-Samuel and his western cronies. They mostly lugged maps and documents even though they contained information about Lightview, not Waters Edge. They had to totally revise their strategy to get to the Capitol from here. Ali-Steven pushed everyone until evening, Emilia's first sundown back in Donegal. She felt good to be back home, so to speak, but she would now be viewed as a usurper with a pack of uncivilized barbarians. Ali-Samuel's poetic words that had made so much sense back in Histomanji now seemed so illogical. They weren't going to be looked at as saviors like Ali-Samuel had described. She was now an enemy of the kingdom; a traitor with treasonous intentions. Emilia also realized Elkridge was many miles and an uncountable number of deaths away from their ultimate destination. They began to set up camp and her paramour disappeared again. Emilia went and sat at a fire with Princess and Pariah.

ELISA

A sharp knock on the thick wooden door surprised the queen in her chambers. She quickly straightened her dress and hair before looking through the spy slot on the brass fortified cedar door. She opened the heavy lock on the door and Sir Anderley Ellsworth greeted her, holding something behind his back. This piqued Elisa's curiosity.

"I know you've told me several times about your missing sword from Burkeville so I came up with a gift for you," Anderley told her. The knight produced a petite-looking sword and said, "My first gift to you."

The queen asked, "First gift?"

"My second gift will be to provide you with an accomplished swordsman to practice with," he said with a smile.

Elisa stared at the stunning object. Anderley had the sword exquisitely crafted down to every last detail, just as she had explained to him. Her father had forced her to leave the original sword in Burkeville when she moved to the Capitol. Aston Burke hadn't even wanted her to have a sword in the first place; he said it wasn't ladylike.

Brehan had gifted the original to her and the sword had become one of her most treasured items. After her family evacuated Castle Burke, she had given up hope of ever seeing the sword again. *Here it is somehow, just the way I remember it.*

The silver blade gleamed as the sun's rays peeked through the window but the jewels encrusted on the hilt and pommel were what caught her eye.

Crushed clusters of beryl, jasper, ruby and obsidian jostled with each other for supreme brilliance and gave the destructive killing device a softer, feminine touch. The black leather grip felt soft and molded to her fingers as Elisa took the sword from Anderley. She stared at the nearly perfect replica. "It's light," she remarked.

"Yes, indeed. So you can keep your stamina in extended battle," he winked and continued, "I had the seamstresses work with the tailors to make you these ladylike breeches and soft leather overshirts that are much more suitable for fighting. I shall return shortly to take you to the practice yard."

The queen got dressed and Anderley returned as promised to lead her to the yard. Despite some strange looks and noble gasps, everyone bowed, curtsied or took a knee as the queen passed.

They faced off with several people gathering to watch. The taller Elisa impressed the crowd as she went on the offensive and showed solid technique. Anderley easily blocked her attempts and she would never win against a trained swordsman, but the queen did flash a few skillful maneuvers. Sir Anderley let her keep swinging away but her skinny arms quickly became tired. She thought about practicing with Brehan and took a wild overhand strike. Her blade collided with her practice partner's and she lost control of the sword. Anderley nearly suffered a heart attack as he watched his foolhardy queen try to catch the fluttering sword.

"NO," he screamed. The blade stuck in the ground and tragedy was averted.

"Perhaps we should call it a day," suggested Anderley.

"No. I promise I will hold onto my sword this time," she pleaded.

Never one to turn down a queen's request, the knight agreed. After a few minutes, more people had gathered and the queen's entire body felt worn out from the unaccustomed physical activity. She took a few more lazy swings, and with feeling running out in her arms, the sword slipped from her hands again. She didn't try to catch it this time but the rotating blade almost clipped the unprotected queen. She saw the look of fear on the knight's face and realized the practice session was over. Elisa knew if Anderley put her in a situation where she could get injured, his father would probably disown him.

Her muscles were already exhausted from the brief bout because she mostly sat around in meetings. Sir Anderley took her back to her tower apartments and the sweaty queen rested for a bit before calling for her hand maids to bathe the stink away.

A few hours later, the queen heard a heavy knock and checked the slot in the door to find the Grizzly Bear waiting outside. She opened the heavy steel barrier and her guard said, "The Lady Victoriah would like your audience."

"Yes, of course. I'll be right there," she responded and went back inside for a moment. She put on a gold bracelet studded with pearls and a beautiful choker of square onyx beads, each one decorated with silver leafing of a bear's face with tiny diamond eyes. It tied perfectly into the dark yet elegant look Queen Elisa and Lady Victoriah sported. She put three silver rings on each hand, slid on her thin black gloves and attached her matching veil. She grabbed her cape and had the Grizzly Bear secure it when she got back outside.

He followed the queen as usual and said, "So have you been over to see your little lover before I kill him?"

Elisa wanted to smack the smirk off the big man's face but answered calmly, "He's not my lover anymore, now that I am queen. I have a certain duty expected of me, unlike you who can do whatever you wish."

"Yeah, this is a great time for me. I get to follow around a girl who busts my stones all the while, I love it. Look, if you are worried about me saying anything, I won't, but you better go see him while you can. The only way you can save his life now is if you call off the fight," he said as they walked down the wide stone hallway.

"You seem pretty confident for someone who was scared originally. Or do you want the fight to be called off to save your own hide?" she posed.

They walked outside to get to the citadel and the sun's lustrous rays shone through her veil and blurred her vision. An early fall breeze caused her cape to stand at attention as they moved across the inner-bailey.

"I like to kill but this will be like fighting a half-man, hells, you're taller than the kid," the Grizzly Bear chuckled.

"Well, I've seen Brehan best men more than twice his height on many occasions so I am sure he isn't worried about your size," Elisa retorted.

"Here's one thing I do know, one of us will be dead in less than a week and sure as shit comes out of men after you kill them, it won't be me," the hirsute guard said and then quickly turned around. The queen stopped, looked back and heard the Grizzly Bear say, "Why you following us closer than our fucking shadows?"

A wiry man with a thin mustache, who looked like a knight said, "I'm not following you. Don't flatter yourself."

"I don't think you are following me. You're trying to get a sniff of the queen's arse. Well, it's not going to happen so make yourself scarce before I get angry," the Grizzly Bear said.

"Come now, Sir Bardo, I just want a few words with our queen. Do me a small courtesy today," the knight pleaded.

"Don't ever call me Sir Bardo again. You don't even see that I am doing you a giant courtesy by not bashing in your fucking skull until your eyes pop out in front of all these lovely ladies. Now go piss up a river," the Grizzly Bear said with spit flying out of his mouth.

"My queen," the man said and bowed before cursing under his breath at the Grizzly Bear as he left.

Elisa realized that even though she had put his life in danger, the Grizzly Bear still protected her from everyone. The skinny knight may not have been a major threat to Elisa but her protector had made certain nothing came of the suspicious behavior.

"I'm sorry I put your life at risk with the duel. I've tried to talk to Lady Victoriah about changing the decision, but she said Lord Ichibod would never do something that comes across as weak. It's not your fight," Elisa said.

"I get paid to protect you. Pretty damn well, too, so you won't find me bellyaching about a little fight. As your guard, I know your little lover would never hurt you but the way it stands, I have to kill him anyway. Only question is, will he even put a scratch on me?" the big man bragged, making Elisa angry.

"You may have been able to hector other men but as I've told you, Brehan will have none of that," she answered.

Elisa and the Grizzly Bear argued most of the time but she preferred that to the assiduous pandering of her followers. She couldn't wait to leave

Lightview and the favor seekers behind. Lady Victoriah had been correct in her warnings. Elisa came to notice that whenever she was nice to someone, within a week's time, they would ask her for help. In the process of trying to distance herself from the people she now considered leeches, Elisa Wamhoff was unknowingly becoming a colder woman. She had become extremely direct, seeming to absorb some of Victoriah's personality and completely shed the shyness of her younger days.

Later that day, Elisa rode a black-spotted palfrey as she followed Lord Ichibod. She now understood why Lady Victoriah had brought her riding pants to wear today. The queen was extremely unnerved wondering about the surprise Lord Ellsworth had promised back at the castle. She knew he would be upset that she had promised the Prograggers freedom without consulting him. Elisa only hoped he wasn't luring her to her death. The pair arrived at the mews. A large wooden structure housed the birds of prey owned by the lord. The long, rectangular building with a high slanted roof was painted black with golden apples in various places on the outside.

Elisa swung her leg over the saddle and jumped down from the stirrup before Ichibod could help her. She didn't want to look vulnerable and had a sinking feeling he was going to feed her to the raptors. She nervously followed him through the main opening. The words 'Ellsworth's Nest' were painted in white over the entrance. She walked into a vast open room with large perches on both sides of the interior. Ichibod signaled for the queen to follow as he walked around and pointed out the birds as he spoke, "Here we have our falcons. We have peregrine, black, rock and blue-eyed falcons. Over here are the hawks. Red-tailed, prince and silver-tipped hawks are the fastest and most easily trained. Then we have our eagles. The sea, black- and brown-beaked eagles. And last but certainly not to be forgotten, are the osprey. We train the osprey and the sea eagle to hunt for fish."

They walked around the entire room and Elisa was impressed and more at ease now as she noticed a look on Ichibod's face she had never seen before. The affectionate gaze he had for all his feathered friends as he described them told Elisa he loved the birds deeply. Elisa also noted the immaculate condition of the mews. She remembered sneaking into the mews in Burkeville with

Brehan during the throes of passion and they were disgustingly dirty.

Her father had kept a few falcons and hawks only because it was expected of a duke. In reality, Aston Burke hated falconry and only maintained the charade to satisfy his false reputation as a sportsman.

She had counted nearly fifty birds when a soft voice carried through the open room, "My lord, my queen, this is quite unexpected. It's my pleasure." The older man gave each of his superiors a respectful bow.

Ichibod spoke, "This is our Master of the Mews, Ollie Rolbacher."

"It's great to meet you, master," Elisa responded.

"Oh no, the honor is only mine, I must say. A queen doesn't visit us every day," he smiled.

It made her nervous again that the master hadn't known they were coming. Ollie Rolbacher walked with a distinct limp and hunched over slightly, looking at the birds with narrowed eyes. He had wild hair that looked like curled silver strings hanging down to his shoulders and the coarse black whiskers speckled on his chubby, wrinkled cheeks were a few days removed from a clean shave. The Master of the Mews was a highly coveted position. The head of all the falconers was entitled to lands and prestige equal to a court member because falconry was considered a regal sport. The Master had seven Lord Falconers who worked under him to train the birds and ready them for the hunts. He also supervised thirty apprentices and five cadgers. Ollie was responsible for finding new birds to add to the nest.

Elisa was excited because her father would never have let her go hawking. "We would like to take a few birds out, down to Red Stag Pond. I want to introduce our queen to the sport," Ichibod said.

"Of course, my lord. Are there any specific birds you would like?" Ollie asked.

"How about Spearhead and Goldeneye?" Ichibod asked. *He named the birds. He really does love these animals.*

"As you wish, my lord. I will cap them now and send them down to the pond. My queen. My lord," Ollie bowed and went to get the birds ready.

They waited outside until a skinny teenaged boy known as the cadger emerged from the mews carrying a mobile perch. A leather harness hung over his shoulders, supporting a square wooden perch around his midsection. The cadger waddled down the hill and Ollie pulled a handcart full of falconry supplies. She met two other Lord Falconers who joined them, their names already forgotten by Elisa. The sharp sunlight coming from behind the stringy clouds caused Elisa to squint to see the quarry at the bottom of the hill. Her veil had always blocked the harsh sun but she hadn't worn it today. She looked around while Ichibod pointed out some prospective prey for his pets.

Elisa innocuously asked, "So is it officially called falconing or hawking?"

"Now you've done it. We've had debates that raged for years over the proper name of the sport. To me it's falconing because the sport is falconry," Ichibod opined.

"Now, now, my lord. I must respectfully disagree. Those who created the sport called it hawking. The Wamhoffs only changed that name to falconry to feed their pomposity. They tried to ruin the sport because they had misnamed the Capitol Falconhurst," claimed the Master of the Mews.

A spirited logomachy raged on with even the young cadger getting involved until Ichibod ended the matter and forbade the conversation to continue. The High Lord reached into the cart of supplies and pulled out a black gauntlet. He handed the leather glove to Elisa and she slid it up to her right shoulder. He tied a cord around her upper arm to secure the gauntlet.

The Master put on the other protective glove and Ichibod went up to the cadger. He untied a falcon from a swivel and brought her over to Elisa. She immediately felt the weight and power of the bird on her forearm and Ichibod helped support her for a moment before letting go.

"Let's get Goldeneye under your thumb," said Ichibod. He tied both jesses around Elisa's protected thumb. "Here, pull down a little," the lord suggested. Elisa was amazed that a slight tug of her thumb could pull the bird closer. The huge female wore quite an extravagant blindfold. A hood made of kip leather, studded with mother-of-pearl and a huge silver plume on top caused the falcon to constantly bob her head around. The master removed the hood and the bird wiggled around, adjusting to the bright light.

The falcon opened her wings and Elisa saw the elegant animal up close. The bird looked to be wearing a black helmet that stopped at a silver breast.

The hooked beak, feet and talons matched the golden eyes but the overall layered pattern of black, white and slate blue-gray extended to the pointed tips of her wings. Goldeneye's underparts had blue-gray spotting and barring and Elisa saw how Ichibod could grow to love these birds. The master untied the jesses around her thumb and the majestic flyer took off into the blue sky with rapid wing beats. The ringing bells tied to her feet sounded soothing even though one of the wings almost slapped Elisa in the face as Goldeneye took off. The bird effortlessly rose to about one hundred feet and the queen marveled at how the animal had just been on her arm. They launched the sea eagle next and Elisa watched the two birds circle above as she shielded her eyes from the sun.

Lord Ichibod pulled her a few feet away and casually said, "I hear you granted freedom to people that don't belong to you."

"People shouldn't belong to anyone. Everyone should be free," Elisa argued.

"I couldn't agree more. So I suppose you will free the Prograggers before we go into battle, right? Or do you plan to make them fight and perhaps die so that you can achieve your personal goal of becoming queen? You *need* them to serve your purpose and you know it. It's quite convenient to have strong convictions before you are Queen of Donegal but you need to understand our realm first. Giving the Prograggers freedom will only fill your yearning heart with goodwill. No citizen of Donegal will see this as a noble action. Unleashing barbarians around the kingdom will not please anyone. Decisions often have a greater impact on those who appear to be uninvolved. While this decision directly involves about two thousand men, it may turn hundreds of thousands against you. Nobody wants to live in constant fear that the barbarian Prograggers will put their family to the spear," Ichibod countered.

"Our kingdom acts more like barbarians than I would bet these men ever have. They do as they are ordered because they are slaves," she said.

"Be that as it may, you can't constantly ruffle a bird's feathers. Concentrate on becoming queen first and then start making promises. Remember, we don't need a queen, only a king," Ichibod said with a wry smile.

Is he going to kill me? Was that a threat?

"Look, my queen," said Ollie, pointing up at Goldeneye. Elisa noticed the raptor making a high-speed dive toward a rabbit in the open grassy field. The speed of flight increased substantially as she closed in on the quarry. The rabbit sensed the predator and took off, changing directions unexpectedly. The bird deftly veered left and right, keeping up with the dodgy moves of the fast land animal. The falcon made a final stoop and sunk her talons into the defenseless rabbit's neck. The group hustled over to see the tri-colored bird mantling over the wiggling prey. Ichibod gave the bird a treat to coax her into releasing the prize. They praised and stroked the predator and tied Goldeneye back to the cadger.

"Look, look," said Ichibod. The sea eagle circled the pond before diving swiftly into the water. The bird disappeared for a moment before rising up with a fish in her mouth. Spearhead brought the trout over to the group to receive her treat. As they walked back to the mews, a great day had been blemished by a few words. Elisa kept trying to figure out what Ichibod had meant earlier when he said, 'we don't need a queen.'

A-BREHAN

He didn't know how many days he had been locked in the cage. He couldn't understand why Elisa hadn't come to see him yet. Brehan wanted to believe she was orchestrating his release but the second guessing tore at his heart and soul. *Why does the love of my life turn her back on me? If she no longer loves me, there's no need to even fight this duel. There's no reason to live with only half a heart.*

Brehan's thoughts consisted of darkness and a constant questioning of the situation. He was starting to go mad running through all the possible scenarios. He wondered if he should have stayed with Kopar and the pirateers. A perpetually flickering candle in a wall sconce provided just enough light to help fight away the rats. He kept hearing the guards telling each other that they were moving out in a few days. Brehan had been hearing short conversations among the guards but he couldn't put all the information together. Nobody talked directly to him. The guards referred to him as bear food. They protested against feeding someone who would be dead in a few days, but always followed the queen's orders. The guards told tales about the Grizzly Bear in an attempt to make Brehan uneasy. It was working. Brehan knew firsthand about the cruelty of the big ogre, and some of the stories were downright sickening.

He heard rumors of Elisa and Lord Ichibod being lovers, Darryg Ellsworth's homosexuality, Jon Colbert trying to usurp the crown and even details of plans to kill an unnamed guard. The dungeon guards assumed

Brehan was already dead so they did most of their whispering and plotting near his cell. It took Brehan a while to understand their vernacular, but now it stood as his only form of entertainment. A bright light appeared before Brehan, blinding him for a moment. By the time he refocused, a vision of loveliness captured his sight. Elisa Wamhoff stood in front of the latticed barrier with a lantern. She looked like an angel wearing black. All the anger and frustration he had felt for the past ten days seemed to melt away. He finally got a chance to speak with the woman he loved and had tried to forget. However, he was still bitter.

"So you finally came to see the prisoner?" Brehan asked.

"You don't understand. Things are so different from when I saw you last. Then, I was just a queen in name. Now, everything is expected of me and then some," she explained.

"Are you saying you no longer love me?" he wanted to know.

"Lower your voice. Lord Ichibod has someone constantly spying on me," Elisa said.

"Of course he does; why wouldn't he spy constantly on his lover?" Brehan told her.

"Lover? Ha, I am not his lover. I'm the farthest thing from that," she laughed.

Brehan retorted, "That's not what your guards seem to think, Queen Ice Heart."

Queen Ice Heart? I thought they called me Queen Black Ice. It matters not, I like both nicknames.

"The men around here talk more than women in a sewing circle, it seems. A position of authority comes intertwined with false rumors concerning every facet of your life. You can trust me. There is nobody," she explained.

"Except me, right? Say it. My first, my last, forever my..."

Elisa cut Brehan off, "Quiet. We said that back when we were careless children. So much has changed since then. I still have strong feelings for you but they have been modified to be more practical. Our stations in life will prevent us from pursuing a legal marriage." She sounded stern, almost cold even through the whispers.

"Love is never practical and last I heard, you are Queen Ice Heart. Kings and queens set the laws in this realm. You set the rules, my queen," Brehan pleaded.

"I can't just change laws that have been in place for hundreds of years without consent from the nobles. They will have my head. I want to but I can't, I just cannot do it. It's difficult to understand fully unless…"

Brehan cut her off, "Yeah, sure, it's too difficult for a stupid bastard like me to understand."

"I would never say or think that and you know it. I've been put in an unenviable position for all those who've never served as queen. All my time is spent in royal obligations. I wake before light and retire deep into the night. I barely get to see my sister who is starting to resent me and I couldn't even get you out of this death match," she said, fighting back tears.

"I don't even care about the fight anymore. Half of my heart just died," he told Elisa.

"No. I'm not ready to say that we can't be together," she looked around and whispered, "I'm only saying that you need to adjust your expectations of this fabled romance."

"Say it," Brehan sternly demanded.

"I cannot repeat our special saying. I've already told you that. I am being spied on by ears and eyes coming from everywhere. You will always be special to me. Is there anything you need for the fight? I want it to be as fair as possible," she said.

"How can it possibly be fair? I'm confined to this cage while my opponent is free to move about, drink and eat whatever he should hunger for. I'll barely be able to raise my sword for this fight. I'm like quarry for the peregrine falcon." The words felt like ice on her spine.

"Are you sure there's nothing I can do for you?" she asked.

"Other than retrieve my sword, some knives and daggers, I suppose I'll give you half your heart back. Wouldn't want that to die in the fight," he said.

Tears streamed down her face and she said, "This doesn't have to end. I don't think I have been completely clear in my words."

"Say it, just say it once," he demanded one last time.

Through the tears, she said, "Best of luck in the fight, good sir. May the Gods be with you." She stared into his jasper eyes that reminded her of the gems in her sword's pommel before turning and leaving.

Brehan cried uncontrollably for hours. The next day, the guards opened his cage and pushed in a cache of weapons and belts. He wouldn't have any armor but Dragon-Bite and the other knives and daggers would have to suffice. An hour later, several guards led Brehan to the fighting arena. His rigid movements started to regain coordination along the walk. Brehan could feel the anticipation of the buzzing audience. The guards made him wait outside the main entrance and he did his best to stretch out his weary body.

ELISA

"Did you give your little lover a kiss, one final kiss?" the Grizzly Bear guffawed.

"Keep laughing. I'd laugh too if I thought I was going to die and didn't want people to know I was scared. And he is no longer my lover. I am married to Ali-Varis Wamhoff, King of Donegal and First of his…"

Elisa was cut off by her main guard. "Save that proper talk for someone that gives a good damn. Are they going to let our wise and powerful King out for the day?" he teased.

"The King shall remain in his quarters today. Seeing you die might overexcite the poor old dear," Elisa fired back.

"Careful now, you're starting to spew icicles that start in that frozen heart of yours," the Grizzly Bear said.

"So you think I've grown cold too?" she asked.

"Aw hells, I like it. I can finally talk to someone who isn't scared shitless of me. I don't get that too often. And last of all, who cares what anyone else thinks. You're the fucking queen. Ruling will turn a person cold. You became the mother of thousands of helpless citizens in the blink of an eye. You may get a better understanding of your awful father soon," he told her.

"I will never be cruel like him," Elisa promised.

"Not yet my queen, not yet," said the Grizzly Bear.

She heard the crowd already going wild as they neared the fighting arena. They walked silently through the twenty-foot-wide entrance. She could feel the energy when they hit the hard dirt in the fighting pit. The soldiers filling the seats exploded when they saw their champion arrive. The circular, open-air arena had a huge fighting pit in the center surrounded by raised stone benches completely encompassing all angles of the combat area. There was a special stage near the main entrance on the ground floor to which the Grizzly Bear led the queen. The Ellsworths were already seated and Elisa took her spot between the lord and lady. About five hundred of her best swordsmen sat in this area. None of them knew that Elisa was rooting for the prisoner.

The Grizzly Bear put on his black bear head helm and pulled his enormous sword to the delight of the audience. He started to pander to his fellow warriors until a chorus of boos rained down. Brehan Castaway was being pushed through one of the small openings into the fighting pit. *This looks hardly fair. The Grizzly Bear is wearing chainmail and a battle helm while Brehan is as good as naked out there.*

She turned to Lord Ichibod, "Why does only one man get to wear protection? This is supposed to be chosen by the Gods."

"Only one man is accused of a crime. Those are the rules of trial by combat as put forth by the Gods. Your prisoner requested a trial by combat, do remember," smirked Ichibod.

As the two men faced each other, Brehan stared directly at the chest of his elephantine opponent. He looked like a boy next to the Grizzly Bear. Her enforcer's shimmering silver blade took to the sunlight much better than Brehan's greenish sword blade. Without realizing it, Elisa's fists were clenched tightly and her palms were sweating profusely. She kept nervously tucking her hands under her thighs. She couldn't believe that one of these men would be dead soon. The reality of the situation finally hit her. She fidgeted back and forth in the seat waiting for the fight to start.

With a blow of a bugle, the death match was underway. Each man sized the other up, patiently waiting to take the first swing. Brehan started to back away and Elisa thought neither man would ever do anything until the Grizzly Bear wound up and unleashed a deliberate strike. The knight from Mattingly easily blocked it and countered without success. The two men went back and forth, the green blade frequently colliding with the huge glinting steel of the

Grizzly Bear. Elisa could barely breathe as Brehan backed away and his opponent chased him halfway across the pit area. Elisa could see the Grizzly Bear panting like a dog and knew he was already getting tired. Suddenly Brehan went on the offensive with a vengeance. He tried a combination of attacks with spin moves but the big man easily fended them off as if he was swatting flies away from his beard. However, Brehan kept up the onslaught and seemed to overwhelm the gigantic man. Elisa felt that Brehan could be on the verge of victory because the Grizzly Bear dropped his sword hand down to his waist. Sir Anderley had taught her that was how men got killed in battle. He said they got tired and couldn't get their swords up in time to defend themselves.

Brehan wound back and came with a mighty overhand swing that was met plum by the blade of his enemy, causing an emerald spark to shoot off the point of impact. The two men awkwardly yanked their swords around until Elisa realized the two blades were stuck together. The combatants stared at each other until the Grizzly Bear lifted his leg and kicked Brehan in the chest. The knight of Mattingly tumbled backward, but quickly jumped up to his feet. The smaller man drew a dagger and flung it at the hairy beast. It harmlessly flew well wide of the target. Brehan heaved three more in desperation without any of them connecting. He had never practiced throwing knives and when the Grizzly Bear started laughing, the queen knew her former lover was in deep trouble. The Grizzly Bear mocked Brehan's knife throwing skills and threw the tangled swords away to the delight of the audience. Elisa realized without swords, the gargantuan Grizzly Bear had an even bigger advantage.

Brehan let out a mighty scream and rushed his opponent and tried to use his shoulder to plough into the big man's legs to tackle him. The Grizzly Bear didn't budge and held Brehan with one hand as he popped off his black-painted iron helm and smashed Brehan in the small of the back with it. The smaller man collapsed face down to the ground and before he could get up, the Grizzly Bear pounced on him. He dropped the helm and wrestled Brehan onto his back and punched him repeatedly in the mouth. A fountain of shattered teeth and blood spurted upward before landing back on Brehan's face. The crowd went wild, screaming for their champion to tear the criminal's heart out. As Elisa had expected, the biggest cheerleader was Lord Ichibod Ellsworth. She liked both men but she only loved one of them. Even though she might never be able to marry Brehan, their love was strong and would always outshine the tough conversations she had with the Grizzly Bear.

Her guard took his sword gloves off and raked down both of Brehan's cheeks with his razor-sharp fingernails. Brehan writhed and wiggled helplessly until a thunderous punch to the right eye caused his head to bounce off the firm soil, and his body went still. *He's dead. He's dead. I couldn't even tell him I loved him one last time. I couldn't even give him that satisfaction. I killed him. I should paint myself in his blood and wear it as shame for the rest of my days as punishment for this.*

Elisa hadn't even noticed that she had been bawling uncontrollably through most of the fight. The Grizzly Bear raised his arms in victory and exhilaration surged through the arena as guilt collected in the deadened soul of Elisa Burke Wamhoff. The queen didn't realize how strong her love for Brehan was until she saw him lying bloodied and helpless under the grip of the Grizzly Bear.

The gigantic man must not have been satisfied because he leaned down and bit off most of Brehan's nose. Elisa noticed Brehan's head and arms start to slowly move again. The Grizzly Bear held up Brehan's nose like a trophy and laughed along with the crowd. He threw the body part into his mouth, chewed it up, and ate the warm flesh as Brehan's blood ran from the side of his mouth. His fans loved this too and screamed for their champion to take the prisoner's life.

A lightning quick motion from Brehan's right hand struck in tandem with a wounded animal yelp from his opponent. The Grizzly Bear jumped up with blood squirting from his head. Brehan had jammed his final short-blade knife into his enemy's eye, all the way to the cross-guard. The big man fell down with a sharp screech of agony and rolled around uncontrollably, lightly touching the knife, unsure of whether to pull it out. His got back up and his left eyeball tried to look for the knife, but the big man only looked cross-eyed as he stumbled around aimlessly. Blood gushed from the wound and collected in his heavy beard before ultimately falling from the long matted whiskers and finding its way to the dirt.

Brehan staggered slowly to his feet with a mangled and completely crimson-covered face. He walked over and picked up his sword. It was still attached to his combatant's blade, creating a V at the top near the points of the blades. Gasps and shrieks from the crowd and Lord Ichibod were followed by shouts of warning to the Grizzly Bear, but the excruciating pain seemed to drown out the volume of the voices. The giant man went to his knees as he hopelessly clawed at the knife. Brehan approached the Grizzly Bear while trying to steady the heavy, uneven weapons. All the frantic screaming for their champion meant nothing as Brehan held both sword grips firmly and made a quick thrust forward with the connected blades. The Grizzly Bear's head hit the dirt before his body collapsed entirely.

The silent and stunned audience couldn't believe what they had just witnessed. Brehan picked up the head by the knife handle.

He held the head up high and screamed, "Here he is. The man you cheer for. Here he is." He spun around and heaved the head into the stands, warm blood streaks trailing like an angry red comet. The battered victor turned to the queen. Brehan dropped to one knee and said, "My queen, I swear my life and sword to protect you. From this day until my last…" The mutilated Brehan Castaway crumpled to the ground and the few counts in attendance slowly made their way over to help.

Elisa screamed at the younger Count Elroy, "Run. Go now. Go get poppy powder. Fast."

ALI-TERSEN

The King of Donegal had nodded off in the meeting again. Sir Oliver Wedgeword placed his perspiration-soaked hand on the King's shoulder and shook him awake. As Ali-Tersen Wamhoff woke up, his main henchman's touch transported him back to the night he had almost leaped from the Dragon's Keep. Sir Oliver had yanked Ali-Tersen back from the ledge and forcefully led him to safety inside the castle. He stared with bleary eyes at the rolled parchments at the other end of the table, hoping one piece of good news had arrived today. The Albino King couldn't stand to even glance at his main advisor after seeing him naked with his son, and his Falconer too avoided eye contact with Ali-Tersen and only spoke when spoken to by the King. To avoid possible discovery of the buggery, he had sent Neron back to Cloverfoot. He had recently realized that his son needed increased responsibilities and thought some time without his parents would be beneficial for the young man. At least that's what he had finally decided after ruminating over the matter for several sleepless nights. The only positive aspect of his life was that the supernatural visions of his bloody predecessor had dwindled over the past few days, but even so, the incessant problems of the realm always reared their heinous heads to haunt the King.

"If our scouts and spies are correct, Jon Colbert marches from the south. Lord Ichibod Ellsworth marches from the east. Warrior Queen Leimur of Goldenfield marches from the west and the bastard usurper from the north. We are not even equipped for a one-front war, let alone trained armies attacking from all directions," said the Falconer.

Two council members had already fled the Capitol in fear. The district of Falconhurst wasn't in a position to stave off a large offense, especially around the Capitol. From smallfolk to nobility, the population had started to thin out as citizens scattered to different compass points to seek the best chance at protection. Everyone took heed of the harbinger of war and knew what the inevitable dark outcome would be. The King's call-to-arms for all able-bodied men had backfired and served as a notification for the people to get as far from the King's Castle as their legs or horses would carry them. A scant number of knights and soldiers chose to risk their lives for the pariah known as King Ali-Tersen Wamhoff. The only members of society interested in fighting were untrained commoners looking to jump several stations in life by defending their King and Capitol.

Conversely, numerous new bands of dissident revolutionaries seemed to form daily. These newly formed groups carried standards hanging from wooden posts that still dripped sap from their recent construction, and staked the most ludicrous claims to the throne. Just the previous day, Ali-Tersen had heard a preposterous rumor about a man who had the audacity to claim he was born in the heavens and sent by the Gods to serve the people and rectify Donegal. The rebel factions didn't present any sort of threat in themselves, but when combined with the four major armies closing in, they served as an equally terrible forewarning. As with most ominous portents, ubiquitous death would soon follow.

He hadn't been winning his battle with insomnia, and kept dozing off while sitting up in well-cushioned chairs at meetings and in court. The King had come to blame his wife for manipulating his fragile emotions. Alvyra had devised all the insidious plans that he had to carry out to become king. Her past arguments had always made sense inside Ali-Tersen's fragile head. She kept reminding him over and over that they hadn't killed anyone, only his guards had, but those words rang empty now. The King of Donegal was drowning in a filthy gutter of compunction. His wife's rationalization of some great plan by the Gods wasn't making him feel any better and he only wore the daily crown when necessary.

"Concerning pecuniary matters, the banks of Arpeppi and Nowa Basha are threatening to crash our shores and violently plunder what they are owed," Derich Bonsfogger said.

"Let them try. They won't make it near the Capitol before they get all their due," Ali-Tersen replied with a coy, unnatural smile.

"We cannot name ourselves a legitimate kingdom if we allow our borders to be attacked. Marauders of all sorts will never stop until we are utterly destroyed," Derich remonstrated.

Ali-Tersen snapped, "It never stops, don't you see. *Nothing* ever stops. *Nothing.* Every blasted meeting is doom and gloom. Not even one singular upbeat item to discuss. *Everything...everything* is downright horrendous, so maybe it's time the rest of the realm gets a taste of misery. Most of them sound like rebellious traitors from the reports, ready to attack the Capitol as we speak. Let those men defend the kingdom they so desperately dream to usurp. Let their dreams turn to nightmares before their very eyes. If there are at least four large armies in every direction, let's coerce the banks to go through them to get to us. Finally, *yes,* this could almost work as a ring of protection until we get back on our feet. It may just buy us enough time to stem the tide of this rough river were drowning in."

"We can't knowingly destroy our own kingdom," Derich argued but with much less fervor than before.

Ali-Tersen shook his head. "You damned fool, listen already. Our kingdom already *is* destroyed thanks to you and those who *helped* rule before me. I'm quite positive all those who depleted the royal treasury have also stacked enough personal coin to reach the sky in the process," the King scolded, almost looking fierce with angry red eyes.

The meeting ended and the despondent King retreated to his royal quarters to find his wife knitting an autumn quilt.

"My King, is your head well again?" she asked.

"A bit better, but not entirely," he responded.

"Alright, my King, what are we to do?" his wife asked.

"Which problem are we speaking of?" he needed to know as he rubbed the bridge of his nose.

"Are we to stay and fight or leave for a while?" she pressed.

"I need to consult a few more lords to make a final decision, but everything looks like an early death if we stay. This isn't what being king is supposed to be. My family has abandoned me, proving they never loved me in the first place. My closest supporters...they have all fled the city. I'm haunted everyday by reminders of the past and new futile accords to deal with. Why would anyone desire to be king?" Ali-Tersen asked rhetorically.

Alvyra set down the quilt and began to massage the King's shoulders. They were soft to the touch, just like the rest of his plump but not obese figure. Exercise and physical feats had only tormented Tersen as a youth and his body represented a gluttonous castle dweller which didn't help his reputation with the citizens.

His consort whispered softly to him as her breath warmed and tickled the fabled drum of his ear, "Unknot your tense nerves, you will know what needs done. You do understand there have been many known instances when a king has been forced to abdicate his kingdom only to return even stronger and rule again. King Elagon of Teretault and King Ratadon of Murkette had to structure foreign armies to reclaim their royal rights. The Gods only test their strongest warriors, so it's no fool's riddle with a surprise at the end that they shall test you the most. You've had to fight for everything to get up to your rightful throne. Why should that differ greatly now?"

"I can't build a foreign army without gold. We have none. I have no military exploits to speak of. I don't exactly carry a great reputation as a king either," Ali-Tersen said.

"You have the birthright and you are the chosen heir to the throne of Donegal by the Gods and that is undeniably supported by all laws and rights," his wife reminded him.

"And that means nothing to a man from Teredez. Why would he fight for a land he has never seen?" the angered albino posed.

"My King and lord, you need to find the warriors who will fight for land and titles. You promise men tangible items and then fill the realm with those who were loyal to your cause, if need should make it so. You need to lie down and rest now. I had the goose feathers fluffed to provide my King with his maximum comforts. The Gods have scripted a plan for you, I've told you many times. There are moments in life when you need to surrender and trust that the Gods have a special destiny for you and they know what's best for us. I've already spoken to Sir Oliver and he will provide steadfast service in whatever decision we have to make. He should be considered a practical travel companion in this type of situation, I would like to think," Alvyra said.

Ali-Tersen blurted out, "I've failed you as a *Queen*, my *Queen*. You should be hosting balls, attending tourneys and traveling your realm and beyond. Instead, you have to endlessly torture yourself about the rotten dealings of a falling realm. My father and brother didn't give me a chance to be triumphant as king. All they did was borrow huge sums of money from new banks to make smaller payments to the banks they already owed. My father called it funny money and said it was part of the game of ruling a kingdom. He said it would never run out."

Alvyra cut him off by putting her finger over his chapped and cracking lips. "Your father was a fool. Your brother, also a fool. You did your best to eradicate their mistakes but you simply could not in only a month. By the way, you should never feel sorry for me. Being a queen by my King's side is enough for me. I knew ruling wouldn't be filled with only sniffing exotic flowers or sorting through gowns and jewels and dresses. Take some time to mark this decision, but understand we can always come back."

The King smelled the scent of another man's love stink clinging to the chilly air before it could escape through the open door of his balcony. *I know she cheats on me, but with whom?*

"How close is Neron to being back?" he asked.

"I believe he is about a week away. I told you not to send him back to Cloverfoot," Alvyra scolded her husband, showing true motherly concern for their only child.

"The boy needs to grow up at some point in time. If he is to rule after me, he needs to toughen up and marry the right bride for the advancement of the family. The same as I had to…" he stopped.

"Don't worry about offending me, my King. I know you were only performing your family obligation to marry a noble woman below your pure royal blood," she said.

"That wasn't how I felt about the matter. You know my family can be quite predatory to outsiders or even their own for that matter. If not for my loving mother, I wouldn't have even survived after birth. Now, if we do decide to leave, it will have to be sooner than a week. Had I known Lord Ellsworth, that pestilent eunuch, would be moving so fast, I wouldn't have sent Neron to Cloverfoot," the King explained.

Ali-Tersen's spies had spun a web of ears and eyes around the Capitol to monitor the actions of his son constantly, and found out that Neron had numerous sexual partners. He was surprised to discover how many nobles, knights, castle workers and even hucksters took part in the illegal amorous activities that were punishable by death in Donegal. The widely detested King couldn't chance rumors of a badling Prince circulating throughout the kingdom. He couldn't handle that being thrown on top of the vast compost pile of problems that mounted higher every day. Ali-Tersen also planned to have all the offenders rounded up and beheaded so Neron wouldn't be tempted to return to this perverse behavior when he came back to the Capitol.

I wish Sir Oliver had let me jump from the Dragon's Keep. There can't be this many problems in the heavens.

He understood why his father and brother had resorted to their tactics under the immense pressure and scrutiny of being king. Ali-Tersen's main problem was he couldn't use any of the former kings' monetary schemes anymore.

If I leave, whoever takes this throne is in for quite a shock. They might leave before even sitting down. I wish I had never done it. What is it all for?

"Isn't it so?" Alvyra asked.

"What?" he hadn't been paying attention.

"I asked if you have given thought about where we can go to escape this mess," she clarified.

"No, I don't think any house will welcome an expelled king and take that risk," he replied.

"I'll talk to Sir Oliver and find out if he knows a way to escape the kingdom. If we do exercise this measure, it will only be but a sentence in the royal account of King Ali-Tersen Wamhoff, the greatest king to ever rule,"

Alvyra said encouragingly. Recently, her words had seemingly changed from silk to sandpaper and did little to soothe Ali-Tersen these days.

Sure, I'll be the greatest king to never rule. You need coin and soldiers to rule and I have neither.

"Was there a man in here?" the King finally snapped, pointing a bony finger in his wife's face. For a husky man, the King's long, slender fingers were out of place.

"No, don't be foolish. Sir Oliver stepped in to escort me to the flower gardens so I could see them before fall sets in and they disappear. My King needs to rest. I shall go to Lady Renbart's quarters and leave you with your thoughts, my King," she curtsied and left the room.

Ali-Tersen went out on the balcony just before the dark of night swallowed up the last bits of a sunny day. The pumpkin sky and pallid clouds seemed to melt into the horizon as stars began to appear out of nowhere like giant lightning bugs. A stiff breeze prompted the King to close the top two buttons of his vermillion overcoat. He rubbed the stitched argent fox over his left breast and decided to go down to the bight on the Royal River. The sound of cascading water always had a calming effect on the King. He turned away a dozen guards' offers of protection on his way toward the river.

For a few moments the water did have a positive impact and his problems began to slip away. In the gathering gloom, his eyes focused on a ripple. He couldn't figure out what was causing it to resist the powerful current. The tide should have easily disrupted this anomaly. The circular ripple entranced the King who couldn't tear his eyes away from the mesmerizing swirling.

The whirlpool became illuminated by the emerging moon and changed color from aquamarine to burnt black to deep mulberry until settling on a bright crimson. The rest of the river remained its normal color which made the King wonder if he was suffering from insanity. Then, a perfectly round, translucent red bubble sprouted from the water with an unidentifiable object in the center. The blood-like bubble popped and the hidden item proved to be a levitating skull, hovering a foot above the water. The moon seemed to magically siphon some bright sun light and temporarily turned night back to day. As the floating deadhead reached the riverbank, the King's bowels threatened evacuation and a sick feeling attacked his midsection. He clenched his buttocks and watched entangled human bones washing ashore and settling near the skull. Seven arrows shot down from the sky and penetrated the moist soil, surrounding the mess of moving human remains. The dull white bones began to do the dance of the dead and assemble themselves into a complete upright skeleton. Flesh began to appear over his toes. The transformation started at the feet and slowly flowed upward like a liquid, instantly solidifying to create a male body and reveal a face. The naked Ali-Ster Wamhoff became magically covered in an aketon and woolen breeches. After that, the red and white patterned armor with gold inlay he had worn in the mini-tourney attached itself to his body. The scintillating colors had diminished and the suit showed a good bit of wear. Ali-Tersen saw the judging eyes of his nephew through the dented battle helm shaped like a fox's head.

"Don't worry, uncle, I haven't come to kill you, or perhaps I will? I haven't yet decided," Ali-Ster chuckled. The former king's voice sounded guttural, like a wire brush slowly scraping against the stone castle walls. It sent a chill up and down every one of Ali-Tersen's bones. However, his nephew physically looked exactly the same as in life. He even retained the healed scars of his death injuries.

"Let's you and me…let's take a little walk," Ali-Ster said. As he passed the King, he slapped Ali-Tersen on the back of the head with tremendous power. The ghost had never so much as grazed him with a finger before and the King became so petrified, a yellow stain began to spread down his thighs and soak his bright white breeches. He hurried to keep up with the determined pace set by his nephew. The brilliant moon returned to normalcy and disappeared behind a streaming cloud as Ali-Tersen fell. He popped up quickly as Ali-Ster led the reigning King to the west wall of the castle near the kitchens. The former king began ramming his shoulder into the thick stone wall of the castle. After a half-dozen plough-like thrusts, the wall started to crumble and after twelve tries, a huge mouth opened up. Ali-Tersen stood in awe of the feat of incredible strength.

Ali-Ster shoved the King in and followed. They stood in the unused storage room of the kitchens and his nephew opened the secret door to go downstairs, way downstairs. He kept Ali-Tersen in front as they descended in total darkness to the Alley of the Heavens. Ali-Ster cracked the creaky door and the formidable stench of decay knocked the King back. He now wanted to stay close to his undead nephew until Ali-Ster's perfectly still elbow sprang back into his uncle's chin. The King fell on his back and felt dazed. He checked his teeth and all were still intact, although his entire mouth rippled with pain and he tasted salty blood. The swirling, sparkling diamonds disappeared from his vision after several moments and he noticed Ali-Ster approaching the altar of Ali-Dus Wamhoff.

Ali-Ster spoke as he looked up at the ceiling, "Great Gods in our heavens, after only a brief stint you've deemed that I must return to earth to assist in one last battle. I humbly accepted and now I shall execute the will of the Gods."

He put his hand on the dead king's head with his fingers touching the crown. Ali-Ster said, "Dear Gods, please send us the soul of this great warrior to fight in the ultimate battle. I humbly ask for the return of Ali-Dus Wamhoff to earth." His hand was blown back from the body as Ali-Dus moved around on the stone slab, stood up and, like Ali-Ster, skin materialized around his body. Smallclothes formed over the nude body. Next came a coat of boiled leather and finally a heavy hauberk of interlinked red ring mail covered the tall, thick body of Ali-Dus. Ali-Tersen heard the troubling rattle of stubborn iron as the First King of Donegal moved around the room, inspecting the chamber. One last transformation took the old man from his mid-sixties to early twenties. Long gray hair returned to the bright red close-cropped cut that the former king had favored during his early reign. He looked like a serious man, not to be questioned, with thick eyebrows, a blunt chin and menacing blue eyes.

Ali-Ster strode over to the memorial for Ali-Sander Wamhoff. He placed his hand on both the crown and head of the former king. "Dear Gods, please spare the soul of this great warrior to fight in the ultimate battle. I beg for Ali-Sander Wamhoff to return to earth," Ali-Ster cried to the ceiling. His hand was blown back by an immense, invisible force again and the dead king stood up. His body slowly formed from bottom to top and glorified all the features of the former king before death. A full-suit of white-colored plate armor with rouge foxes addorsed on the chest shaped itself around his short stout body. Ali-Sander had died close to fifty years of age, but his body reverted back to his days as a late teen.

Ali-Sander's bones and armor cracked as he stretched, and asked, "Are we here to restore the Wamhoff name?"

"In a certain vein, yes we are. It appears that my brother needs us. We have been sent by the Gods to protect every man, woman and child on earth. Every person's lives will depend on us. We will first stalk the earth to uncover all the other preserved Warrior Kings whom we can bring back from the heavens. We will assemble the Noble Army of Undead Kings. We will first stop at the Androsi Isles to see if any of our ancestors might want to join us," Ali-Ster answered. The curled-up King of Donegal noticed none of the former kings wore their crowns, humbly relinquishing them for battle helms.

Ali-Tersen cowered as the Undead Kings started to leave. Ali-Sander stopped and looked down at the pathetic-looking excuse for a King, "Can we kill this one for ruining our family name?"

Ali-Ster swiftly returned, "*No*, we aren't here to take part in the internal or external warring of any kingdom, even our own." He turned his attention to Ali-Tersen, "You should vacate the Capitol right now if you are preferential to keeping that pasty skin attached to your bones. Luckily for you, we haven't been sent to kill humans, we've been sent to kill demons." Ali-Ster Wamhoff kicked the Albino King as he walked by.

Damian Doome

Pandemonium broke loose on Venom Island. Damian Doome had just recited a rousing, rallying diatribe against the humans to the demon warriors. He had received word from Travibero to launch the attacks. Nervous excitement rushed through the leader of the demons. The majority of the army would set sail on the morrow. The higher-ranking demons would fly on dragons when the ships got close to the Gama Traka border.

"Great speech," Ephesi said, patting Damian on the shoulder.

"Thank you. I have something else planned to keep our black blood stirring," Damian stated. Ephesi still seemed off, so Damian decided not to send him on any skin-changing adventures anymore. The ill effects appeared to have caused irreparable damage to his friend. Ephesi's memory had suffered the most damage. His closest ally couldn't remember recent occurrences and Damian felt responsible for sending him on the missions. The mustard-colored demon walked away and Damian looked out at the crashing waves.

He had secured all the animals and cross breeds to the southeast but now started having thoughts about moving them farther inland as the waves poured in closer to the living quarters cave. The snarling beasts were ready for action, but a long boat ride loomed ahead. The soldiers, siege weapons, animals and smaller arms would travel across the Sea of Green to Gama Traka. The demons hated open water and Damian wasn't sure how the animals would react to the sea, so he designed boats with a lowered deck and high sidewalls to pen them in. He even had his men craft special ships to carry the enslaved one-eyed giants he had captured from Heldoor.

This would be a much different attempt than his last. His army was bigger and better trained but he knew little of the prowess of his opponent. He couldn't be sure if every man on earth would band together to stop his demons. He walked with a reserved air of confidence. The opportunity to become a Plade after death had increased the pressure on Damian. He didn't want to spend eternity trying to explain an epic loss to his fellow deities. His legacy was on the line.

Damian found Ephesi and took his friend down to the dragon chamber. They walked into the fiery pit and stood in the center of the room. Two rows of chained-up dragons lined both sides of the enormous room.

Damian spoke in the old underground tongue. "The time to attack is upon us. We will launch a preliminary strike tonight to let the world wonder which direction we are coming from. My friends, you can set fire to anything you should desire. Find the biggest castles on the highest mountains. The centers of towns or cities. Places full of happy humans. Men, women, children. There are no restrictions. Kill them all the same," Damian told them.

The chains started to rattle as the malevolent beasts became excited. "Eat what you want. Pillage what you must. Cause as much destruction in every direction as demonly possible," Damian instructed.

He walked around the room, releasing the bonds of his fire-breathing friends. He instructed each dragon about the extent of the area he or she was responsible for wreaking havoc on. He finished unchaining the beasts and led them up through the large crevasse before they went skyward. The dragons fired out celebratory flames as they departed and Damian could hear more excitement among the soldiers. He walked around the hill and back over to his demons with Ephesi.

The pressure started to build inside him again but he remained strong as the leader. He made his rounds, spouting his usual propaganda against the evil humans. The basic message was that the humans had stolen the earth and were solely responsible for the demons' cramped life. It always had a great effect on the men, getting them even more ramped up than they were before.

Damian needed the men to maintain this energy level for an extended period of time but it didn't look like it would be a problem. The warriors seemed more excited than the men had been five hundred years ago.

Damian heard a creaking sound and turned around to see the pens containing humans being wheeled out of the cave. Each pen had four humans crammed into the tiny structures.

Damian orated over the rowdy bunch as he pointed at the naked humans, "This is our enemy. Nothing is sweeter than eating the flesh and drinking the blood of the enemy. These humans have caused hard times for us. It's time to get a taste for human blood before we depart."

As soon as Damian finished, the men started hollering again and one cage was opened. The demons poked the emaciated bodies with a stick to push them out of the cage, where the humans were instantly engulfed by demons that proceeded to rip them apart. The humans begged for mercy but their visceral cries fell on deaf ears. The soldiers passed pieces of the bodies around for everyone to get a taste. They opened the seventh and final cage and Damian helped remove a man's head from the rest of his body. He drank the blood from the messy neck and passed it to Ephesi. Damian became troubled to see the hesitation in his fellow demon and was shocked to see Ephesi gag on the blood and have to spit it out. The yellow demon passed the head to the next man but Damian was alarmed.

After they sucked out all the ceremonial blood, the demons used their strong teeth to chomp through the skull and bones. The only thing they couldn't chew was the teeth of the humans. The demons savored the flavor and left to take a short rest before the sun came up.

Damian went to his small room and looked over the maps of the Sea of Green between Venom Island and Gama Traka. He needed to use the dragons to fly out and survey the sea to make sure everything was safe for departure. He planned to use his dragons to fly over his fleet and ensure the safety of the demons. Damian wanted to time it perfectly so both units crashed the shores simultaneously. He also had the water dragons to worry about. Without sea dragons of his own, he didn't know what to expect.

The next day, on his way out of the mountain, Damian heard the mighty flapping of his returning dragons. Every dragon returned unscathed and told stories of causing massive destruction. *The warning shot has been fired. Now it's a fair fight. Hopefully, they will pull all the warriors from that school to save everyone from future dragon attacks. The earth will soon be ours.*

Damian sent the dragons back out to find out if they should set sail. The dragons returned a few hours later and reported that the waters were rough, but nothing out of the ordinary. He walked toward the shoreline and before too long, he stood on the southern coast of Venom Island. Most days were dark and gloomy on Venom Island but the sea was angrier than normal today. Huge waves bounced the metal boats up and down wildly. He watched the entire fleet embark and hoped for the best. Land and the underground were always the comforts of the demons.

JON

Jon Colbert's contingent rumbled toward the Capitol, shaking the earth in the process. Jon rode with Ruxin and the men from Bottomfoot. They kept the horses at a quick trot. Jon had promised Camelle he would keep himself and the family out of direct danger. About five thousand men traveled ahead of Jon and countless thousands more followed behind. Ruxin kept trying to nudge Jon farther toward the front. They were already well into enemy territory and hadn't hit a bit of resistance yet. The Fox Chapel residents they had passed were all on their knees, begging for their lives to be spared. White flags of surrender had been planted in front of most houses and several had crude drawings of a bull on them.

Jon Colbert was many things; a husband, father, warrior, Duke, brother and conqueror. He had killed men and given the command to kill but luckily for the citizens of Fox Chapel, Jon wasn't a human butcher. He didn't kill for the fun of it. Every man's life he had taken was because of the oath he took as Duke. He always erred on the side of mercy but knew that laws needed to be enforced or there was no reason for them.

The Duke didn't expect much resistance but he was always on guard after the last ambush. As they got relatively close to the Capitol, Jon recognized the familiar area of the Royal Road. He was surprised it wasn't still drenched in blood. Gone were the lively colors. Vapid brown leaves crackled under the horses' hooves and even the rolling pastures of green grass looked faded. Some rusty foliage still clung to most branches above despite the swirling fall breeze.

The only thing that Jon could still see shining was the burning treachery he had encountered on this part of the road. He could still visualize the scene in his head, but he tried to push the thoughts aside and look forward.

The stiff wind ruffled Jon's snowy goatee protruding from the bottom of his golden bull battle helm. Slow rolling clouds tinted the shine on his knights' plate armor as they bounced up and down in their saddles, majestically charging their way to the King's Castle.

The rest of the family traveled near the back of the pack. Jon had some of the best swords available guarding his family. They rode about three quarters of the way to the back of the group with most of the wagons and coaches. Jon had appointed a small army to make sure no harm came to his loved ones.

His numbers had grown unabated since invading Fox Chapel. Citizens proudly rushed to the usurper's side and marched along with the infantry. As he got closer to the castle, Jon became extremely worried about an ambush. Even one small uprising on the way would have made Jon feel a little more at ease.

He started to fear a major sneak attack. *Where's the chicanery? He knows he cannot beat my forces head on.*

He pictured his entire family huddled in the dungeons, trying to kill rats to eat. His mind then flashed to the suckling pig he had seen at the market place. Suddenly, the babe was yanked away from the teat. Then, a vision of Camelle breast feeding Baby Jon had the same pair of hands yank the child from his wife's nourishment. Jon's chest stared to tighten and he became short of breath. His clammy hands gripped the horse's reins tight as extreme dizziness threatened to toss him from the animal. Jon closed his eyes and tried to make the feelings dissipate. Panic continued to attack his body for another minute and then simply disappeared. Other than a full-fledged sweat, Jon seemed perfectly normal again. He didn't have a clue as to what had just happened, but he knew they were getting extremely close to the castle.

"You best slow up if you want my help, nephew." Jon recognized the voice and turned around to see his hypercritical uncle Hambone.

Jon asked, "And what brings you up here?"

"Now I know you prolly won't need me fer nuthin', but this is the smart way to go see the Wamhoffs." Hambone pointed around at all the surrounding soldiers and continued, "I gotta warn you now, as old as I am, I prolly aint worth nuthin' with a sword no more."

Jon noticed he didn't even carry a knife in his waistline like almost every other man in Donegal. His uncle said, "But if battle breaks out, I'll fight til I die, like I did with your daddy."

Jon bowed his head a bit and responded, "That is the greatest honor you can give me, good uncle."

The sun escaped the shade of a streaming cloud and Jon heard a ruckus up ahead. *Finally, the King is going to stand up for himself. If he fights with honor, I will grant him an honorable death.*

Jon had the urge to forge ahead to assess the situation but he practiced restraint. If it was a real threat, Jon knew someone would have sounded the horns. The prospective king did realize that it would be foolish to serve in the vanguard. He remembered when he had rushed into action like the cavalry members streaking by. Jon looked over to talk to Ruxin but the young man was gone. Straight ahead, Jon saw the fluttering surcoat of Ruxin, speeding toward the front. *What am I to do with my overzealous son? How would I explain this to Camelle if something happened to him?*

Anger ate at the Duke of Mattingly. He had repeatedly warned Ruxin not to go ahead. *He has a child of his own to think about now. The boy is brave, I'll give him that, but he must use better judgement. He is a true Colbert, but I need to put a stop to this before he kills himself. I have to teach him the difference between smart-brave and dead-brave because it tends to be a fine line.* Jon began to calm down until the noise ahead grew louder and he began to worry about his overenthusiastic son. Jon was stopped by three guards that said they needed to talk to him.

A-TERSEN

"We cannot wait any longer," pleaded King Ali-Tersen.

Sir Oliver ignored him and looked at Queen Alvyra. The royal couple sat on a small bench behind one horse with a small, linen covered wagon hooked to the wooden seat. The Albino King could hear the enemy closing in and had started sweating profusely on the brisk autumn day. He loved his son, Neron, but above all else, Ali-Tersen loved himself and was terrified to have to answer for his sins after death. His spies had told him that Jon Colbert was less than an hour away. He wanted to leave but his wife wouldn't acquiesce.

How did all this happen? I was King. This is rooted in the time Alvyra convinced me to kill my father. It all culminated when she convinced me to kill Ali-Ster and take the throne. Why didn't I say no? How could I let a woman tell me what to do?

King Ali-Tersen's final days of rule had consisted of blaming everyone including himself. He stared at the castle's north facade as the disturbing noises got louder. He pulled the black hood over his chalky eyebrows to deflect the sun's dancing rays. The King wore a modest woolen cloak, rough spun and night sky in color, scraping the ground. The tunic and breeches underneath protected his ghostly skin from the scratchy cloak. Sir Oliver had ditched his King's Guard attire for simpler, unaffiliated protection. Ali-Tersen's wife wore a plain black dress without any berets or jewelry. Ali-Tersen knew that Oliver's father would pay a fortune for the contents of their wagon even though there were only a few bare hides and food. The plan was to stop by First Foot and sell the items to the High Lord Wedgeword, then set sail for Gama Traka.

The King tried to hide as the citizens ran by in their tattered duds. He wished he were as filthy as the peasants' faces so he could avoid detection from low- and high-born citizens. Ali-Tersen actually felt bad for the displaced poor but his mind quickly shifted back to himself and survival.

"Can't believe we're just going to let someone take it," remarked Sir Oliver as he looked at the King's Castle.

Total chaos filled the crisp air as the lowest ranking citizens dragged hemp sacks of their belongings as they raced north. The King was relieved nobody had recognized him or it might have been a nasty repeat of the King Ali-Stanley funeral march. Ali-Tersen didn't want to be clawed and quartered by the people he hated most in the world, the poor. He instinctually pulled the hood down, almost covering his easily identifiable red eyes. His royal following had been reduced to the only two people he believed he could trust. The bugles and bull horns raged louder and louder and Ali-Tersen's stomach tightened.

"We must leave now," the King commanded.

Sir Oliver gave him a blank stare and responded coldly, "You can leave whenever your little heart wishes. We leave when the Queen says we leave and not a moment before."

Ali-Tersen addressed his wife, "My dear Alvyra, I love our son as much as you, but…"

She snapped, "But nothing. You say you love our son but the one chance you have to prove it, you want to run away. You only worry about yourself. I should have expected this with the way you handed away my kingdom so easily."

Her kingdom? I thought it was our kingdom.

"You should consider yourself the luckiest king who can barely hold a sword. If Sir Oliver and I weren't looking out for you, you would be dead by now. We will wait for our son until I give the order to leave," Alvyra said.

From the hill, he could now see the bannermen of Jon Colbert on the southern city's outskirts but his wife stood firm. The King was stunned but couldn't utter a single word of objection. Ali-Tersen realized she was right. He was now a huge liability and a target. He knew there would be a hefty reward to deliver his head to the new King of Donegal to gain immediate favor. Ali-Tersen Wamhoff needed Sir Oliver and his wife but they didn't need him to escape alive. In Donegal's entire history, no king had ever abdicated the throne willingly. There had been several close calls of usurpers almost breaching the King's Castle, but they all had been snuffed out. This was the first time a Wamhoff didn't stand up and fight for his realm. *What if I run back to the castle and challenge Jon Colbert to a duel? I'll show my wife I can swing a sword.*

"I'm afraid I have to say it's time. We must go," the Queen stated emotionally with tears streaming down her rosy cheeks.

They began to slowly roll northeast, just off the beaten path. Luckily, they blended in with the lowborn except that they were on horseback and everyone else was on foot. As his castle began to disappear behind him, the harsh reality finally set in. The impact of the situation began to crush Tersen Wamhoff, now former King of Donegal.

I ruined my family name. For what? Over four hundred years of the Wamhoff dynasty out the garderobe and into the moat. I let Alvyra turn me into a monster and I now need her just to survive. I was the King. I was the King.

B-RUXIN

Ruxin sped up on his brown destrier to check on the commotion ahead. His father's loyal men had someone surrounded. Ruxin jumped down from his horse and moved toward the front of the action. He saw a knight, clad in white armor, and a short, fat, red-headed teenager.

The White Knight said, "Let the prince go. You may have me outnumbered but I could beat any of you in single combat."

Ruxin spoke up, "There isn't a living knight from Fox Chapel that could even beat a child from Mattingly." All the men laughed at the insult.

"Prove it," dared the White Knight.

"I need not prove anything to a white-livered hoddypeak," Ruxin rebutted.

He loved to test his sword skills and the White Knight had unknowingly tapped that nerve. Being the youngest brother made Ruxin constantly eager to prove himself, which sometimes put him in some rather dangerous situations.

"Let's say this; you fight me in single combat. You win, your Prince and you are free to leave and have all the badling fun you desire," Ruxin said as his men erupted in boisterous laughter again.

Ruxin had heard of the White Knight. He had a dual reputation as a great swordsman and Neron Wamhoff's sexual partner. Ruxin couldn't believe that someone who loved men could be skilled with a sword. He also assumed that people in Fox Chapel were useless with a sword.

"My lord, you don't have to do this. We have them grossly outnumbered," Bryan Caughleigh reminded him.

"Men from Mattingly act with honor. This man challenged all of Mattingly with his words and I will represent our home with my sword. We don't run from a fight and I will indulge his request for a fair battle. We all know the Gods would never side with this pair," Ruxin said as he stared down his opponent. Mattingly and Fox Chapel residents never saw each other but both sides heard all the rumors from the enemy region.

Ruxin wore brown, layered, lightweight fibers of armor over his entire body and a silver war helm shaped like a bulldog's head. His black surcoat with a golden bull's head the size of his chest proclaimed his allegiance. Both men pulled their swords simultaneously, causing the surrounding men to back away and increase the size of the fighting area. Green grass below and a bright blue sky above provided a gorgeous setting for the deadly duel.

The Mattingly men worked themselves into a frenzy with spit flying from their mouths as they called for death.

Ruxin spoke from behind his lowered helm, "Alright, it's pretty simple. You win, both of you are free to go. You lose, and the little Prince here, well, let's hope he's not afraid of the dark or rats for that matter. I'll leave it at that."

The White Knight turned to Neron and said, "If they don't pull any tricks, I'll win and we will leave in peace."

"There will be no tricks. You must be used to fighting the cheats of Fox Chapel. When a Mattingly man gives you his word, it's worth more than gold," Ruxin assured the White Knight.

The two men faced each other for a few moments and the taller Ruxin was full of confidence. For only being fifteen, Ruxin harnessed the strength of a grown man.

A voice from behind Ruxin said, "You really don't have anything to prove to us, Lord Ruxin." *I have something to prove to myself.*

"Thank you for the concern, but I'm sure I'll be quite fine. Enjoy the fight," Ruxin screamed to the surrounding crowd.

The combatants tapped blades, signaling the official start of the action. In a flash, furiously moving swords collided in mid-air several times but neither man could gain an advantage. Ruxin quickly determined that this wouldn't be an easy victory. Both men traded volleys back and forth but couldn't land a significant blow. Ruxin tried high, low and every point in between to no avail. The White Knight deftly backed away like a dancer, ducked an attempt from Ruxin and spun around with a powerful side swing. Ruxin maneuvered his sword a moment late and the deflected blade of the White Knight rattled his bulldog helm and scrambled his balance. His hazy vision saw three White Knights with trails streaking from their bodies. All three men attacked and a pensive Ruxin blocked the wild strikes as the White Knight transformed back into one man. He tried to refocus but the White Knight kept up the offensive, not giving Ruxin a chance to get a grip on his blurry vision. Nervousness shot through Ruxin who hadn't been up against anyone as supremely skilled as the White Knight. Ruxin had heavily underestimated his opponent and couldn't find a vulnerable area in the White Knight's armor to attack.

He noticed that the earholes and eyeholes in the White Knight's helm were the only open areas. The two men sparred back and forth until finally Ruxin landed a strike in the White Knight's protected left shoulder. To his surprise, the Dragon Steel ripped through the metal and pierced his enemy's skin, causing blood to spurt out and spray the golden bull on Ruxin's chest.

Amazingly, this injury didn't seem to slow the White Knight down. Ruxin tried to land a few unorthodox shots with the flat of the blade to his opponent's earholes but didn't have any success. Everything he tried, failed. The knight anticipated his every move and Ruxin began to run out of energy. He had foolishly started the brawl at breakneck speed, expecting an easy victory. Ruxin had never been scared for his life until now. He thought about his wife and unborn child and wondered why he had acted so hastily to start this fight. The two men's swords banged into each other again and the White Knight pushed Ruxin down to his knees. He tried to hold off his opponent but he knew this couldn't last much longer. "Yield," demanded the White Knight but only silence ensued.

The men looked on in horror as their leader looked to be on the verge of death. *I won't yield in front of the Mattingly men. I'd rather die.*

Ruxin looked up into the eyes of death. He wanted to get a good look at the man who was going to kill him. He was surprised to see dainty blue eyes and a powdery complexion. A piercing scream came from the White Knight just before his tight battle helm filled with thick red liquid. The pale face of death was now splattered in blood after Bryan Caughleigh shoved a knife into the White Knight's earhole. The lifeless man fell to the ground with the handle still protruding from his head.

"Who did this?" Ruxin yelled.

"I did, my lord. You were about to be killed. You were gonna lose," Bryan Caughleigh answered.

Ruxin walked up to the young lord and grabbed him by the shoulder. "I was not about to lose. I was consolidating my strength. Even if I had lost, which I wasn't going to do, at least I would have died with honor. There's no honor in his victory. This can't even be counted as a victory. I should release the Prince on principle alone. You're lucky I don't have your head for this, Lord Bryan." Ruxin's anger quickly disappeared when he saw his father ride up on his horse with a reddened face and pursed lips.

C-JON

Jon made his way through the parting sea of men and up to his son. He said, "We need to have a talk in private, now."

He got down from his mount and dragged Ruxin away. Jon stopped and stared right into his son's eyes, "You cannot be reckless any longer. You need to think about your lovely wife, your unborn child. How would I explain this to your mother and wife? What, I would have to tell them that only one man died in the takeover because of staunch foolishness? No, it seems you won't be happy until you're the bravest dead man in all the kingdom. We fight only when there is no alternative. Have I made myself clear, son?"

"Yes, father," Ruxin somberly responded.

Jon could already see the remorse on his boy's face.

"I did think of my wife and child, but it was after the fight had started, my King," confessed Ruxin.

His son's formality reminded Jon that the kingdom was his. "Let's go see our new castle," Jon told Ruxin.

The two Colbert men got back on their horses and headed for their new dwelling. Jon first saw the House of Eternal Light and the King's Castle positioned behind it. Boisterous soldiers were screaming and pillaging until Jon Colbert yelled over them, "MEN, we are not here to destroy our own kingdom or its history. We came to end injustice through the realm and return Donegal to prominence again. All soldiers will be handsomely rewarded in the new structure of *our shared* kingdom."

Most conquerors would have killed the men, raped the women and pillaged anything they could from the existing citizens. This was a civilized takeover in every sense of the word with very few casualties. The simple threat of the Duke of Mattingly's power saved more lives than it lost. Jon rode down the Walk of Kings and crossed the bridge to his new castle. He didn't need to utilize his mobile bridges to get across the Royal River. Jon was shocked that the wooden bridge hadn't been set aflame in the evacuation. The new King trotted up the slight hill, through the open main gate and under the raised portcullis. He saw the fox decorations and thought, *We will need to remove some of this foxy décor but I won't destroy my own Capitol. We will write the history the way everything happened, not the way the Wamhoffs saw fit.*

When he entered the castle, Jon saw what he expected, a messy scene portraying a rushed exit and a quick attempt to snatch up anything of value. About twenty or so castle workers were on their knees outside the grand hall. He got down from his horse.

Jon saw a man with a long, twisted moustache and asked, "You're a count?"

"I am. Served this castle for over five decades. My name is Count Silzeus," the man responded.

"I've heard of you, obviously. Worry not, good Count. I will need you to assess the current state of the kingdom," Jon promised.

The man smiled and said, "I know who you are and I shall loyally serve you as I have every other king I have known. My king."

Jon assured all the other workers that they were safe.

There hadn't been a ceremony to officially mark his takeover but Jon Colbert was now King of Donegal.

He could hear his father speaking in his thoughts. *My son, it will be either you or me. We will one day become king of this great land, but our rule shall be short-lived. My father prophesized that I would become Duke of Mattingly and I or my son would sit on the throne as king. It is our destiny. We cannot run from it, this is what the Gods have planned for us. We will make matters right in this realm once again.*

Jon realized his father's prognostication had finally come true and he hoped Jasper Colbert was looking down with pride from the heavens. *We did it, father. You laid the groundwork and I followed. We did it.*

Jon entered the throne room and saw various remnants of the hurried flight scattered about. Even the throne had been knocked over in the madness. His loyal men re-erected the heavy silver seat to a normal upright position. They urged the new King to sit down. Jon obliged and immediately realized the chair wasn't comfortable. Out of nowhere, his chest tightened again, his face reddened and sweat poured from his chin. He became extremely dizzy and thought he was about to stop breathing. Jon could only see black and white spots. He heard voices; they sounded scared and prayed to the Gods for someone's survival. Jon wondered whom they were talking about. His head and chest eventually returned to normal, but Jon felt like he had just woken up.

He opened his eyes; color rushed in and painted a vivid picture of grizzled war veterans hovering over him. Jon lay on his back, next to the throne, with concerned men surrounding him. A collective sigh of relief was released as Jon sat up. Jon's men told him that he had fallen off the throne and had probably hit his head on the stone floor. Jon got up and sat down on his throne again. This time he didn't experience any of the earlier symptoms. He couldn't even venture a guess as to why he had blacked out as he rubbed the developing lump on the back of his head.

"My King, we haven't been able to locate the Seven Crowns of Donegal," Sir Rosebud reported.

"Keep looking. We will craft a new crown if need warrants. And this time we will only have one crown, not seven. The overindulgence and gluttony needs to be stopped for this kingdom to succeed. We will meet at first light tomorrow to discuss the plan to resurrect our realm; not my realm, our realm," Jon said.

About an hour after sundown, the rest of Jon's family finally arrived at the castle. Ruxin rushed over to his wife and gave her a kiss and hug. Jon put one arm around Camelle and rubbed his son's cheek with the other.

"Not a single person on our side died. This was a great success on all accounts," Jon proudly disclosed to the family.

"I'm still not sure. If people are willing to give up a kingdom this easily, there must be some serious problems ahead. However, I am pleased to hear that no blood has been shed," Camelle said.

"I am already thinking about ways to make certain nothing happens to us while we stay in this castle," Jon promised, even though he had already noticed some geographic defense issues that needed immediate attention.

He didn't worry because Jon knew he had the manpower and resources to handle the problems. The royal couple tried to settle into the King's apartments but Jon couldn't get fully comfortable. He thought about all the corrupt dealings that had taken place in this castle and mentally vowed to put a stop to it. He finally got to sleep just before dawn.

Four days later, Jon sat in the council meeting as Count Silzeus delivered more bad tidings. "Now, we don't have to pay off the full amount of these loans, but we have to pay all the delinquent and current payments. And that amount would be, uh…" he ruffled through the documents on the stone table and said, "That would be one hundred and twenty-two thousand gold rounds."

"Pay it off," the King said to his new Master of Coin, Enric Plast and the older man nodded in agreeance.

Ruxin spoke up, "Why are we paying the former king's debts? I say we tell them to find Ali-Tersen Wamhoff if they want their money."

"My son, when you take over a kingdom, you take responsibility for everything involved. That means we assume all debts. Right now, we have four internal armies coming toward the Capitol. Unless they all back down, we can't afford an attack by sea. We now control the coastline from Bottomfoot to Waters Edge. That's too much space to protect as we focus on the area around this very pregnable, so-called strong hold. I've already sent builders and masons with enough raw manpower to start the wall around the castle. We will start with the east and west. Lord Ichibod and Queen Leimur are reported to be closest. The bastard in the north hasn't made it to the Blue Caps. We've already sent a welcoming party to delay their journey even further," Jon told his staff.

"I suppose we don't have to worry about an attack from the south. Unless your brother tries to attack you," said Hydell Kenzy, his Grand Lord of Defense and everyone laughed.

"Our spies in Elkridge have spotted several ousted Wamhoffs camped out on the beaches. They are having a standoff with the bastard and employ an army of barbarians," Jon reported.

"Are you saying that Ali-Tersen Wamhoff has surfaced in Waters Edge with an army of foreigners?" Lord Kenzy asked.

"This is where it gets interesting. They say its Ali-Steven and his son Ali-Samuel along with the former queen Emilia. Not the Wamhoffs everyone expected but these ones are more dangerous than that Albino King," Jon said.

Lord Kenzy needed clarification, "And they have an army of barbarians?"

"I hear they are from Histomanji," Count Sproul said.

"Strange time in our beloved kingdom. Perchance they will slow the bastard usurper down until we can easily eliminate him and the bastard Wamhoff usurper. There are a few other matters we haven't yet touched on, my King," said Count Silzeus.

"Go on," Jon told him.

"During his short reign, Tersen Wamhoff raised taxes on the lowborn many times, many, many times. The poorest of the poor were uprooted during your rush into the city and…"

Jon cut off the Count, "I've heard enough. I realize it's necessary to ameliorate relations with the common folk. Lower their taxes to be equivalent to Mattingly's. Send out as many criers as can be spared to report this to all the poorest areas of Fox Chapel."

"It shall be handled, my King," promised Count Silzeus with a nod and a smile.

Despite insuperable odds, Jon seemed equipped to handle all aspects of repairing the broken kingdom. The new King's biggest issue was the multiple armies still marching on Falconhurst. He had never been involved in a large-scale war and the debt of the kingdom had nearly wiped out his vast savings. Jon knew the cost of war during cold weather was always higher. More fires, heavier clothing, better footwear, blankets and for some reason men always ate more during the winter season. The King didn't perceive these challenges as insurmountable and quickly dealt with problem after problem in his early rule.

As he crossed the bridge, a familiar voice greeted him. Uncle Hambone said, "I come to say I believe its bout time for me to get on back to my Black Hills. Coffee and tea ain't as good up here. I'll have to send some of the good stuff up north for my new King," he smiled. "Look, I know I flung a bunch of my beliefs at you over the years, but I only did it outta family love. Truth be told, I couldn't be no prouder of my nephew. And even though me and yer daddy had our differences, he'd be proud of you too, boy. You got a chance to make this kingdom something special now." Hambone tightened his lips and pushed away the emotion as he continued, "So don't you go doin nothin stupid and get yourself kilt. You hear me now, boy?"

"I hear you quite clearly, good uncle," Jon replied. The two tough men shared a brief but genuine hug. Men in the Colbert family rarely hugged each other and Jon took a step back after the embrace.

"I just want to say…" Jon was cut off by Hambone, "Ima stop you right there. I know what you is gonna say and you know what Ima say back so let's just skip over all that. You got a beautiful family, you hear? You take good care a them now. I'll be back to check on you fore too long."

"I wouldn't have it any other way," Jon responded. Hambone hopped on his horse and took off before things became emotional again.

Jon's guards escorted him to the west side of the Capitol. Along the way, Jon recognized the former High Priest of Mattingly. Orian Vangor had decided that the religious system had become too corrupt and resigned from his position but Jon had plans for the elderly man. The older man served and wept for the lowborn of Donegal.

Orian appeared to be in his early sixties, evidenced by his wrinkles and the frequent grimaces he made while walking. His dirty, close-cut silver hair and unkempt wiry whiskers gave his frail face a pearly glow. His bushy eyebrows were scrunched down to hide his blue eyes that had been dulled by years of seeing injustice and discrimination. He wore a knee-length kirtle of assorted animal hair that rubbed his body raw from the coarse fibers. The kirtle looked battered and blood stained with holes in random spots. He carried a wooden stick that was connected to a leather whip with three metal tips that had been rounded and spiked. True to his style, Orian orated over some citizens who wore cheap, poorly sewn duds.

Jon listened to the man. "Ofttimes we must pray for the Gods to gain us wisdom and that we shall apply that wisdom to find new homes. However, if need should force it to be, we will surely frolic on Mother Earth and take nourishment from her bosom. The only direction to go is along the path of the Gods and to follow and praise their precious words and lessons. Stay true to your soul, pray, believe. My precious souls, your day in the sun will surely come. Don't forget, supper can be had at The Mother of Mercy citadel. Now go apply the wisdom of the Gods."

The small crowd of forty people quickly dispersed.

The King wasn't wearing a crown and approached Orian, who looked unimpressed. "Aahh, our new King," said the older man without a customary bow.

Jon's guard, Elfson, said, "This man is your King. You need to address your king, your highness, with the proper respect, old man."

Orian Vangor turned and faced the guard and spoke slowly, "Highness. That means you see him above all other men. Most men serve kings, this is known to be true. However, I serve the Gods first and all men equally. I don't give more courtesy to a man who wears gold on his head. For, it doesn't appear he needs many prayers, but the man who lives in squalor is the one who needs my assistance."

Elfson's voice became sterner, "You need to show the proper respect."

Jon spoke up before Orian could get angry, "That's enough, Sir Elfson. I need some privacy with this man I've known my whole life, please."

"But I know you better, Jonathan Colbert. Being older, I've known you since you were a babe," Orian said with a smile. All the guards backed away and moved out of hearing range. Vangor asked, "Why don't you wear gold on your head? You are king, no?"

"I am the King, yes. A crown is being crafted and sized as we speak but that's the least of my concerns," Jon said.

"I should hope so. Did you see those citizens, your citizens? Innocent prisoners in their own kingdom, being thrown from side to side by the powers that be. Your deeds might ultimately measure as honorable, but I've met some displaced citizens that could argue that point," Orian told him.

"I didn't light any of those fires. That was the Wamhoff regime on their way out of Falconhurst. I couldn't stop them from doing that," Jon argued.

"He said, she said, they said, who said? You could have stayed in Mattingly and lived a comfortable life in that region as duke," the old man pointed out.

"That is true. I could have easily stayed in Mattingly and lived a very comfortable life. The only problem is that situation doesn't help the hopeless and lowborn citizens of the kingdom. If the Wamhoff dynasty had continued, do you really believe the plight of the poor was going to improve? I came to you to talk about helping me improve the lives of the poor. The commoners have been put down for too long in our kingdom. I understand the skepticism with your belief that all dukes and kings are corrupt. Yet you know my father to be a man of common birth and you saw with your own eyes how I minimized corruption in Mattingly. I couldn't straighten out the church but that was the only area I failed in," Jon said.

"These words please my ears. I know you, Jon Colbert. I know you are a good man. I know you to be a loyal man. I wish you the best of luck in straightening out Donegal," Orian said.

"Wait, I need your help to straighten out the kingdom. I don't know of a man who is better suited to serve as High Priest of the realm," Jon offered.

An extended silence worried Jon until Orian cleared his throat and spoke, "Jon Colbert. I remember saying to myself a long time ago, that's one of the most intelligent boys I've ever encountered and that still holds true till this day. I watched a boy grow into an even more intelligent man and then duke. You now seem to be wise with only one fault of judgment. Surely you know I wouldn't have the faintest interest in trying to pull all the evil weeds of the church. They grow too many and with no power of repercussion, I am left to lose my soul amongst the demon's garden," a disheartened Orian Vangor said.

"I can give you the proper tools necessary to punish the corrupt priests or parishioners. I need your help. I understand why you wouldn't be initially interested in my offer, I really do, but I also know that you want nothing more than to improve the situation for the poor. I am working to do that but I need your help," Jon pleaded.

The old man shook his head, "Power on earth can only serve to weigh us down in the heavens. I don't mean any offense."

"I take none. This is your chance to help the poor. If I appoint anyone else, what do you think will be the result? More corruption?" Jon raised his voice.

"There will be no fancy churches. There will be no salvation for sale. Every man will be judged equally by the Gods without regard to birth status. We will get back to honest services of faith," Orian demanded.

"Aye, of course. This is exactly what I want as well. We can burn down the opulent church in the Capitol as a reminder that overindulgence will not be tolerated," Jon offered.

"All grown up but you still think like a boy. It would make little sense and prove quite wasteful to burn down that building. Instead, make it a sanctuary for the poor. In every decision we make, we must think of those that need the most help and put them above ourselves. Only then will the Gods truly smile upon us. I trust you more than most men so I am cautiously going to accept your offer," Vangor said.

"I understand the hesitation. We can meet soon to forge out the details," Jon promised.

"I'm sure you've been lied to, yes?" Orian asked.

"Most men can attest that I have been," Jon responded, showing his missing pinkie fingers.

"The most difficult task we face in life is deciphering whether a man is lying or telling the truth. That is why we trust, but do so with reserve. When the green serpent sleeks in the summer grass, we can all be judged as fools. We can only fully trust our Gods and principles," Orian closed the conversation and walked away without bowing.

Two days later, Jon lay in bed with his wife. He asked, "Why haven't you been wearing your crown?"

Camelle shook her head in disgust and replied, "That blood crown? Is that what you mean? No, thank you."

Jon questioned her with a calm demeanor, "There was blood on the crown?"

Camelle turned and looked out the window before saying, "Not physical blood. It's the fact that the gaudy circlet that represents the royalty of Donegal has been steeped in the kingdom's blood for years. This entire castle has for that matter."

Jon talked to the back of his wife's head, "Then we will have it cleaned or a new one made like they are doing for me. It's tradition for a queen to wear a crown."

Camelle kept looking out the window and said, "Well, there are many long-standing traditions like murder and rape that need to be broken."

Jon tried to defend himself, "That is totally different. The citizens expect to see their queen in a crown. It uplifts them." Jon knew the words weren't true, but he was running out of things to tell his wife to cheer her up.

She snapped at him, "The citizens are only worried whether they will be able to make it through a harsh winter with enough supplies to survive. Seeing someone wearing an object on her head that could be sold to solve all of their problems doesn't uplift anyone. You have lost your priorities, Jonathan Colbert. We need to put a stop to these silly traditions that are followed just for the sake of doing so. We must instead be critical of supporting everything because it has been done before. Blindly supporting dissenting traditions is the epitome of stupidity and I have always thought you were a smart man."

Jon had never heard his wife go off like this before and hoped it was only the stress of taking over the entire realm. He said, "I thought all this might make you happy again, after all we've been through."

Camelle finally turned and faced her husband with tears running down her cheeks. She uttered, "I can never be fully happy again unless our entire family is together and back in Mattingly, our only home. This will never be home. I had thought I would never love Riverfront when I first arrived, but it only took me a few days to realize it was my true home. I've tried to like this castle and city but you can only have one true home and it will never be here. "

D-MARIAH

Mariah Colbert and Torvald Malik held each other's hands as they walked into the King's audience chamber. As they sat down on a red cushioned bench, Mariah knew something was amiss by the troubled looks on her parents' faces.

Jon and Camelle sat across from the young couple and the patriarch spoke, "I originally summoned you both to discuss plans for the wedding. Those thoughts were swept aside when a dark raven just arrived with some terrible news. There have been dragon attacks around the kingdom and I am sorry to say that one of the beasts hit Housemont. Torvald, your parents are believed to be dead. I am so sorry."

Mariah felt Torvald's hand tighten and his breathing become deeper and faster. He didn't cry. He looked like he was about to burst into tears, but instead, Torvald Malik stared blankly at a painting of Jasper Colbert hanging on the wall behind Jon and Camelle. "Are we certain?" Torvald asked with pain in his words.

"I hope not, I really do, but these sources have scarcely been wrong before. We have accounted for all of your friends' families," the King tried to console his future son by wedlock.

"We can put the wedding on hold if you need to return home, of course," said Camelle.

"If a dragon cooked my home, there is no reason to return immediately and risk a repeat performance. I will make sure it is safe before I go look for my parents' bodies. They loved Mariah, especially my mother, and I know she would want the wedding to proceed as scheduled. They will look down from the heavens on our special day. I'll return home after the wedding," Torvald said as he still kept his composure.

Mariah on the other hand, started weeping when Torvald talked about Lucille. She couldn't believe that two of the greatest people she had ever met were now dead. Mariah wept because she knew Lucille would have loved Falconhurst and the King's Castle. She didn't even realize she was talking when she said, "Are you sure, my love? We can wait until we return from Bottomfoot if you wish."

"I'm sure we should move forward as planned. This is sad but my parents lived a great life, much better than most. There are so many great times to remember that they will never be truly dead to me." Torvald fidgeted in his chair but never shed a tear.

"In times of need, I find it helps to stay close to the Gods. Let them guide you and remember, we will always be here for you," Jon said.

"I appreciate the advice, my King. We need to go tell the others," Torvald whispered to Mariah. "If you would excuse us," the well-mannered Torvald said to Jon and Camelle.

Mariah wiped away her tears and tried to put on a brave face before going to meet the others.

"Of course, if there's anything you need, be sure to ask. We're family," Jon reminded him, and Camelle added, "Anything, Torvald, anything."

The couple walked to the east end of the castle and found the Bottomfoot crew eating dinner in the great hall.

"Wait until you hear this one," Chopkins cheerily said until he turned around and noticed Mariah and Torvald looking distraught.

"It's going to have to wait, my friend," Torvald said. The mood tensed around the long table and everyone stopped eating. Torvald looked around and spoke, "There's been a dragon attack in Bottomfoot. Ridgetop and Housemont have been burned to the ground. None of your families were in either of those areas, so they are all safe. However, everyone near the top of the mountain is suspected to be dead, including my mother and father."

"Bullshit," screamed Sir Bastion as he slammed his hand on the table and bellowed, "I'll slay the damned dragon that did this. I'm leaving right now."

Torvald had to grab and forcefully push Sir Bastion back into his seat as he screamed, "Sit down. Nobody is going anywhere. We will all go back after the wedding to inspect the situation for ourselves. Until then, I know this is sad, but we will carry on. We will enjoy a great wedding the way my parents would have wanted us to do."

Despite the encouragement, Chopkins was bawling and J. Everson had to blink away a salty stream from his eyes. Callice started singing a soft requiem as his lips quivered in sadness. After about an hour of crying, Mariah and her friends from Bottomfoot began to drink in honor of Lucille and Edword. They drank, danced, mourned, consoled and told stories of the late Duke and Duchess of Bottomfoot with Callice softly playing the psaltery and singing in the background. Mariah finally went to bed only a few hours before sunrise.

The next morning, Mariah's handmaid was already cleaning her quarters when she woke up. Jon made Torvald and his daughter wait until they were married to share a bed. The young woman rushed a silk robe over to Mariah and hurriedly lit some more candles around the room.

The handmaid spoke with her accent, "I hear about what happened. I am sorry for your loss, my Princess."

"Thank you, Deydranna," Mariah answered. The exotic young woman from a far-off land had been assigned to Mariah's service. She had told Mariah that she expected to die the day Jon Colbert took over the castle.

"Can I ask you a question?" Mariah asked.

"Yes, my Princess," Deydranna answered.

"Please don't think I am trying to be rude, but are you pregnant?" Mariah pointed at the bump on her handmaid's midsection.

Deydranna became defensive, "No. I just…I just eat too much, too fast."

"You don't have to hide it. We won't have you punished for being pregnant. My father isn't like any of the previous Wamhoff kings, except for maybe Ali-Ster," said Mariah. Deydranna looked down and avoided eye contact. Mariah pressed her, "You can tell me."

"If I tell the truth it could be very dangerous for my baby. Many people will want the child to die, even your father," Deydranna pleaded.

Mariah was intrigued by these words and said, "There are many things that I am downright lousy at. One thing I am good at is keeping secrets. You can tell me. I can see it is weighing you down."

Reluctantly, Deydranna started to talk as she brushed Mariah's frizzy hair. "He was King of Donegal and he was a great man." *That eliminates Ali-Stanley and Ali-Tersen straight away.*

Deydranna went on, "He come to me for help. He want to marry Queen of Goldenfield to unite kingdoms but he never pleasure a woman before. He want to use me to make him better. We only make love one time but the King is strong. I cry for three days after he die. King Ali-Ster is the greatest man I ever know and I have his baby."

"From all I've heard, Ali-Ster was a great man," Mariah responded. She was blown away by this confession.

"You shouldn't tell. If you tell, they will kill my baby," Deydranna uttered frantically.

"I promise I won't tell a soul about this," Mariah said, realizing this would be a hard secret to keep.

"Can I tell you a secret?" Mariah asked.

"Yes, yes, anything," Deydranna responded.

"I don't know if you know about how King Ali-Stanley attacked my father last spring," Mariah said.

"Yes, I remember when they drag him into the castle. Blood cover his face and body. Ali-Ster say his father send him away so he can con…con…conduct dirty actions," Deydranna told her.

"Yes, he was probably sent away because he had too much honor. That seems to be the fastest way to get killed in this realm. Well anyway, it was believed that I was coming to the Capitol to be wed to Prince Ali-Ster. Little did I know, I was being used as bait to lure my father in to further his grudge with King Ali-Stanley," Mariah started to get emotional.

"I've been here ten years now. I came as little girl. I see and hear so many bad things. The only time I see hope was when Ali-Ster puts on the crown. I love him still with my whole heart. I will never need a husband. I have a King, always in my heart." Deydranna talked glowingly in one breath and with agonizing heartache in the next. Mariah could easily see that she genuinely loved Ali-Ster. Deydranna continued to talk as she helped Mariah get dressed. The handmaid then led Mariah to the dining hall to break her fast.

Mariah saw a teary-eyed Chopkins Haddock first. She sat down next to her stoic betrothed and kissed him on the cheek. Nobody spoke about the Duke and Duchess and the subdued demeanor of the normally high strung group showed a true sadness. Callice slowly plucked at his psaltery to break the silence but the rest of the meal drew a somber tone. After breakfast, Mariah excused herself to reprise an activity she had practiced in Mattingly.

Being a staunch servant of the Seven Gods, Mariah often went and prayed for the most destitute of the Gods' creatures. She grabbed a large candle and headed for the dungeons. Most of the condemned men wouldn't talk to her after finding out she was only there to pray for them, not release them. Mariah still prayed for the men, begging the Gods to show them the eternal light so they could seek forgiveness before death. She came up to the last cell and noticed a plump, ginger-haired young man.

"Merciful Gods in the heavens, please guide this prisoner toward wisdom. Help him to see the light…"

Mariah was cut off by the prisoner, "Merciful Gods, ha, no such thing. If the Gods were merciful, I wouldn't be starving in this cell."

"You are in the dungeons for a reason, I am sure," Mariah reminded him.

"I am. And I'll tell you the reason. My greatest crime is being born Wamhoff. How do I change that? I can't change who I am. No, the merciful Gods decided that because of my father's mistakes I should stand and answer. I had nothing to do with any of his plans as I was sent away to Cloverfoot. Now I wait for the new King to make a spectacle of me in a glorious public killing. I know I have no value for a ransom, so what will it be? Hanged, beheaded, quartered perchance? Yes, the people would love to see Prince Neron Wamhoff's head on a spike," the prisoner revealed.

"My father is not like that. He put you here because you are a Wamhoff, that is true, but he has no intention of killing you. You have to understand that your father and uncle tried to kill him and our family. He may provide you with better accommodations when you prove you can be trusted," Mariah told Neron.

"I suppose that's a touch encouraging. Have they captured my father yet?" Neron asked.

"No, but they aren't aggressively hunting him down. Your father doesn't serve a threat to the kingdom right now as there are others coming after the crown. This may seem queer to hear but you may be safer in this dungeon than on the run with your father. That man will be lucky to escape the kingdom alive," Mariah said.

"I get mad at people judging me for being Wamhoff, but I always judged my father for being born albino. He loved me greatly, but everyone saw me as the little albino. I was always looked at as my father's son, not Neron Wamhoff. It mattered not that I had the true red hair of a Wamhoff. When I failed with a sword, everyone said, 'he's definitely Tersen's son'. But now that he's gone, I realize he and my mother were always by my side, protecting me. Now, I have nothing. I have no one," the young man started sobbing.

"You have me and you will always have seven friends. When everyone abandons you, it's best to stay close to our Seven Gods. When I was lost and alone in the Fox Chapel woods I saw death as the most likely outcome. I prayed and prayed and the Gods sent someone to rescue me. Now the Gods have sent me to help you. I will talk to my father about putting you into some nicer accommodations. But if you act out of order or do anything foolish, you'll be sent right back down here. Remember, stay close to the Gods and accept them into your heart," Mariah said.

"Thank you," Neron returned.

Mariah turned around to leave and saw a dirty-faced man approaching.

The man spoke, "What in the heavens is a beautiful young woman doing in these grungy dungeons?"

"I come to pray for the desolate. Every man and woman is loved by the Gods and deserves to have their final pleas heard," Mariah said.

"What a charming attitude to have. Wait, are you…?" he held his lantern closer to Mariah's face and talked again, "Why are you, you're the Princess of Donegal?"

"Yes, I am. And who are you?" Mariah questioned him.

"My name is Orian Vangor and we seem to share the same conviction. Hope, faith and charity. Your father has asked me to reform the religious order of the realm. A princess who displays the same values as yourself could be a great rallying point for all the lower citizens. If they see a princess who puts them on equal ground as her King father, hope could flourish. Faith could spread and others will be encouraged to be charitable with their poorer brothers and sisters. Stories would spread and this movement could bloom like a beautiful daisy. Think on the matter. You could be instrumental in making religion pure again in Donegal. Princess," the man said without bowing and walked away.

Mariah remembered her father talking about Orian. Jon had said that he had almost gone mad because of all the corruption in the church system. Mariah viewed him as a man with strong conviction, and the offer intrigued her.

The Man with the Golden Sword

"I think that to be a foolish idea," Gamelda opined.

The Crippler quickly retorted, "And when did we start taking battle advice from a woman?"

"Enough, both of you. I get it already. You hate his ideas and he hates your ideas. If we can set aside these petty quarrels and get back to winning a war, that would be superb," The Man sounded more like the teacher than the student.

His war council sat in a makeshift meeting room near the Blue Cap Mountains. The pavilion rippled from the swirling wind gusts coming in from the raging waters of the fjord and the constant sound annoyed The Man.

He stared at the map-covered table as he spoke, "How many men can we sacrifice here and still make it to Falconhurst?"

"That's an almost impossible number to arrive at but the unfortunate fact remains we can't afford to lose any men. With the news of Duke Colbert's takeover, the Capitol is under much better protection. Why couldn't the coward albino king stay and at least kill a few of our new enemy?" Benroy asked listlessly.

"We waited too long. I called to leave all along, but everyone said we weren't ready. We would have been in a much better position if we had taken the King's Castle and tried to protect it from Jon Colbert. What's the situation with the hills, Benroy?" The Man wanted to know.

"Advance scouting has spied a few hundred men around the passes. If these tunnels and secret exits are real, then we can easily surprise and crush the enemy, but we must act fast. The time to move is now," his advisor said pointing at the map of the secret tunnels.

The Man was pleased with the progress of the army of men. They were ahead of schedule for the current march and The Man with the Golden Sword remained confident that he could defeat the new King in battle. His worry was that only one high lord had supported him but with a new regime, Lord Harolg Cuthbart could shift his allegiance. The Man swore that after he took over as king, he would kill all the nobles who had turned their noses up at his offers. The meeting ended and the folded canvas opening revealed that the sun had been lost for the day.

He followed Gamelda to his tent, went inside and sat on the bed. He peered into her green eyes and said, "Let's look at it again. I know I'll see something this time."

"No. You need to relax and stop worrying about it so much. When the time is right, you will know," Gamelda said.

"I think the time is right, right now," he pleaded.

"Perhaps you won't know when the time is right if you think it's now. I can tell you, it's not going to happen right now. Your soul is becoming lighter but there is still some weight that needs to be shed. I can see it in your eyes, my love," Gamelda smiled.

The Man became quickly irritated because he hadn't got his way with the future skull, and sourly said, "This nonsense with you and the Crippler has got to stop."

"Then tell him to stop constantly attacking me out of jealousy of what we have," Gamelda responded.

"Enough. You're not going anywhere and neither is he, so you are going to have to work with him. We cannot have constant squabbling in every meeting. I will talk to him and demand the same civility from him," The Man stated.

"I am always civil…alright, I will try," Gamelda started and corrected herself with a sexy smile. The Man jumped on his lover and began to pull up her dress.

A screaming voice came from outside, "My king, there's a dire matter to discuss."

"Go away or die," he screamed toward the door.

"Urgent matter. Life or death, my king," the voice of Tucker came through the massive tent.

"This will be your death if I don't deem this as urgent," The Man muttered as he went through the opening.

Tucker saw the angry look on the king's face and talked fast, "My king, this could be your life or death. We've just received word that an army is marching toward the Ridge Cliffs in an attempt to seize the capitol. We don't have the castle or city very well protected except for the city gates. If they breach the gates, they will gain a powerful stronghold. If we move ahead and they trap us in the passages, we will be slaughtered like sheep from both sides. But if we go back, we get farther from the King's Castle."

"Who leads this army?" The Man asked.

"Someone we know all too well, Ali-Samuel Wamhoff," Tucker responded.

The Man's heart sank. He didn't fear Ali-Samuel in battle but he did consider the great warrior an equal on the killing field. "He must know something we don't. How close are they to the gates?" The Man wanted to know.

"They landed up shore but they are approximately as far away as we are. We need to race back if we want to hold Elkridge," Tucker counseled.

"Who knows about this?" The Man asked.

"Just you and I, unless the messenger had opened it and perfectly resealed the parchment," Tucker replied.

"Wake everyone. We need to hold Elkridge from Ali-Samuel. He presents a greater threat to us right now," he ordered.

"Are you certain, my king?" Tucker wanted to confirm but a stern look from The Man proved his conviction. Tucker ran off to alert the men of the new plan.

The Man with the Golden Sword went back into the tent and said to Gamelda, "We need to leave now. We need to find the fastest horses and get to the northern gates." He noticed she had already been readying herself to leave when he entered the tent. A frantic scene ensued as the chosen soldiers scrambled to hustle back to Elkridge.

The Man and Gamelda galloped for fourteen hours before stopping to rest for a few hours. They got back on their mounts and repeated this pattern twice before The Man saw the southern gates of Elkridge. The guards let him in and his destrier bolted across the city limits. He was so exhausted, he couldn't imagine fighting a battle, but he pressed on. The Man navigated through the panicked city and fought against the people rushing south. As he neared the north gates, he heard the ear-crunching sounds of wood pounding wood. The Man became nervous when he saw the tall city gate bending in as a battering ram methodically slammed into it. Splinters shot skyward in the fire-lit night. His dutiful men were being knocked backwards violently as they valiantly tried to hold out the enemy.

The Man with the Golden Sword looked around quickly and started shouting orders, "Get the siege towers over there. Push them up against either gate and put the trebuchets behind them." Saddle sore and worn, The Man helped his men move them in front of the collapsing doors. The trebuchets were moved in and another siege tower was placed behind that for good measure. Suddenly, the pounding stopped.

A-Emilia

The ramming sounds slowed and finally came to a stop. The city gates were at the top of the steep cliffs but Emilia could barely see what was going on. She had run to a hilltop to get a better look at the action despite numerous warnings from Ali-Samuel to stay on the sandy plateau below. Emilia saw the men angrily slam the boat they were using to bash the gates to the ground, shattering the wooden vessel. She noticed the group moving back down the hill and rushed to beat the crowd. She arrived back at the safe area and joined Pariah and Princess. The disgruntled officers came back muttering to each other. The evil look on Ali-Samuel's face prompted Emilia not to engage him in conversation. An eager young squire who was left behind foolishly asked, "Sir Ali-Samuel, did we get in?"

The despondent knight calmly walked over to the young man and punched him square in the jaw, knocking the squire out. "Stupid boy," exclaimed Ali-Samuel before storming off.

They retreated down the hillside until they hit another level area to set up camp for the night. They had lost the ships carrying the camping supplies, so most of the people had to sleep under the stars. The Histoman didn't seem to mind but the western men weren't coping well with the rugged conditions. They were used to much nicer accommodations, even on the battle front.

The next day, the group traveled down the hill and set up operations on a beach with a nearby port. Emilia sat in an ill-crafted pavilion to meet with the war council. Ali-Steven spoke, "Both northern and southern gates are on a hill. They can be easily defended by the bastard now."

"What if we juth march around them?" posed Sir Ralph.

"We will just get squashed in the Blue Cap passages. That's why The Man with the Golden Sword came back. He must know something we don't to back away from his ultimate prize. Why is this stronghold so damn important?" Ali-Samuel rhetorically asked.

"He must know we can't lay siege to the city, but how much food can they have inside those gates? Can they survive a harsh winter?" Ali-Steven wondered aloud.

"Can we lay thiege? If we take control of the Beachwood Port, we may be able to stharve them out," Sir Ralph said.

"We would have to steal from most of the vessels and they would stop coming to the port once word got out. We should try to buy grain and send scouts to look at the surrounding cities for items we could take if necessary. I just don't see us being able to lay siege to that city. We don't have the resources to sustain a siege," opined Ali-Steven.

A balding man popped his head into the pavilion, then entered carrying rolled vellum over to Ali-Steven. The elder Wamhoff broke the seal and moved his lips as he read the letter silently.

He lowered his head and spoke softly, "This is awful news. If this is true, we have a new king. Duke Jon Colbert is a duke no longer. King Jon rules the realm and his younger brother now serves as Duke of Mattingly. Instantly, we have to defeat a mighty enemy, the likes of which we aren't currently prepared for."

Maybe this wasn't meant to be. First, we lose half our fleet. Then we can't take this city that seems to be so important, and now this. The odds are stacking against our cause. Ali-Samuel and I should escape this nonsense and go to an exotic land to live out our days in peace. That's what he promised me but we appear to be getting farther away from that dream. Maybe now that the Wamhoffs aren't ruling and revenge has been removed from the scenario, he will soften his stance and simply walk away.

"Can we scale down the beach and move around the Blue Caps?" Emilia asked.

"We would have to get around the fjord and back to the coast but they will be well-defensed once word of our arrival reaches Falconhurst. Our hand seems to be forced on this issue," Ali-Steven answered.

"Are there any lords or ladies that we could form an alliance with?" Emilia asked.

"If we had landed with full forces, then maybe. With this mangled operation full of perceived barbarians, no one will want to ally with us. We are going to have to take the castle by force, not diplomacy," Ali-Steven said.

"What about The Man with the Golden Sword?" Emilia questioned.

"What about him?" Ali-Samuel snidely retorted.

"If our forces are shattered, why not work out an alliance with him. Offer him the position of Falconer, lands and gold," Emilia offered.

"I know the man too well. It won't work. There can only be one king and I know for fact that he will never accept that offer. He would expect one of us to take the position of Falconer and bow down to him. He's not the type of man to quickly change his mind," Ali-Samuel said.

Emilia spoke, "But he has no claim to the throne."

"And he will argue that neither do we. Ali-Stanley is now three kings removed. Any or all ties to his claim have been washed away. Jon Colbert had no claim to the throne yet that's where he sits right now. The Man with the Golden Sword wants to usurp the crown. He cares little for anyone's claim, especially ours," Ali-Samuel spoke from his experiences with his sudden enemy.

"The King Colbert factor does change the situation now. The bastard may see that the task has just hardened tenfold. Sometimes alliances come in the strangest of ways. It wouldn't hurt to send an offer and see where he stands," Ali-Steven recommended.

"It will be wasted time, vellum and a scrivener's services, but we must do as our council wishes," Ali-Samuel said.

"Do you have any positive suggestions or only harsh criticism? Help us solve this problem," Emilia told her lover.

Ali-Samuel shot a stern look her way before speaking, "We need to appeal to his narcissism. He doesn't have a proud family, only himself. That's his only weakness that I know of, which is why he wants to be king. Use heavy flattery in your request," Ali-Samuel suggested.

After the meeting, Emilia sat on the windy beach with Pariah and Princess. "So does everyone still hate me?" Emilia wanted to know.

"No. Most don't like the Ali-Samuel. Blame him," Pariah told her.

Good. The more I think about it, he seems to be the one behind everything, even pushing his father along.

"Rolog, he no live in this land," Pariah said.

"What do you mean by that?" Emilia asked.

"He no on water and he no here. No Rolog. He no help us here. We pray, we pray, we pray. No help. No nothing. If we stay, we all die. I know. I see in my sleep," Pariah started rambling.

"No need to worry. I've seen horrible visions in my dreams that didn't come out to be true. Everything has gone against us up until this point and we are still here. When luck shifts to our side, we will make our mark and you will see that Rolog can go anywhere," Emilia tried to calm her down but the words weren't working well.

"Me hope. Me want go to Histomanji but no on water. Evil is water. I stay here forever until dead," Pariah morbidly told Emilia.

Sunny

Sunny tossed around in his sleep, rolling back and forth on the moist dirt floor. An army marched toward him. He tried to run but he was buried in red sand up to his ankles and couldn't budge. He looked ahead at the oncoming horde. They carried enormous banners of a crowned skull on a black field. The banners rippled in the breeze and served to scare Sunny even more. The wild, screaming men marched right up to Sunny, stopped and lined up. They were a strange group. The men moved like living bodies with ravaged flesh and pale blue skin with red splotches. Most were covered in armor or some type of mail but the exposed areas of skin shocked the boy. A tall warrior garbed in red and white with a fox helm walked through the soldiers and approached Sunny. The man took off his battle helm and looked almost exactly like Sunny except for the cleft palate. The man dropped to one knee and began to speak but Sunny's eyes shot open.

Sunny had been having lucid dreams ever since the masters had started allowing them sleep for six hours a night. The School of the Learned Warrior sensed the oncoming battle and wanted the students to be better rested. Sunny had never remembered his dreams until he started to sleep longer.

The day's activities remained strenuous, filled with exhausting mental and physical lessons. The bell sounded and several of the students were permitted to take leave. Sunny still worried about Ollor and wondered what had happened to his father figure. Muriel and Sunny were no longer allowed to leave together. Sunny walked alone to the beach that he now called Dragon

Beach. The small pink pebbles rolled under his feet as he reached the water. The waves were huge and the tide had come in significantly since the last time he had been here. The dark and stormy day kept Sunny on edge with random lightning flashes and thunder strikes.

He wished the dragons would come out of the sea but didn't know how to summon them. He stood and stared blindly at the crashing waves. Sunny wondered if he would ever be permitted to get married and have children of his own. He had pledged his life to the School but if he survived the Ultimate War, they wouldn't need to train any longer. The only female he had really known was his younger sister. He didn't know how to properly treat a girl, but even at only twelve, Sunny was intrigued by the prospect of a family.

Something caught the corner of his vision. A large object washed ashore and lay harmlessly on the sand. Sunny slowly moved in for a closer look. He saw the dead body of a man he recognized, Ollor. A lifeless body that wore the same clothes Sunny had last seen him in.

He must have drowned in a storm while fishing. My father…at least, I will always consider him my father. How am I going to explain this to Muriel?

The sorrow was short-lived as black hands sprouted from the sand to grab at Ollor's body. The hands started to pull the body under the pink pebbles until a silver flash in the sky startled Sunny and he sprang back from the peculiar site. The dark clouds parted and a blue beam of light shot down from the opening. The brightness stunned Sunny's eyes and when his vision readjusted, he saw a battle for the body in progress. The upright body of Ollor was buried up to his midsection and the underground hands pulled him down further. The tugging battle continued with the body moving up and down until Sunny looked up and noticed a gold adumbration of a giant man in the sky. The beam changed from blue to gold and Ollor started to rise up. The underground hands disappeared and the golden beam carried Ollor up to the heavens.

Did the Gods just pull him up into the heavens? I knew he was a good man, worthy of the Gods. I wish I could have said goodbye.

The clouds closed back up and darkness reigned once again. Most of Sunny's life had been filled with inexplicable occurrences and this new one baffled the boy. He suddenly realized he would never see Ollor again and started to cry until another great sight appeared. Dolpho, the blue sea dragon, peaked through the raging waves and extended her tongue. Sunny stood on the smoky tongue and the dragon pulled him into her mouth. The fiery underwater trip seemed to take longer this time and just when he thought he would burst into flames, they arrived at the secret cove. Dolpho's mouth opened and Sunny could see the other dragons. He walked down the tongue and the cordial dragons greeted him.

"I didn't realize I was allowed to come without my sister," said Sunny.

"The time is much closer than most think. The demons will crash the shores of Gama Traka within the season. The humans think they are ready but Damian Doome will bring a war unlike any seen before. We detecteth a demon amongst thy School. Beware, you must. The predatory wolf dons the dress of a sheep, ready to strike without warning. We do not know who the inflicted human, but you need to figure out the mystery. We have a message to deliver to Muriel," Dolpho said. Sunny listened intently as the dragon spoke, "Be certain of all who surround both of you. There will be many people to trust but a demon lurks in the sand. As I have said, the disguised demon will try to destroy anyone who holds or knows the holder of the Pearl of Wisdom. Muriel doesn't hold a physical object but her internal ability could put her in grave danger if the secret is exposed to the wrong person. They will look to kill her or infest her body to use her special forces for evil. You must watch over her and protect the young girl. Without her, your life will be at the mercy of Damian Doome. I wouldn't want my fate determined by a blood-thirsty demon," Dolpho instructed.

Several of the dragons poured more information into Sunny's ears, and he promised to relay the information to his sister.

LEIMUR

The Queen of Goldenfield and her contingent moved through Burkeville. Leimur had brought a smaller army than planned to navigate stealthily through an invaded kingdom. She witnessed the squalor of Donegal and not a single citizen seemed to care for King Ali-Tersen. The people peacefully let her pass through and some wished her well along the way. This slightly concerned Leimur that an army would be able to walk right through her kingdom and capture her princes. Several men even took up with her cause and pledged to fight against the tyrannical Ali-Tersen Wamhoff. She had heard the names, 'White Demon, Albino King, King Killer, Ali-Tersen the Treasonous, Albino Snake and Ali-Tersen the Hunter King' used to describe him. She didn't hear any positive words about the King of Donegal during the entire trip.

This is going better than expected. We are well ahead of our travel plans and our sources report very little standing in our way. We need a quick victory so I can see my brothers and Ali-Tiste.

Leimur had never expected to fall in love with her sworn enemy. She had never understood what love truly felt like. A captain once told her, 'When you can't stand to be parted from them and they are all you think about, you are in love.' If this were true, Leimur was deeply in love and felt the rotten side of being separated from her partner. She had been slightly under the weather for a few days and the condition exacerbated her worries about the defenseless boys back at the palace.

The leaves were changing shades on a daily basis and deep scarlet and banana yellow caught her eyes as they passed through a bosky. Her horse trotted along as she looked back to see the cavalry following behind. The destrier's hooves started to sink and stick in the ground and Leimur knew they were coming up to the Pyesville Marshlands. Ali-Tiste had educated her on this area near the Fox Chapel Border. A crucial decision had to be made so she called for a quick meal before moving on. Her real motivation was to have a meeting to discuss how they should move forward.

The men constructed a pavilion and even though it wasn't perfect, the Queen knew the structure would serve it's short purpose. General Rigby and Captain Tetine propped up a portable table and Leimur set maps on the top. Captain Salina sat down and the quaternion got started. Leimur wasted no time pointing at the maps as she spoke, "We have two routes we can take. The first would take us well north around the Marshlands and much, much farther from our destination. On the other hand, if we cut straight across the smallest section of the Marshlands right here, we could surprise the king and have an easy takeover. The first way will take us far from Falconhurst where they can bring the fight to us, and they know the land better." The Queen tried to sell her idea arbitrarily rather than explain both sides.

"Countless thousands of Goldenfield soldiers lie under those marshes from ill-advised attempts at crossing. As long as my voice has a forum, I will advise against it. It's a death wish. No one has ever successfully crossed the Pyesville Marshlands," argued Captain Tetine.

"But those people didn't have inside information like we do. It won't be easy, but we will have to wait for more men-at-arms to arrive from Goldenfield if we go up and around," Leimur pleaded.

"A message has arrived, my Queen," said a voice from outside that Leimur recognized as her guard, Thadley.

"Bring it in," she yelled toward the door.

Thadley walked in, bowed to everyone, and handed a rolled scroll to Leimur. She read the message and lowered her head before speaking, "Our hand may have just been forced on this matter. There is a new King of Donegal. King Jon Colbert. Looks like he beat us to the prize but that doesn't mean we won't take it away from him."

"I say we wait for backup forces and then go up and around the Marshlands. We need more men to defeat the new King and I don't want to walk over our fallen brethren," General Rigby counseled.

"No. If we cross this narrow strip, we can get to the Capitol before the King has a chance to garrison his surroundings properly. The reason no other Goldenfield officer has been successful is because they have been trying to cross at the worst possible points," argued Leimur.

"I'm sorry, my Queen, but I've heard this argument before and we lost some good men to that marsh after General Hambauer said almost those exact same words." Captain Salina told her.

"But we have inside information that nobody else had," Leimur pleaded.

"Are we certain we can trust this Wamhoff woman?" General Rigby asked.

Leimur answered quickly, "This Wamhoff woman has gotten us across Burkeville completely unscathed up to this point. It's not her fault a stronger king has emerged from the rubble. Besides, it's not her decision whether we cross the marsh. She simply pointed out the best place to cross. She has no idea if we will even use that counsel. Ultimately, the decision comes down to me."

"Yes, well, remember what happened when you refused your council in the past, my Queen," General Rigby reminded her.

"Sorry General, but my mind is made on this matter. We will press on through the muck. Three-quarters of our forces will cross the narrow strait and the rest will head south for a diversionary tactic. We need to be craftier than this new King. We'll camp here for the night. We *will* make it across these mud lands," Leimur said.

General Rigby started to raise a hand in protest but Leimur talked before he had the chance, "Please don't try to debate me on this matter, General, my decision is final."

She left the meeting and went to her personal tent. The rain had picked up as nightfall approached and Leimur could hear the pitter patter of heavy drops over her head. Tolaya entered with some blankets and set them next to the Queen. "Go fetch a scribe. I must send a letter," Leimur ordered.

Her dutiful servant ran off to locate one of the scribes. Tolaya returned quickly with a young man who set up a trestle table, laid out his paper and massaged it flat, then waited for Leimur.

The Queen saw he was ready and dictated, "Dearest Ali-Tiste, We are making progress even faster than expected but we've run into a problem. King Jon Colbert presents an extremely dangerous element for a returning Wamhoff. It pains me to say this but perhaps you should stay at the palace with our boys. If you are to be caught in Donegal, the usurper king wouldn't hesitate to kill all of you. For these reasons, please stay in the safety of Goldenfield and the royal palace. I have sent instructions to Bero Sandway to increase security around the palace. This new situation also brings to my attention that the extreme possibility of death exists. If that were to happen, I would like you to take custody of Huber and Romer. My wish would be for you to rule Goldenfield as regent until Huber is ready to be king. Raise them well. Don't be easy on them, but shower them in love. They deserve it, our boys deserve love." She looked at the scribe and said, "Now make sure that gets to the palace."

"Yes, my Queen," the scribe said. He waited for the Queen to affix her signature before he broke down his equipment and left.

Leimur didn't sleep well that night. Her last major decision had ended in disaster and she worried about the marshlands all night long. Ali-Tiste had never taken an army across the Pyesville Marshlands or even traversed them herself. Leimur's wise men assured her that the footwear they had designed should work in the swampiest of conditions. In theory, everything should work out, but everything should have worked out on the Rushing River. She realized that if she got more men killed because of a bad choice, she could face a mutiny.

The next day, they packed everything up and split into two divisions. The horses were fitted with their special, oversized shoes that were secured around their ankles. Crosshatched strips of bamboo were tied together with sinew and hemp string to distribute the weight evenly and allow the mud to handle the pressure better. The infantry used smaller shoes to get across the sinking earth.

The marshlands were sticky, slimy and muddy at the same time. Black trees grew out of the muck and their twisted branches only made the crossing even harder to navigate. Legs and arms in various stages of decomposition stuck out of the mud and kept the area infested with bugs. Leimur could already feel them inside her armor and layers of clothes. The insects made her sweat even more in the sultry marshlands. The smell of the bodies started to hit her and make her gag. She wanted to throw up and strip her clothes off to swat away all the biting and pinching bugs. Despite experiencing the most uncomfortable feeling of her life, Leimur Leluc pressed ahead.

Shunning objections from anyone with a voice, the Queen heeled her horse and didn't look back. General Rigby and Captain Tetine kept pace with Leimur. The special gear worked well as the sounds of crushed leaves and twigs below the horses' shoes mingled with the buzzing of the insects and whistling of the birds. It got much hotter and more odious as they went farther and the sounds of the birds disappeared as the bugs became much louder. They got about one hundred feet into the steaming sludge and the horses adjusted to the awkward footwear. Leimur was starting to feel confident when she spotted a problem. The busted, fallen brush and leaves were matting into the small square openings. The shoes were sinking much deeper than before and the ground seemed to be getting looser as they moved forward.

Leimur ordered everyone to stop and dismount to clean the brush from the horses' shoes. The insects had an insatiable appetite for blood, constantly attacking any exposed skin. The panicked Queen managed to close her eye just in time before a mosquito stung her eyelid. Blurry vision had to be moved down the priority list as she frantically tried to avoid sinking. The Queen of Goldenfield pried the leaves from her horse's feet. Getting back on the horses proved to be quite a chore for everyone. Leimur dragged her body up with both hands on the saddle. She kicked her leg over, but the tar-like substance was all over the Queen when she got back on her mount.

She looked back through one eye and saw the other men struggling to get onto their animals. As they forged on, the conditions became worse and the horses sank deeper with every step. Leimur hoped she would wake up from this nightmare soon, but knew this wasn't a dream.

General Rigby shouted, "My Queen, we're not going to make it. We can still go back. We're going to die if we continue ahead."

For the first time, Leimur waffled about what to do. She could see the green grass on the other side of the marshlands but if the terrain kept deteriorating, they would surely sink into the marsh. She froze, with the bugs still pestering her and a throbbing pain in her eyelid.

If I should die, I know Huber and Romer will be fine with Ali-Tiste. At least I can say I lived with honor and always put Goldenfield ahead of my own intentions. I know I am leaving the kingdom in better condition than when I took over. But I will never be remembered like Marius Leluc.

"Stay the course, move ahead," screamed Leimur.

"Are you trying to get us all killed?" General Rigby yelled back. Several others demanded that the Queen turn back, but Leimur stood strong.

"I said we continue on. Forward march," she ordered.

The horses struggled mightily and some sank down to their ankles, making movement almost impossible. Leimur Leluc, Queen of Goldenfield, closed her eyes and wished for the best but expected the worst as she kept heeling her horse.

ELISA

Elisa and Lady Victoriah traveled near the back of the group. The enclosed wooden coach with plush interior served as a mobile meeting room on the way to the King's Castle. Elisa rubbed her choker, made of connected onyx squares.

Her Lord of Defense had a defeated look on his face as he jumped into the slow moving coach. Lord Wendell Deerheart relayed messages from Lord Ichibod to the ladies. The man bowed his head and spoke softly, "My queen, my lady. High Lords Wedgeword and Lolat are pledging fealty to King Jon Colbert."

"That dirty usurper has no rightful claim to your throne. He killed Jermar Lolat on the Royal Road and he just chased Sir Oliver Wedgeword out of Falconhurst. How can these houses stand behind him?" Victoriah complained.

"Regardless, he's obtained quite an army and didn't suffer a single casualty when he usurped the crown. The other high lords haven't responded to our request to clarify their allegiance," the defense master told her.

The excitement of leaving for battle had taken a sobering slap in the face when the news arrived that Jon Colbert had assumed the throne. Elisa had never seen Lord Ichibod as angry as when he heard about the takeover. He fed the raven that delivered the message to his hawks. They continued to move forward as planned but Elisa realized the task had become much more daunting.

"I can't believe that sleaze, Lord Nanbert!" Elisa exclaimed.

"Oh right. He did send a letter confirming his position of support for our claim. He's the only lord we really need to get to the Capitol. Without Pigeon Bridge, we have a much more arduous route to our prize," Lord Wendell reported.

"Pigeon Bridge? I fear you mean Pigeon Shit Bridge. Beware of the flying white waste; I hear it feels like a hammer hitting you on the head. We'll stay in this coach but the men might want to wear their battle helms. I'm glad Lord Nanbert is still on our side but I don't want to see his ugly face again," Lady Victoriah said.

"I second that sentiment. Send a letter to Jon Colbert and do not address him as king. Tell him that we thank him for his efforts in trying to rectify the kingdom but he can cease and desist. Let him know that the true heir of Donegal will forgive him if he relinquishes the throne. The rightful king will allow him to serve as Falconer and nobly serve the realm. Sign the letter in the hand of Ali-Varis Wamhoff, first son of Ali-Stanley Wamhoff, and the Gods' choice to be King of Donegal. Let him know we won't back away from our claim," Elisa stated confidently.

"You do understand he is going to reject this outright?" Lady Victoriah asked her.

"Of course. I want him to worry about why we are so confident in our stance. We could use a bargaining piece. If only we could capture one of his family members, we would have something," Elisa uttered. *I cannot believe I just said that. Is this how my enemies think about Telly? Mayhaps I am becoming cold and cruel?*

"Have the other false claimants renounced their stakes to a claim?" Lady Victoriah asked.

"I don't believe any have backed away which could help or hurt. Ali-Samuel Wamhoff and Queen Emilia have washed up in Waters Edge. They are rumored to have Krys Colbert in tow. If could get to him, that is if he is actually with them, now that's a bargaining piece," Lord Wendell said.

Elisa felt betrayed again as her co-conspirators appeared to have hatched a plan to retake the throne without her. She knew they had been using her to take the fall for King Ali-Stanley's death.

"It should seem they are camped out near Elkridge. The bastard usurper holds the castle and the two armies are at a standoff. This works to our advantage. Keep them both up there. I've been to war with both men and neither will blink on this matter. My only concern would be them banding together," the defense master told them.

I hope the bastard crushes her army straight into the Sea of Green. I knew I couldn't trust Ali-Samuel but I can't believe Emilia played me for a fool too. I pray to see that backstabbing bedswerver just one more time.

The coach came to a stop for an afternoon dinner. The leaf-covered road was flanked by sprawling stretches of grass trying to hang on to that bright summer green. Elisa would never admit it out loud, but she missed the services of the Grizzly Bear. She was still disturbed by the images of the trial by combat as she removed her veil to breathe the smells of horses and crushed leaves. Petyr, her new guard, barely talked to her. He always sported a gawky smile and stuttered when talking to the ladies. It seemed unusual for a hulking man to be intimidated by women. Petyr the Powerful lit the braziers and open fires while keeping an eye on the queen. They traveled with fourteen cooks who quickly got to work butchering and roasting some game. The amenities weren't as nice as the castle but she could hardly claim that she had been suffering the rigors of war. She was dirtier than usual because the travel tub took quite an effort to fill with hot water. She was thankful that they would soon pass several castles that would love to let a queen bathe.

She noticed Darryg Ellsworth sitting alone and went to talk to the young man. "Nice day, isn't it?" she started the conversation.

He responded, "Quite nice. Jealous as well." Elisa gave him a queer look.

"Jealous it could never be as fair as our lovely queen," Darryg said with a perfect smile. He was a charming man and always respectful to Elisa.

"It must be killing you to have to ride back here and not up front with all the men," she said. He gave her a strange look as Elisa realized her words could have been misinterpreted. "No, I didn't mean it like that. I meant that you probably wouldn't want to travel with the women. Alright I am just going to stop talking right now," the scarlet-faced queen said.

Darryg grinned to break the tension. The future King of Donegal had been ordered to stay away from any possible action by his parents. Conversely, Lord Ichibod planned to have his eldest son, Anderley, serve in the vanguard.

"Can I share something with you?" Darryg asked.

"I've kept all the other secrets we share. I can't see why not," Elisa told him.

"I'm nervous about this. I never served my military duty. My parents paid the tribute to keep me alive. I was supposed to go after Penrose but when he decided to serve in the King's Guard, my father didn't want the heir of Lightview getting killed defending the Wamhoffs. I've never killed a man and I don't know if I could do it. I would think about the mother or wife of the man, or even his children. I shouldn't be choosing when men die. I'm not a God. It's not right for me to decide another man's fate," Darry said with misty eyes.

"It's a shame more men don't think like you. There wouldn't be any silly wars and men could finally stop killing each other," Elisa said without realizing that her actions were only perpetuating the eternal problem of war. The queen looked over to a poplar and started to get angry. "Please excuse me, Darryg. It should seem I've got to get my sister out of a tree again," she curtsied and rushed away.

"Telly, you get down from there immediately," Elisa ordered.

"What for? This is the only fun I get to have. None of the kids in my carriage can even talk," Telly said in a snotty tone.

"Look, it's too dangerous for a girl to be climbing trees. It's unbecoming of a princess," Elisa chastised.

"I'm not your daughter, I'm your sister. I am not a princess," Telly said, as she climbed higher.

Elisa snapped, "Well you still need to act like one. Now get down from there this instant."

The younger Burke sister slowly worked her way back down the tree until she hit the ground.

"Now I know you don't get to do everything you want but I also make sacrifices every day. I never get to do anything I want. The faeblors tell tales of queens doing whatever they fancy but it's only a story, and a cruel story at that. Real queens have to make sacrifices and guess what, so do their sisters. You'll be able to have all the fun you want once we take over the realm. I promise," Elisa said.

"I was going to tell you something important, but since you're being mean to me I don't think I will tell you," Telly said.

"With mother gone, I am a sister and mother to you. I know you don't want me to worry about you but I have a duty to make sure you stay safe. You know I want to be nice to you all the time, but I have to correct you sometimes just like mother corrected me when I was your age. It doesn't mean I love you any less. I could have sent you away to any lord's castle in this entire kingdom. You could have been sworn to a marriage with a stranger but I wouldn't do it. You're my sister and I will need you to rule this realm someday. Now what do you have to tell me?" Elisa asked emotionally.

"Lord Ichibod is always mean to me. I want you to tell him to stop," Telly said.

"How is he being mean to you? He is barely around anymore," Elisa responded.

"When he is around, he yells at me for playing too rough with the little ones," Telly said.

"I've seen you around the kids and there are times when Lord Ichibod could have a point," Elisa told her.

Telly began to get very angry and asked, "So are you going to talk to him?"

"I'll tell you what. If he keeps it up, let me know and I will talk to him," Elisa promised.

"Well, that's not all of it. He also said some stuff about you," Telly said.

"He talked to you about me, did he?" Elisa needed to know.

"No. I was up in a tree and heard him talking to another man. He said once he takes the King's Castle, they were going to kill Ali-Varis," Telly informed her.

Now Elisa started to get riled up and asked, "Who was he talking to?"

"I couldn't see the other man but he had a laugh like a woman. Lord Ichibod told him that once Darryg took over as king, they would have no need of an overbearing queen. He said they could manipulate Darryg like a puppet, just like he was doing with you," Telly revealed.

Elisa was now seething and asked, "What else did Lord Ichibod say?"

"He said he was going to cut out your tongue and make you wear it as a necklace for a fortnight," Telly told her.

"I can't believe that man," Elisa said.

"That's not all. He said only after he let every soldier rape you, would he grant you a painful death in front of everyone. He said it would show what happened to those who challenged the Ellsworths. Lord Ichibod said it would show their power and be the perfect beginning to the long rule of the Ellsworths. I told you he was evil," Telly said.

"Who else have you told about this?" Elisa wanted to know.

"No one. I mean, just you, that's all," Telly swore.

"Don't tell anyone, promise?" Elisa waited for her sister to confirm.

"I promise, but you better be careful. What did you get us involved in?" Telly stormed away before Elisa could render an answer.

Elisa couldn't move for several moments. *How could he betray me? I should have known something was amiss when he took me falconing. I should have seen right through his recent bout of niceness. Has Lady Victoriah taught me nothing? And people think I am becoming too cold. It's quite obvious I'm nowhere near cold enough. I let my guard down with one man and he plots my death behind my back.*

The confused queen wandered around wondering if Lady Victoriah was privy to the plan. Elisa tried to catch a strange look from a guilty guard but nothing aroused suspicion. Count Pettice approached and said, "My queen, we are about to take off the bandages and assess the wounds."

"Alright then, I'll follow you," Elisa said. Sir Petyr was lurking as always and Elisa told him, "Sit and enjoy some food. I'll be fine to walk over to that wagon with the Count."

"Yes, my queen," said Petyr with a bow.

They neared the wooden wagon with the champion laid out in the back. He had several linens wrapped around his entire body. The count started to pull back the bandages and expose a severely bruised chest. Count Pettice peeled away the blood-soaked white bandages around Brehan's head. Elisa didn't know what to expect. His face had been covered in blood when they had rushed him to the Count's quarters after the duel with the Grizzly Bear. Elisa couldn't stand to watch the process and had gone to pray for Brehan's recovery instead. She had only seen him awake a few times since the death match. He remained unconscious as his face started being exposed. Count Pettice pushed open Sir Brehan's eyelids to expose cloudy gray eyes with occasional blood spots. Elisa jumped back in horror as the count uncovered Brehan's nose, or lack of one. The Grizzly Bear had ingested most of the nose during the brawl. The deep gashes on his cheeks and the overall lumpy look of Brehan's head made Elisa ill. *He looks hideous. He's like a pig, almost demonic-looking. He used to be gorgeous. I did this to him. I turned him into a monster.*

The count opened Brehan's mouth and it got even worse. Almost every tooth was either knocked out or shattered. Elisa turned away. The body stayed completely still as the count looked over the rest of Brehan.

"My queen, there is a strong chance that he will never regain full mental faculties. Eating will obviously be a challenge and we cannot repair his nose," Count Pettice informed her.

"So he is going to be grotesque?" she asked.

"His looks will not improve much from here, I am afraid, if that is your question," the count said.

"That was the question. Thank you for your service, Count Pettice," Elisa uttered.

"As you wish, my queen," the older man said.

Elisa nibbled on a few pieces of braised elk shoulder before getting back into the coach. Her mind bounced back and forth from Ichibod to Brehan. *Lord Ichibod has all the power. There's no way I could have him killed. The Grizzly Bear was the only man I could convince to do something like that. Is there anyone else who would be willing to help? What about Anderley? Brehan is the only one who would help me unconditionally out of love but the count said he may never be the same again. I need to take care of Lord Ellsworth before he takes care of me. And as for you, Lady Victoriah, you better hope you aren't duplicitous in this endeavor.*

Elisa tried to stare through the black veil and get a read on the lady. She couldn't see a sign of quilt on her so-called friend who had vowed like a noble knight to protect her always. Elisa thought about Brehan and realized he was the only person she could truly trust in this world.

TERSEN

"Again, we seem to be getting ahead of ourselves and forgetting who is king here," Tersen said when he couldn't take any more insults from Sir Oliver.

"Jon Colbert is king from all I see. I think you're forgetting that you are no longer king of anything. Out here, where you make the wrong turn and your throat gets slit, I'm the king. You can run off on your own and be king of the damn forest if it makes you feel good, and I wish you the best of luck with that. Now, if you stay, stop complaining and be happy you're still alive," Sir Oliver exploded at him.

The former king had no rebuttal. He wasn't suited for the outdoors. Traveling through dense woods and under the canopy of changing leaves prevented the sun from attacking the albino. However, he was harassed incessantly by insects. The bugs seemed to be the only citizens in the land that were willing to get close to Tersen Wamhoff. Even his wife sat as far from him on the wagon bench as she possibly could. "I think we are all going to die if we go to Castle Cuthbart. He's the one who sent all those slanderous letters around the realm," Tersen said.

"He also loves money. We sell him the crowns and he gives us a guarded entourage to escort us to my father's castle. Once we get there, you two will have no problem getting to a nice ship to go away for a while. It's all pretty simple," said Sir Oliver Wedgeword.

"I don't think we will get out of there alive," responded Tersen.

The former king was used to living in plush environments so he couldn't snuggle up and get any sleep on mother earth. He could hear Sir Oliver snoring almost every night while he stared at the moon and stars. Tersen kept whining, "They also said he backed the bastard usurper during our rule."

Sir Oliver screamed at the king from his mount, "Enough already. Don't make me shove a scarf in your mouth to quiet you."

Tersen couldn't believe the way his guard was talking to him. A month ago, he would have used other guards to kill Sir Oliver for the disobedience. Tersen didn't like it but he realized power had quickly shifted. This trip humiliated the man who carried a feminine reputation. He felt as worthless as possible. He couldn't light a fire, kill game or lead the sumpters on a beaten path. Every flying bird or sounds of rustling leaves caused Tersen to pull the hood of his pelisse over his face. He was constantly scared for his life. He knew how many people would like to see him dead.

The next day, they arrived at the outer gates of Castle Cuthbart. Tersen stared at the menacing black stone castle. The wide bridge was covered with moss and roots and there were several giant gargoyle statues made of ivory that had weathered over the years. The moat stunk like there were dead bodies in it and a quick peek showed four floaters before Tersen turned away. Giant columns with babery chiseled into them and red ivy wrapped around them from top to bottom flanked both sides of the bridge. As they neared the castle, they saw that demons, unknown symbols and downright scary creatures were carved into the facade of the castle. The detail was amazing and the grotesques stood out in high relief.

They wheeled the cart right up to the front steps of the castle. Porters came and carried their belongings inside. A smiling Harold Cuthbart greeted them on the bottom step. Tersen's heart raced even more as the young lord stared intently at him. Harolg finally wiped away the devious smile and bowed. He said, "Welcome, my esteemed guests. Why don't you come inside?"

"Thank you for the hospitality, my lord," Alvyra said as she passed the teenager.

"Thank you for the generosity, my lord," said Sir Oliver as he passed the young Cuthbart.

Tersen refused to bow down to a man of lesser station and silently passed the husky young man. Even though every man who was born to a lord bore the right to be called a lord as well, Tersen ignored this custom and walked by without even a nod of the head. In his mind, and only his mind, he was still a king. Lord Harolg invitingly pointed the way and followed the trio up the steep stone steps, through the lifted gate and into the south entrance. The wide foyer was lined with armed guards against two walls. The men had their swords in their right hands with the blade diagonally across their chests. Tersen started to think that he was about to be sacrificed.

"So how were your travels, my king?" Lord Harolg asked.

"Majestic. There's nothing like tangling with nature now and then," he lied.

"I see no reason why we shouldn't move straight to business," Alvyra said.

Harolg responded, "She has beauty and keeps her mind on the task at hand. Quite a queen, I must say. Open up those barehides and let's see what we have."

His guards pulled crown after crown from the leather cases and laid them in a row. Lord Harolg spoke, "One, two, three, four, five, six, seven, eight, nine, ten. There they are in all their opulence. The Seven Crowns of Donegal and the three captured crowns. I suppose these carry some value. A raven told me that what you seek is gold and an armed guard to take you to Castle Wedgeword. Did my ears hear the right words?" Harolg asked.

"That is indeed true, my young lord," Tersen decided to indulge him.

"Bring it in," Harolg told a page who ran off to relay the message.

Moments later, Harolg's men carried in seven rectangular wooden boxes. He slid open the tops to expose neatly stacked gold rounds. Tersen thought he saw countless thousands of the coins. The three visitors moved in for a closer look and the gold proved to be real. "The one hundred men you see will be included as well. They are some of my best men, so don't get them killed. Does this offer appeal to you, my king?" the high lord asked.

"We graciously accept," Tersen blurted out.

This offer is ridiculously rich. The crowns are valuable but this will help me raise an army.

Hope was instantly injected back into the former king. This quantity of gold could raise an army of free swords to come back and reclaim his throne.

I might have Sir Oliver killed if he keeps treating me poorly. My wife better wise up too. At least this little lordling is showing me the proper respect. It's only a matter of time before I return to put Jon Colbert's head on a spike. I will resurrect the Wamhoff name as Alvyra prophesized. I will be the king again.

"Alright, so everything is settled. You can stay for the day or be on your way if there's nothing else."

The young lord shook his finger and continued, "How forgetful of me. I forgot we had one more piece of business to negotiate."

What is he talking about?

"What is the going rate for a deposed king on the run? I know whom we should ask," said Lord Harolg. The one man Tersen wished to never see again entered the foyer.

"How about a hunt, good uncle?" asked Kryen Wamhoff.

Tersen tried to bolt like a horse but was quickly overtaken by the surrounding guards who kept taking unnecessary shots at the former king. One of the guards noticed a dirty look coming from Lord Harolg. The guard shrugged his shoulders and said, "I never got to punch no albino before."

"Oh now, where do you think you are going? We haven't even started with you yet, my king," taunted a smiling Harolg.

Two more rectangular boxes of gold coins were added to the deal and Alvyra gladly accepted.

"You betrayed me. The two people I trusted more than anyone," Tersen lamented.

"I maximized your worth right now just as I have our entire marriage. At least you can rest comfortably knowing you'll keep me a rich woman for the rest of my days. Now I can begin my life with a real man," Alvyra told him. Sir Oliver leaned down and kissed the former queen. She spoke to Tersen, "Your suspicions were valid. We started our affair the moment you appointed him Captain of the Guard."

"That's bigamy," shouted Tersen.

The voice of Kryen entered the conversation, "It's only bigamy if you are alive, good uncle. You never know what can happen on a hunt," Kryen taunted the former king.

I am as good as dead. My wife sold me like a common slave. I used to be the King of Donegal.

"Kryen is going to ask you a few questions and your answers will go a long way in determining whether you will be alive tomorrow," Harolg said and turned to Sir Oliver and Lady Alvyra, "I can't thank you enough for this gift. Won't you stay for the night?"

"Certainly, we'll leave on the morrow," said Sir Oliver.

"Great. We will have a grand time this evening. Reinholdst, show these fine nobles to the guest apartments. Thanks again and I will see you in a bit," stated Harolg as Tersen's travel mates were whisked away into the castle.

Tersen was still being held by the guards when Kryen asked, "Why did you do it? Why did you kill my father, brother and Ali-Ster?"

Tersen started crying, "All I ever wanted to be was king. I was kicked around by my own family my whole life. Then it was so close and my wife kept pushing and pushing. Look at me, I'm an albino, a worthless albino is all. I didn't see it as killing your father or brother, they were just names in the way of me becoming king."

"Just names in the way, huh? No one defended you more than my father. He denounced Ali-Ryen and any chance to rule the realm to support you. When everyone criticized you all the time, and I do mean all the time, he was always quick to defend you," Kryen told him.

"My wife, it's been my wife, you heard her before. She convinced me that Ryen never loved me and that he talked constantly about me behind my back. It was all her," Tersen explained.

"Blaming a woman. And a lovely one at that. I know you may still be upset that she sold you away to be tortured, but that was minutes ago," laughed Harolg. He continued, "Oh, did I say tortured? I guess the secret is out."

"Do you even feel sorry for what you've done?" Kryen asked.

The sobbing Tersen said, "Every day, every night and even when I sleep. If there is anything in my life I could take back, it would be that day in the King's Woods. I pray to the Gods for forgiveness every day."

"Perhaps you should pray harder. I don't believe him," Kryen said.

Harolg turned to the guards and spoke, "Take this man down to the board and strap him in to be stretched out. Kryen and I will be down shortly to have some fun. We must first check on our guests. We'll have a few chalices of wine and then show our king the respect he deserves."

Tersen was dragged down the steps as he thought about how long he would remain alive. Less than a fortnight ago, he was King Ali-Tersen and now he was thrown into a rat-infested room with several torture devices scattered about.

JON

King Jon tried to get comfortable in his new meeting room as he wiggled in the chair. The room had been stripped of all Wamhoff mementos and the circular table and chairs seemed almost too plain for a prominent room in the King's Castle. Jon looked down at the piece of parchment and read over the list.

King's Council
Falconer-Lord Kelvyn Harros
Master of Coin-Lord Enric Plast
Grand Lord of Defense-Lord Hydell Kenzy
Admiral of the Sea-Lord Errol Swansmore
Foreign Overlord-Lord Rance Perry
Master of Spies-

Jon wrote 'Count Silzeus' in the blank space left for Master of Spies, and completed his new council. All the new members were in attendance along with Ruxin Colbert.

"Who is most likely to arrive first?" the King of Donegal asked.

"Lord Ellsworth's party touting Ali-Varis Wamhoff as king should arrive first from the east. The Queen of Goldenfield shouldn't be too far behind them from the west. We seem to have hit a spot of luck in the north. There is a standoff between two sizable forces. Let them slaughter each other, I say," Lord Kelvyn reported.

"We need be careful they don't band together. Three opponents would be nearly impossible to fend off," Jon Colbert added.

"Yes, my King. We have received word that the construction of the protectionary wall is going faster than originally expected. The wall to the east is making rapid progress so we can keep that barbarian horde away," Hydell Kenzy said.

"Are the pyromancers working in conjunction with the building process?" the King asked.

"Indeed they are, your highness. The vast number of workers is moving this project along nicely," Count Silzeus told him.

The King's days had been filled with meeting after meeting, but securing the castle and Falconhurst were paramount. He hoped that at least one of the contenders for the crown would give up after he took the throne. He had to be on constant alert with the ever-present threat of an invasion looming large.

Jon instructed his council, "Let's concentrate on the east and west sides of the Capitol and leave the north alone for now. The only thing we need to worry about in the north is plugging the Blue and Silver Cap Mountain passages."

"On another matter, the lowered taxes are reaping results. Morale is starting to rise amongst the poor. The citizens appear to support their new King," said Lord Enric.

"Lowering taxes will make some people like me, aye, but it also upsets those who collect the taxes. We need to keep the nobles happy but also make them understand this policy will be enforced strictly. There won't be any roguish increases when the king turns his back. Any lord caught extorting from his subjects will be tried for treason. The days of phantom policies for the sake of inflating reputations are over. My father proved what could happen when the common class has a strong leader. The poor rise up in unity and the numbers will always favor the poor," Jon informed his council.

"We will need to keep a close watch on a good many lords. Scared citizens would never disobey their liege lords. We'll have to catch them in the act. It should take only one greedy offender for us to make an example of, and the rest will fall in line. Everyone needs to see that the laws will be enforced," Count Silzeus said.

"All laws will be enforced. I don't put up with nonsense, my good count," Jon reminded the old man.

Count Silzeus' words often made Jon curious about the previous rulers. The castle veteran's warnings and concerns were common sense that his predecessors must have lacked. A page entered the room and whispered in the King's ear.

"Men, we must reconvene at a later hour. I have a pressing matter to tend to. Thank you for the time; you are all dismissed," Jon said.

The men rose, bowed and left the meeting. A barefoot, dirty man entered the room in a tattered kirtle. He slowly slid his bare, black-soled feet across the stone floor as he walked, and spoke when he neared Jon, "Quite plush accommodations."

"I am the king. I need to present a position of power," Jon Colbert explained.

"There's that word again. Power. I grow weary of most men who wield that word. Religion is faith, almost a blind hope. We ask people to believe in Gods they cannot see. We ask worshippers to believe in the heavens which they may never see. In good faith, these principles are realized after we die, but there is no substantial proof to back this up. Kings are much like religion. Citizens must have faith in their king. They must believe. They want to believe in a king that will treat all men equal. I firmly believe no king will be able to accomplish that task, so I ask myself who can come the closest. I trust you are pure in your intentions. My skepticism from last week has waned as I have seen the vision. The Gods have selected you as King of Donegal. I searched deep in my soul and asked the Gods why you presented me with this opportunity. All moral inclination pushed me far from the proposition until I had a revelation. If there could be a king who will stay committed to his people, all his people, I could help a man driven by this passion," Orian told him.

"Is that when you realized I needed you to correct our church system?" Jon asked.

"Not quite. I still had doubts until a met a lovely Princess in the castle dungeons. Your daughter's soul might shine brighter than a sinless newborn.

Sin can chip away at a person while good deeds and strong faith only fortify us. We all sin, most from a very young age, but living by the Words of our Gods can outweigh our immoral intentions. I accept your offer to attend your daughter's wedding ceremony, albeit for a short time. I will perform the ceremony and would like to talk to the young couple and advise them to live by the Words of the Gods. I also accept your offer to rectify the religious order of the realm. It shall be a purging resurrection. There will be no high priest, only pure creatures, dedicated to delivering the proper message. I will be equal to every man who accepts the holy vows. All churches will be stripped of excessive decoration. We must get back to an emphasis on prayer and holy service rather than elaborate buildings and magic devices of trickery. Men and women will be spiritual again, not just claim they are by throwing gold at a brother or sister of the Faith. Donations will not grant special favors either. I shall cleanse the land and remove all the wayward priests known to sell their souls for false salvation. The Faith shall also reserve the right to try any wrongdoers and punish the guilty accordingly. The king will have his laws and the Faith must do the same. Sometimes, a gentle man needs to make hard decisions for the benefit of the whole and I am certain none understand that more than you. Our Gods do not grant exemptions to repeat sinners and we must be swift to purify the faith," Orian Vangor finished his demands.

"You will have my backing on everything. The only problem I foresee is not having a hierarchy to solve internal problems. You need a higher voice to settle disputes among the priests," Jon said.

"I have already established The Council of Seven to reach verdicts on major issues. I make everything sound simple at times, but I would never accept an offer had I not already set up a strong interior system of balances. The Council met yesterday to devise ways to praise the Gods without turning it into a status symbol. The Faith of Eternal Light shall remain as our religious order but the delivery of the holy messages will change drastically," the old man smiled.

"You can talk directly to my Master of Coin, Lord Enric Plast. That should speed matters up when you need money. I will alert him to grant any request you may have," Jon told him.

"That is a genuine endorsement. I hate that we need money to fix these problems caused by money, but we will only take what we must. I also have a request for uh…uh…some larger men to help me enforce the faith. I prefer men who worship our Faith but any man whose ears are open to the words of the Gods will suffice. Again, the unfortunate side to being a father to the people. But just as a father disciplines his child, so must a king with his citizens and a priest with his repeat sinners," Orian said.

"Aye, I'll direct you to my Training Master. He can provide further details on which men have strong faith. How many men do you think you will need?" Jon asked.

Orian scratched his head and said, "A good one hundred men will make for a good start. The Words of the Gods just aren't enough anymore."

"That shouldn't be a problem. Is there anything else I can do for you?" the King wanted to know.

"I have told all the crooked priests to evacuate the House of Eternal Faith. They returned with an angered argument containing vulgarity that is very unbecoming of a servant of the Gods. I may need you to flush these men from the House. We need to make a public display of sinners being cleansed from the Capitol. We need our citizens to see the impoverished members of society being offered accommodations over the nobles. Symbols, actions, stories, offerings, statements. Any of these can send a strong message to the people. There are times when words will be enough to convince the people but this isn't one of those situations. We need to send a message of action, not empty words, this time," Orian instructed.

"I couldn't agree more. If you should require anything else, I believe you know where to find me. If you set up in the House, I could come see you upon request," Jon said.

"Oh, no. I need to spread the word. I need to travel the lands and see exactly what needs to be repaired. I'll be leaving soon enough. The Words of the Gods have boundless wings, and those wings need to fly. I will stay for the matrimony of your daughter. I wish to recruit her to join me in spreading the gospel. The faith runs pure in her. You should be well proud to have produced such a fine daughter. I will be happy to bless her union," Vangor offered.

"Thank you, I will have my guards escort you back to…well, wherever you need to go," Jon said.

"Much gramercy but I need no escort. The Gods will watch after me and decide when they need to take me. I must apologize for missing your coronation. I heard it was a modest, understated affair and I must commend you on this. You obviously have my blessing as king. I only hope you don't expect me to sink to a knee or treat you any different than the poorest man who believes in the faith," Orian warned.

"I understand completely," Jon told him.

The frail man slowly rose and exited the room.

Jon walked across the Capitol to visit Tormel's new site for building weapons and armor. Jon arrived out of breath and wished he had taken a horse as he walked up to the door. He could hear hammering and construction as he entered and was greeted by the King of Scholars in his usual tattered epitoga and accompanying body odor. Jon looked around and saw a quiet young man in the corner who appeared to be patiently layering fabrics for a winter shirt. The small man first pressed down and patted over the entire area of a layer of fabric. He picked up another layer of woven fabric and brushed it with resin. He kept adding more layers to create a very unlikely armor jacket. Jon didn't understand exactly how the fabric jackets worked better than iron or steel, but he had seen the results firsthand. The protection was extremely lightweight and gave his side an advantage in battle. The only downside was that a person needed help from at least one other and maybe two to secure the tight-fitting jackets.

Jon asked, "What happened to those…those little things that explode?"

Tormel spoke slowly as usual, "The incendiaries have run into a problem. On our travels to get everything we needed here, our wagon wheel busted and one of the necessary ingredients was lost. We are waiting for some more to arrive from Ton Abelisey."

Jon wanted to know, "So do you have any completed right now?"

A rank smell emanated from the underside of Tormel's armpit and filled the air as he scratched his head and said, "Approximately fifty, but we won't be able to produce more for at least another month. And as I have told you, it's quite the volatile process, to say the very least."

Jon made a promise, "I'll only use them if the need should be dire."

Jon woke up on the day of his daughter's wedding in a cold sweat. He had a slight buzz in his head. He hadn't been getting any crippling headaches since the imprisonment and saw it as the only positive taken from the experience. Jon went and ate breakfast before going to see his little girl prior to the ceremony, but he walked in on a grown woman.

She was in a small perfume room with four makeup tables and flowers covering all the walls. Jon could barely breathe from the heavy smell of the freshly cut stems and lively petals.

Her jewelry, dress and make up made Jon see her in a new light. "Father," Mariah greeted Jon.

"Hello there, are you getting nervous yet?" he asked.

Mariah nodded to her father with a reserved smile. Deydranna stopped working on the bride's make up and left the room so father and daughter could have some privacy.

"It's natural. At least you had the chance to know Torvald before the wedding. I only knew your mother from a few conversations. You two will be just fine today," he reassured her.

"Thank you, father," Mariah said.

"I still can't believe this day is upon us. I remember when I could hold you in the palm of my hand. The first time I held you, I never wanted to let you go. I looked at you and saw perfection. That tiny baby grew into a child who loved to argue with her father. I commanded rough and rugged men twice my size who never gave me half as much trouble as you. That child grew into a teenager…she still loved to argue with her father," Jon smiled as tears welled up in both of their eyes. He continued, "And that father wouldn't have it any other way. I couldn't be prouder of you and I love you even more now than when you were a perfect little babe. I used to dread this day. I could never envision a young man worthy of my perfect daughter. I have kept you close by my side for good reason but I can't think of a better man to give you away to."

"I just wish his parents could be here to see this. You would have loved them. I know you would have, I just know it," Mariah told him.

Jon rubbed his daughter's frilly shoulder and said, "I'm sure I would have loved them, my dear. I'll bet they are looking down from the heavens with a big smile for the both of you."

Mariah rubbed the golden bull hanging from her neck that now caused her to think about Lucille and said, "I never thought this day would come. I remember the day I heard you and mother had been killed. That nightmare shifted to a dream before my very eyes when I saw you both again in Riverfront. I thought this could finally be the way to impress you."

"Impress me? What could you mean by that?" Jon asked.

"With the boys, they have other ways of impressing you with swords or longbows. I never had that chance to accomplish something like going away for war duty," she said.

"Oh, my sweet dear. You don't need to impress me. You've always impressed me. Being able to grow up with your brothers is an impressive feat in itself," Jon smirked.

"Thank you, father," Mariah told him.

"It may seem like I give you a hard time because I am used to dealing with rough and tumble men most of the time. It's hard to switch back and forth from gentle father to disciplinarian duke with the snap of a finger. With that said, I've failed as a father if I've ever given you the impression that you disappointed me," Jon told her.

"No, it's nothing you've done. It's not you, it's me. I just feel like I haven't accomplished anything worthwhile up to this point," Mariah said as Camelle entered the room.

She looked at her mother in a plain yellow gown with an extremely conservative neckline and long sleeves. What must have been the least decorated gown at the wedding brushed the ground. She didn't wear any make-up or jewelry. The long gown covered up Camelle's shoes, which were Mariah's favorite part of the outfit.

"We may need to cancel the wedding, my love. Our daughter's gone mad. She's somehow under the impression that she has let us down," Jon said.

Camelle seemed rushed and quickly said, "We don't have time to worry about this nonsense now. And that is absolute frippery, Mariah. Now, the

King needs to leave so Deydranna can finish our daughter's extravagant make up. The poor girl is pacing back and forth outside the door. She's worried there won't be enough time to finish, so goodbye father," Camelle said as she pushed Jon out the door.

He stopped and gave his daughter a hug before being hustled out. He heard Mariah say, "I love you father." He wanted to return the courtesy but the door shut again.

A-MARIAH

Deydranna rushed over to her supplies and got back to work. She finished the gold leafing around Mariah's eyes and forehead. An exotic, swirling pattern of glowing yellow accented by concentrated streaks of silver made Mariah look like a foreign princess. When Deydranna had first proposed the idea to Mariah, she had rejected it. Deydranna had then painted the face of a new member of the Queen's court named Lady Morgaine and showed her to Mariah. The princess fell in love with the look and even Camelle approved. It took Mariah about an hour to convince her father to give permission. Mariah wanted to distinguish herself from all the previous princesses of Donegal on their wedding days. Her father was a traditional man but as long as she agreed to sport golden bull accoutrement, Jon went along with it.

Deydranna attached the choker, and the object lived up to its name. A snug, uncomfortable fit became immediately annoying. Her mother pulled the charm on her golden bull necklace, looked at it and gently placed it back near her daughter's heart. *I wish Lucille and Edword were here. If you can hear me from the heavens, we love you. We will always love you and wish you were here.*

Deydranna grabbed the long white lace ties and wrapped them around Mariah's arms to produce a beautiful crossing pattern. Her shoes had matching strings that extended and intertwined up her legs and were hidden under a dress that hung to the floor. The rich purple material had seven crowned bulls' heads stitched in Goldenthread around her midsection.

"Seeing you like this takes me back to my special day. I arrived in Riverfront to meet your father the night before our wedding. Take deep breaths and enjoy everything. You only get one wedding to remember forever. I thought mine was grandiose until I inspected these party plans. This should prove how much your father loves you. I would have never expected your father to approve these plans, let alone add to them. It scared him more than he is willing to admit when he almost lost us. Now, he sees what's important to you and he supports it," Camelle said.

"It's no secret that you had a lot to do with it, I'm sure. I know I've always been a handful and I appreciate everything you've done for me over the years. I'm not always quick to say thank you to father and you," Mariah confessed.

"If you think you were a handful, you better hope to the heavens you never have any boys. Keeping up with their antics of constantly harassing Ruxin kept me busy enough. You were a treat to raise for the most part. You don't need to thank a mother for what she is supposed to do. As a mother, it's days like this that gives us all the satisfaction we need. Just think, your brother's official wedding celebration with the family will be next week," Camelle said.

"I can't believe he is going to miss today, my wedding day," Mariah complained.

"Your father and brother are under the assumption that the soldiers won't fight if one of them isn't out there. That's the foolish thinking of men; get used to it. I had a long argument with your father over this and he said he sent Ruxin to the west where there's no chance of conflict. Ruxin thinks he is doing this for you so your father can attend the wedding," Camelle explained.

"Two weddings in two weeks. Your children have all grown up," Mariah said.

"Both of you aged years in mere months. Hardship will do that to a person and although it may have been good for you, I hope you never have to face anything like that again," her mother said.

"Me too, but I wouldn't be getting married to Torvald if I hadn't experienced that. Is it true that Krys is with the Wamhoffs?" Mariah asked.

"I think it's only a cruel ploy to manipulate your father. I hope this is true, nobody does more than me, but the Wamhoffs demand your father give them the kingdom in return. No one has confirmed that they have Krys and, until someone does, I fear this is only the dirty tactics of war. No, don't cry, your face will run," Camelle warned.

Mariah tried to hold back the tears, "I just wish there was something I could do to help."

"There is. You can go enjoy your day. If your brothers were here, they would be so happy for you. They had a strange way of showing it, but they loved you. I can remember a time at the markets when the boys overheard George Ropert saying he kissed you and played under your blouse," Camelle said, to protect Mariah.

George had insulted Mariah for having big buckteeth that she had since grown into. Camelle knew the real reason would make her daughter self-conscious so she conveniently changed the story but all the rest was true.

"Your brothers warned him that he better stop but the little chatter mouth carried on with his stories. Ruxin, the smallest of your brothers, grabbed the boy by the throat and pushed him up against a storefront. George reluctantly agreed to stop and Ruxin let him loose. I probably should have stepped in and stopped him, but I was a proud mother watching him defend his sister like that. If the situation were ideal, Ruxin would be here for you. Ruxin thinks he is protecting you today, just like he did back at the markets with George. As you spend more time with Torvald, you'll find that men act in unusual ways. Your brother, even as a very young man, demonstrates these signs," Camelle told her.

She finished talking to her mother and Deydranna placed the multi-flower chaplet secured with lace over Mariah's head. As the time neared, Mariah walked in circles around the tiny room.

The rest of the day was an overwhelming whirlwind of events.

Her father had proudly escorted her up to the altar in the castle chapel. Mariah looked around the room as they moved toward the stage. A lot of the guests looked like they were going to fall asleep as the ceremony closed in on about three hours. She continued as the people threw flowers in front of her path. She looked ahead at Orian and felt guilty about the flower throwing despite his toothless grin. Her attention moved to her husband-to-be.

Torvald Malik wore the perfect outfit of shiny, dark blue hose to show off his powerful legs and blend in with the color of his bride's dress. His black doublet had seven argent rams sewn around his belly and lower back to match Mariah's dress. Her father let her arm fall before grabbing and kissing her hand. He looked her in the eyes and said, "I love you. You make me so proud." He kissed her hand again and held it against his heart for a moment. Mariah could feel her father's excitement as he extended her hand to Torvald. The smiling young man from Bottomfoot eagerly grabbed Mariah's hand as she still looked at her father and they shared one final loving gaze. Jon kissed and hugged his daughter before taking his seat next to Camelle.

Mariah's next memory was walking out of the rectory with Torvald to the thunderous cheers of the attendees. The ceremonial throwing of ground wheat wasn't Mariah's favorite part of the ceremony as the grains got stuck to her body and in her dress. The grain was to encourage a fertile family but Mariah wished there was a better custom.

The next thing Mariah knew, the guests were starting to sit down in the grand hall for supper.

She saw Orian approaching and greeted him with a curtsy.

He said, "I'm afraid I must take leave."

She was almost offended and asked, "Why? Are you and your friends not having a good time?"

He shook his head and replied, "Too much it should seem, and that's precisely the problem. I need to become scarce before I indulge too greatly in these good times. There are too many handsome women here to prevent my thoughts from remaining completely pure. I don't want to whip myself to death, right here on your celebration day."

Mariah disagreed, "It's not sinning if you don't act on it though. Just thinking about sin is natural."

Orian raised his prominent eyebrows and said, "I like that word. Natural. If we think about sinning over and over, we will start to act on it eventually. Thwarting temptation can prove a fruitless endeavor despite the greatest of effort being given. Thinking about sinning is the first step toward the deed itself. It becomes natural and we make rationalizations to justify our sinful actions. Then, we start lying to cover up the other sins and madness takes over as a vicious wheel spins out of control. Have fun, my dear, but remember salvation is most often steeped in selfless acts of humility." He looked around at the expensively decorated hall and went to leave.

Mariah asked, "Are you sure you and your friends don't want to stay and eat? I can have part of the meal brought out early if you would like."

He turned to face her and answered, "I've already taken full advantage of the servants with their trays of treats but my friends would like to stay if you would permit."

Mariah immediately reassured him, "Of course, I would be happy to do so. I will make sure they are well taken care of. In fact, I am going to take any food that is left over to Kimberton to distribute to the people."

He looked at her and wrinkled his nose before he responded, "I suppose that will bring smiles to a good many, but it will depend on the gluttony practiced in this hall prior to delivery. Now if you would be kind enough to excuse me, I must atone for these impure thoughts I've been having. My dear." He nodded and walked away as Mariah looked around the hall.

She really started to see the money wasted that could have been put to a more charitable use.

Several jugglers on low-stilts approached the married couple and heaved several large, fragile vases in the air. The surrounding crowd held its collective breath until the fragile objects landed back in the men's hands. They continued to rotate the vases and even tossed them back and forth for added difficulty. The autumn wedding called for warm clothing, and most of the women's attire consisted of a combination of ermine, pean, vair, potent, fox and squirrel fur mixed with various colors of layered charmeuse, chiffon, duchess satin and crushed velvet. She looked at the corner of the room with the barrels of wine from all around the world stacked high against the wall. Every course of the twenty-one course meal was to be matched with a special wine to enhance the flavor of the dish.

It wasn't until the fifth course that Mariah started to feel guilty about the expense of the grand event again. She bit into a chicken liver on a piece of stag horn that had been sliced thin and fried in lard. She thought about her brothers and fought away tears wishing even one of them could have been present.

After the dinner was served, there were tables set up with dessert items for the guests to serve themselves. Everyone got up and walked around and Mariah found herself surrounded by her Bottomfoot friends. Callice marched up to the group and started to sing,

"A pair can pair for all of time,

For no reason or no rhyme,

Perfect man with woman to match,

The strongest love, now watch it hatch,

A pair lived with honor and died so too,

They touched so many, not just a few,

We've cried, we've wept and mourned the loss,

That mighty bridge, we cannot cross…"

Callice stopped singing suddenly and she heard gasps coming from the crowd. Mariah couldn't understand what was happening until she stepped out from behind her husband and nearly passed out. The same feeling hit her as when she had seen her mother in Mattingly, after believing her to be dead.

Tears liberally fell to the matted rushes. Beyond the dance floor, Mariah could see her father approaching with a ravishingly dressed woman. She rubbed her eyes and almost fainted. Callice stopped singing and silence snared the tongues of the stunned crowd. There stood Lucille and Edword Malik, alive and well. She didn't pass out this time, and ran over to Lucille and Edword to give them a big hug as the couple was being swarmed by awestruck family and friends. The euphoria lasted several minutes and the group hug was finally broken.

Mariah asked Lucille, "How are you…? What happened? I thought…"

Lucille pulled her in for another squeeze and whispered in her ear, "We weren't in the castle when that awful dragon attacked. We were out paying tribute to the families who lost sons in the Fox Chapel attack. We were in the Laurel Lowlands, far from the attack, but it still breaks a duchess' heart to find out about something like that. This is your day." Lucille whispered something into her ear and Mariah looked around.

She spotted a band of instrument players and yelled, "Play something that we can all dance to."

She grabbed Lucille's arm and the two listened as several musicians tried to play all at once until one song drowned the rest out. Everyone started to move to the music except her mother who stood off to the side near the wall holding her baby brother. Mariah saw her mother look away quickly as she made eye contact. She detected a look of jealousy and excused herself from Lucille and walked over to her mother.

She grabbed her hand and said, "Come dance, will you?"

Camelle spoke fast, "No, I can't. You go, I've got little Jon to worry about."

Mariah dragged her out from the wall and said, "Stop making excuses. Little Jon will love it."

She started to feel happy again until she noticed Haley with a forced smile and wished Ruxin could have attended.

B-RUXIN

Ruxin threw the wooden stick out onto the grass. Jasper ran over, scooped it up with his mouth, and brought it back to Ruxin. He sat on a tree stump and continued throwing the piece of wood to his dog. Ruxin tossed the stick again but the dog ran by it and over to the edge of the hill.

The dog started barking. Ruxin told Jasper to stop, but the dog wouldn't listen.

"General Taker, get the men ready. Send word to the next unit to be on alert. We may need backup," Ruxin said.

"What? Where is this coming from?" the general asked.

"Do it now. That's an order from your prince," Ruxin commanded.

Ruxin walked over to the incline and looked down. He saw screaming soldiers rushing the bottom of the hill. Ruxin assumed this was a scare tactic to draw them down into a trap. He thought the men would rush halfway up the hill and retreat. As the enemy passed the halfway point, Ruxin's men began to assemble along the precipice. Ruxin drew his sword and his men followed.

Who are these fools? They have the purple tiger banners but she can't be this foolhardy. Does she think we only have one hundred men? Nobody would attack uphill like this.

Ruxin looked behind him and saw his count of soldiers growing by the second. Ruxin wasn't going to allow the enemy to get to the top, so he screamed, "ATTACK."

The men rushed down like wild banshees and Ruxin quickly overpowered a fat soldier by driving his sword into the man's unprotected chest. Moving downhill, Ruxin killed liberally and often, massacring the enemy with ease. He couldn't understand why they would attack uphill. As the utter slaughter pressed on, Ruxin realized that all the men were normal soldiers. No one wore the colors or decoration of an officer. He killed four more men and looked around the hillside. Bodies covered the normally romantic landscape, soiling the purple-leaved bushes and littering the dense orange soil. Very few of Ruxin's men had been lost until it hit him.

I smell a red herring. This has to be an illusory attack.

There weren't any high-ranking members of an army and most of the so-called men looked younger than him. His suspicions were confirmed when he saw boys who looked like pages or squires dressed in the special surcoats of officers but lacking the sufficient armor or body protection.

A frantic Ruxin ran up the hill, stumbling on dead bodies and hacked-up pieces of men. He tried to work around the carnage but that proved impossible. After wading through and over the bloody mess, he reached the top.

He saw two messengers and yelled, "Get the fastest horses. We need to leave now. We need to get word back to the castle, immediately."

C-LEIMUR

"ATTACK," screamed the Queen of Goldenfield. An explosion of pent-up aggression followed and her troops rushed south. The vanguard smashed into the unprepared opposition. Her army had been permitted to pass through the city gates after bribing a sympathetic lord. She could hear shouts from the enemy. Calls for retreat, sending word back to the castle and her favorite, surrender, rang in her ears along with the banging blades around her. They herded up a group of men that yielded without much resistance and the Queen continued toward her prize.

She hoped the false attack would force the King of Donegal to send forces to the west and leave the northern area unprotected. Leimur hoped the attack was still going on. She had only left instructions not to attack uphill. She knew the smaller force would ultimately be defeated, but if it could extend the battle for at least an hour and draw men out of the Capitol, it would go down as a wild success . When Leimur had learned that the new King would be at his daughter's wedding today, she knew it was the perfect time for an attack. She worried about more people being in the Capitol but most of them weren't fighting men. Dusk slowly stole in, which was fine with Leimur, who didn't mind fighting in the near dark.

As they rambled down a slight hill into a level valley, another faction of soldiers stood in her way. Her warriors shredded through the enemy with ease and raced across the open plain. They came to another hill and the cavalry raced ahead as the Queen preferred to fight on foot. The bowmen set up at the bottom of the hill and the Queen thought back to the Marshlands.

Just when Leimur had thought it was her fate to be sucked under the murky earth, the ground firmed up and allowed her horse to make it safely across. The worst of the swampy area proved to only span about fifteen feet. General Rigby thanked her for not taking his advice and retreating. They made it into Fox Chapel undetected, traveling under the deep cover of thick forests. Her spies had noticed only small units randomly placed in strategic areas north of the castle. Her informers had found heavy forces to the east and west, but the north side seemed to be forgotten. The Queen's unlikely plan had paid off so far but looking up this hill made her worry. She tried to get her men up to the top as fast as possible because she hadn't seen much of the enemy yet. All reports told her that Jon Colbert was a brilliant battle technician. She was on edge wondering where an attack could come from. Her contingent made it to another level area. Leimur heard a sound like a thundering herd and looked at the next hill in front of them to see a heavy unit racing at them.

The two forces crashed into each other, sword on shield, and the wild warring commenced. Leimur whirled her battle-axes around and traded failed attacks with an older man with a long sword and shield. She ducked a wild swing and rose quickly to bury one axe into the man's helm, right at the bridge of his nose. The cold steel caved the iron helm inward, creating a mortal wound. She pulled her weapon out of the dead man's face and continued killing. This proved to be a lower skilled unit and Leimur's soldiers crushed the enemy quickly.

I can taste the throne already. All the reports of Jon Colbert being a battle expert seem to be lies to create a false mystique. I wish I could send a letter to the palace and tell Ali-Tiste and my boys to leave for the castle now. This is as good as Goldenfield's.

Another small force of very green teenagers tried to stop Leimur. They only delayed the Queen's ascension to the top of this series of hills. Blood dripping from both axes, Leimur started to traverse the next hill. This was the final summit to the King's Castle. With strong numbers behind her, Leimur didn't see anything that would prevent her from taking her prize. The last hill was the steepest and darkness had fallen fully, creating a tense atmosphere, but the Queen marched forward fearlessly. Leimur laughed at King Jon's desperate attempts at defense. The last few groups of boys couldn't have been much older than fourteen and they were getting younger by the minute. The Queen hacked her way through the brave but foolish boys and farther up the hill.

I will let Ali-Tiste be Queen of Donegal and she can hold the throne until Astrid is ready to rule. Then she can come back to Goldenfield so we can grow old together.

The stars and moon provided just enough light through the lingering clouds to expose the towers of her new castle. She could barely see, but the gate towers and barbiment looked void of defense. Suddenly, she saw a screaming horde of silhouettes. A massive attack of cavalry backed by infantry raced downhill at her. Now Leimur worried that she had fallen into King Jon's trap to lure her in and surround her. She ordered the troops to retreat to flat land to fight the battle. At this point, that looked like her only chance at victory.

D-MARIAH

As Mariah enjoyed her wedding dance with her father, she couldn't have envisioned a more perfect day. Everything seemed almost magical. She had married a wonderful man and felt like the Gods were smiling upon her again. They had spared Lucille and Edword from the dragon attacks and made sure they could make it to the reception. An armed guard pulled Jon Colbert away from his daughter. Mariah thought her father was going to assault the guard until the man whispered something into Jon's ear. That's when everything changed.

More guards, knights and soldiers invaded the room and it didn't take a scholar to realize there was a huge problem. The music had stopped and the minstrels left their instruments behind in a dash to leave.

Jon made his way back to his daughter and said, "You stay here, right here. Where is your...*Camelle?*" Jon yelled, looking around for his wife.

Through the mad chaos, he spotted her, ran over and told her something, then ran out of the room.

Camelle rushed over to a confused Mariah and she asked, "Mother, what is going on?"

"It may be nothing, but we may be under attack," Camelle said with a firm grip on Baby Jon.

"Attack, who is attacking us?" Mariah wanted to know.

"That's not important right now. We just need to stay here until our escort arrives," her mother instructed.

Torvald and her Bottomfoot friends came over to Mariah as everyone was being whisked away through the south entrance. Mariah was terrified and kept stumbling over her lengthy dress. Jon ran over and noticed the problem and stopped Mariah for a moment. He pulled a dagger and cut the dress away unevenly just above his daughter's ankles. This broke Mariah's heart. This was supposed to be her perfect day but now it might be the day her family and friends died. She continued rushing along until they were outside, exposed to the ominous black sky and swirling gray clouds. The clouds had increased and now covered the moon and stars to create an inhospitable escape scene. The only thing not hard to see was the utter madness. Mariah looked around for her new husband and his parents, but couldn't spot them in the melee. Nobles in expensive silk and samite dresses were running for their lives, screaming to be spared by the Gods. Jon Colbert had his family rounded up and got them to the southern stables. He quickly procured a small army of knights to guide his family back to Mattingly. Mariah sat up on her mount, gripped with fear.

E-RUXIN

Ruxin raced for the entrance to the castle when the unsettling sight of a mass evacuation became apparent. He worried for a few moments until he spotted his loved ones surrounded by some of the best knights of Mattingly. He dismounted and rushed over to his wife.

"My darling, Haley," Ruxin said, and bear-hugged his wife and unborn child.

"I was so worried when I heard about the attack," Haley said.

Ruxin's wife licked her forefinger and wiped some of the dried blood from her husband's speckled cheeks.

"I am perfectly fine. No need to worry, my love, our child will grow up with a father," Ruxin promised while rubbing his wife's burgeoning belly.

His father tapped him on the shoulder. "Ruxin, we must defend our castle. The rest of you go back to Mattingly until we crush this small uprising."

Camelle objected immediately, "No. Both of you are coming with us. We stay or leave as a family."

"We cannot call ourselves the King and Prince if we turn and run while our castle is being attacked," Jon argued.

Ruxin helped his wife up into her saddle and all his family members were on horses now except for his father and him. He wanted to stay and fight.

"Well if that's the case, then a Queen and baby Prince should fight too. Someone give me and my son a sword and shield so I can fight and die," Camelle stated emotionally.

Before she could continue with her stunt, Jon slapped her horse's hindquarters and screamed, "Be off, I love you all."

Ruxin watched Torvald pass with Baby Jon in his arms and in a flash, his family was gone.

Jon turned to Ruxin. "We need to hurry. We don't have time to get into full armor, so return to your quarters but only for a few minutes."

Ruxin barely reached his room before his father arrived wearing mostly the same get up from the wedding. He noticed his father had a sword belt, his battle helm and gauntlets to the elbows. Ruxin grabbed a large triangular shield and handed his father a buckler. The royals ran back through the castle and headed for the north side.

They saw Bryan Caughleigh and Jon questioned him, "What's the situation?"

He reported, "Waves of enemy soldiers keep coming up the hill. Just when we think we killed them all, more start running up, ready to die. Must be several thousand, at least. I don't know how they got in the gates but they won't be able to get siege towers up the hill. We have seen ladders moving in toward the north wall. We need men on the ground and up in the parapet walks."

"I have word out for men coming from the east and west, but who knows when they will get here? It looks like this battle is up to us," Jon said.

"Then we are at a strong disadvantage from a numbers standpoint," Bryan stated.

"We better get to action. Let's go kill this bitch of a queen. Ruxin, you go down on the ground level and I'll head up to the walks," Jon ordered.

His father assumed the fighting on the ground would be safer for his son but the real possibility of death lingered everywhere.

"Yes, father," Ruxin answered and took off. As his father left, Ruxin could hear the savagery getting closer by the moment.

F-LEIMUR

Warm blood decorated her tainted golden armor as Leimur made her way to the top of the final hill. Her plan to back up to level ground had worked and they quickly defeated the enemy force and moved up the hill unmolested. Her men were throwing up ladders and climbing the castle wall. She couldn't believe they had fought their way up several hills to reach this point. Goldenfield had suffered some big losses and the Queen had left some of the force behind to avoid getting completely surrounded. After seeing the lack of skill of the enemy, Leimur's confidence brimmed.

The battle still raged behind her on the hill as Leimur rushed for a ladder. The soldier in front of her only made it a few steps before a pot of boiling grease rained down, burning his eyes and exposed face. Leimur kicked him aside and steadied the rocking ladder. She quickly climbed the creaky wooden construct. She found crenellation at the top and easily stepped onto the narrow walk way. There weren't any archers still alive. Their bodies were strewn about on both sides, littering her path to the throne. Leimur needed to navigate down the walk to get to the Dragon Tower and into the King's Castle.

As she fought, the Queen heard the booming voice of General Rigby from below, "My Queen, heavy enemy forces have arrived from the east and west, they're crushing us on both flanks. We need to retreat north. We will all die if we stay and fight, they will trap you inside the castle. Get out now."

Leimur peeked down to see the General running off, shouting instructions to the soldiers. Leimur wasn't willing to make it this far to turn back now. *If I can just take this stronghold, I have enough soldiers in Goldenfield to break any siege. I just need to take control of this castle and the realm is ours.*

She also knew that the enemy was likely to give up if she took control of the King's Castle, so she forged on. Leimur took a quick glimpse down the hill and saw her flanks being heavily assaulted but it didn't look as dire as General Rigby had made it out to be. She slaughtered three more men and neared the opening to the main castle. The next man who stood in her way wore fancy clothes and held a long sword and small shield. The odd-looking man took almost a full minute for the Queen to dispatch, the stiffest opponent yet. The next man she faced wore fancy clothes featuring golden bulls and a golden bull helm. The Queen could tell this man was a high noble because that kind of helm took many hours to craft.

The short, stocky man wore gauntlets but no signs of armor. Leimur slashed and dodged with both battle-axes whizzing through the air. The early exchange showed Leimur this man had a lot of power. As the two carefully attacked each other in the narrow space, they came to another crenellated area. Leimur glanced down and saw her forces being massacred. She quickly focused back on her opponent but could hear the blood curdling cries of her loyal men being slaughtered like sheep. Unfortunately, their bravery wasn't being rewarded at the moment. The Queen tried to land her axe in the exposed body of her enemy but the slick man with a gray-blonde goatee proved to be supremely skilled. He blocked everything Leimur could throw at him. The stocky man used his little shield extremely well to block the whirling battle-axes.

Every tactic that had worked in the past failed against this man. She wanted to kill this noble and rush the castle but the indomitable man wouldn't budge. An irresistible force had met an immovable object as both unleashed their best attacks to no avail. The tiring stalemate raged on as sparks flew from a sword being blocked by a battle-axe, but neither could land a clean blow. Leimur was running out of stamina after all the fighting and racing up the hill. She became desperate as she finally realized who her opponent was. She let loose with a final furious assault that culminated with an overhand swing that stuck in her opponent' buckler. She made a quick attempt to slash the man's throat with her other axe but he slapped it away at the last moment with his sword. The axe did make light contact with the man's shoulder, drawing blood. The greenish blade of her opponent matched his eyes as Leimur stared at him. In one motion, Leimur leaned down with her shoulder and thrust it into her opponent's chest, knocking him onto his back. Leimur felt someone tugging at her shoulder but her only thought was to end the life of this stubborn enemy.

F-JON

The King of Donegal lay flat on his back, eyes closed. He couldn't believe he had been bested by a woman. He feebly covered his face with the tiny shield, leaving his entire body exposed. The brave warrior disappeared and he accepted that death was imminent as panic attacked his chest. The terrible screams, echoing sounds of steel and battling bugles were flushed out completely and a disturbing silence settled in Jon Colbert's ears. *What will she attack? My chest, my neck, or will she open my belly and let my guts fall out? Just end it already.*

Jon thought about Camelle and the rest of the family. He focused on the good times like the perfect wedding today that had been disrupted so he could die. Being King Jon Colbert seemed like a dream only hours ago, before this sneak attack. His noble intentions were focused on making the kingdom great. Jon wasn't sure if he was dead or not. He didn't feel any pain but either his eyes refused to open or the world had gone black.

At least I got my family out in time. They should be safe but did I get Ruxin killed? Hopefully, I didn't die in vain if I saved most of my loved ones. They will never understand, but this was the right thing to do.

The chaotic sounds of war began to fill his ears again, and Jon heard, "My King, my King." Jon's eyes shot open and he saw one of his loyal men. Sir Gallante said, "I almost had me a heart attack thinking you were dead. I yanked her away from you, but that strong bitch drove me back and jumped down that ladder before I could stop her. They should capture her before she can get outside the city gates. We have her trapped now."

The young knight extended his arm and helped Jon to his feet again. The King looked through an opening at the Queen of Goldenfield and her glimmering gold armor running down the hill.

Jon thought of Ruxin and hustled down a ladder to find his son. He jumped onto the blood-stained earth and tried to avoid bodies of men that were living only minutes ago. This task proved unavoidable so the King did the best he could to traverse the dark organic graveyard. He drew his sword and charged down the hill, but the battle was all but over. Even in the black of night, as the moon broke through briefly, and Jon noticed reflective blood stains extending to the bottom of the hill. Jon was in a panic as he screamed, "RUXIN."

Bryan Caughleigh approached and said, "He's farther down the hill, my King. There wasn't enough killing for that one at the top. You should be right proud, your boy must've killed at least a dozen of the enemy."

Concern trumped a father's pride as Jon ran down the hill. The smells became worse and Jon's worries increased as the death count rose. Jon had a sinking suspicion he would find the body of his son along the way. He got to the bottom and an open flat area appeared. He yelled, "RUXIN."

"Yes father," returned a voice close by. Jon spun in circles before his son touched his shoulder.

"Now, now, that's some killing. We chased that bitch right out of here," a proud Ruxin exclaimed as Jon turned and faced him.

Ruxin's eyes were wide open and he seemed to be on a battle high. Jon couldn't believe it. Ruxin only wore a few pieces of armor and although his entire body and face were soaked in blood, barely any of it was his.

G-LEIMUR

Leimur ran with her back to the ultimate goal. She had set out to take the castle, but now she would be lucky to leave the Capitol with her life. Captain Salina and Leimur found a few horses in the darkness and jumped on them. Both women heeled the animals and took off for Ali-Sander's Gate. The Queen knew that if she got caught inside the city walls it would spell death. She thought about how close she had come to sitting on the throne of Donegal. She wasn't even certain that they were going in the right direction to find the only viable exit. The pair made it back to the gate and reined up on the horses before entering the lighted area. She recognized the oddly dressed Lord Undertow waving her along as he went to open the gate. The lord struggled with the enormous wooden door but the opening started to widen and the ladies darted through. Leimur breathed a sigh of relief as they trotted back into darkness until twelve mounted men from Donegal appeared out of nowhere and surrounded the women. Leimur still had her battle-axes but this fight would equal suicide. Captain Salina and the Queen got down from their horses. Two men approached and stripped them of their weapons.

"Looks like we got the biggest prize of them all, fellas," laughed one man. Another man chimed in, "Wait till our new King see's this present."

Leimur had been through many near death experiences in her short stay on earth, but this was the only time she truly believed death couldn't be dodged. The men bound the women's arms behind their backs and started to march them back to the King's Castle. A familiar roar captured the night and

Leimur could see tigers' eyes glowing in the dark. The fierce yellow eyes started to move and the men from Donegal started to back away.

"Cut us loose, now," yelled Leimur.

A man gingerly came up to the Queen and cut the thick rope from her and then moved to Captain Salina.

Leimur went up to the man who had taken her axes and reclaimed her weapons. Captain Salina retrieved her sword and daggers as the men stayed completely still. The two women walked away and the convoy of tigers followed. They marched quickly in an unknown direction for over an hour. They started moving through a dense forest that Leimur didn't recognize. She heard another group of people and cautiously approached. The Queen of Goldenfield looked down a slight hill to a welcome sight. There were several hundred of her men with a few fires going.

General Rigby got up and rushed over to say, "Another loss. You seem to be making a bad habit of that. Now, you've almost gotten me killed, and I've supported you more than any."

He spit on the ground and stormed off. Leimur understood her track record wasn't stunning in battle as Queen, but she hadn't lost her own kingdom; she had only failed in conquering the neighboring kingdom. The unit moved into Burkeville before sundown and took refuge for a while in an open plain. They seemed safe for the moment.

RUSSELL

"My mother told me he was a man of honor. She said he died defending her. Lord Turnbush slapped my mother across the face. Most men would mind their place and let the lord on his way. My father wasn't most men." Russell's face lit up as he talked. "A fight broke out and didn't end until my father choked the lord to death. The next time my mother saw him was at Lord Turnbush's front gate. She saw his head on a spike." His tone saddened.

Riceros tried to cheer him up and said, "Sounds like a great man."

"He truly was. The queer thing is that I have no idea what he looked like. My mother described him often but I still can't fully picture the man. I used to hope when we went to market that my mother would point to a man and say, 'That is what your father looked like', but that never happened. She said he was one of a kind, a unique soul, she always called him." Russell still couldn't figure out Riceros and the hump on his back that he habitually scratched.

"Where is your mother?" Riceros asked. As the words left his mouth, Russell lowered his head and slowly shook it.

He took another moment before speaking, "She worked in the castle, doing various tasks, a do anything really. One of her duties included being a food taster for the duke and duchess. My mother actually loved it. She got to eat the same food as a duke even if it were only a taste. 'Nobody wants to kill Duke Etburn,' she used to tell me, but I felt she was trying to convince herself more than me. Ali-Pari told me it was the turtledove soup that turned her face blue and locked up her throat. The count couldn't do anything to help and said purple hemlock was the culprit. I was eleven." Russell was on the verge of crying but did not let the salty liquid loose. He straddled the line between pride and pain, bouncing back and forth when he talked about his parents. "I'd ask about your parents but I pretty much know the story. There is something you might not have known that the Lady Ali-Pari told me while she was steaming mad one time. Before your mother married your father, Duchess Ali-Pari tried to arrange a marriage between Camelle and Ali-Varis Wamhoff. She fought with the duke for weeks over the matter, Duke Etburn preferring an alliance with Jon Colbert. You already know the end of the story so I won't bore you with those details but you almost never happened."

"That's not true. Turns out the Colberts raised me but they aren't my real parents. I am a bastard from the Seventh Island. My father has a complicated story that I can't detail with this many strange ears about." Riceros kept scratching the lump on his back.

Russell looked at his new friend and understood there had to be something special about Riceros, but he couldn't see it. He was a little boy, and scrawny at that. Dragon-Eyes had tried to tell Russell about Riceros in the brief time they had away from the group but the Imp kept falling asleep. He felt much more at ease with the Cyclops on their side than the tiny kid.

Russell knew he still had to be the leader of the group. Most of his concern lay with the Imp Wizard. What if the wizard's friend had left Gama Traka? Dragon Eyes had told Russell that he hadn't talked to this mystery man in years. There were no guarantees they would ever find more Fuji Dust. Russell also needed the Imp to direct them to the School of the Learned Warrior but the man could barely speak anymore. Russell was amazed at how the Imp had almost reverted back into the ugly creature he had discovered in the Frozen Forest.

The perilous journey continued over the endless, humongous waves. The aquatic graveyard known as the Sea of Green had seemingly eaten the sun and spit out gray clouds that dominated the skyline. Russell held his stomach as the ship dipped down another valley of water. The battered vessel was holding up, but the old wooden ship wouldn't last if these conditions persisted.

The uneasy sounds of moaning wood and loud splashes of water created another variable. Riceros tried to break the tension and asked, "So you're saying Dragon-Eyes can't fly?"

"It's like I told you, he can do some pretty amazing things, but most of the stories are made-up tales. I had only heard two stories about him before I met the man. One was about how he married one hundred princesses in one hundred consecutive years. The story said he kept his wives in the stables with the horses. Supposedly, he went to the stables one day to find the bodies of horses with the heads of his princesses attached," Russell said.

"I've heard that one," Riceros said.

"He told me that was a bold lie. He's never been married, not even once. The other story I heard was about him fighting off an army of demons with only his thoughts. That is closer to the truth," Russell said.

"I heard that one too," Riceros commented.

"Also false," Russell revealed.

"Well then, I guess fire doesn't come from his eyes, does it?" Riceros asked, disappointed.

"That actually does happen. He can do that and I've seen him move heavy objects with only the strength of his mind," Russell told him as he looked around and whispered, "He is very well-versed in the craft of magic. My eyes have witnessed some impressive feats I once thought impossible." Russell Seabrook wasn't quite ready to reveal that he was favored by the angels and shared in their magic.

His feelings for Gamelda persisted but they were shoved aside with the passing days as he focused on the mission ahead. Confusion clouded his mind because he wasn't sure exactly what the 'secret mission' entailed. Dragon-Eyes didn't have a firm grasp on anything and only provided vague details of what lay ahead before falling back asleep. More than anything, Russell needed some privacy with Riceros to find out what the special boy knew. The nightmares about the men he had killed on the Pearl Islands started to fade, but those events still weighed on his conscience. He slept better on the open waters than on dry land, which surprised Russell.

He shared a tiny cabin with Lizeria but could barely get her to talk. She seemed more comfortable with Shireez as Russell looked over at the two, holding hands near the burn barrel. Dragon-Eyes slept next to the girls, curled up in a blanket near the fire. Dioneer stood in the middle of the boat. The unsteady action worried the Cyclops who didn't want to throw off the balance. Russell thought the boat was big enough for the big man to stand wherever he wanted but also understood the reasoning.

Russell looked at the young navigator and didn't even bother to go over and ask how close they were to Gama Traka. If he heard the captain's recycled line of, 'Couple of days now and we should be there. Steady as she goes,' he was going to toss the little teenager into the depths of the murky waters.

"So what happened after your mother passed?" Riceros asked.

"I stayed on as the spurrier's apprentice before the Duchess Ali-Pari seemed to take an interest in my story. She put me up in nice quarters and I became a 'do anything' around the castle. 'Lucky you're a cute one,' Lady Rotondo used to tell me all the time," Russell said, almost embarrassed.

"Well, good for that or you could still be smelling horse dung. We all get lucky in one way or another and we shouldn't be ashamed of it," Riceros reminded him.

"Yeah, after that I started to work better jobs and by thirteen, the Duchess treated me like her own. I know Edburgh resented me for that and for all the affection his mother poured on me. I didn't ask for any favors, but I'm sure he saw it otherwise. I thought Edburgh would lose his mind when I was knighted by his father in a special castle ceremony," Russell revealed.

"Pray, why didn't you introduce yourself as Sir Russell Seabrook?" Riceros wondered.

"Because I've renounced the title. Yes, I would have eventually received lands but I didn't want to defend rotten kings anymore. I also realized that as soon as Ali-Pari died, everything I had attained through her might disappear. Not might, everything would disappear. That's when I met Dragon-Eyes in the Frozen Forest and realized there's more than just defending false principles," Russell said.

"I've always wanted to explore the Frozen Forest," Riceros told him.

"I've been there countless times and unless you find a wizard, the Forest isn't that exciting," Russell said with a grin.

His stomach started to feel better until a bone-shattering wave slammed into the port side of the boat, knocking everyone down. Russell smacked his head on the mizzen mast and when he got his bearings straight, water rushed up, past his ankles. The boat tilted and Russell tried to find his friends. As he looked for Dragon-Eyes, his ears were filled with the haunting sound of stressed and cracking wood. The front end listed hopelessly, and Russell realized evacuation was imminent. Some frantic passengers dove into the enormous waves.

Russell started to strip off his baldric and ring mail as he looked for the Imp Wizard. Half the ship had been gulped away and the tilt became more severe as Russell moved to the top. He removed all excess weight that could lead to an instant drowning and plunged into the chilly waters. Russell assumed the sea would be warm. He looked back as the last tip of the Red Kraken went under and now Russell Seabrook was at the mercy of the Sea of Green. These waters were fabled to have killed more men than the Gods themselves. *If a boat can't handle these conditions, how can I?*

Russell slapped at the choppy waters, barely staying afloat. He rode down a wave as the speed increased dramatically until it reached the bottom. The tide grabbed hold and pulled Russell into the salty brine. He frantically worked his way back above and sucked in a glorious breath of air. Unfortunately, he fell back under and drank some nasty sea liquid. He bobbed up and down, nerves going wild, and regretted skipping all the swimming lessons Ali-Pari had set up for him. Russell had come up with an excuse to get out of every session. He had never been a strong swimmer even in still waters and these waves seemed to have the strength of a thousand sea warriors. After being tossed around violently for several minutes, Russell started to tire. He was expending all his energy just to keep his nose above the water.

He felt ashamed because he was supposed to be the fearless leader. The leader had no idea if any or all of his companions were alive or dead. However, Russell started to think the group would soon need a new leader as he started to go under more often and drink more of the salty cocktail of the sea. His arms flapped slower and slower until they barely moved through the rippling waters. He stressed every muscle to keep his neck above until he finally ran out of strength and began to plummet. Just as he accepted death, an angelic, soft forearm hooked his chin and dragged Russell Seabrook above again. He gasped and pulled in deep breaths until he steadied himself. The sun pushed through the dense black clouds and provided enough light for Russell to see two things. Lizeria had been his savior. Somehow, the tiny girl with arms as thin and light as feathers held the grown man above water. The other welcoming sight was a pink-pebbled beach in the distance.

Land looked so close but the tide seemed to be pushing them farther away. Lizeria rotated her body and hooked her arm through Russell's, locking them together. The two lay on their backs as Lizeria tried to teach him better technique with his feet. She then demonstrated how to use his off hand to paddle. The quick lesson paid instant dividends as the uneven pair powered its way through the treacherous conditions. Russell closed his eyes and tried to maintain the pattern of the movements. Being on their backs helped conserve energy and Russell thought he could keep going for a while but eventually his stamina would run out. Lizeria seemed like she could swim forever and Russell thought more about the amazing courage of this tiny creature who had saved his life for the second time.

Russell felt something hit the back of his head. His eyes shot open, and he panicked. He had heard the stories of sea monsters and turned over, but his knees must have hit the beast also. A smile came over Russell as Lizeria stood next to him. They were on the sandy pebbles of an unknown land, but they had survived for now. His pounding chest and heavy panting were the only after effects of the ship wreck. Even his head had recovered fully and Lizeria looked no worse for wear. His excitement quickly died down when Russell couldn't find any of his travel companions.

There were dead bodies scattered on the beach and more were washing in with each passing wave. The smell indicated that some of the unfortunate sea goers had been here for a while. The gulls and crows fought for fodder around the dismal graveyard. Russell saw up close and personal how unforgiving the Sea of Green could be. The two started a morbid search up the shores but they didn't find anyone from their party. This created a good and bad scenario. Russell rejoiced that they hadn't found any bodies from their group but he also knew that nobody could survive very much longer in the angry sea.

RICEROS

Dioneer inadvertently slapped Riceros' leg as he tried to grab the boy before being thrown into the water. The giant's hand caused Riceros to be tossed in as well. Riceros could barely move his leg and he used his black board to keep above the waves. He sank under occasionally but the flotation device always pulled him back up. Dioneer was the only person he could see and the giant was already running out of energy. The Cyclops wasted too much movement and kept dipping below. The two started to drift apart and they ended up on opposite sides of a wave. He couldn't see anyone now and with the sun finally shining down, he was all alone.

He looked at the board for answers from the dragons. None came. He hoped one of the mermaids would show up to help out. None came. Riceros wondered if the noble dragons were watching and had already dispatched the water dragons to come help him. None came. With a dead leg and no swimming skills, Riceros wished the strongest swimmer he knew would magically show up. Jasper did not. He had found out that the air dragons were very susceptible to lightning and decided they must have lost track of the ship. He couldn't see anyone in the vicinity.

A fifteen-foot-high wave threw him down with tremendous force and pushed him below. He struggled mightily to get back up while holding onto the black board. He finally got to the top and sucked in the sweet air. Just as he almost caught his breath, he felt the power of the ocean plunge him under, even deeper this time. He fought again to get to the top and when he saw light, he took a deep breath but swallowed more salty water. He emerged to find some air and a thought hit him.

He kicked his feet to get on his stomach. He pulled off his shirt and tucked it into his pants. With his back exposed to the air, he closed his eyes and concentrated. A bloody pearl emerged from his back and beat like a heart before giving birth to something else. Golden reptilian wings slowly spread out while Riceros kicked liked crazy despite the throbbing leg. He focused even more, and the wings began to flap. They started slowly, building up speed and sound. The loud whooshing sounds of the wings started to pull Riceros from the dangerous waters. He rose about ten feet and scanned the sea for Dioneer and the rest of his group. He didn't see anyone and flew higher.

Riceros knew he had to be careful about who saw his wings, but his friends' lives were on the line. He didn't see anyone and after a few minutes, his hopes started to wane. Riceros suddenly spotted some bubbles on the surface and the Cyclops popped out of the water. Riceros zeroed in on his struggling friend and fought the gale force winds to get to Dioneer. The Cyclops had saved his life several times before and Riceros vowed to repay the favor. He slid the black board into his shirt and watched Dioneer sink back under. He flew over to the area but the giant came up about ten feet away. He went to that spot and fished for his friend as he hovered over the water, slowly flapping his wings. How could he miss the huge man? He should have been able to see some part of the Cyclops, but he bobbed up seven feet away this time.

Riceros couldn't factor in the moving current before the big man went back under and became invisible. He floated up several feet higher in the air for a better view and when Dioneer surfaced this time, he sped over to grab his friend before he could go under again. Too late. He pulled Riceros under and both of them nervously fought the ocean to get back above. He emerged and mightily flapped the dragon wings to hold Dioneer above water. Riceros' strength drained quickly due to the extreme weight. He told the one-eyed giant to swim on his back and hold his arms above the water. He held onto one of Dioneer's arms while the big man paddled with the other. This offset some of the heavy mass, but they both kept plunging under the water occasionally. They rode down a huge wave and were thrown under again. It took every shred of his remaining power to keep Dioneer above water.

"Are you alright?" Riceros asked. The giant threw up a small sea of his own before he eventually nodded his weary head. "I can't hold you up much longer. Let me know when you can swim for a few moments," Riceros told him.

Dioneer gathered himself, spit out some green water, and said, "Go now. I can do it."

"Take this, it will help you float," Riceros said as he gave Dioneer the blackboard, but seeing how tiny it looked in the giant's hand, he doubted his assertion.

He flew up a little bit and stretched out his numbing muscles. He went up even higher and a wonderful sight filled his vision. Pink sand lay a few hundred feet away. He looked back down at Dioneer who was struggling to stay afloat. Through the raging waves, Riceros worked with the giant man to beat the elements. Riceros flew above, dragging Dioneer, who kicked effectively to move toward their destination. Riceros wished his Colbert brothers were here to see this physical feat of strength. The wings empowered the unathletic boy and gave him a confidence he had never felt before. After several exhausting minutes, Dioneer's hands scraped the small pebbles.

Riceros let go and flew onto the beach before collapsing in the sand. He retracted his wings and the Pearl of Wisdom sank back under his skin. He put his shirt back on and tried to gather himself. He could barely breathe, every muscle throbbed in pain, his heart was on fire, and his skin felt icy. Dioneer stumbled over and fell down next to Riceros. The two lay there for a while until they had recovered from the epic struggle with the sea.

They searched up and down the beach, sorting through the washed-up bodies, but couldn't find the others before sundown. They went to sleep hungry and with worry filling their hearts.

Riceros woke up before sunrise and paced around the snoring Dioneer. When the giant awoke from his slumber, Riceros said, "I have an idea, but it could be dangerous."

Dioneer sat up, yawned, and said, "I'd expect nothing less from you. What's this dangerous plan?"

"Much like yesterday, I could use my wings to scan the beach and look for our companions. Trouble is, if the wrong person sees me flying, we could all be in grave danger. What do you think?" Riceros asked.

"If I get to stay here and sleep while you fly around, I don't care if it puts us in danger." Dioneer's statement shocked Riceros until he saw the goofy grin on the big man's face. "Of course, I won't allow you to fall into danger. Let's find some fish to eat before we leave," the giant said.

After eating some raw clams and sea trout, the two searched the entire day with no luck whatsoever. They slept on the beach again and repeated the search for two days. Riceros was ready to give up hope.

The dark and nasty day set an ominous tone but they kept walking around the dead, looking for signs of the living. In the distance, two shadowy figures appeared, one tall and the other tiny. As bodily details became defined, Riceros recognized Russell Seabrook and Lizeria. The foursome spent the rest of the day searching for Dragon Eyes and Shireez, but had to stop at nightfall.

They found a small school of red snapper and Dioneer started a fire to cook the fish. The giant ate the entire fish while the rest ripped at the tender flesh and stuffed their mouths with the juicy morsels.

The next day, the search for the two missing group members continued, but they also started to collect supplies from the bodies. There were bloated bluish bodies scattered over the pink pebbles of sand. Riceros felt strange taking a knife from a dead man's belt but practicality outweighed the morality of the situation. His belly was full from snapper and he had slept well on the soft sand. Another day ended with fruitless results.

The day after that, Riceros and Russell were the first to wake up. Riceros asked, "How long should we continue to look for Dragon-Eyes and Shireez?"

"There's no right answer for that seeing as how he is the only one who knows where the School of the Learned Warrior is located, we need him desperately. Without him, we will be lost looking for a secret entrance to the School in the middle of a sea of sand. And if we found the School, there's no guarantee we would be allowed entrance," Russell explained.

A loud yelping that Riceros assumed was a seal caught their attention.

They looked at the waves, expecting to see an animal, but instead saw a small woman on a broken plank of wood dragging another object behind her. Shireez was struggling with the harsh waves. Riceros scanned the area for other living people. He didn't see anyone and unleashed his golden wings and used them to fly out and guide Shireez back to safety. He noticed Lizeria and Russells's eyes looking like they were going to pop out of their heads as he rose into the air.

They got back to land and Russell asked frantically, "Is he still alive?"

Shireez' unreassuring silence and nervous look didn't instill hope for the best. Russell and Riceros inspected the still body. Riceros checked his neck and wrists for a pulse but couldn't find any beating. He put his finger under the half-man's nose and felt the tiniest wisp of warm air come out. Dragon-Eyes' chest wasn't moving but Russell managed to stand him up and pat him on the back. The young knight also got the wizard to bring up most of the water he had swallowed. Russell quickly swaddled his mentor in one of his shirts and they immediately moved inland. They tried to force-feed the Imp mashed fish, but he kept spitting it out. He did show signs of life though. Eventually, the discombobulated Imp Wizard recovered enough to direct them toward their destination again. However, the little man was so out of it, Riceros couldn't be certain the directions were correct.

Five days later, Riceros swore they had passed this exact area one hundred times already. Everything looked the same out in the desert. They were nearly out of water and food. The group would die if it tried to get back to the Sea of Green and no one knew if they were anywhere near the School of the Learned Warrior.

SUNNY

Sunny looked at Muriel and still couldn't figure out a way to tell her about Ollor. The musty training room that stunk like aged sweat consisted of a dirt floor and undecorated stone walls. Wall sconces held candles and torches to brighten the room. Simulating a night battle was never a problem, but they needed to fully light every wall to replicate a sunny brawl. Even in the glowing room, the effect wasn't nearly the same as being outside. Sunny had only seen daylight for a few hours every fortnight for the past few months and had become used to fighting by firelight.

Muriel was besting a much larger man in combat, but Sunny contemplated whether he should tell her. *She can defeat grown men in fights, yet I know this will tear her apart. What to do, what to do? She still thinks there's a chance he's alive. I will need to tell her eventually, but I don't think that time is now.*

They finished the single-combat portion of the day and went to their respective sleeping areas to rest for the night. Sunny lay awake as his stomach growled with hunger. He thought about every student's bold proclamations about how the war against the demons would play out. Men bragged about how many demons they would kill and how long it would take to achieve victory. Sunny and Muriel were among the humble few to simply listen to everyone else's boastful claims.

Sunny didn't believe the stories anymore because numerous students had said that the battle would begin over a month ago. Yet, nothing happened.

Others called for action a fortnight past. Yet, nothing happened. The students remained on high alert, which was the only certainty that Sunny could rely on. The warriors constantly cleaned and sharpened their personal weapons as they waited for the call. The School of mostly men and a few women chomped at the bit to test their skills against the ultimate opponent.

The next day, Sunny completed half of his classes and Master Kazu let him go outside. The leader of the School warned him that the demons would attack from the north shores of Gama Traka. He made Sunny promise not to go to the northern beaches. The twelve-year-old agreed and went straight to his usual spot on the northern beach. The dark day couldn't hide hundreds of dead bodies or the rotting smell coming from them.

He normally watched the sun set over the water but the giant fire in the sky couldn't be found today. The black clouds lined with silver had seemingly inhaled the fiery blaze and refused to exhale. He stood near the exact spot Dolpho had told him to return to. He waited. He waited longer. He grew very impatient as he waited frustratingly longer. Sunny started getting angry and decided to go back to the School of the Learned Warrior.

Before he turned to leave, a shady outline of a distorted mammoth creature rushed toward him with the oncoming waves. The huge mass began to take shape and an odd stomping sound accompanied this anomaly. An army of men-at-arms walked on the waves. The standard-bearer carried the flag Sunny had seen in his dreams. The wind gusts held the flags, pennons and pennants at attention as nearly five hundred men came to a stop as they hit dry land. Sunny wanted nothing more than to turn and run, but his frightened body remained still.

There was something wrong with these men but they looked to be from all different backgrounds. Sunny spotted choice weapons from various parts of the world. He had learned about the sword and sleeveless leather vests of the soldiers of Teredez and saw about twenty men carrying them.

He noticed several men with Irello wooden war shields. The connected vertical planks featured a golden eagle on a red field.

The men wearing mail jackets as long as hauberks with semi-hidden quillon daggers had to be the Black Jackets from Livingstone.

Men wielding decorated maces with wooden shafts covered in snakeskin were from Havasu.

The streaks of black ash under their eyes and around their mouths coupled with a trusty poleax indicated Kipissee had representation too.

A man in red and white armor walked up to Sunny and knelt down. The boy noticed the exposed areas of the men's' skin and it had a pale blue tint to it. The men had the look of death.

Before he could think about the skin any further, the warrior rose back to his feet and spoke, "Don't concern your mind with trying to figure out if we are dead or not. We are. Well, maybe not as dead as those people over there." The soldier pointed at a collection of beached bodies. Despite the joking nature of the comment, the dark, deep tones of the man's voice scared Sunny.

He took off his fox shaped helm and Sunny thought it might be his own reflection.

They looked tremendously alike and the undead man spoke again, "We are the Noble Army of Undead Kings. We are a collection of rulers, once perished, and now banded together to help stop the demons. We are here to serve you. My name is Ali-Ster Wamhoff of Donegal. I've rounded up these great warrior kings to fall under your command in the final war. I know you've been told that you would lead a great army to defeat the demons, so how do we look?" Ali-Ster smiled.

"Well now, let's see, you arrived by walking on water. How could I not be impressed?" he stumbled with the last word and smiled through his cleft palate.

Other than the ghastly facial scar, Ali-Ster looked like an older version of Sunny. The dead King said, "There is much more to discuss in our future meetings. Know this now, the demons have hit the Sea of Green on a course to land right where we stand. We will try to delay their progress but the time has come to defend the world. I've been given a great deal of wisdom, so I know you better get back to the School before you are beaten again."

The entire army knelt in unison, rose and turned back to the water. They seamlessly knifed straight through the waves to get back out to sea. Sunny sprinted back to the School. Out of breath, he found a strange crew outside the secret door. A Cyclops, one young man, two children and two dwarves were impatiently waiting as the giant desperately pounded on the entrance. The door opened and Master Kazu emerged with a look of concern. He took a closer look at a wrinkled dwarf and said hurriedly, "Get him in. Now."

Everyone rushed inside and Kazu had the normal sized man carry the dwarf back to his private quarters. Sunny had never seen anyone but the Master of the School go in there. Kazu went inside for a few minutes and then reopened the door.

Everyone started to rush in but the Master put his bony fingers into Sunny's chest and said, "You must stay on the outside, I am afraid."

The door was shut in his face and he was left to wonder who the people were.

The Man with the Golden Sword

The Man sat at a table made of cherry wood and sharpened one of his daggers. He stared at fly walking around a dark knot on the tabletop. He continued to stroke his blade over the coarse side of a flat oilstone.

His concentration broke when the Crippler said, "It's been several days now; we have to send a response."

He set down the dagger and replied, "I know, I know. I've given thought to a thousand different ways to handle this situation. We could race over to the Blue Caps, praying that the secret tunnels really exist or haven't collapsed, but we all know that if we get caught in the passes, we'll be ripe for an easy slaughter. The Wamhoffs would be two days behind us, but their cavalry could catch our infantry and we would lose too many men. I rejected any alliance they have proposed. They are ousted Wamhoffs, supposedly treated like bastards, but that dirty royal blood still rushes through their veins. We will all be dead within a fortnight if we sign any peace accord. Now they camp on top of our biggest reserve of hidden gold. Depending on their resources, we might not be able to starve them out without that gold. I've already put a moratorium on all incoming ships to the Bonewich Harbors. They'll soon take control of other harbors, I would presume, but this is a start. We need to stockpile any resources we can and prepare for a siege."

"It will be done, your highness," Benroy said.

The Man with the Golden Sword went back to sharpening as he continued, "The only way to get rid of this problem is flattery. Just as Ali-Samuel has tried with us, using every possible compliment in his letters. I know Ali-Samuel. He will never stop short of his dream. He lusts for power. Gold and jewels can buy power. I propose we send him gifts to entice him to move down the coast of Fox Chapel to launch his invasion. Have the carpenters craft a giant fox passant with several doors on the sides of the body and open storage inside the doors. We will stuff it with riches to get rid of them so we can get to our buried gold that has one hundred times the value. If all goes accordingly, they take the money and leave, we get our gold and get back on the move to the Capitol. Our sources tell us security around the realm increases by the day especially on the other side of the Blue Cap Mountains." The Man had been taking firm control of the meetings and sounding more regal by the day despite not studying with the Crippler anymore.

The meeting room was different now. The whores had been expunged from the castle and only ewers of water sat on the table top. The Man hadn't been drinking much wine lately to keep his head clear and wanted his subjects to do the same. He felt the men had been enjoying themselves far too much before victory.

"Give me one hundred good archers, oh hells, they don't even have to be that good. I'll take 'em down Griffins Pike and we'll rain fire on those Wamhoff followers," Terry Underling suggested.

The Man stopped for a second to ponder the thought. He didn't want to resort to dirty tactics but Ali-Samuel had already tried to break down the city gates to kill him, so nothing was off the table anymore. He said, "We will wait for his response to our peaceful proposal, but if he refuses, we will dispatch your attack."

Two days later, a raven arrived back at the rookery with a sealed letter embossed with a fox. The enemy rebuffed his offer and stated that he could come reclaim his gift personally if he wanted it back. They refused to move and strongly suggested The Man accept their original offer. He became incensed and went straight to Terry Underling to authorize the attack. *If he doesn't want to listen to sense, I'll show him I can beat him without losing a single man. Why is he being so foolhardy?*

He and Ali-Samuel had called themselves 'Battle Brothers' when they fought against Goldenfield and The Man was extremely disappointed in his one-time friend. In his rage, he gave Terry the services of two hundred archers that would stuff Griffins Point, the small overhang that looked down on the Wamhoff campsite.

The anger still swelled as he walked back to his quarters. His journey to the throne had been delayed again. Patience was never one of The Man's virtues. Force had always been his friend, not waiting. He entered his room to find Gamelda reading a leather-bound book with old, cracked yellow pages and faded ink as she sat on a cushioned teal couch. She kept reading but said, "We need to leave or you will die."

He retorted, "No, if we leave, *we* will die."

She put down the book, looked at her lover, and said, "Oh, is that what you see in your spirit ball? Look at me."

"I am," The Man responded, staring at her chest.

She raised his face to meet hers and said with a concerned look, ""I've seen the great fire, inside these city walls. Your body is burning."

"Are you sure it's me?" he asked.

She calmly answered, "I was certain when I saw a blond man wearing a crown that turned out to be King Jon Colbert. My spirits are never wrong. If we stay, you will die."

He looked away and didn't want to believe this could be true. He said, "The Crippler says we should ally with our enemies because King Colbert is a whole different animal than Tersen Wamhoff, more like a dragon actually. The Queen of Goldenfield snuck through the city gates with a full host and couldn't breach the castle. They'll be expecting our attack, and our soldiers can't be much better than hers, if even that. You have to look into that crystal skull again and see me on the throne. You *will* see me at some point; I know it."

"Look at me," she said pulling him back toward her before continuing, "What if I never see it?"

"No matter. You can see it with your own eyes, in real life. It'll be much better that way," he said with a forced smile.

Everyone could see the stress building inside the new king. He knew being a supreme monarch added more responsibility to the constant grind, but the decisions were starting to tax his mind. He wanted to get to battle, a situation he could excel in.

"The Crippler's had visions of me as King of Donegal," The Man added nonchalantly, knowing it would bother Gamelda. He hoped it would give her motivation to see him on the throne in her skull.

"What other lies has he told you? Have you ever seen that man bleed, I ask you?" Gamelda pressed him as she suddenly became agitated.

He answered, "I think so, but I don't specifically remember."

"Was it black or red? I hope you remember that," she remarked.

The Man couldn't truly remember but said, "I think it was red. I would've remembered if it was black."

She shook her head and warned, "You think so, do you? You better be damn sure he doesn't bleed black or that might be why your soul seems tainted by darkness."

"I've never seen lots of people bleed, but I can't just go around pricking people to check," he said, staring into her intoxicating eyes.

Gamelda seemed to sense that he was passively referring to her. She stood up and held an open hand in the air. A sheath on The Man's hip unlatched its own buckle. The knife escaped the holder and flew across the room until the handle safely landed in Gamelda's right hand. With a smile, she nicked the top of her other hand in between her thumb and forefinger. The crimson zest of life dripped down on the floor. She said, "You are the king. You could make all your subjects line up to check the purity of their blood. You are a king but if you wish to continue with that status, you must beware of the Crippler."

B-Emilia

"So we all agree that we can't lay siege?" Ali-Steven asked to confirm.

Nobody objected in the rickety meeting room on the blustery beach. Fall on the Elkridge coast was unlike anything the Histoman had ever seen. Their native land stayed warm to hot all year long and they weren't used to such harsh winds. Their tents and belongings kept getting blown all over the sand and into the water. Luckily, it had rained the night before, so the nasty sandstorms weren't blowing.

"What else can we do? The Harbor Master told me that The Man with the Golden Sword has ordered a halt on all incoming trade to Bonewich Harbors. We'd have to move camp miles down shore to find the next harbor," Ali-Samuel reported.

Emilia suggested, "Maybe we should take his gold and add it to ours and move down to Fox Chapel to buy more allegiance."

Ali-Steven immediately refuted, "We can't. If we had the ships, which we don't, we'd be wide open to attack. We might not even get to land before our entire fleet is sunk. With King Jon controlling the coasts, we would never see firm ground. Even if we could land and make it inland, we stand to lose too much to try to regain through alliances backed by gold or promises."

"We thtill have our bethed tholdierth, but they've never ethecuted a land invathion. I think it bethed to find a way to defeat this bathdard," Sir Ralph said.

Emilia asked, "How much provisions do we have?"

Ali-Steven answered, "Even with the hunting teams faring well, winter is looming and we eventually need them to fight in battle if that day should ever come. We would ultimately need to start raiding bordering towns and cities. That's a reputation we don't want to gain this early, if we wish to harbor support from any lords."

Emilia thought out loud, "What if we play into his vanity? What if we sent him a request for an old-fashioned duel? His best man versus our best man. Loser leaves." Emilia knew she had a good idea when Ali-Samuel raised an eyebrow and sat up straight.

He said, "Now that would appeal to his self-pride as a soldier and a leader. Yet that fool knows I would best him in a fair fight. He probably won't go for it."

Sir Ralph said, "Won't hurt to try."

Ali-Steven closed the topic by saying, "Send a letter."

"What about the Colbert boy? If the King doesn't want to believe we have his son, maybe we should send him a few body parts as a friendly reminder," said Ali-Samuel.

Emilia was livid and said, "That's quite cruel. Besides, the boy's survived a dragon attack. He is unrecognizable from his former self."

Ali-Samuel thought for a second before saying, "I have it. Make the King send a representative by sea to dock in the harbor and Krys will go talk to the representative to confirm his identity. That man can send verification to the King and then, then we have our bartering chip. We could use his help to rid us of The Man with the Golden Sword."

Ali-Steven said, "Send a letter."

The meeting ended and Emilia went outside to see the Histoman struggling to maintain the fires and braziers. She heard two Histoman screaming in primal agony when an entire kettle of boiling liquid came crashing down on them because the tripod wasn't set up properly. The nasty looks were common now and Emilia had learned to ignore them as she put her head down. Pariah and Princess were the only ones she cared about anymore. She approached the two girls who were shivering despite being attired in thick, long-sleeved cloaks made of layered linens. Emilia invited them into her tent to warm up. The small area didn't offer much except protection from the wind bursts that now ruffled the fabric walls of the tent. The three sat on her tiny bed and Emilia handed out blankets to help her friends stop their shaking and teeth chattering. Emilia had experienced the extremes of every season in Burkeville and Fox Chapel.

They played castle cards and talked for hours before falling asleep on the same bed. Emilia was startled awake by horrible sounds of destruction. She poked her head outside the tents to see glowing purple fire everywhere. People were running around, fully engulfed in flames. Pariah and Princess were awake and screaming but didn't want to come out of the tent. Pavilions, tents, humans and horses were all ablaze and the frantic calls for help came from all sides. She didn't need Pariah to translate the desperate pleas that broke all language barriers. The other girls finally crawled out of the tent.

Emilia panicked amidst the chaos. She didn't know whether to get back inside or make a break for the caves. She just stood there holding onto her best friends until Pariah tapped Emilia and pointed up. She looked up to see a fiery hell of amethyst flames descending down from the heavens. Suddenly, someone slammed into the girls and pushed them under a circular wooden table with its legs dug firmly into the sand. Krys Colbert guided the girls to safety just as the beach was peppered with more destruction. The table had been set ablaze and Krys grabbed the women and pulled them toward the caves. Emilia looked back at the burning table and almost tripped. She looked up again and saw another round of fire-breathing missiles headed for the earth. Then all she saw was darkness.

Krys had guided them into an opening in the mountain. The small crevasse was almost completely full of screaming Histoman. She wondered about Ali-Steven and Ali-Samuel and her blood started to boil as she remembered the suggestion to torture Krys Colbert and further disfigure the boy. Ali-Samuel's cruelty had seemed to go unnoticed until they left the Capitol. He had hidden it well in the early stages of his relationship with the former queen.

The bombardment stopped and they came out of the caves. Emilia watched as what must've been over one thousand arrows finally flamed out, but the purple fire blazed on even longer. Emilia found the Wamhoff men, who were absolutely fuming.

"Dirty tactics. Attacking innocent women and children," Ali-Samuel lamented, without bothering to check on the condition of his future bride.

None of the survivors slept that night. Some mourned, some vowed revenge, but everyone kept looking up, expecting another attack. The members of the war council tried to mount a plan to continue toward the Capitol as they gathered around an open fire.

"Have you seen Ali-Samuel?" Emilia asked Ali-Steven.

The older man looked puzzled and said, "He didn't tell you? He went on a mission to defeat our enemy."

The former queen shook her head in disgust and said, "No, he didn't tell me, *again*."

Ali-Steven spoke in measured, careful tones, "He was outraged that someone he served with would stoop to fighting this way. It's hard to understand unless you've been to war."

She asked, "Am I not at war right now? I could have easily swallowed a flaming arrow if Krys Colbert hadn't saved Pariah and me. Yes, the same Krys Colbert your son discussed cutting apart and sending to the King. The same Krys Colbert that saved your wife's life."

Ali-Steven had a dumbfounded look on his face and spoke, "War. The war you are involved in comes attached to dirty games that only get increasingly worse as every year passes. Common sense would tell us that you aren't supposed to use a man like a chess piece. You aren't supposed to attack women and children. War is only winnable if you are willing to go farther than your enemy. Then, and only then, can you take a crown."

Emilia asked, "How long will he be gone for?"

The scar-faced older man answered, "About four or five days."

Disappointment started to settle in her eyes and it seemed like Ali-Steven noticed and said, "I know my son has certain problems with sharing his thoughts properly. That, it pains me to say, has much to do with me. I wasn't there from the beginning of his life. Even if I could have come back and rescued him when he was eight or ten or even twelve, I could have made a difference. Just some time to be there for my son. Some time to influence him not to be so cynical of everything. I could have taught him to take deep breaths and step back, rather than jump to action. I could have made him such a better man than my brothers did, but I didn't. I failed him and it seems now I have failed you in turn."

Emilia agreed with part of his statement. She thought Ali-Steven was a much better person than his son and would have been a positive influence.

She said in a soothing voice, "It's not your fault. You had to leave Donegal."

Ali-Steven looked at her intently before saying, "That's what I've told everyone for all these years. My king father was angry with me, but I know he wouldn't have killed me. Without my wife, I thought life in Donegal was over. I barely thought about Ali-Samuel when I was fleeing. I know that's terrible but all I could think of was my wife's head, not connected to her body. I often think of what could have been had I stayed and reconciled matters with my father. I think after some time, he would have named me heir again. I could have been King of Donegal way back when, had I only stayed."

"It's never too late, you still have a chance to be King of Donegal," Emilia said, but she understood this would be a much harder path after looking around at the utter destruction. She went to sleep alone by a fire while wondering about Ali-Samuel's secret mission.

Elisa

The coachman sat next to Petyr the Powerful on the front bench of the moving coach as Queen Elisa and Lady Victoriah talked to the Lord of Defense. Elisa looked out the opening with the golden silk curtain drawn back.

"Just because she failed, doesn't mean we are going to fail," Lady Victoriah said.

The Lord of Defense spoke fast and seemed unsure, "Yes, well, it does show that even an unexpected attack can be thwarted by our new King."

Elisa interjected, "She doesn't know the Capitol and castle like we do. Has there been any progress on the Krys Colbert situation?"

"Two spies from Waters Edge reported that infiltrating the Wamhoff's operation would be near impossible. The sources haven't seen anyone who resembles the description we gave them. The Wamhoffs only have a small group of western men as war officers. The rest are Histoman. They know that no one would be anxious to rush to their side to support a barbarian effort, so sending in one of our men would raise serious suspicion," the Lord of Defense said.

"What about our people in the Capitol? What's the word on the Princess effort?" Elisa asked.

The Lord of Defense looked embarrassed, lowered his head and said, "Our sources have changed allegiance to the King, it would appear. We haven't received word back from over ten sources."

As they neared Pigeon Bridge, Elisa never thought she would have to lower herself to these unclean dealings, but she could almost feel the crown on her head. The lust for power changed people. "Were my mother and brothers with Queen Leimur?" Elisa asked.

The Lord of Defense answered, "She had been staying at the royal palace and some reports speculate that she was going back to Arigold to reclaim her castle. Our people in Sevring reported seeing her leave but no one seems to know how to follow a woman, it should seem. Some say Queen Leimur took a real liking to her and supplied her with a small army to reclaim Arigold."

I don't know how the Queen took such a liking to her. If only mother knew she was widely regarded as a bitchy Princess. How could she make peace with our sworn enemy? She saw how those pigs butchered our citizens in the border wars. They maimed our brothers and sisters of Burkeville and she reconciles and sleeps in our enemy's palace. She left Telly for dead and couldn't care less about me but she was certain to rescue the boys. My father was too much of an influence over her. She makes my blood boil. I truly cannot believe I came from her.

About one quarter of their contingent had crossed the bridge that intersected the Deerfield River. They came to a stop as the narrow passage backed up the brigade. She thought of what to say if Lord Nanbert offered her the hospitality of his castle for a night. *Oh no, we are already behind time. We couldn't possibly put you out like that. Sorry, but we have a throne to capture to make sure you have that lofty appointment.*

She looked out the window and could only see green grass. Elisa still couldn't figure out if Lady Victoriah was setting her up. After what had happened growing up and at the King's Castle, Elisa had become defensive and expected that everyone would try to use her again. She couldn't peer through her veil and the lady's to see a crack in her armor. *I won't let you use me. I've tasted salty tears for far too long. It's time to taste victory no matter the cost.*

About one-half of her party had made its way across. Elisa heard a thundering stampede and the earth began to quake. She thought it was Lord Nanbert's men coming to greet her, but they were screaming wildly. Her heart sank when sounds of unforgiving steel on steel echoed in her ears. Next came the primal screams of men either dying or being severely injured.

"That crapulous son of a bitch has ambushed us," Lady Victoriah announced and pulled out two short daggers with leather sheaths that were stashed under a pillow.

She handed one to Elisa and clutched the other in her right hand.

Lord Deerheart proclaimed confidently, "I'll go put a stop to this."

He jumped out of the coach and Elisa quickly shut and locked the door behind the Lord of Defense as Lady Victoriah boarded up the open window. She received a sudden jolt when a spray of blood stained the thin canvas door. Lord Deerheart's dead body crashed into the coach, slid down to the ground and lay still.

A bloody sword blade cut through the curtain of an open window and a voice said, "Come out peacefully and we won't kill you. Stay inside and you can play dodge the incoming sword. Not a fun game, but it's your choice, ladies."

Lady Victoriah looked at Elisa and said, "Hide the dagger. They won't kill us, I hope. We carry too much value."

The lady opened the door and the two women slowly emerged from the coach into a scene of utter chaos. Elisa could hear the sounds of fighting from all directions in the near distance. The ladies were immediately surrounded by seven men wearing boiled leather and ring mail jackets with green sleeveless surcoats emblazoned with the Nanbert perched cardinal. Their drawn swords deterred Elisa from trying anything with the dagger in her waistline.

Out of nowhere, Sir Petyr the Powerful caught one man from behind and took his head clean off. The man's gambeson wasn't properly secured and Petyr seized the opening. The Cloverfoot soldiers moved to surround Petyr but the giant's enormous sword was making looping strikes around his whole body to provide a natural shield. Petyr kept pirouetting to keep his opponents at bay.

Elisa didn't understand this fighting. All the songs and stories talked about how two honorable men fought a one-on-one battle. The winner would then face another man but six on one was hardly chivalrous. Two men simultaneously rushed Petyr, but her hulking guard defended it gracefully.

He crouched to avoid a blade to the head and attacked with a long cross stroke that sliced the knees of three men standing too close. The soldiers of Cloverfoot had a gap in protection around their knees because they thought it slowed a man down on the march. The battle raged on around her as the three remaining men tried to fell Petyr. A short soldier rushed at her guard and he used the back of his sword hand with lightning-strike quickness to knock off the opponent's battle helm. Petyr used his left hand to draw a long dagger and thrust it into his dazed enemy's chin. Petyr drove the blade in and left the knife to step back and defend himself. Petyr the Powerful was now tiring and the two men seized in on him and attacked with reckless abandon.

Her guard had little trouble fending off the dual offensive until he slipped on something and went down to one knee. He tried to jump back to his feet but his opponents were relentless. One of the men hit Petyr on the earhole with the flat of a sword blade. He stumbled to his feet, only to fall again, never to get up. The bloodied men were breathing heavily as they turned their attention back to the ladies.

Why didn't we run? But where would we go? Elisa's scattered thoughts and erratic heartbeat caused her to sweat on this brisk autumn day. The Cloverfoot men pushed the ladies near the edge of the coach.

A particularly ugly man with missing teeth licked his lips and said, "Guess who's going to King Jon? And guess who's gonna be a lord soon? We gonna be wealfy for the rest of our days I should think."

The other man said, "You thought your giant could save you, but you was wrong."

Elisa corrected the man, "It's we're wrong not was. It's proper speaking."

The ugly man started to laugh and said, "I don't fink you is in any type a standing to correct us right now. Pretty soon your whole army will be dead. So unless you want us to only take your pretty littl' head back to the Capitol, keep that mouf shut."

Elisa stared at the man and said, "I will never."

A wide green blade sliced through mail, boiled leather and bone, emerging from the chest of the ugly man.

A-Brehan

His body screamed at him. Give up. Stop now. Kneel or you will die. Brehan ignored the excruciating pain and struggled to pull Dragon-Bite out of the dead man. He gave up and grabbed the fallen opponent's sword before the other man could seize a chance. The bigger sword proved to be even heavier than his, and Brehan struggled to fight off the attack of the last remaining Cloverfoot soldier. Love allowed him to hold onto life. He thought this heroic act might change Elisa's heart and make her love him again, and if he died trying, then so be it. He fought valiantly with every last bit of courage he could muster but knew it would all be in vain. Despite the long battle his opponent had already endured, Brehan's pre-existing injuries were going to lead to his death. A loud thumping noise caused his enemy to drop his sword and go down to his knees. Brehan looked around to see a couple hundred oncoming members of Elisa's cavalry. Brehan started to see bright lights and streaks of different colors while his body felt like it was on fire. He collapsed and twitched for a few moments before lying still.

Elisa

Elisa screamed for someone to get a count or apothecary to help Brehan. Elisa's soldiers tried to get her and the lady into the coach until she realized something and stopped the men. "Has anyone seen my sister? Oh Gods, where is Telly?"

Elisa started to cry until a huge knight came up on horseback with her sister and the queen dried her tears and hugged Telly. Elisa commanded her men to help get Brehan into the coach. As Elisa entered the coach with Telly, she peeked back and saw that hundreds of men had formed a wall around their queen.

Her heart raced out of control as she waited. Brehan was barely breathing and she hated herself for being the cause of his hideous looks and almost getting him killed again. Another hour went by and Elisa periodically looked outside the cabin to make sure her guard was still at full force. The close sounds of dying cries became more muffled with passing time. She waited another hour and her guard still stood strong as the sounds of war switched to those of victorious, but angry and injured warriors.

The door swung open and a stunned Elisa realized she had forgotten to lock it. Sir Anderley stood outside and asked, "Has anyone heard from father?"

Lady Victoriah had a nervous look in her eyes as she answered, "No, not yet."

Anderley ran off but Elisa had seen that the knight's face was clean courtesy of his battle helm, but from the neck down, he wore a collage of other men's blood. The golden apple on his surcoat looked like it was drunk on a deep burgundy wine. The black bear looked evil with red eyes.

Elisa and Lady Victoriah got out of the coach and surveyed the scene. Luckily, they had managed to remain just far enough away from the heavy fracas to avoid catastrophe.

The lady said, "Sir Willam, Sir Denton, Sir Larwell and Sir Ean will stay to protect the queen. The rest of you go find Darryg and Lord Ichibod. Do not return without them."

This was an emotional cry for help that went against the cold lady's normal behavior and she was nearly in tears by the end of her plea. Elisa could see the panic clearly through both veils but other thoughts crossed her mind.

I know you want Lord Ichibod to be rescued because your devious plans against me won't work with him gone. I can read you like a storybook written for children.

Elisa put her hand on Lady Victoriah's shoulder and said gently, "I'm sure he's fine. He is a tremendous warrior."

The lady said in a softened voice, "Was."

Elisa replied, "Excuse me?"

"He was a great warrior. Was. He is an old man now. Look around this outfit, you won't find a great deal of older men. They die before they grow old if they spend too much time in situations like this. You won't see too many older than him in the fighting ranks. I don't know what he was thinking, trying to lead the attack. And my Darryg, where is my sweet, innocent Darryg?" Lady Victoriah uttered emotionally and Elisa saw large drops stream down her cheeks, escape the secrecy of the veil and cascade down onto her breasts.

Ironically, before Elisa's training with Victoriah, she would have taken great sympathy on the lady. She seemed heartfelt in her sorrow but Elisa didn't know what to believe. Elisa took pleasure in the misery of her mentor. It felt strange to enjoy someone else's pain and suffering, but Elisa needed a way to get rid of Lord Ichibod before he got rid of her. Depending on the final casualty count, this could turn out to be a positive ambush by Lord Nanbert.

Those thoughts were dashed as the Ellsworth men rode up together. Anderley vaulted down off his mount and went to help his father.

Lord Ichibod had a painful look on his face but he brushed him away. "Get off me, I am a man and I can do this myself."

"Let me help you, father," Anderley said in a tone and manner that commanded respect.

The former King's Guard member was always soft spoken and Elisa had only heard him raise his voice on a few occasions. Lord Ichibod slowly swung his leg over the saddle and stood in the other stirrup for a moment. Sir Anderley took his father's hand and helped the older man down. Darryg had a crazed look in his eyes and had to be told three times to get down off his horse. Lady Victoriah disposed of the veil and ran over to hug and kiss her son before moving on to her husband. For the first time, the lady didn't seem to care who saw her in a weakened state. Elisa stayed as cold as a glacier. Her tears had now turned to ice and winter hadn't even arrived yet. She hugged the Ellsworths and showed the proper concern for them, but she also knew that at least one of them was plotting her death. Lord Ichibod winced in pain and Darryg looked like he had seen a ghost. Elisa noticed he hadn't blinked since arriving back at the coach.

Ichibod talked with disdain in his voice, "Stupid cunt thinks he can ambush our family. Where has honor gone in this kingdom? I am going to find that porknell and skin him alive."

Sir Anderley grabbed his golden battle helm and said, "Father, I will go find this traitor." Anderley jumped on his destrier and rode away.

They just let him go without any type of concern for his well-being. Oh poor Darryg, poor Ichibod, oh you can go muck the stables, Anderley. They treat him as if he's not even part of the family. I'll bet I can turn him against his parents. He was willing to kill King Ali-Stanley for me. Lady Victoriah even said her son would do anything for a fair face. I'm starting to pick up on this game, so look out Lord Ichibod and Lady Victoriah.

Two guards helped Lord Ichibod get into the coach, followed by Elisa, Telly and Lady Victoriah. The lady had to yell to Darryg to get inside with one of the guards pushing him toward the coach.

"What is HE doing here?" Lord Ichibod asked, referring to Brehan.

Elisa shot him a mean look and said, "HE saved your wife and your queen's lives, so you owe him a lot. We would both surely be dead or captured if he hadn't valiantly defended us after Sir Petyr met an unfortunate end."

The extended coach provided barely enough room to sit comfortably with Lord Ichibod and Brehan laid out but it was the only place Elisa felt safe right now. She feared Lord Nanbert might have more tricks to pull and being surrounded by hundreds of her warriors made her feel slightly better.

"What in the seven hells happened?" Lady Victoriah asked.

Darryg remained silent, steadily shaking his head as he stared at the wall.

Lord Ichibod spoke gruffly as he cleared his throat, "That rat waited until we had about half our men across the bridge before he struck like a coward. He hit us from the front and back on both sides of that shit-stained bridge. We lost many a precious sword and staff due to these dirty tricks. The Prograggers weren't quite ready for something like this, although they did serve their purpose and the elephants helped chase the Nanbert men away for good. We probably lost over a thousand Prograggers and many knights and valuable soldiers were killed or badly injured. That ugly son of a bitch hit us hard, that's all that is certain right now."

He didn't show any visible injuries or blood stains from battle but wore a face of pain. Elisa assumed his gout must have been acting up.

"Are you alright, Darryg?" Elisa asked.

He stared at her with a distant look in his eyes, "I saw…I saw things. I never wanted to see those things. I saw men being butchered much like a stag or goat. We're all just full of hidden blood. Cut us open and watch us die."

His blank stare made him look even scarier than his normal grim appearance. *This man is supposed to be a king? Not my king. Sir Anderley is a much greater man than Darryg, despite his softness toward pretty women. Lord Ichibod knows he can control Darryg. I'm starting to figure out your entire plan, my good lord.*

"You're a brave man," Elisa said in a soothing tone.

She pushed his hair to the side and wiped away some tears with her fingers to encourage him to stop crying and be a man. She liked Darryg but could see he would only be used as a pawn even if he sported the crown of the kingdom on his head. Elisa was slightly confused. Flayed bodies permanently lined Moonlight Road, which was the only way in and out of Lightview. *How could the lord and lady keep their son away from that? After seeing impaled bodies moaning, how could it be so shocking for him to see men being killed in battle?*

Everyone fell asleep on top of each other except Elisa. The awful sounds from the afternoon kept replaying in her head. The agonizing screams of the men haunted her. She carefully moved Darryg's hand so she didn't wake him, and got out of the coach. There were about thirty guards that all bowed to the queen.

She walked away from the coach and two guards followed closely. In Elisa's eyes, the night sky sang a song of sorrow with a melancholy moon and somber stars to cap a horrendous day. Open pit fires and braziers illuminated a picture of pain and loss. The healers tried to treat all the injured, but their good intentions greatly outweighed their skills. Even the trained apothecaries and medicine men weren't ready for this carnage. This deep into the night Elisa expected that all the wounded would have long been taken care of, but the makeshift treatment area still had men shrieking in pain while the overmatched apothecaries tried to ease the suffering.

Elisa focused on a man whose arm had been removed just below the elbow. The apothecary tied a tight band above the wound and held the injured man's arm steady. Another soldier pulled a sword from the fire with the blade glowing like a dragon's molten eyes. He touched the burnt blade to the stump of the injured man's elbow.

The wounded man jumped back and knocked the skinny apothecary to the ground. Another soldier handed the man a goat skin of mulled spirits. His good arm shook so violently that he ended up spilling most of the stiff booze down his chin and onto his blood-soaked surcoat of a golden apple hanging from a tree. The Ellsworths used their own standard but anyone with a visible golden apple depicted in any manner fell under his protection. Unfortunately, Lord Ichibod hadn't been able to protect this man from losing his arm.

Elisa started to feel sick as she watched the crude medical techniques and teeth-clenching amputations. Her icy heart started to warm. She had an epiphany. *I caused this. These men were fighting for their queen. It used to only be a phrase, but now I see the reality. Have I turned into a monster?*

She hurried back to the coach and jumped inside. She couldn't sleep and when the sun rose several hours later, one sentence rang over and over in her head. Elisa remembered when Telly had told her that she overheard a soldier saying, "We'll be the ones getting a sword blade shoved in our ass while the queen polishes her crown."

When she got back out of the coach, the scent of decaying bodies hit her nose.

The sunlit scene was even more heartbreaking. Some of the bodies from the mass carnage had been thrown into piles that were taller than she was. Soldiers dug graves for the men without association. All residents of Lightview who died honorably would have their bodies returned to their families. Elisa knew this would set the effort back even more. Officers sorted through bodies trying to identify the fallen. As Elisa walked among the scenes of misery, she experienced even more heartache. She knew men had died for kings and queens on a regular basis for thousands of years, but she had never been the reason for any of those. Amongst parts of men and bodies alive just yesterday, she decided to leave.

Some of the passing men spoke to the queen, "We got them bastards for you, yes we did, ya highness."

"Long live our queen."

"Here's to your first battle victory," one man remarked as he held up a skin of wine.

Victory? If this is victory I should surely hate to face defeat. We've lost thousands of soldiers. I don't even know if we should press on if there is more of this to follow. The soldiers aren't just pawns or numbers anymore.

She went back near the coach and gave Telly a hug and kiss on the cheek. Telly dragged her into the open field and Elisa looked across the blood-stained grass and felt the piercing stare of Green Mamba.

Elisa knew she had to go talk to the man and excused herself from Telly. He shook his head in disgust as Elisa made her lonely walk, trying to avoid the red splotches.

He shook his head and spoke as Elisa approached, "You can't free dead man. You say you free my people, they free now." Green Mamba pointed around at the piles of dead Prograggers. Elisa didn't know what to say, but the man with dirt and blood covering his body continued, "The pale man fights with no honor. Attacking when it's not expected, stabbing men in backs. That's not battle, that's disgrace. Pale man push us into each other and attack on horse."

Elisa finally gained the courage and said, "I'm sorry. This man gave me his word that we could cross his bridge in peace."

Green Mamba said, "Man is only worth his word. I'll kill this man if I see him."

Elisa replied, "I will kill him myself for all the mayhem he has caused."

The two awkwardly stared at each other until she said, "I still plan to free all the remaining Prograggers. I can't give them back their brothers but I will provide plenty of land to live on."

Green Mamba just shook his head again and went back to the other Prograggers.

Elisa saw the Ellsworths outside the coach when she returned.

She spoke to everyone, "I'm not sure if we should press on."

Lord Ichibod immediately retorted, "Whoa, let's not say anything hasty. This was an unmitigated disaster, there is no denying that, but a strong queen must press on. This is war. These men died defending the highest honor, their queen. They didn't die in a tavern brawl or getting shivved at the markets by a complete stranger. All men want to die defending their queen or king."

Let's hope you share that sentiment too. I wouldn't mind if you died while defending me.

Elisa didn't have time to press the issue as a small coach slowly pulled up and a man ran over to Lord Ichibod.

The guard said, "Lord Ichibod, we found him."

Ichibod said, "Thank the Gods, we almost lost a key piece of our claim."

The guard lowered his head and softly spoke, "We did lose our king, my lord."

The lord buried his head in his hands and let out a cacophonous scream.

He went to the coach and the rest of the group followed. He pulled open the door and everyone saw the butchered body of Ali-Varis Wamhoff lying in disgrace. He had stab wounds extending from his face and ears right down to his knees. Elisa barely recognized the man she had married a half-year ago. For some reason, she didn't feel sorry. The ice must have started to reform around her heart. She decided to press on in her attempt to take the throne.

Tersen

A bucket of cold urine rushed down over Tersen's head and body. This had been the normal wake up call for the last few days.

The toothless torturer asked, "What's a matta, gettin' sleepy is we?"

Tersen wanted to die. He was strapped to a device they called the stretcher. A flat board had four holes with loops of hemp rope coming from them. The tied areas were positioned for a person to hold his hands above his head and legs spread apart. His body had been tied securely in place for about half a day. The torturer looked over the former king in silence. Only three men in the castle had caused physical pain to the former king: Harolg, Kryen and Balsam.

The latter asked, "What should we do today?"

Balsam stared at the wall of pain devices. One side had long swords, maces, morningstars, daggers and one-handed war hammers. For more delicate work, Balsam moved to his left. The shelves on the wall contained fine razors, small spikes, metal hooks, steel clamps and metal thread. The sparsely lit room had a soiled dirt floor with moldy stone walls and stunk terribly.

The portly man with missing teeth took his time looking over the painful devices and a sadistic smile ran across his face.

"Let's us go fishin'," Balsam said. He started to laugh until he noticed Tersen had nodded off. He rushed over and booted the former king right in the crotch. The kick was excruciatingly painful for Tersen because the previous day, Kryen had performed a crude, painful procedure to be certain the Wamhoff name wouldn't be tarnished further by any offspring of Tersen's.

The agony jolted Tersen awake but he could barely stay conscious. He could see Balsam with a long hook coupled with a look of devious intentions.

The jolly torturer said, "Me said we is goin' fishin', yes I did. Now me, I never liked me no albino fish. Bad luck daddy always said. Now me daddy wasn't never a king or no station like that, but methinks he was right. Ima try me a catch anyhows."

Balsam twirled the hook in his left hand before clutching it tight. He drove the cold steel under Tersen's left nipple and pulled up. Tersen shrieked and pain shot from his chest to the extremities of his body. This intense smarting was different than the constant, life-draining stretching. Tersen had begged all three of the men to kill him, but none were willing to grant his wish. Every time his breathing had almost stopped from the taxing effort, they would let him down to recoup before strapping him back up. The routine had been repeated over the last week and a half. Tersen hung by his limp wrists, rubbed raw and bloody from the harsh hemp rope. He had never experienced even a fraction of this kind of physical pain in his entire sheltered and pampered life.

Balsam twisted the hook and an angry river of dark blood flowed out of the former king's ghostly flesh. The piercing gave Tersen a shot of energy and he was fully awake now. The only time he felt truly awake was when the three men were conducting the disfigurement. It seemed that Tersen's life lay in the tiny hands of a volatile sixteen-year-old high lord. He knew he could be sent to the new king as a gift to gain favor. Right now, that seemed like a better prospect as Balsam removed the hook and moved to the other side of Tersen's chest and dug in.

"Me dunno. This don't look like no keeper to me boys," Balsam said as he looked around the empty room. "Methinks you'll get sick and die if you eat the albino fish. Better throw this one back." Balsam guffawed at an unseen audience. The man wore an old black cloak that had never been cleaned, secured with a wide belt of cracked brown leather that held on for dear life just below his huge gut. He yanked the hook and Tersen passed out again.

Later that day, Kryen Wamhoff entered the room. He thought Tersen was sleeping so he gently slapped his uncle's face. That didn't work so Kryen slapped him harder. When no movement followed again, Kryen unstrapped Tersen's arms and the body fell to the ground. Kryen tried to gently set his uncle down, but underestimated the man's girth. He untied Tersen's feet and pushed him onto his back. Kryen put a finger under the former king's nose and felt nothing. He looked for any kind of movement of the chest to signal breathing and saw nothing.

Jon

"I was worried about my family at first, until she knocked me down. She could have easily killed me. I was lying there with little protection from her sharp axe. Why was I spared?" Jon asked.

Orian Vangor had already taken on several nicknames from the High Raven or White Raven to the Father of the Poor and the Raven of Light.

The old man rubbed his bushy eyebrow. "Why is anyone *spared*? There have been reports of dragon attacks recently. Why did they attack Housemont and Kimberton? Why didn't they attack the heart of the Capitol, the true center of greed and sin in the kingdom? Why were all those dirty souls spared? The Gods, they work in queer ways. Our minds are too fragile to even imagine the reasoning of the Gods. Be joyous in the fact that you still wake every day, and spend less time trying to figure out why. You'll simply drive yourself mad."

Jon tried to let it go and asked, "How is the resurrection coming along?" The resurrection was the name given to the holy reclamation process.

Orian answered in his normal, drawn out manner, "Slowly, but steadily. We finally flushed most of the waste from Falconhurst, or so I thought. It should happen to seem that some priests who had been ousted for unscrupulous practices are less than happy. A few have been causing problems for our new brothers and sisters. They threatened a woman and me whilst we were simply walking by. Imagine if that was your daughter by my side. If I give over the names, can I depend on you to help with these problems, so king and church can stand united?"

Jon gave his word, "Give me the names. I will put an end to these trouble makers."

The Raven of Light had struck a chord by mentioning his family's safety. He knew Orian hadn't just stopped by for a friendly chat. Jon started to realize the White Raven was much shrewder than he ever remembered in Mattingly.

"Sin needs purged," the old man said as he whipped his back. The Raven of Light had suffered for his sins for so long, he barely moved when the spiked ends broke the skin. His battered body looked like he had been through many bloody battles.

Jon had been receiving a large number of complaints over the new practices. The nobles didn't want to share their churches with the poor, but the new system treated everyone equally. The wealthy members also complained that the new brothers and sisters had stripped the rich decorations from all their churches. They had even removed the cushions from the benches and kneelers. The new leader of the Faith stressed that people needed to get back to upholding the words of the Gods and forget about who had the fanciest church. None of the new policies meshed with the rich citizens who used to be able to buy promised salvation. They now had to pay for their sins on earth before being ready for the trials of death.

Suddenly, Rick Rosebud busted into Jon's audience chamber, bowed and stated, "Highness, High Raven." He looked at Jon and said, "We have him. Lord Undertow will be arriving any moment now."

Jon jumped out of his seat and cried, "Bring him to the King's block in the inner bailey. Fetch my sword from my quarters and meet me out there."

Jon's face turned purple and boiling blood coursed through his body.

He had forgotten the Raven of Light was still there until the old man said, "What is the meaning of all this?"

Jon turned and answered, "We've caught the traitor who opened the city gates for our enemy and helped sneak her through Fox Chapel."

The White Raven started to say, "But who are we to judge? If we have repeated the same actions as others…"

Jon interrupted him sternly, "No, we're not doing this. I leave you to dole out punishment for sin as you deem fit and I am helping you to punish the people on that list that you've judged as guilty. This man put my family's life at stake. He put your life at stake. You punish your sinners and I'll punish my citizens. Good day, High Raven."

"Do as you must," Orian said in a haunted tone as he whipped his left shoulder. One of the spiked ends got stuck in the bruised and bloodied flesh that was visible through his shredded kirtle.

Jon watched him pry it from his body as he walked out. "Good day, High Raven."

He rushed out the door and found the closest steps. Four guards trailed Jon as he moved briskly down another stone staircase. The King tried not to let Orian's words sway him and thought about when he had been forced to evacuate his only daughter's wedding and had almost died at the hands of the Queen of Goldenfield. He remembered the looks of terror on his family's faces as he said goodbye for what could have been the last time. He stood firm in his decision again as he hit the inner bailey. He looked across the grassy yard and saw Lord Wolter Undertow for the first time.

The upstart lord wore a flamboyant powder blue and magenta themed outfit with gold necklaces and enough silver bracelets to make a princess jealous.

His dark eyes looked nearly shut as he said, "I am just as much a traitor as you who calls himself our king. I am and always will be loyal to the Wamhoffs."

Sir Rick handed Jon his sword and Jon realized he had forgotten his crown on the table in his audience chamber.

He didn't need a crown to carry out this sentence and said, "You pledged fealty in a letter because you couldn't attend the coronation in person."

The man with a curled mustache that hung to his stomach, spit on the ground and said, "I never knelt in front of you or kissed any hands. Anyone could have forged that letter. Perhaps one of my scared sons sealed it with my standard."

Jon cleared his throat. "Your lies won't work here, I'm afraid to inform you. You got over a thousand men killed around the gates and more than three thousand killed in total by letting our enemy though."

"And I'd do it again if I had the chance," Lord Undertow said insolently.

Jon looked him in the eyes. "You will never receive that chance, Lord Wolter."

Jon's guards pushed the bound man to his knees. A square wooden block sat in front of the condemned man.

"Lord Wolter Undertow, you have been determined to be guilty of treason at the highest level. In the name of King Jon Colbert, first of my name and grand protector of the realm, I sentence you to die. Do you have any last words?" Jon asked.

"You will die soon enough. All your followers will die soon enough. You have more enemies than you could ever imagine. Fast they rise, fast they fall. See you in the seven hells, you dirty usurper," Lord Wolter said in an ominous tone and followed it with a demonic laugh.

The lord placed his head over the edge of the block and the guards pushed it out even further. Jon looked at Green Fury and lined up his stroke with a few practice swipes. The sword rose above the King's head and the blade caught the shine of the sun before dropping down to end the life of Lord Wolter Undertow. A buzz ran through Jon's body and he felt justice had been served. He only wondered if the lord was right and more enemies loomed. The two parts of the body were taken away, blood streaming from both. Jon didn't believe in putting heads on spikes. He thought it was an outdated barbaric activity that didn't serve any purpose. He finally stopped shaking as he went back into the castle. Jon had expected Lord Wolter to plead for his life, but the smugness of the man surprised the King.

He walked up to an open door of a storage room and caught sight of something that almost made him ill. The room contained paintings from the previous regime. They had been taken down when Jon captured the castle. He wanted to look at them before burning or disposing of them. He focused on a painting of a duel between a young King Ali-Stanley and his father. The former king stood over his cowering father, ready to deliver the death blow.

A gentle voice from behind said, "Quite an atrocity, yes I know."

He turned to see Count Silzeus. The ancient man with a heavily wrinkled face was hunched forward as usual. Scraggly silver hair and a long matching mustache ran down to his plump belly. The rest of his body was skinny, although hidden under his loose black cloak. The elderly gentleman walked around the castle in pain despite the help of a hickory cane. He was notorious for refusing assistance from anyone.

"Why don't we sit down in the next room over there? We haven't had much of a chance to talk individually since…since I arrived," Jon suggested.

He almost said took over but the term takeover didn't sound right in his head. Jon viewed it as more of a liberation for the good people of the realm.

They sat on fox fur-edged brown chairs around a circular stone table. The room hadn't been fully decorated because Jon's focus had been on other matters.

Count Silzeus, breathing heavily from the brief walk, said, "That business of false paintings was all started by King Ali-Baris at the end of his reign and unfortunately grew even bigger under the next two kings."

Jon asked, "If you don't mind my asking, how old are you, my good man?"

A slick smile came over the count's face as he licked his lips. "I am afraid vanity won't allow me to answer that fully, but I was present for the end of King Ali-Pharell's rule. They called him the last of the good kings and you shall never hear me argue that. I was spoiled as a young chap into thinking all kings acted like Ali-Pharell. A great man and better king, well respected too. His son Ali-Baris couldn't have been more different."

Jon sprinkled some salt into a cup of water and handed it to the count, who grabbed it with a shaky hand and continued, "Where was I? King Ali-Baris, yes, his reign was synonymous with gluttony and unfortunately he taught King Ali-Baster to rule in the same manner. Schemes and hoodwinks was how they ruled. The banking borrowing game only hurt the kingdom, but they pressed on with the funny money system. As for those paintings, Ali-Baster took false royal propaganda to an unthinkable level."

The old man paused a lot and sipped his salted water often to keep his dry lips from sticking together. Jon enjoyed getting an inside viewpoint on the exaggerated history of the Wamhoffs.

The count continued, "He spent the realm's coin commissioning the top artists and he had more painters in his court than viable advisors. Ali-Stanley let the practice die down of late with the financial woes of the royal treasury, but he held viewings early in his reign. They would display the paintings by the Walk of Kings. The despicable atrocity you just laid eyes on became one of the main attractions and remained constantly on display. Fifteen guards made certain the thieves didn't develop impure motives before they were taken down for the day at dusk. Citizens starved just outside the castle walls, while close council meetings centered around propaganda art and buildings to increase the royal reputation, no matter the grand falsities contained within."

Jon asked, "So what is the real story about my father's death?"

Count Silzeus' face became flushed and he drank half of his large cup of water. "It pains me to tell this story. King Ali-Baster and Duke Patrick Beverley were great friends, so obviously he wouldn't be very fond of your father's rebellion. King Ali-Baster tried to organize several overthrows of Mattingly, but your father crushed them all. He tried until his dying day to kill Jasper Colbert to no avail."

Jon stopped him for a moment and asked, "That's another debated story. How did King Ali-Baster really die?"

"He was found in the privy after complaining of great stomach pain. I examined the body and found that he had been poisoned. He held all the signs of death by purple hemlock. Yet, the rest of the Wamhoff family didn't want to believe it. They put out a statement saying that the king had died while sitting the throne, and I was one of many sworn to push that lie. Even stranger, the family didn't want to believe my opinion. Quite odd, I remember thinking," remarked the Count.

The King said, "So back to the story of my father."

Count Silzeus rubbed his closed eyes for a moment and spoke, "Yes, right you are, where were we in the story?"

Jon answered, "King Ali-Baster had just died on the chamber pot."

"Aahh, yes, yes, that's correct," the old man chuckled. He continued, "Jasper Colbert showed up at King Ali-Baster's funeral services and entered the tournament. This absolutely enraged Ali-Stanley. The new King had been experiencing awful stomach pains and for a few days, we thought Ali-Stanley had been poisoned too. I knew the ground dragon horn could possibly drive him a bit mad but it was our only hope to save a dying king. His stomach pains finally did persist, but his head became twisted and warped. Had I known the resulting effects, I may have never prescribed it. I often think of what would have been if Ali-Stanley had died back then. Ali-Varis would have taken rule as a teenager; a boy who couldn't remember to swallow his food was set to be our new king. Sorry, uh, back to your father. He dazzled in the tourney, ultimately being named Grand Champion. He easily defeated the best knights that Fox Chapel could throw at him. This drove Ali-Stanley over the edge. He concocted a devious plan that every advisor tried to talk him out of. He planned to ambush your father's troupe of one hundred. That phantom duel never took place. That balderdash was all part of a mad faeblor's story. King Ali-Stanley sent five hundred of his best warriors for an easy victory. It was anything but as only twenty-six men returned and most of them were injured. They said your father cut down one hundred men in the least before succumbing to defeat. He obviously died that day and I fear I bear some of the blame. I prescribed the dragon antler knowing it might make the King mad. He didn't have me in any meetings concerning your subsequent ambush on the Royal Road but I understand if you must punish me for what happened to your father."

Jon quickly quelled the old man's fears and said, "That's wildly unnecessary. You are a good man who served his kings in the best manner possible. How could I punish you for that? Just do the same for me is all I can ask."

The count played with his long mustache and said, "With honor, your highness."

Later that night, Jon lay in bed with Camelle and Baby Jon. Most parents put their baby in a crib but Jon liked to have his defenseless son close to him.

"So I need to send Ruxin west and I will be going to the eastern front shortly. The Queen of Goldenfield is on her way back to Sevring, so Ruxin won't see any more fighting. Lord Ichibod is our greatest threat now but I will be staying out of the action. I have a plan to avoid fighting altogether," Jon said with a sweet smile that was broken by a wrinkled frown.

Camelle wanted to know, "Why are we doing this?"

"Doing what? Defending our kingdom?" Jon asked.

She raised her voice and said, "Yes. This is exactly what I told you would happen. We have a target on our backs now. Did you think all the others would just back down once you took the crown?"

Jon immediately answered, "I knew there would be a struggle in the beginning, same as my father's rebellion in Mattingly. But once we establish ourselves, it'll all disappear. Don't worry, nobody is going to get hurt. I am sending Ruxin to an area of safety. I am not going to make his wife a widow."

She rubbed Jon's cheek and said, "Don't make me a widow either, let's not forget about that. You cannot forget your father's prophecy too."

Jon became agitated and spoke in short bursts, "You think I could forget something like that? I think about it every day, several times a day. Either my father or I would die soon after becoming King of Donegal. He never became king. Yeah, I remember what he said." He continued in an annoyed tone, "I cannot, no I will not, live scared. We're all going to die, but if we serve a strong purpose…"

Camelle shook her head and said, "Now you sound like your uncle Jasine. If only he were still around; he would agree with me."

"Oh you think so, do you?" Jon asked and gave his wife a soft kiss on her velvety lips. He looked down at the baby in between them.

"Do you think the Wamhoffs really have Krys?" Camelle asked.

"We're going to do our best to find out soon enough. I just sent Rick Rosebud and Sir Antery Blackburn to meet in peace to identify Krys. They say he's been burned by dragon fire so he looks nothing like his former self, but our knights know what questions to ask our son."

Camelle got a rare gleam in her eyes as she said, "I really want to believe it is him. Do you think it's really Krys?"

Jon slowed down his talking as he answered, "I don't know. I just know we can't give up the entire kingdom for our son."

"Yes, we most certainly can. Let them take this forsaken castle and we can go back to Mattingly where we belong. Our son is much more important than something as trivial as power," she said with tears forming in her eyes.

Jon tried to be delicate and spoke in a soothing voice, "It isn't about the power. I would throw it all away at a moment's notice for our sons, but did we just risk our lives to rid the realm of Wamhoff tyranny only to hand the crown right back over to them? There has to be a negotiable price that doesn't include a throne."

Camelle just shook her head in awe before saying, "And what if that is the only option for our son's life? We let our son die? Have you no heart?" She rolled over with her back to Jon and the baby.

Jon started scratching her back the way she liked over her silky night gown. He whispered in her ear, "I don't have my entire heart. It will only be complete when Ryno, Krys, Riceros and Brehan return. Now I hear rumors that Brehan has sworn allegiance to Elisa Burke's cause. Do we give up the kingdom to have him come home too?"

"That's completely different. He swore his sword to her. Krys is a prisoner against his will," she said.

Jon lowered his voice and said, "I knew he loved the girl but I never expected her to rise to power so quickly. We may have lost Brehan to love, but I will do anything to get Krys back."

Camelle rolled back over and looked into Jon's green eyes. "Then give up this wretched realm."

Jon shook his head and the two went back and forth for about an hour before finally falling asleep. The next day, King Jon wanted to take his son on his first horse ride. They walked down to the stables and Jon had the spurrier saddle an ambler for him. He had asked the King of the Scholars to design a sling to wear over his shoulders that Baby Jon could sit in and be held securely. It looked like a sleeveless leather vest with four slots for the baby's arms and legs in front. Jon made sure his son was perfectly stable before using the stirrup to spring up on the dark amber horse with black points. He started with a slow walk to let his son get used to the cadence of the horse. He heeled the animal ever so gently to get her up to an amble and worried as she neared a canter. Jon was about to pull up on the reins but he looked down at his son. The boy was clapping silently and Jon could feel his boy wiggling around, seemingly enjoying the ride. Jon let the ambler maintain speed as a grin as wide as the Royal River came over his face.

Jon's father had taken him on his first horse ride when he was a baby, so this meant a lot to him. He would often see babies at the market and Jasper would tell Jon that he was younger than they were when he went on his first ride. He just realized that this horse was faster than he had expected and had to pull up again. The two kept riding in circles around the plain grass field.

This is what life should be about; enjoying the first ride with your son. If only the rest of life could be this simple. Why does everything have to become so complicated?

Most men would have found the ride boring, but Jon viewed it as the best of his life. He could feel his son moving up and down and the excited boy made gurgling sounds that made Jon smile even more. He lost himself in the moment and thanked the Gods for the chance to enjoy this bonding experience with his son. When he had been locked in the dungeons, Jon never expected to have this moment. The imprisonment taught him to cherish every experience with his family, even the fights with Camelle.

He had lost track of the time of day when Sir Harris rode up and screamed, "So sorry, your highness, they are looking for you in the meeting that you supposedly called."

Jon yelled back without slowing the horse down, "Go back and tell them I am on my way."

His trusted guard asked, "Would you like me to take your boy back to his quarters so you can go directly to the meeting?"

Jon looked at him like he was crazy and replied, "No. My son is more important than being a few minutes late for a meeting."

The King took the Prince back to his mother, and apologized for his tardiness as he sat down at the table to start the meeting. Of course, everyone told him there wasn't a problem with his late arrival.

Jon started the meeting by saying, "Have we figured out exactly how the Queen of Goldenfield rolled through Fox Woods and our walled Capitol?"

Kelvyn Harros said, "I've found out a great deal from my many birds. First, we found out that she crossed the Piper Marshlands to sneak into Fox Woods. That is where Lord Undertow came in and coordinated quite an extensive effort to guide the rival Queen straight to your castle. We've captured all thirty-four men involved in the plot and they are being held in the dungeons. That was how she marched unmolested around our realm. The surprising matter was that the bribes were relatively low for the risk of treason. The conspiring group apparently has taken issue with you lowering taxes on their subjects. That's what we've found so far."

Jon quickly said, "Thank you, good lord. I will punish all of them in the inner bailey at five bells."

Count Silzeus cleared his throat and spoke in his old, raspy voice, "A raven arrived with words of an ambush of sorts constructed by Lord Jerian Nanbert on the Ichibod Ellsworth contingent. He says it was a gift to the new King. Another report tells us that Lord Nanbert was eventually overtaken but they did cause heavy damage to the enemy."

Jon shook his head and spoke in an angry tone, "I never sanctioned anything like this. This is the first I've heard since the lord sent a letter pledging fealty. I would never authorize an ambush; that type of action goes against everything I believe in. What happened to honor in this realm? The ambush tactic is more popular than the monogramed purses the nobles seem to love so much. What happened to two generals meeting and agreeing to a fair fight? What happened to chivalry?"

His Falconer softened his tone and said, "This won't probably please your ears then, your majesty. The bastard in the north has sent down a storm of purple fire on the Wamhoff's campsite, destroying nearly everything. Our people in the north tell us that the Wamhoffs have already been crippled and no longer pose a legitimate threat to the throne." Lord Kelvyn became more excited toward the end of his report.

That's why they want me to believe they have my son. They are getting desperate already. I hope they do have Krys but can I really give up the entire kingdom for him? Jon stared at Ruxin as he thought about this. The meeting ended and Jon asked his son to remain behind.

RUXIN

Ruxin wondered why his father wanted to talk. King Jon Colbert started to speak as soon as everyone left, "I am sending you west to ensure the Queen of Goldenfield doesn't try to pull any more of her tricks. Now, I don't want you up front. A Colbert needs to be out there, but I won't have you getting killed."

Ruxin retorted, "Then why go? So I can cheer the other men along? I'm a fighter. I fight."

Jon spoke with a calm demeanor, "Not this time. You could have died several times over in the past fortnight. Enough is enough. The men, they know you're brave. You don't have to prove anything to your older brothers anymore. Queen Leimur is likely to just go home so there probably won't be any fighting, but if there is, you are to stay in the back. King's orders."

Ruxin mockingly said, "Yes, your highness."

He didn't understand how his father could command him to act like a coward. He thought avoiding the action would only serve to embarrass the Colbert name. Ruxin was full of youthful exuberance and wanted to lead every attack. He walked back to his quarters and found Haley working on needlepoint as she sat at the low table. He pushed a chair next to hers and kissed her on the cheek. She always brought a smile to his face.

He asked, "How are you, my queen?"

"Still getting used to you calling me that," she shyly exclaimed.

"One day you shall be a queen, my queen. We will rule this realm together and travel the world with our family," Ruxin said as he rubbed her burgeoning belly and felt some movement. He leaned down and kissed his wife's midsection over her dress. He pecked his lips all over her round stomach and turned his head to listen to the baby. He whispered, "I hope he's a boy."

Haley smiled and said, "I don't care whether it's a boy or girl, so long as there aren't any problems. With the stories of princes and princesses being cast away for slight disfigurements, I hope our baby is fat and healthy."

He straightened up from her stomach and said, "I will love our child regardless, but we will need a male heir to pass on our legacy. Our son will one day be king."

He gave his wife a kiss. He decided this was a good time to tell Haley about his impending departure. He said softly, "I have to go back out west to make sure Queen Leimur doesn't try to come back this way."

She shook her head and said, "No, no, no. You've dodged death too many times to try again. Not so soon. Wait until your baby is born to go back out there."

He tried to calm her fears as he said, "All this fighting will only happen in the beginning of my father's rule. Besides, our King has ordered me to stay near the back, like a craven."

A slight look of relief washed over his wife's face as she commented, "I agree in total with your father on this one."

"This isn't funny. I can't sit in the back and simply hope that the men will pull out a victory without their leader fighting with them. I need to be up front so the men will fight harder," Ruxin told her.

Haley argued, "You can't help anyone if you die on that battlefield."

Ruxin rebutted, "Actually, the men will probably fight even harder to avenge my death."

She shook her head rapidly and said, "No, stop. You need to stay in the back on this one, my love."

His wife gave him a kiss on his cheek, which had newly sprouted facial hair.

He still lamented, "My father never stayed near the back. Neither did my grandfather. They always fought up front. That's what Colberts do."

She asked him, "So will we constantly have to worry about the next Colberts?"

"What do you mean?" he needed clarification.

"Your grandfather usurped the dukeship of Mattingly. Your father usurped the throne. Is it only a matter of time before someone else takes over?" a concerned Haley asked.

He hugged his wife and whispered into her ear, "That's not going to happen. My father will be a fair and just ruler. I will be a fair and just ruler. If you keep your people happy, they have no reason to rebel. The Beverleys were just as bad as the Wamhoffs from what I've been told."

She cut in, "And you know I've been told the exact opposite."

He continued, "I do and I know your stories are wrong."

Ruxin playfully squeezed his wife's chubby sides, tickling her and causing her to squirm in the solid oak chair.

He smiled as he spoke in a lowered voice, "My grandfather realized if you couple the anger of the common man with the greed of nobility, you could leverage the most powerful of families. My father called together the top lords of Mattingly to make certain everyone was as unhappy as he with King Tersen. As I said, if you keep people happy, the rest is all fun and fantasy. I'll be back before you even have time to miss me. Our enemy is going home with their tail betwixt their legs."

His wife said, "I miss you when you go to the privy, so you can't return soon enough. I hate worrying about you constantly. It can't be good for our baby. You should try to convince your father to stay here instead of just lurking in the back of the battle. Please?" she begged with hope glimmering in the golden flecks of her eyes.

He brought her hopes back to reality by saying, "A Colbert has to be there. My father is going east to stave off any advances from the Ellsworths."

A loud knock at the door interrupted the conversation. Ruxin acted surprised and went to investigate. He opened the door and smiled as two harpists entered, followed by dulcimer and rebec players. Finally two men, each with a psaltery, assembled near the other instruments. His wife still didn't know what was going on. Haley had always talked about how the stringed instruments were her favorite, so Ruxin had arranged a private performance for his pregnant wife. The six men and two women were extremely skilled and even Ruxin enjoyed the pleasing sounds. He put his arm around his wife who had been standing in shock since the musicians entered the room. He gently rubbed her side as tears cascaded down her lovely face and gently dripped to the floor. Ruxin had only cried when he found out that his mother and father had died, although he liked to tell everyone he'd never cried. He had been forced by his brothers to be tough and he never once cried from the rough love. The sweet slow song sent a gentle melody out the open window and into the chilly autumn air of the inner bailey.

"It would be impossible for me to love you any more than I do," she whispered into his ear.

Later that night, Ruxin couldn't sleep, so he took a walk around the castle. He went to the ground floor and walked past the dimly lit throne room. His father had left some of the previous kings' busts on the assorted pedestals. The current King had removed several of the statue heads of monarchs who didn't deserve the honor. The silver throne shimmered in the dying torchlight as Ruxin approached the front steps. He walked up and sat on the uncomfortable chair. He closed his eyes and thought about how he would change the throne once he took over as king. He knew it would be a long time from now, but he still liked to dream. He planned to use gold gilding to decorate the entire throne and widen the seat for comfort. He wanted to put gigantic golden bull horns on the top of the back of the seat. He also thought about a nice silver silk pillow stuffed with goose feathers to sit on while he ruled. He anticipated a long run as king so he wanted as much comfort on the throne as possible.

I'll show Haley how to be a just ruler. If you treat the citizens with respect, nobody will have reason to revolt. I shall be the greatest king to ever rule, and she, the greatest queen.

He heard footsteps and opened his eyes to see Chopkins Haddock stumbling around the room. He was playing with the face of King Ali-Dus when Ruxin said, "Hello there, good man."

The intoxicated joker started to spin around and looked up at the ceiling. "Straight to the stables, who said that?"

Ruxin got up and walked down the steps as the stocky jester focused on him.

Chopkins slurred his words, "Prince Ruxin. What are…what are you doing up this late?"

Ruxin answered, "Couldn't sleep. And what's your excuse?"

The young man stared at the Prince before answering. "Same. Exact same for me." He slurred his words through his red wine-stained teeth. Even in the dark, Ruxin could see the funnyman's eyes were glazed over. Chopkins said, "We're going to have some fun in this castle, you and me."

Ruxin glared at the young man before saying, "No. You will have fun in my castle while I go and fight for our kingdom."

Chopkins shook his head with a strange smile before saying, "I'm going with you when you leave to defend the kingdom."

Ruxin looked at the staggering man, specifically, his soft, round belly, and asked, "You are going to fight with me?"

Chopkins nodded confidently and said, "Sure as seven hells, I am. I'm Torvald's squire. He told me we were leaving with you when you move out west. Truth be told, I'm a tiny bit scared about the whole endeavor." He put a finger on his lips and winked at Ruxin. It turned out to be more of a blink as the drunken man couldn't control his eyes.

Ruxin said, "Worry not, little man. As luck should have it, we've been ordered to stay out of the action. You are going to be just fine."

A slight look of relief came over Chopkins' face as he said, "That's pleasant news because Torvald and I have never been in real battle. I can keep the men's spirits up, but that's about all I am good for."

Ruxin thought for a moment and told him, "We'll give you a pike. You can poke 'em with the pike. Now let's get you back to your quarters."

The next evening, Haley and Ruxin prepared for the special supper with the entire family and friends of Bottomfoot. Ruxin walked over to his bride and presented her with a beautiful necklace. A silver charm with a mosaic of shined turtle shell, crushed crystal and carnelian hung from a golden band. He secured the clasp behind the back of her neck and looked at the streaming rainbow of colored lights coming from the charm.

He held out his arm and Haley put her arm through it. They walked down the hallway and descended the steps to get to the Grand Hall. Almost all the attendees were already there and the couple took their place at the table. Jon sat at the head of the rectangular table with Ruxin to his left and Camelle to his right. Haley sat next to Ruxin and the rest of their side consisted of Edword, Lucille and Orian. Ruxin looked at the opposite side and saw Mariah, Torvald, Sir Bastion, Chopkins and J. Everson. The long maple table, one of many in the hall, was the only one occupied and the chatter at the table echoed throughout the open area. Baby Jon sat on Camelle's lap as she fed him tiny spoonfuls of mashed carrots and onions. Ruxin grabbed his wife's hand and squeezed as Callice rolled a giant harp into the hall and began to serenade the guests.

As the meal commenced, he noticed his sister kept arguing with Torvald and giving him dirty looks from across the table. The faces full of judgment became more frequent and when the meal ended, Ruxin went to talk to Mariah.

MARIAH

Mariah immediately berated her brother, "Why is my husband suddenly going off with you to fight? Did you talk him into this?"

Ruxin stepped back and answered, "I didn't even know he was coming with me until I saw his little jester stumbling around the throne room last night. All I know is Chopkins told me that he and the Bottomfoot men will be coming along, all except Edword, who is going with father."

Mariah talked in an angry and annoyed tone, "So that's who it was, father? He's making Torvald go into battle, isn't he?"

Ruxin answered with a slight grin, "It's Torvald. Torvald is making Torvald go into battle. He's a man. Men fight and women have children. That's how the stars shine. I think he wants to go because that's what real men do. You should be pleased you didn't marry a coward."

Mariah moved closer to her brother's face and said, "Yes, look at me; I'm basking in joy over the matter. He can die a hero on the battlefield, yet that still leaves me a widow. There's no joy in that. He's not a fighter and most of the young men from Bottomfoot aren't real warriors. They all tell me Torvald will excel in battle and while it may be true, I don't want my husband to risk his life out there."

Ruxin smiled and said, "You don't seem too concerned that I am risking my life out on the battlefield...again?"

She shook her head and said, "Not right now, I don't. Someone put my husband up to this. He comes from a land of neutrality. I know he wouldn't want to leave me."

Mariah turned and walked away only to immediately bump into Lucille.

Lucille looked her up and down. "You look angry, my precious dear. Whatever is the problem?"

Mariah showed her teeth in a fake smile and responded, "Nothing really, just a slight disagreement with my brother about dragging the Bottomfoot men away to war. What if they are gone for months or even a year? I've heard about how unexpected things can happen during a war."

Lucille pulled her in for a comforting hug and whispered into her ear, "Listen to me, you precious thing, men are going to do strange things constantly that will drive you absolutely mad."

Mariah asked, "But what can you do?"

Lucille brushed Mariah's hair over to the side with lavender fingernails poking out and soothingly said, "You can love him, support him and pray for him if he should be away for reasons of duty. Apart from that, you can only worry."

Mariah wondered, "When did you stop worrying about Edword?"

Lucille laughed and answered, "You never stop, sweet dear. Being a wife or a parent is different. For some inexplicable reason, you dream or imagine of horrible events involving the people you love the most. The more you love, the more you will be scared to death that something horrible is about to happen to those you hold dear. For the boys, well, they like to play rough, so every time Edword left the castle without me, I was as nervous as a sin-filled soul on judgment day." She laughed again and broke the hug with Mariah as they stared into each other's eyes.

"So there's not really anything you can do?" Mariah asked.

Lucille put her palm on Mariah's cheek and lightly tapped her neck with her silky smooth fingers. "Find activities that will fill your day and fill your heart. Find friends that share the same interests. You are a princess now. You can do anything your soul should desire. Love your husband, but don't become dependent on him to take care of everything. Walk on your own, my sweet dear. Regardless of all that worry I see behind those sparkling eyes, you look absolutely beautiful, sweet dear." Lucille gave her a kiss on the cheek and left some crimson smears from her makeup.

The White Raven came to say farewell for the evening and Mariah queried, "May I please have a few moments with you in private?"

The old man slowly answered, "Of course, where do we need to go?"

Mariah pointed and said, "Just over here, a bit farther away from the music." She led Orian to the other side of the hall. The instruments still buzzed in the background but now the High Raven could hear her without straining his ears.

He started by asking, "Have you had enough time to make a decision on my offer?"

Mariah ground her teeth together and her stomach started to stir. She didn't want to disappoint the highest-ranking religious official in the land. She didn't like to disappoint anyone. She talked through the developing lump in her throat, "I have, and I must respectfully decline."

Orian pressed her, "And why is that?"

Mariah took a deep breath, looked into the White Raven's dull blue eyes. "I would love to join you in traveling the kingdom to spread the word of the Faith. Unfortunately, I need to carry out my duties to the realm as a princess."

He nodded slowly before licking his brown lips and saying, "Our duties aren't owed to any realm. Our duties are only owed to the Seven. Salius, Patriah, Josevius, Nunce, Cleon, Radial and Numa. They are the ones who bestow the great gifts upon us. The Gods will be judging your soul when that fateful day should arrive. We help the realm, but we don't owe any piece of land our allegiance."

"My father is the King of this piece of land and it is to him that I owe my allegiance. I can't bring my husband here to the Capitol and just leave on him with my family while I travel around." Mariah finished with a playful frown on her face.

Orian smiled and tapped his lip. "I hardly think anyone would shed a tear for a man stranded in the luxury of the King's Castle, but that is a matter for another discussion. I asked that you give thought to my offer and you did. I hoped you would join me in this venture but I can tell you have given a good deal of thought to the matter. Perhaps if a next time should arise, we shall see each other again."

Mariah smiled at the gentle man and said, "Yes, this is still a turbulent time for our kingdom."

The White Raven took a drink of water from his sheep skin vessel that was slung over his neck. He wiped his mouth with the back of his hairy hand. "Indeed it is. That is why I must spread the word with even more vigor. A great many people are going to die soon and I must help guide the pure souls to the heavens. I must help the tainted souls denounce a life of sin and set out on the straight path to the heavens. I must travel the kingdom and educate our brothers and sisters. *That* is my duty."

The old man chuckled, bowed and pulled the wooden end of his whip from his tied belt. He took a few steps away from her, transferred the wooden handle to his right hand, and stopped to whip his left hip. Mariah cringed as she noticed blood spray out after the third strike. The repentant man adjusted his belt and kirtle around his midsection. He looked around and continued his slow, slouching walk out of the Grand Hall. Two hands met Mariah's shoulders from behind and she immediately knew they belonged to Torvald. She turned to look at him with a scowl of defiance. His loving smile started to warm her heart but she still felt betrayed.

"Did my father force you to go with my brother?" Mariah questioned.

Torvald shook his head and said, "No, nobody forces me to do anything I don't want to. My father is going with yours to defend the east and we will be going west. We have to defend your kingdom."

Mariah quickly asked, "My kingdom?"

Torvald took a moment to gather his thoughts before replying, "Our kingdom. Is that better? Look, nothing is going to happen. We are going for moral purposes so the men can see that the son of the king and a duke will fight for their kingdom. We just have to be there."

Mariah retorted, "Men have fought in the past without kings and princes on the battlefields. I've read many stories that would support that."

Torvald said, "Our past two kings did not fight in battle. Look at the state of *our* kingdom. A man doesn't want to defend a king he will never see. The men will fight solely for self-preservation and only for that, and that is a bad way to fight. Think about King Ali-Baster. He wasn't a warrior and nobody wanted to fight for him. Then we had Ali-Stanley. Not a warrior and no one would fight for him either. Ali-Ster went to war for four years instead of the required two. Men remember that. It isn't surprising that men ran to the Capitol to help King Ali-Ster. He fought for his kingdom and by doing so, he fought for his men. They would do anything for him. There's no choice to be made here. I have to go. That scare on our wedding night will never happen again. We were caught in a queer situation where we were unaware of the attack. There are no secrets now. Not to mention, we've been forbidden to join the fray should anything occur. I'm telling you, you're worrying about nothing."

Callice broke the tension by serenading the couple with their special song. Torvald leaned down and kissed Mariah, causing her anger to subside.

After the song, a drunken Chopkins stumbled over, held his finger in the air and said, "Alright, alright, what did the bald rabbit say to the horse?"

Everyone just looked at him as he spilled wine on his puffed ivory sleeves due to his shaking hand. He held his finger in the air again and spoke, "He said, I wish…I wish I was more like a hare. Or is it what he said to the hare?" The confused young man jumbled and slurred the words.

"My, you certainly are taking a strong liking to the wines of the Capitol," Mariah inferred.

Chopkins looked up at Mariah and shook his clear goblet around, spilling even more on the floor. "What difference should it make? All us men could be dead bodies in only a few days from now."

Torvald immediately scolded him, "Shut your mouth. I'll have no talk like that. If you are scared, you can stay behind."

Sir Bastion came in to pull Chopkins away before the young man said something he would come to regret. The knight told Chopkins, "Let's get you into that nice soft bed of yours."

Mariah started to get angry again until Torvald softly rubbed her lower back with his thumb. She could see his flushed face return to normal as he pulled her in for a hug and kiss. The evening wound down and the couple held hands as they walked back to their quarters.

As soon as they closed the door, Torvald picked Mariah up and carried her to the bed. They began to kiss and undress each other passionately. Mariah got lost in the moment and didn't realize how long it took to shed all of her layers. Her fiery body reacted to the chilly air in the room and became even more aroused as Torvald pushed her onto her back and got on top.

He started out slowly, but initially all Mariah could feel was pain. From this short preview, she didn't think she would like sex, but the pain progressively shifted to pleasure. As each moment passed, her internal bliss seemed to multiply. She could see Torvald's brown eyes in the flickering firelight as he continued to drive her wild with excitement. She wrapped her legs and arms around Torvald's body and pulled him tight as he kissed her neck. His warm breath on her ear made every hair on her head tingle and then spread through her entire body. She could feel their hearts beating in unison and truly felt like one with her new husband. She let go, fell back again and the overwhelming passion lasted for a few more minutes until an explosion of love preceded Torvald's collapsing on top of her. The heavily panting couple lay on their sides and lovingly gazed into each other's eyes. The wash of ecstasy began to dissipate but she had never been more in love with her husband. Mariah pushed Torvald onto his back and put her head on his chest. He put his arm around her, making her feel secure. They talked and giggled until they fell asleep later that night.

LEIMUR

The Queen of Goldenfield stared at the sky, which was streaked with hues of pink and baby blue. Some of the clouds mixed together for a deep lilac that matched some of the inlay coloring on her armor. She desperately needed to know what had happened to Ali-Tiste and her brothers. Nobody knew where they were and it was driving Leimur mad. She couldn't comprehend how her guards could have lost the future king. Thoughts she didn't want to believe kept crawling back into her head.

Ali-Tiste wouldn't double-cross me, would she? We have something special. No, she wouldn't do it.

Leimur had survived the near mutiny by her men, although her tigers had saved her from being torn apart by the angry mob. Her forces had been severely diminished and those who remained wanted to go back to Goldenfield. Leimur still believed they could take the crown if they stayed and fought. She had secretly sent a letter to request that another four thousand troops meet them outside the Capitol of Donegal. A raven carrying confirmation had arrived a few hours ago and the Queen had a sudden jump in her shattered confidence.

The crew of less than one thousand had tentatively marched west, but Leimur planned to change that today. They stopped to set up camp and Tolaya approached with the words Leimur had been dreading, "My Queen, the General and council want to speak with you."

She just nodded her head and got ready to deal with an unhappy group of advisors. Leimur entered the newly erected pavilion and sat down at the head of the rectangular table. She saw General Rigby, Captain Salina, Captain Tetine, Sir Randolf and Sir Pierre.

"Alright, I'll make this quick. *We* are going back to Goldenfield. I'll save you the trouble of trying to convince us that it is a good idea for you to send us back to our deaths," General Rigby said sternly. He looked down at the table and avoided looking at the Queen.

Leimur stared at the circle of baldness on the General's tanned head and spoke, "We can *still* take the King's Castle."

Rigby shook his lowered head as he talked, "We couldn't take it by sneaking up on them. We walked in right behind an unprotected, unsuspecting king, and we couldn't slit his throat. Now he'll be in full armor, anticipating our every move."

Leimur smiled and said, "Good. That's exactly what I want. We aren't going to take the castle from the King. We are going to cause a battle to capture the King of Donegal."

Captain Tetine jumped in and sharply announced, "We hardly have any forces left after the last slaughtering."

Leimur rebutted confidently, "A huge army of skilled warriors marches this way as you make talk about running home. You can leave as you will, but I shall have that crown by season's end."

Captain Salina asked sheepishly, "My Queen, what is the grand plan this time?"

"That is the beauty of the entire plan. I've been trying to play the games of crooked kings and queens. I forgot who I was, what Goldenfield stands for. I am a warrior. We are all warriors. We'll start a big battle in an open field and do what we do best. We will make it a priority to capture their King at any cost. Then the crown will be as good as ours. I realized I had been putting all of you in unfamiliar situations. You aren't sneaky, tactical fighters. Now I will let you be the open field warriors we all know ourselves to be. Go home right now if that's what you wish, by all means, but I'm not leaving without a crown." Leimur looked around and still didn't think she had sold the proposition.

"I'm going home," declared Sir Randolf.

"I'm staying," Captain Salina chimed in.

"Leave," announced Sir Pierre.

"I'll stay to fight a real fight," Captain Tetine said.

General Rigby finally looked up and made eye contact with Leimur as he asked, "What makes you believe we can win in open field battle?"

The Queen smiled and said, "Track records. When was the last time you lost in open field battle?"

The General shook his head quickly and responded, "Never."

She proceeded to point to Captain Salina and Tetine, who both responded in the same way as Rigby.

Leimur said, "There you have it. Everyone is sure to lose at some point, but not all on the same day. We almost took their castle. I know we can win in open warfare and once we capture their King, we can retreat if necessary. We don't need a resounding victory."

The General scrunched his eyebrows together, giving the appearance of deep thought. "I'll have to give the issue some further thought but it's hard to refuse a proper fight for once, not trekking up mountains before even entering the battle. I was so damn tired by the time we had reached the King's Castle, I could barely hold my sword. I'll let you know soon."

The meeting adjourned and Leimur raced to get back to her tent. She saw Tolaya waiting outside and asked, "Any messages?"

Tolaya looked disappointed and answered, "No, my Queen. I will check again." The petite assistant ran off to check the message tent.

Nothing still? Where in all the kingdoms in all the world could they be? What am I supposed to think? I couldn't even imagine that they are...no, they are perfectly fine. No harm has befallen them. They are just traveling outside the range of eyes and ears. That's all. Tolaya will return any moment with a letter from Ali-Tiste.

Tolaya returned out of breath but wore a big smile. Leimur got excited, looked behind the young woman, and asked, "Any letters?"

Tolaya said, "No, my Queen."

Then you should wipe that stupid smile from your face before I slap that smirk away. Why would she do that?

Leimur's anger had manifested because she was stewing over the lack of communication from the people she loved the most. She wanted to win the crown of Donegal, but she had always planned to put the coronet on Ali-Tiste's head. Her lover would rule until Astrid was ready to become a proper king. Now the capturing of a new kingdom took on a bit of a hollow meaning. The will to press on became less imperative when compared to finding her brothers. She had sent a few search parties out to find the group, but no one could locate them. The Queen barely ate anymore and her stomach almost always writhed in pain. Holding down food was a real chore.

SUNNY

Sunny looked across the open room at the crew that had stumbled through the door about a week ago. Kazu kept telling him that everyone in the group was very special and could be the key to victory against the demons. Sunny didn't see it. He felt secure going into battle with the Cyclops and Russell, but everyone else was so tiny or frail, he couldn't envision them serving a purpose in live battle. Muriel had become fast friends with Lizeria and actually got the shy girl to start talking more. They both spoke Lizeria's native language of Nowa Bashan, which the new girl seemed more comfortable with.

An instructor put his hand on Sunny's shoulder and whispered, "You are free to take your leave. Be sure not to go north, the demons are lurking."

Sunny hated to break the rules but he headed straight for the northern beach. He arrived and stared into the oncoming waves rolling in. He hoped Dolpho or Ali-Ster would show up to provide some more insight into the overall situation. Being sequestered at the underground School always made him wonder about what was happening outside.

The twelve-year-old warrior pushed away the worries about the upcoming battle. Nobody had thorough details on the fighting styles or weapons of the coldomores other than handed-down stories that seemed to stretch the limits of the truth. The demons had only participated in two major wars and the last one had been five hundred years ago, so most of it sounded like pure fantasy to Sunny. When they had studied the armies of different kingdoms in class, they had been provided with detailed notes on the battle tendencies of different forces. None of those behaviors had been chronicled in any of the battle records of the demons. Sunny only hoped that the demons weren't well-versed in the battle tactics of the humans.

A man appeared to be walking on water and coming toward Sunny. He recognized King Ali-Ster Wamhoff gliding up and over the waves as he continued coming in to the beach. Sunny waited for the rest of the Army of Undead Kings but no one else appeared. The former monarch sloshed up onto the pink pebbles and approached Sunny. The boy asked, "You've come alone today?"

Ali-Ster chuckled and said, "What gave you that idea? The rest of the Army is scouting the demons and their progress. I've come to tell you that they are stuck in between Venom Island and where we stand right now. You aren't going to see Dolpho because the water dragons are working together to keep the tides swirling around in a big circle. The demons cannot move forward or return home. Their boats move along the outer edge of this ring, but are unable to break out and continue to Gama Traka. That is the good half of the news. The other half is that they are bringing a force of coldomores, dragons and wild animals unlike anything the earth has ever seen. They are well prepared for an all-out fight. Their army is huge and supplemented by three ships of flesh-eating beasts."

Sunny had to ask, "Why don't the water dragons just come up to the top and sink their entire fleet?"

Ali-Ster answered, "I had that same question too. The dragons have come up and sunk a few ships but Damian Doome's aerial dragons have moved in to protect the coldomores. Their dragons keep diving into the green waters, attempting to catch our noble friends. We thought they might starve out there but they don't eat much and have already sacrificed some of the smaller animals for the greater good."

Sunny had a question. "Can the water dragons keep them inside the circle forever?"

Ali-Ster quickly shook his head and replied, "Highly doubtful. There aren't enough of them to control a fleet of that size. They will eventually find the small openings and break through to land right here. Most of us are surprised they haven't broken through yet."

Sunny wanted to know, "So you are here to tell me that they could arrive at any time. We've been hearing that for months now."

Ali-Ster laughed and said, "Yes, but the Army of Undead Kings has seen the demons firsthand, not through some storybook or poets' words. We will come ahead to warn you, but always be ready. I don't know how much advance notice we can provide."

Ali-Ster said, "You're scared. Not to worry, it's perfectly natural. I had all the training a prince could ever ask for before I was sent away to war. It did little good as I rode into that first battle and thought my heart would bust through my thumping chest. You will see the overwhelmed men start to die and you will either join them or you will feel the burning rage inside, stirring around your body. It will precipitate you to do anything possible to not end up like your fallen brothers. Once you sink your sword into a few of your enemies' bodies, you'll become numb to all the killing and death. Once you realize that someone else's sword can deliver the same destruction, something is set off in your head, your eyes widen and you'll do whatever it takes to stay alive. All the physical pain you have caused your opponents in practice will pale in comparison to the first man or demon you lay down forever. It's easier to kill a demon, I should think, but don't allow it to swallow your mind. That is your most important weapon on the field of battle. I watched some of the most legendary swordsmen die because they gave in to that fear. Don't allow it to happen. Luckily, I don't have that problem as I am already dead."

Sunny asked, "So you can't be killed?"

Ali-Ster returned, "No, what I meant was that it's hard to be scared of death, if you've already gone through it. The Army of Undead Kings can be killed just as easily as a living human and to top it off we aren't even guaranteed we will get back into the heavens. An oath and sacrifice we accepted to help save the world."

Sunny realized he had been gone from the underground lair for a while and said, "I must return to the School but when will I see you again?"

The former king said, "When the time is right. I need to move inland to see the rulers of Gama Traka."

Sunny quickly asked, "The Triumvirate. Why?"

Ali-Ster explained, "I need to recruit a greater number of warriors to fend off the demons. I don't believe the students of the School can stave off this advance on their own."

Sunny tried to warn him, "But the Triumvirate has a long-standing reputation for not granting any requests from their citizens, not to mention the cruelty and injustice they practice. They could kill you just for asking."

Ali-Ster gave him a goofy grin and said, "They could, but this is a chance to save all of mankind. This is much bigger than just me and if I have to sacrifice my life again, I took the oath. I can't turn my back now as this might be our only hope to secure victory. I must take action. This could end up being more valuable than the actual fighting."

Sunny closed by saying, "I wish you the best of luck and truly hope to see you again."

The two redheads walked in silence until Ali-Ster veered to the right and Sunny continued toward the School. He entered through the back entrance and walked down the main hallway. He saw the new group sitting around a long rectangular table made of driftwood in the library. He entered to see Kazu, Dragon-Eyes, Russel, Dioneer, Riceros, Lizeria, Muriel and Shireez.

He sat down as Dragon-Eyes said, "Sunny, I need to have a few words with you and your sister."

"Alright," Sunny agreed and immediately popped back up. The Imp Wizard jumped down from his chair and landed awkwardly. He used his hand to brace himself and get back onto to his feet. The old man moved slower than a sloth bear as he led them to Kazu's quarters.

They sat at a small table made of reinforced bamboo. Sunny wondered what this reverse aging man wanted to say. The Imp gave a warm smile and started by saying, "Look at the two of you. I never thought I would see you again." *See us again? Who is this man?*

The dwarf continued, "I am here to tell you where you both have come from. Ollor was a father to you, but he was never your true father. I know you are probably tired of hearing that you are special, but you are, and it might have to do with the mystery of your births. The long and the short will reveal that you both come from royalty."

Muriel and Sunny perked up as Dragon Eyes continued. He looked at Sunny and said, "Ali-Sundry Wamhoff, Prince of Donegal, trueborn son of King Ali-Stanley and Queen Emilia. You were sent away because of your deformed lip. The King wanted to keep his own hands clean of the matter, so he had his men put you out in the woods to be eaten by hungry animals. Ollor and I searched the King's Woods to save you from a sad end. We split up and I finally found you. However, wolves and rabid foxes had you surrounded. I panicked. I shot fire from my eyes and engulfed the entire circle of animals in flames. In my haste, I also severely burned a newborn child. I looked down on a charred black body but I didn't even have a chance to shed a tear. Before my tiny eyes, I saw your transformation back into a normal, living baby boy. The dead animals provided enough warning for others to keep clear and Ollor eventually stumbled upon you."

I'm not so sure I believe this guy. Dolpho said to be wary of a dark spirit. Maybe this is the demon I have been forewarned about. His eyes look fiery but I hardly think he has dragon-like qualities. Stories can inflate the skills of a warrior or wizard.

He remained silent as Dragon-Eyes went on, "Ollor's wife couldn't produce a child, which made you very special to him. Ollor raised you in Donegal until it became too dangerous to harbor an expelled prince in his native land. He took you to Goldenfield to stay for a brief period until you were ready for Androsi. I came across Ollor and you when the vital piece of news arrived."

An excited Muriel asked, "What news?"

Dragon-Eyes smiled at the little girl and said, "The news of another member of a royal family being cast away. The new princess apparently had an issue with her feet. King Pascal Leluc and Queen Harla planned to send their baby down the Rushing River on a floating bassinet. They were certain the nasty beasts of the water would devour their daughter and therefore, they could avoid the curse that comes with killing a castaway. But luckily, Princess Muriel Leluc, sister of Leimur Leluc, wasn't quite ready to die. Ollor rescued you from certain death as well. He kept you hidden in Goldenfield until you were of age to be moved to Androsi. So as you both can see, you are indeed very special children. I was convinced you were the ones who would lead the water dragons. Ollor was to deliver both of you to this School to prepare for the eventual battle against Damian Doome. You look a little overwhelmed, my dear, do you have any questions?"

Muriel stuttered, "I…I…I don't know."

Sunny needed to know and asked, "How could our parents throw us aside so easily?"

The calm wizard tried to explain, "Widespread belief in both kingdoms was that children born with deformities could be demons or demonic creatures in human form. Most believe them to be inherently evil but don't want to actually do the killing themselves because the curse has been said to transfer to the killer. So they send them away to be sorted out by the Gods. Most parents find this to be the easiest solution. Look at the both of you, poised to save the families that once sent you away."

Muriel made an observation, "If we had been raised as a princess and prince we wouldn't be anywhere near here. We'd be sitting in a castle praying for someone else to save us from the demons."

Everything surprisingly made sense to Sunny. Now he knew why he looked exactly like Ali-Ster. He didn't get mad about being cast away because he had never known castle life and what he had missed out on. He worried about Muriel and how she would react to this news.

The Imp spoke in a gentle voice, "Have you seen Ollor lately?"

Sunny told Dragon-Eyes all the stories about Ollor including the final time he had seen his father figure.

A-RICEROS

Riceros sat in the library of the School of the Learned Warrior. He felt the eyes of the old man staring at him again and quickly glanced over. Kazu looked away and Riceros wondered why the old man kept doing that. Dragon-Eyes had taken Sunny and Muriel away to talk to them. Everyone endured an awkward silence while trying to look around without making eye contact with each other. Riceros looked at several books that he would like to read after the battle. He pulled out his black slab and looked down. His eyes widened as he read the words, "We must see you before the war. Sneak outside and be absolutely certain you are alone before you draw your wings and fly up to our lair in the sky."

Riceros looked around the table and said, "I need to go outside for a bit."

Kazu narrowed his eyes and asked, "Why?"

Riceros stumbled with the words as he said, "I need to see the sun again before we go off to battle. My senses are a bit off." *Why did I just say that? That was so obvious. They'll never believe that.*

Kazu responded, "That is fine. Do be careful."

Dioneer spoke up, "He need not be careful. I will escort him to fulfill the oath that I took."

Riceros told him, "No, I need to go alone."

Riceros looked around the table, expecting to hear somebody object but all he saw was an ugly smile come across Kazu's wrinkled face.

The old man warned him, "Please make this brief. There is no telling where the demons lurk anymore. Where is it you will go?"

Riceros didn't know how to respond but he blurted out, "Nowhere in particular. I just need to be outside."

This time everyone objected and begged him not to go or at least wait for the Imp Wizard to return. Riceros had to perform his secret duty. The new group followed him to the door, still trying to talk him out of it but Riceros stepped out into the sun-soaked desert. He looked around and didn't know which way to go. He chose a random direction and tried to walk that way with confidence. He kept looking back to be sure no one had followed him and couldn't see anyone. He walked for about twenty minutes into another deserted area. He checked for people before closing his eyes. He concentrated as the Pearl of Wisdom burst through the skin on his back. The golden wings started to form from the radiant object and a soft flapping sound hit his ears as he rolled his shoulders to move the wings.

The speed of the wings increased rapidly as he thought he noticed someone to his left. Riceros rose up into the cerulean sky. He flew toward the sun and soon reached the clouds. He kept rising and spotted a silver dragon out of the corner of his eye. He followed the dragon to the gray lair and walked along the bridge to the castle, through the main gate and under the rising portcullis. Several dragons greeted him as he walked down the long hallway and into an open room with Ikeros and Rosambell.

The golden dragon greeted him, "Welcome back. Is the plan moving forward down there on the earth's surface?"

Riceros didn't know what to say but he answered, "I guess so but I couldn't truly know. It seems that the special group you mentioned before has come together at the School of the Learned Warrior. However, even the wizard Dragon-Eyes doesn't know when the demons will attack."

Ikeros let out a sigh and said, "The demons were never reputed to be an intelligent bunch, but I am confident that they will attacketh without warning or announcement. It is a rather clichéd statement, but stayeth ready, young one. I hate to belabor this point but the demons are unpredictable. Dost thou knoweth how the demon race came to be?"

Riceros knew a great many facts and he said, "I've been told they came from inside the earth."

Ikeros waved his head back and forth and spoke, "That is true to a certain extent but there is much more behind the story. Salius and Travibero, two names I am sure thou art familiar with, were brothers and the first men to live on earth. They lived happily for years, enjoying the bounty of nature. One day, the boys went to explore Mount Genesis. They foundeth two enormous blue eggs with scales covering their surface and took them back home. They gaveth the eggs love and warmth until two dragons hatched from the shells. Babies, they were, but the brothers continued to nurture the tiny creatures until they were too big to stay in the caves. A golden male and black female greweth into adulthood and started to have children. It is said that the dragons started to feel guilty about having families when the two men who had raised them couldn't enjoy the same pleasures. The dragons fleweth up into the heavens and didn't actually find the Gods, but they did stumble upon two women, perfect for each man. They brought down the two, known as Esther and Patriah. Both ladies quickly fell in love with the charming Salius, which obviously enraged Travibero. The angered brother captured Esther and stole away with her and the red and black baby dragons. He went to a place that he knew to be safe and forced Esther to bear him children. She gave him seven children and he promptly killed her after the final birth. He took his children and dragons and sank into the earth. Everyone assumed he would never be seen again. The jealous sibling lay waiting underground for the perfect time to strike. He saweth the war of the First Families as the best opportunity to retake the earth for himself. Unfortunately for him, all of his dragons perished in the failed attack. He lost the war and retreated back underground. Many centuries have passed and Travibero has transformed himself and all the demons into the current form. Their looks were molded over time and their blood turned black. The rest of Salius' story has been well chronicled in the Words of the Gods."

Riceros was blown away but he had to ask, "Wow. So how did the water dragons come to be?"

Ikeros sat his body down before continuing, "Inquisitive, thou art. That is a fine question. When Travibero stoleth the baby dragons, their parents searched everywhere for them. Understandably distraught, they looked all over before depression set in. As they flew over the Sea of Green, warm tears fell from their eyes. Even for a dragon, those tears are tiny drops compared to a vast ocean. Those fateful tears miraculously foundeth each other and mingled together to create a male and female water dragon. The parents had no idea of this event and only met their children over fifty years later. Most people know that a rogue black dragon left the noble effort to joineth the likes of Damian Doome. Feeling underappreciated, Brute proved to be a rogue and simply up and left one day, but I still don't know how he bred with no female counterpart. Somehow, Damian Doome has built up a heavy force of angry dragons. He also has cross-bred the dragons with other animals to create some very wild and scary creatures. He captured an army of Cyclopes from Heldoor and convinced them to fight for his side. Be careful of where you put Dioneer on the battleground. He may have trouble killing a former brother or sister, just like anyone else."

Riceros looked into Ikeros' flaming eyes as the dragon went on, "I think this is enough new information to fill thy mind for now. I will try to layer these revealing stories so they don't overwhelm thou. Most men would wholly dismiss these revelations but thou knoweth they are the truth as thy has seen too much."

"Why are you telling me this?" Riceros wanted to know.

Ikeros answered without hesitation, "Because thou are a young man of knowledge. I knoweth thou like to understand the reasoning and background stories behind these decisions. This will probably be our last meeting in this lair. I need to give thou something."

From the inside of Ikeros' wing, a small hand with three bloody, opposable fingers protruded from the reptilian skin. The hand reached into the cloudy wall and the dragon pulled it back out. Riceros watched the sharp nails of the dragon move across the room to stop in front of his face as the hand opened. A tiny golden flute appeared and Ikeros' eyes and face prompted the small boy to jump up and grab the magic whistle. Ikeros retracted his hand back into his wing and gazed at the boy in silence for a moment.

Riceros asked, "I assume I need to blow into this to summon the dragons?"

Ikeros responded, "You are a small one, but a wise one nonetheless. Now you better return so as not to raise any more suspicion than you already have."

Ikeros sent Epalon to guide Riceros back to Gama Traka. He landed in the same area that he had left from and couldn't find anyone lurking as he surveyed the desert. The wings and Pearl retracted into his back and he started to walk toward the School. After about five minutes, a small man appeared ahead and looked to be moving quickly toward him. His heart raced until he recognized the man as Kazu and a sense of relief came over the little boy. As the old man got closer, Riceros noticed he had a serious, if not angry look on his face. Riceros sensed trouble and turned to run, but Kazu increased his pace. He spun around to see how far away the old man was and looked at a pair of demonic yellow eyes. He kept running until a swarm of yellow, red and black hands jumped out of the earth and grabbed at his legs. They pulled him underground to his knees and held him there. Kazu walked up with an evil smile and stared at the young boy. He used a black silk cord to tie Riceros' arms behind his back. Kazu pulled his feet out of the ground and tied the boy's legs together. Riceros tasted the sand as the old man dragged him away. Kazu stopped for a moment and grabbed Riceros' feet and pulled the light boy up a mountain. As twilight threatened, Kazu stuffed Riceros into a cave and covered the entrance with a huge rock.

B-RUSSELL

"I know the land. I'll make sure the boy is safe," announced Kazu as he stood up and started for the back door.

A confused Russell sat at the table in the library of the School of the Learned Warrior. He looked around at the unlikely team that had been taxed with saving the world. He couldn't envision a more unlikely bunch as the group sat through another long period of complete silence. The Imp Wizard waddled into the room, yawning and shaking his head to try to stay awake. The ancient looks had completely switched to give him the normal aging features of a fifty- or sixty-year-old man. His confidence and attitude had improved greatly from the use of the Fuji Dust. Russell barely had a chance to speak with Dragon-Eyes since they had arrived at the School. He had mostly been conversing with Sunny and Muriel about the training they were under. The dwarf propped himself up onto a wooden chair and asked, "Where are Kazu and our little blond friend?"

Russell answered, "Riceros said he had to go outside for some reason."

The little man's jaw dropped and he spoke in a monotone, "And you just let him walk out that door? How could you do that? You let him leave by himself? None of us should travel by ourselves."

Russell tried to calm him down and said, "Don't worry, Kazu went to keep an eye on him."

Dragon-Eyes asked, "Kazu?"

Russell told him, "Yes, Kazu. Tattoos on his neck. Short, older gentleman. You know him."

Dragon-Eyes shot him an angry look and chastised, "This is not the time for japes. There's been something different about Kazu, I have noticed."

Sunny exclaimed, "I'll round up a few of our best students and we will bring him back." Sunny and Muriel left to organize the search party.

Russell tried to calm down the frantic dwarf and said, "I think you may be overreacting. He is going to stroll in that door any moment, I would bet."

Dragon-Eyes shook his head and said, "Oh, that's what you think, is it? Well, there is much you and I need to discuss. Some harsh realities have come to light. Ladies, Dioneer, may we have a few moments of seclusion, please?"

They left the room and Dragon-Eyes had a puzzled look on his face as he started speaking, "I'm not entirely sure how to say this. It appears I was wrong about one matter. You will not hold the Pearl of Wisdom. That's why I am racking my brain over Riceros leaving. He is the true holder of the Pearl. Remember the phrase, 'the Pearl lies within'? Well, that gross lump on his back is holding the most beautiful object in the world, at least once all the blood is wiped away. He doesn't just hold the Pearl, he is the Pearl."

Russell shook his head and couldn't believe it. *So a big, strong man like me can't hold the Pearl, but a scrawny little boy can? This makes no sense.*

Russell wondered, "So what now, I'm worthless. I should head back for Waters Edge and see if I can find Ali-Pari to take me back in?"

Dragon-Eyes spoke in a soothing tone, "No. No. No. You are still a vital member of this team and we will need you for victory. I know it sounds strange and you are disappointed but this a wild, ever-changing journey we are on."

Russell spoke in a somber tone, "I'm just sorry I let you down and couldn't live up to your expectations."

A serious look came over Dragon-Eyes' face and he said, "What? No. Russell, please tell me you don't truly believe that. You've invigorated my soul. Other than that bout of rapid aging, you've provided an excitement this old man desperately needed. This war has been building for five hundred years. It's no coincidence that you helped me make it here. We were meant to be here, together. It might not be the ideal situation we anticipated, but we will still be an integral part of saving the world."

Russell confided in his friend, "I'm just…I'm just a little worried. I know the spirits will be with me, but I've never been in a battle before. I don't want to end up as a tasty drink for the bloodsucking demons."

Dragon-Eyes paused for a moment and said, "What happened in your first swordfight to the death?"

Russell looked down at his little friend and replied, "I won, but I had practiced that scenario before. I had been trained for that situation."

The Imp Wizard spoke slowly, "All the training means nothing if you don't have the ability to put it to use. You have been trained for this. Rockarius entered his first battle and nobody thought with his inexperience that he would win. It would have been a fool's bet to wager on that little man, to be perfectly frank. This battle isn't going to turn you into a hero. You already are a hero. This test will expose that even further. You've already battled the demons at the site of the First Battle. Nobody else in the world has any experience in fighting the coldomores. Your entire life has been building up to this moment; you just have to believe."

Now I am supposed to trust you. You were wrong about me being the holder of the Pearl.

Several hours passed and Riceros and Kazu still hadn't returned. Dragon-Eyes' motivational speech did little to spur Russell's confidence. He had trouble coming to grips with the fact that he wasn't the chosen one, and would never hold the Pearl. *If the spirits should abandon me, I am just a young man against an army of demons and dragons. I'm as good as dead. One-on-one combat is very different than fighting a force that carries no honor in battle. I could be stabbed from behind in a flash and that's it.*

The night moved along and Sunny and his search crew came back to the library. Russell watched the shaggy red hair bounce from side to side as Sunny shook his head. His mouth appeared tightened with the cleft palate but his unsatisfied look made words unnecessary. The pacing wizard started to mutter under his breath and looked angry. Russell had only seen him this upset when he had spilled all of his Fuji Dust. A few more students left during the night to find Riceros, but the boy with the Pearl never returned and Russell felt worthless.

He woke up the next day and felt even worse. The only thing everyone talked about was Riceros. Russell wondered if there would be this level of concern if he had gone missing. He doubted it. He moped around after breakfast and saw Dragon-Eyes deep in thought as he stood against a wall with his eyes shut. He wanted to talk to the dwarf but didn't want to listen to him whine over Riceros' disappearance. Russell would never openly admit it, but he was jealous of the boy who held the Pearl of Wisdom. That was supposed to be Russell Seabrook.

He went to the library and sat down at one of the tables. To his surprise, Shireez entered the room and walked toward him. He looked at her welcoming pudgy face and bright eyes as she sat down next to him.

She spoke in her normal, soft-spoken voice, "I know you are disappointed and I am probably the last person you wish to speak to, but you are missing out on why you were sent here."

Russell commented back, "I know why. I'm here to distract the demons with the spirits so the others can do the real fighting."

She smirked before saying, "Real fighting? You've already killed several men and demons alike. You aren't a distraction, you are the real fight. Don't think for a moment that the demons won't bring all those dark spirits we saw on Fire Island to help them. Without you and your gift, the humans stand no chance, dragons or not. I still think you are the most important person involved with this war. Remember, you can hold the Pearl, Russell."

He looked into her eyes and said, "But I can't. The Pearl is embedded in the kid. Riceros Colbert is the Pearl."

Shireez reminded him, "So if he is the most important piece to this battle, then what is the most important task you can carry out? You can still hold the Pearl and show why you are here."

Later that day, Dragon-Eyes entered the underground kitchens as Russell rummaged around for dried foods and breads.

The dwarf came closer and asked, "What are we doing?"

Russell simply replied, "Gathering supplies."

He stuffed some salted camel sausages into his bag and the wizard said, "I will not let you leave for Waters Edge. I insist that you belong here."

Russell paused for a few moments and said, "I can't go home because I never truly had one. I am going to find and bring back the Pearl of Wisdom."

Dragon-Eyes sported a confused look as he reminded Russell, "We already know who holds the Pearl."

Russell looked down at the dwarf and said, "I understand that. I am going to find Riceros. Why do you think I am here?"

Dragon-Eyes nodded his head in approval. "That's great. Are you venturing out with Sunny and Muriel's group?"

Russell smiled and simply stated, "No."

The dwarf tilted his head to one side and asked, "So who are you going with? Please don't tell me you aren't thinking of a solo quest through this land that you know nothing about."

Russell shook his head and responded, "Come now, you know I wouldn't be that foolhardy. I'm taking Lizeria."

The wizard's eyes widened as he objected, "Please smile and tell me this is another one of your jests. The girl is practically defenseless."

Russell said with a serious face, "Defenseless. I thought so too. That was until I watched the bravest girl I have ever met kill a demon. I ask you, have you ever killed a demon in all your years?"

The Imp pursed his lips and replied, "Don't try to be cute. You should take Dioneer with you."

Russell disagreed, "If something has happened to Riceros, someone will be looking out for a rescue effort. Dioneer could be easily spotted or heard. Even his breathing is loud. Think about it, Kazu and Riceros are tiny. I might need a person of similar size to help find them. Facts. I'm leaving with Lizeria. We are going to find the Pearl, and if necessary, I will hold and carry the Pearl like we had previously talked about. This is just a different way of doing it."

THE MAN WITH THE GOLDEN SWORD

"There shall be plenty of time to spend with women once you sit on the throne. I fear becoming too attached to a woman right now could be detrimental to our efforts," the Crippler warned.

The Man snickered and said, "A king should be equipped to handle both, and I think I can surely do that."

The Crippler pressed on, "Many have uttered those same words only to be forgotten forever. Nobody remembers the losers or the men that almost became king. They only write and sing about the winners. You must win."

The Man announced confidently, "We will win."

The Crippler kept arguing, "Not in the direction we are headed. We are going to need to exercise your mind again. Do you remember how well everything was going until that…that succubus arrived?"

The Man waved his finger in the air and warned, "Careful now, Duke Crippler, let's not allow ourselves to become too rabid."

The Crippler wouldn't stop. "Rabid or not, this needs to be heard. Always remember that matters were much better, just a short time ago."

The Man stared at his homunculus friend as the pair sat across from each other at a small table.

"What would you say if I asked to see you bleed?" he asked the Crippler, who instantly started to squirm in his smooth pine chair.

His mentor asked, "Are you insinuating that you wish to cause me harm?" The Crippler acted offended at the request.

The Man looked right at his friend's dark eyes. "You know what I mean. Don't dodge the simple question."

The Crippler started to wave his arms around and progressively raised his voice. "I'd say that's the most ludicrous thing I've ever heard. Do you really need to see me bleed? I've been right by your side when everyone else said, 'let that bastard die'. Me, I've been there to teach you how to be a king, how to be a man. I could have taken all that gold for myself. I gave you all the gold that I stole from those castles. I've given you everything I have to offer. Don't throw all that away for a woman you just met. Remember, Tarasoni Alber, remember you swore to never love again. Is this your will or someone else's?"

The Man rubbed his temple with his fingers. "It's my will, I mean, I just…I just don't know who to trust anymore."

The Crippler responded, "You are right to mistrust people. Just make certain they are the correct ones."

The Man bluntly asked, "So why should I trust you?"

"Did you not hear what I just said? I've been right here the entire time. I shouldn't need to prove myself to you or anyone. When no man wanted to follow you, I'm the one who encouraged you to go for the throne. You said it was impossible. I was the man who instilled confidence in you, remember? I said you could take Waters Edge. Do you remember? Do you remember the days when you doubted you could lead an army or kingdom? I helped you get past that. And now you call me a demon?" the Crippler sounded hurt.

The Man quickly countered, "I don't doubt your allegiance or service to me. I don't believe you are a demon, but I've seen too many seemingly impossible actions to dismiss anything."

The Crippler said nothing as he rose from the table. He bowed and backed out of the room, making sure not to turn his back on The Man. The awkward interaction didn't make him any more confident that the Crippler was telling the truth. He couldn't really handle the thought that the Crippler was actually a demon.

The Man rushed back to his quarters to be with Gamelda. He caught her scent from down the long hallway and speeded up his pace. He was still trying to lie to himself and pretend he wasn't in love with Gamelda, but a blind man could clearly see the mutual infatuation between the two. He got inside and kissed his lover.

She asked, "Are we leaving right now, right this moment?"

He replied, "We have their army ready to give up. A few more attacks, and we will be on our way back toward the Capitol. Won't be too long from now."

Gamelda spoke with concern, "I'm seeing bad visions in my ball."

The Man huffed and told her, "You always see bad visions in that shiny skull of yours. So you were right one time about one thing. I can't make our men vulnerable to an easy death because you saw a vision that no one else can see. My head will be on a spike so fast it would be like suicide, and then you will be alone."

"Come, look with me," Gamelda said and grabbed her crystal skull from the end table.

She set the skull on a large table and made The Man sit down. She sat on his lap and they both looked at the skull. A fire was burning on the opposite side of the room and the crystal seemed to attract it. The Man glared at the skull as fire collected and swirled around the sunken eyeholes. The flames became bigger and circulated around the entire frame of the skull. The orange blaze created a permanent ring around the outside of the head as visions began to appear in the middle of the face.

Fires burned in a driving rainstorm at night. Two men were locked in a sword fight as the clanging of the blades rang in The Man's head. He recognized the combatants as they parried back and forth until one man gained the advantage. *No, it can't be. That could never happen. This is all fadoodle.*

The Man slapped the crystal skull from the table in a fit of rage. The fragile object tumbled perilously toward the stone floor until it stopped and remained suspended a few short whiskers from the ground. Gamelda used The Man's chest to forcefully push herself up and retrieve the prized possession. She shot him an evil look as she put the skull back on the small table.

She asked in an annoyed tone, "So did you see him bleed yet?"

The Man took a deep sniff to clear his clogged nose. "As a matter of fact, I did. He was more than willing to put the rumor to rest."

Gamelda lowered her eyes. "Really? I am shocked. You wouldn't be lying now, would you?"

"What? Why would you think that?" The Man asked.

She quickly responded, "The fact that I know you are lying tells me. I know when people are lying. From everything you've seen from me, do you believe I cannot tell when a man is lying? You have to find out whether his blood runs pure or that black cloud will hang forever over your head. If we can get rid of these ugly spirits, the visions in the skull might change, but only if you flush out the negative power."

Every day that they weren't marching to the Capitol increased the possibility of losing the crown, and the pressure had started to take its toll on The Man. He swam courageously in the overflowing river of stress and hadn't consumed wine or ale for over a week, which probably didn't help his normal ornery state.

Later that day, Benroy and The Man sat at an ornate octagonal table in the audience chamber. The Man complained, "I've got one person advising me one way and the other saying the complete opposite."

Benroy said in his soft voice, "That's why you're the king. You need to take all the information and make wise choices based off that knowledge. If you keep intelligent and loyal people around you, everything will be fine."

The Man smiled and said, "You're a good man, Benroy the Builder. Have you set plans for after we conquer the kingdom?" The Man could see hope in his friend's wide eyes.

Benroy rubbed his chin. "With my new title and salary, I assume I'll be able to find a decent wife. A nice castle life for my sons wouldn't be a terrible upbringing either. My children will have everything that I never had. I hate to get back on task, but if we don't leave before winter, I don't think any of these plans will matter."

The Man became angry again. "Those damned Wamhoffs. They cannot win. They *know* they cannot win but those stubborn foxes won't go away. With their depleted force of barbarians, they don't pose a true threat to the crown. "

A serving girl entered with a ewer of water and two clear green chalices. The young woman filled the glasses, pinched some coarse grains of salt from a golden dish and broke up the crystals into both of the chalices.

She looked at The Man until he said, "That will be all."

She curtsied and left the room.

"Jon Colbert grows more powerful with every passing moment as we languish in this backwards region. We need to finish off the Wamhoff party once and for all, and soon, or we can forget about putting the crown on your head," Benroy warned.

"I know. He's going to have every opening along the Blue Caps well garrisoned. If we take these secret tunnels, we could be crawling out of these holes only to be butchered. The longer we stay, the more the problems will mount. Even if we don't lose a single man in dispatching off the Wamhoffs, just the delay in time will hurt nearly as bad," The Man lamented.

"Hopefully, our sons won't have to face these problems," commented Benroy before taking a big gulp of his water. "And our daughters too, I should suppose," said Benroy as he started to cough.

He grabbed at his throat and took another drink from the green chalice. He choked and spewed out the water as his face turned a deep plum color. His bright scarlet eyes started bulging out of his head. He coughed again and blood shot out of his mouth and nose. The Man watched helplessly as Benroy fell out of his chair and landed face down on the floor. The Man crouched down and turned the dying man over. Benroy's desperate eyes searched for the fleeting bits of elusive life and The Man knew the struggle would be in vain. He held Benroy, one of his only true friends, as he stopped shaking and let death take over. His top advisor closed his eyes and finally went completely still.

The Man with the Golden Sword immediately thought the serving girl had poisoned Benroy and ordered his guards to track down the tiny woman. Before too long, his guards came to his quarters with the serving girl. She denied every accusation but there was no other plausible explanation for the poisoning.

The Man started to draw his sword to kill the girl when Tucker burst into the room.

"Stop, highness, stop right there." The Man turned with sword in hand and heard Tucker say, "It's spread all throughout the city. The entire supply of water has somehow been poisoned. I've already sent messages all over to alert the people to stop drinking the water."

By the time the messages circulated, nearly five thousand soldiers had died as well as several hundred people from the castle. The Man didn't feel safe and worried even more about the woman he loved. He had just lost one of his closest companions and got a bitter taste of dirty war tricks. He now understood that the city walls were meaningless if they didn't protect the city.

How did someone get inside and poison our entire water supply? There are over ten different wells, all heavily guarded. Ali-Samuel, you bloody bastard, you've infiltrated my castle. Now, I'll be certain to kill you myself. Now, it's even more personal. No more of these filthy games, it's time to end this with honor.

The next day at the somber council meeting, The Man announced, "Due to recent circumstances and our delayed march, I am inclined to accept the offer of a duel."

The Crippler spoke first, "We don't need to do this. Our enemy is nearly defeated."

The Man rubbed his pommel and said, "That is the problem. Ali-Samuel Wamhoff has been nearly defeated many times over in his life. He always comes out on top. We have to kill him or events like the poisoned water will keep occurring. The man is relentless, but he can't be relentless if he's dead. I'll have to kill him in a duel."

The Crippler disagreed, "I must say, I think this is a foolish move."

The Man looked around the room and asked, "Does anyone else wish to give another opinion that I didn't ask for? This isn't an open forum where this matter is up for debate. I will fight and kill Ali-Samuel Wamhoff. Have everything packed and ready to move out because we march immediately after the victory."

"Pardon my questioning, your highness, but if you say he always wins, how can you be so confident?" Tucker asked.

The Man replied, "He is much better when using tricks and surprise. We are as evenly matched with a sword as you could ever imagine except for one matter. He is well older than me. I will wear him down and claim victory due to my stamina. I wouldn't accept a fight I didn't know I could win. I will defeat him in single combat where he can't use any shifty tactics."

A-EMILIA

A rare smile crossed the lips of Ali-Samuel Wamhoff as he said, "Hot damn, he accepted our offer of a duel. What a fool!"

The excited man dropped the parchment and the paper rolled itself back up. *You mean my offer, it was my idea. How soon you forget about others' contributions.*

The war council sat at an uneven table with its legs dug deep into the moist gray sand. The flapping walls of the pavilion made everyone speak in a louder tone. Emilia and Ali-Steven looked at each other and a smile came over the former queen's face.

Ali-Steven spoke barely loud enough to be heard over the whipping wind, "Listen my son, it pains me to tell you this, but you will not fight in the duel."

Ali-Samuel looked around in disbelief and asked, "What in the good Gods do you mean I'm not fighting in the duel?"

Ali-Steven composed himself for a moment before he said, "Do I think you can beat this man in a duel? Absolutely, I do, but we've both been in many wars. We've seen battles. We've seen firsthand, some of the greatest warriors lose their lives to the hand of a lucky strike of the sword. Whereas I have confidence in your victory, we can't lose you to a lucky defeat, or unlucky as it should be."

Ali-Samuel was still incensed and snapped, "I can't lose. This is certain."

His father retorted, "But you can lose just by being involved in the fight and for that reason, Cobra shall slay your old friend. Cobra has been exposed to the western ways of fighting. He knows how to defend himself against a long sword. I don't think the bastard has faced very many Histoman warriors. Not to mention, Cobra is the best of the best, battle tested scores of times over."

Ali-Samuel just shook his head. "I am the only reason he accepted the offer of a duel. If I hadn't risked my life by sneaking directly into the teeth of our enemy's territory to poison the water, we wouldn't even be having this talk."

The elder Wamhoff raised his eyebrows and pointed at Ali-Samuel. "There it is. You performed the activity you specialize in and you performed the task rather well, I must say. Cobra became the leader of the Histoman by fighting duels; that's his specialty. Trust me on this matter. Making decisions, that's my strong suit. This is the correct choice, whether you like it or not."

Ali-Samuel muttered something under his breath, crossed his arms and rested them on his chest.

"After the victory, we will need to capture all the enemy's resources. Food, coin, soldiers, we need all we can get our hands on. We will need to raid the Duke's Castle unless our predecessor has already cleared out all the valuables. We cannot truly mount a real offensive on King Colbert unless we convert all their supporters," Ali-Steven informed everyone.

Ali-Samuel responded in a monotone voice, "And none of this plotting will mean a thing unless we win the duel."

Ali-Steven yelled, "Stop it. Stop it right now. You're too old for these childish antics. You're a fine warrior, always have been, yet still hopelessly foolish to match."

Ali-Samuel lowered his head like a scolded child and didn't look up.

Emilia spoke in a voice that was almost a scream to be heard over the rippling wind. "I have an unorthodox plan. We win the duel, of course, and claim Waters Edge as our own kingdom. We make Jon Colbert come to us. Make him cross the Blue Caps so we can easily pick off his men as they come across."

Ali-Steven bobbed his head back and forth and said, "Only problem is that he could attack by sea and our fleet and shore protection are basically nonexistent. He would crush us easily and it wouldn't even be fair."

The former queen argued, "If we establish ourselves and heavily garrison the coast and mountains…"

Ali-Steven cut her off, "We don't have enough men or resources to do so. The King will eventually find a way in. Waters Edge doesn't seem to be in great condition if a usurper can come right in and conquer the region. We can reassess these ideas once we see the inside of the castle, to say the least. I do like the idea of drawing them to us somehow though. We might need to tweak the implementation."

Sir Ralph said, "What if we created a War of the Nobleth thenario? We know the Capitol and King'th cathle."

"What is the War of the Nobles?" Emilia asked.

Ali-Samuel didn't raise his head, but said, "My, my, my, how soon they forget. We sacrifice our lives so they can get drunk and not remember our grand deeds."

Ali-Steven explained, "The jade crown that hangs above the throne of Donegal was taken in the War of the Nobles."

Emilia looked confused and asked, "I thought it was won in the Battle of Parismore?"

Ali-Steven reassured her, "Yes. That is the other name for the war."

Emilia was skeptical. "How or who could infiltrate the King's inner circle and gain that much instant favor without cause of alert?"

Ali-Steven responded, "We don't have anyone yet. But if we take over the region, that would open a new set of possibilities. I suppose we shouldn't get ahead of ourselves and remain focused on the duel."

The meeting came to a close and Emilia walked back to her tent.

As soon as she entered, Ali-Samuel barked at her, "What was that? You think I didn't see that smile you gave my father before he announced I wouldn't fight in the duel. Is all this funny to you? Is everything a great big joke to you? You told my father to keep me out of that duel, didn't you?"

"I just don't want you to get killed. I couldn't take something like that happening. I was doing it for your own good," Emilia told him.

He grabbed her by the throat with his right hand and spoke in a dark, gruff tone, "Don't you ever get involved with my affairs."

Emilia gagged as slobber poured out of the corners of her mouth and her face started to turn a strange mix of midnight blue and burgundy. Emilia felt like she would never take another breath until Ali-Samuel relinquished his grip and stormed out of the tent.

I cannot believe he put his filthy hands on me. How dare that animal? And he looks down on the Histoman. I thought he loved me? He only cares about one thing, himself. Maybe I need to only look out for myself now?

Emilia left the tent and went over to an open fire with Pariah, Princess and Krys Colbert sitting around it. The chilly fall air breezed through her short hair and rippled the orange flames of the fire. Emilia didn't have a chance to sit down before Sir Ralph came running up.

He said, "Kryth, your suppothed friendth from Mattingly have arrived. I will take you down to the port to meet them on the Ruthdy Rudder."

Sir Ralph had twenty armored guards prepared to escort them, but Krys looked uncomfortable even with all the protection.

He turned to Emilia and asked, "Will you come with me?"

She answered, "Of course, I would be honored." The former queen hooked her elbow into Krys' arm and could feel the young man shaking. She could easily understand why he would be nervous. Sir Ralph led them toward the Rusty Rudder as the mid-sized ship bobbed up and down in the water. Emilia could see about six men on deck as they approached. Two of the men jumped down onto the wooden dock and walked toward her. They looked like knights, plated in armor, and wearing black surcoats emblazoned with a golden bull. Both men smiled as they gazed at Krys, who wore his golden dragon mask and loose robes.

"Do you know who we are?" the taller man asked.

"I do. You are Sir Richard Rosebud, and you, Sir Antery Blackburn," Krys said, pointing to each man as he said his name.

Sir Antery asked bluntly, "Is it true that your brother, Ryno…is gone?"

Krys didn't speak; he slowly nodded confirmation as his mask reflected the sun's golden rays out onto the dancing emerald waters.

Sir Richard hinted, "That dragon attack looks pretty vicious."

Krys stared out at the sea and said, "Quite vicious. Nearly burnt me to death."

Sir Antery asked, "What about your back? Did your back get burned by the dragon?"

Krys smiled through the mask. "I cannot see behind me, but I don't think my back has been burned."

Both men grinned as Richard Rosebud remarked, "Good. We need to check a birthmark on your lower back. You father told us what to look for. You don't look or sound anything like the last time I saw you, but I know birthmarks don't wash away."

"I don't see a problem with that," Krys responded.

Sir Ralph stepped in and said, "Yeth, well, take a few thepth back. Guardth, if either of thothe men make a move toward Kryth Colbert, kill them. You may protheed."

The guards positioned themselves to protect Krys as Emilia helped to lift the loose burgundy linens. She tried to cover Krys' bottom but also expose his red, but not blistered back.

"There it is," exclaimed Sir Antery as he pointed at a giant freckle on the small of Krys' back.

Emilia dropped the robes again and Krys turned to face the men.

Sir Richard said, "Prince Krys Colbert, I swore an oath to your family. The Knights of Mattingly apologize for letting you fall into this situation. We will return directly to your father to work on your release."

The men were about to leave when Krys asked, "How is my father?"

The men slowly turned back and Sir Richard said, "He is as well as a man can be who's had his family ripped apart. He has been reunited with your mother, sister and Ruxin but he yearns to have his entire family home, well the new home in the King's Castle. Your entire family prays for your safety at every chance. We all do. We can't wait to see the safe reunion of the Colberts."

The men waved farewell and got on the Rusty Rudder. One of their crew mates untied the ship and jumped on as the boat drifted slowly back out to sea.

Emilia started to cry. She wanted to release Krys right then and there. He belonged with his family, not being used as a prisoner in war games. She understood that they had to receive some sort of compensation for Krys. She had never been directly involved in war, but she knew the way it worked. None of the stories or songs ever talked about kind gestures of good will and faith. Normally, the most ruthless side won the war. Emilia assumed Krys was crying as the anchor came aboard the Rusty Rudder and the ship really started to sail away. She couldn't see inside Krys' radiant mask, but tears liberally streamed down her rosy cheeks. The former queen wanted to take the Colbert boy straight to the King's Castle by herself.

The wind let up a bit as they walked back to the base. Emilia spotted her two female friends shivering by a fire and invited them into her tent. They sat down on the bed and Emilia noticed a defeated look on Pariah's face.

"What's wrong?" she asked.

Pariah answered, "It's, no. It is not a thing."

Emilia tilted her head and lowered her eyebrows. "You can tell me."

Pariah took a deep breath as Princess jumped up and said, "ET TOM EET AU TU."

The little girl scampered out of the large tent and closed the cover behind her. "What did she say?" Emilia asked.

"She want to play outside by mountain, she say," Pariah informed her.

"Alright, now you can tell me what is the matter," Emilia insisted.

The young woman said, "When before we know that Cobra fight a man to win, nobody happy. Histoman, for first time, they question Ali-Steven. I get scared. I am Histoman but Ali-Steven is husband."

Emilia casually commented, "Well, you will always have a place with me, if need should be."

She had uttered the words as if she was still the Queen of Donegal. She suddenly realized that she truly had nothing anymore. As queen, Emilia always had supporters who would have helped her out of duty to the kingdom. Now she needed to stay with the Wamhoffs to survive. She had come full circle from her days as a child on the horse farm. She had basically nothing then and she truly had nothing now. The realization irked her as the conversation continued.

Pariah said, "I thanks. Histoman, we want go back to home. Most say no Rolog live here."

Of course, a barbaric foreign god isn't lurking over Donegal. We have proper Gods here. The true Seven. I can't believe they would question Ali-Steven though.

That could present a huge problem. Cobra better win this duel because if not, we might lose our army too.

"Do you know whom you would choose? Would it be Ali-Steven or the Histoman?" Emilia asked because she needed to know whether to prepare for a full-fledged mutiny.

"I no know. Make me sad to have to choose," the young woman responded.

Emilia made a statement in the form of a question, "But I thought you and the others looked at Ali-Steven as a demi-god."

Pariah bounced her head back and forth as she answered, "Is son of Rolog and live on here, not heaven. Some Histoman now are think Ali-Steven is not son of our god. Say he is not true to brings us to a bad land. He take us over water that kill most of our family. Histoman is angry."

Emilia thought for a moment and asked, "But you said they were excited about the Cobra fight?"

Pariah nodded in agreement before saying, "Yes, now is better for Histoman. They say Cobra is win again."

Emilia snorted out a half laugh and said, "We all better hope he wins. Let's go find Princess. She must be freezing out in that swirling wind."

The two women found the tiny girl near the mountain base. Her white, rough linen coverings and body were covered in sand and mud. Princess said, "EP VAR SA LOH PO RIN."

Pariah turned to Emilia and translated, "She say there is something… uhh…uhh, shiny inside the ground."

Princess pointed to a small crack in the mountain and crawled in. Pariah tried to follow her but couldn't quite fit. The petite former queen squeezed into the tight opening. The path became wider and higher as she pushed farther into the mountain. She took short breaths to avoid the foul taste of the dusty, stale air. Total darkness prevailed as she kept pressing forward. She ran into Princess who had stopped. Several small cracks in the tunnel walls allowed some precious sunlight to trickle through and illuminate a great treasure. Princess handed her a gold bust of the God, Cleon. Emilia's hands dropped under the extreme weight of the solid gold object. The shelter contained more gold than she had ever seen in the royal treasury. Princess kept handing her objects until it became difficult to breathe and they pushed back through the tunnel to the outside world. The sharp daylight shocked Emilia and it took her vision a moment to adjust to the brightness. Her vision came back into focus as she stared at her hands, which were holding the two biggest gold nuggets she had ever seen. The Histoman quickly crowded around and Ali-Samuel sauntered up to inquire about the gathering.

Over the next few days, a group of experienced diggers widened the tunnel to extract the treasure. They discovered an assorted cache of gold in every shape, size, form or fashion including outrageous party jewelry. They purchased food from neighboring towns and had a small feast on the blustery beach. They didn't spend much to improve the living conditions because they planned to stay in the castle after the duel. She went back to her tent after the feast and found Ali-Samuel reading on the bed. He closed the book and smiled at Emilia.

He covered his mouth and said seriously, "I have to apologize."

Emilia said sarcastically, "Really? Now is when you want to apologize? Coincidentally, a few days after I helped discover the gold that might save our entire effort. Odd timing to apologize, I must say."

Ali-Samuel took a deep breath through his nose before answering, "It is pure coincidence. Come now, we've argued and fought before and I always realize the errors I've made and apologized."

Emilia looked away and said, "Alright then, get on with it. Go ahead and apologize."

A confused look came over Ali-Samuel. "I already have."

Emilia shook her head and countered, "No. You said you have to apologize, but you never actually did it, so go ahead."

Emilia enjoyed watching Ali-Samuel squirm before he said, "I'm sorry, alright? Are you happy now? This should be no different than our other arguments."

Emilia started to get angry as she said sternly, "No, this is very different. You've never choked me until I thought I would die until this last time."

Ali-Samuel argued, "I said I was wrong and I meant it. Nothing I do will prevent what has already happened. All I can do is to promise by our Seven Gods that it will never happen again. You have my word as a Knight of Donegal."

That didn't make Emilia believe him. She had known many venerated knights that performed the most despicable activities known to mankind. She just stared into his blue eyes. *What good is your word anymore? The more I hear about this decorated hero, the more I find out he prefers to stab someone in the back. A man without honor should never call himself a man. What have I gotten myself into?*

ELISA

Elisa waited inside the stopped coach with the Ellsworths. The horses needed to rest on an unusually hot autumn afternoon. Lady Victoriah sat next to Lord Ichibod, who insisted his injuries were too severe to return to the front of the pack. The queen didn't believe the lord and had a feeling he was faking to avoid being near the action. Darryg sat next to Elisa. The young Ellsworth still hadn't recovered from his brief stint in battle. His crazy-looking, staring eyes, frequent crying episodes and inability to maintain a normal conversation concerned Elisa. Darryg was supposed to be her king. He looked like a king in appearance only, while Sir Anderley demonstrated the actions of a king. The knight had left a few days ago to head one last search for the treasonous Lord Nanbert. His previous efforts had proved fruitless, but the dutiful Anderley had promised Elisa he would bring the traitor to her. The only normal passenger missing was Telly Burke. She had become friends with Brehan and had been riding in the old wagon with him. Elisa wasn't very keen about her younger sister being friends with her secret lover.

She didn't know what to do about Brehan. Part of her still loved him, but she knew the dream to rule together that they had shared and believed in only months ago was a fool's wish. The notion seemed almost silly now. The number of people Elisa trusted dwindled on a daily basis, so she planned to keep Brehan around in some capacity. She knew he would always protect and never betray her. Unfortunately, Elisa didn't know if she could say the same for herself. She still couldn't get over his ugly appearance. Elisa had never considered herself a shallow person, but Brehan's transformation was monstrous.

The coach began moving again on the dirt path, flanked by green plains, as they headed through Cloverfoot. Only a few clouds were out and the sun attacked the earth from high above in the sea blue sky. The passengers sat in a rare silence. Elisa thought about the conspiracy Telly had alluded to in connection with Lord Ichibod. She guarded every word she uttered around the lord and lady. Ichibod became angrier with each passing day because a constant stream of messages were filled with news of increased security around the Capitol and King's Castle. She didn't know what the man with a cruel reputation could be capable of and she remained constantly on edge. The daily messages also made her realize that her path to the throne would be a strong uphill battle. She knew thousands of men would have to sacrifice their lives for her to even have a chance to get anywhere close to King Colbert. The slow moving coach came to a stop and Elisa got a bit worried about another ambush.

"We found him. We found that son of a bitch." She recognized Anderley's voice and everyone rushed to exit the coach.

The queen didn't see Lord Nanbert, only the former knight of the King's Guard. Four horses appeared on the hill, hooves flinging chunks of dark brown soil from the torn up path. Elisa identified the four riders and noticed a pig slung over the back of Sir Alwell Jater's black war horse. The animal approached the Ellsworths and snorted at them. The pig turned out to be the one and only, Lord Jerion Nanbert. Sir Alwell jumped down and pulled the rotund lord to the ground. He squirmed around in a black hooded cloak with his hands and feet bound.

He stood up with the help of Sir Alwell and looked just as disgusting as she remembered.

Lord Ichibod hobbled his way through the gathering crowd and screamed, "I'm going to kill him." Ichibod approached the traitor, who fell to the ground in apparent fear. Sir Alwell kicked him a few times and yelled at the lord to get up. Lord Nanbert wiggled around for several moments before gaining traction and getting to his knees. This made Elisa smile.

Sir Alwell kicked him again and said, "Let's go, you porknell, up to your feet."

"We had a signed deal," Lord Ichibod said with venom latching to his words.

The bound lord looked up with his ugly face and responded, "I had no deal with you. I had a deal with the girl. The whore queen, as she has become known as."

Elisa's blood started to boil. *Whore queen? I never slept with you or anyone other than Brehan. How dare that pig?*

"Excuse me?" Elisa said as she moved to her left to stand in front of the captured man.

He looked up at her and spoke, "Little piece of advice for you. When you best someone in negotiation, the correct practice is not to brag about it, girl. I only signed our agreement based off an implied basis of trust; you never held up your end of that."

Elisa yelled, "We had a deal. You signed the parchment."

The dirty man peered at her for a moment before speaking, "Deals are voided when one of the person's involved brags widely about how they lied to gain signature."

Elisa mocked the lord, "Oh, I'm sorry, did I hurt your feelings? Now I am going to kill you myself. Sir Anderley."

He immediately answered, "Yes, my queen."

Elisa ordered, "Bring me my sword."

I never bragged about anything. Did the lord and lady spread the word around Lightview? It would of course spread further and reach Power's Run eventually. Did they brag about tricking him? It had to be them. They are the only ones who knew about it.

Lord Nanbert started laughing as Ichibod jumped in and asked, "You are going to behead a man in that frilly dress? Now, now, I need to carry out this punishment. I was there when the men died. I need to exact their revenge."

Elisa disagreed, "And the men died defending their queen. What kind of monarch am I if I don't carry out justice for my men?"

Lady Victoriah whispered something into Lord Ichibod's ear and he didn't seem to like the words.

He tightened his lips and unenthusiastically said, "Alright then, you can carry out the queen's justice. Good luck getting all the way through that fat neck with that tiny sword of yours."

The smug man said, "You have no reason to kill me. I pledged my fealty to a strong king. If you were to become Queen of Donegal, not some upstart claim with barbarians fighting on your side, I would do the same for you. Tersen Wamhoff was king when I made the deal with you, remember that."

Elisa stopped him by saying, "Enough empty talk for now. You ambushed our forces. There is no defense for that. On with the proceedings." Elisa's heart thumped along with her whole body as she waited for Sir Anderley to return with her sword.

Can I cut through his gigantic neck? I think I can, but this blade has never seen human flesh yet. Anderley would tell me if the blade couldn't handle this. I surely don't want to embarrass myself in front of everyone.

A huge crowd had now gathered to witness the execution of a High Lord of Fox Chapel. She noticed Brehan and Telly up front and rugged-looking men in every other direction. Anderley slowly walked up to the queen. He held her sword with two upturned hands and knelt to present her the weapon. She grabbed the grip and carefully pulled the blade away, trying not to cut Sir Anderley.

Elisa's head started to spin as she got caught up in all the hollering for death. She thought she might pass out until words navigated around the lump in her throat and started to come from her mouth, "Lord Jerion Nanbert, High Lord of Cloverfoot, you've been found guilty of treason at the highest level and you are set to die today in the name of Queen Elisa Burke. Do you have any last words?"

The lord looked up and said, "You're still as stupid as they come. You are a Wamhoff, when will you get that?"

Elisa pushed his head back down with her plush slippers and said, "Actually, my husband died gallantly in your ambush so I am a widow now. Say hello to him when you see him in the seven hells."

Elisa lined up the stroke by taking a few exaggerated practice swings to make sure her dress wouldn't hinder the process. Sir Alwell came up and moved the lord's head so his neck was straight. The queen took a few more practice strokes and decided now was the time. She raised the sword high and used her wrists like Brehan had taught her as she stroked downward toward her target with all her might. The blade cut straight through and the men erupted in unbridled excitement as they watched the top of the lord's head hit the fading green grass. She stood in place, shaking wildly and squeezing the sweaty grip of the sword with both hands. Sir Anderley came over and pried the weapon from her as Elisa watched her men drag the body of Lord Nanbert away.

I just did that. Me. I killed a man. I don't see what the big deal is. The Grizzly Bear kept harping on about how I was going to throw up over it. Well, my apple buns, honey-dipped cinnamon bread, dried apricots and orange slices are sitting just fine, thank you.

The boisterous crowd heartily congratulated the queen as they made their way back to the march. Her chest still heaved in and out as her intense breathing continued. She noticed a different look in the men's eyes after the execution. Some seemed in awe and others gazed with approval at their queen of action. She thought Brehan was smiling at her but she wasn't sure because of his severely damaged face. Telly sported a smile from ear to ear and her wide eyes gave the impression that her little sister approved of the execution.

Two days later, Elisa seized on the moment she had been waiting for. Sir Anderley sat by himself and took a huge bite out of a salt cured duck leg. He tore the meat away from the bone and needed to use his hand to support his overflowing mouth as Elisa approached him.

"May I?" she asked with a perfect curtsy and pointed to the spot next to him.

Sir Anderley wiped his mouth, bowed his head and said, "Of course."

They sat on a rickety bench made of pine and Elisa kept thinking they were going to fall through as she took off her veil.

She began, "I must congratulate you on bringing in Lord Nanbert so he could pay for his treason."

The modest knight gave a slight smirk and responded, "It wasn't very difficult. I'd make a pig joke, but they have been plenty exhausted in the past few days."

Elisa smiled at him and looked the shorter man in the eyes. "Even if finding him wasn't difficult, you were the only Ellsworth to uphold his duty to his queen and kingdom. I just want you to know that I respect your bold actions and I won't be quick to forget them. I wish I could say you were just like your father but…" *Alright, plant the seed and watch it grow.*

Anderley told her, "My father used to be a great warrior. I know it may be hard to believe but he also used to smile all the time. I think he will come around once we take the King's Castle. He'll smile again."

No. No. You are supposed to bad mouth your father, not take his side. Time for the next seed. She smiled and batted her eyes. "But ask yourself if you will be there to see that smile. I know Darryg will. Your family has little problem throwing you into the heart of the battle, yet they watch from the outskirts. I've heard from several knights that shall remain nameless that Lord Ichibod never even entered the fray. They say he grabbed Darryg and ran for safer land."

Anderley started to get tears in his eyes as he spoke softly, "Darryg is a gentle boy. He's my little brother. He never should have been anywhere near that action. My father did the right thing by dragging him away; he is the future king. Poor Darryg is going to have visions and nightmares for the rest of his days, I must warn you, my queen."

No. No. No. This is not going well. We have to go straight after his biggest weakness.

"Your brother is a great young man, there is no questioning that, but is he really a king? A real king tracks down and punishes wrongdoers with no regard for his own well-being. You know, someone like you," Elisa said and tried to appeal to the knight's weakness for women as she brushed her fingers down Sir Anderley's unshaven cheek. *Come on. Come on.*

"I'm flattered but my father would never oblige," Anderley told her.

Alright, let's see if I can sculpt anything out of this man of stone.

She asked, "So how can we fix that problem?"

The happy look on Anderley's face disappeared as he looked down and answered, "We can't, I'm afraid. We are who we are. You are the queen and I'll be in the King's Guard again, most likely. I'm not going to fool myself into thinking that my father will recognize my actions, regardless of how noble they shall be. And I'm obviously not going to kill him." Anderley chuckled and Elisa knew she would need to look elsewhere for her accessory.

She fake smiled and responded, "Of course, obviously."

Damn it all straight to the seven hells. Just when I thought he would do anything for me, he's too afraid of his father. Let the old man push you around forever if that's what you want.

She lowered her head and flickered her eyelashes as she talked with a lowered voice, "It's strange that you mention that because I've heard a few rumblings about how your father plans to dispose of me after the war, win or lose." *Come on, get angry.*

Anderley shook his head and replied, "Probably just useless chatter among the men. You get some of those talkers together and it's worse than wine-filled women in a needlepoint circle."

Elisa stood up and forced another smile. She curtsied and closed the conversation with, "Yes, I suppose you are probably right. I shouldn't be worried at all. Now if you will excuse me."

All the Ellsworth men are heartless and they might all be conspiring against me after that conversation. I had to listen to Anderley complain endlessly about how much he hated his father the entire trip to Lightview and now he defends the man at every turn. Anderley is useless to me now. Who would take no issue with me asking him to kill another man, no matter the circumstance? Who would be comfortable killing someone for me in the first place? Who is someone that would never break my trust?

Elisa looked across the field at Telly and Brehan, her one and only. First, she had to be certain of the situation. Elisa walked up waving, and asked, "Hello, can I talk with my sister, please?"

Brehan responded in a dejected tone, "Of course, your highness."

"Walk with me," Elisa said to her sister.

Telly rose slowly and started to walk slightly behind her as the queen led her to a deserted area. Elisa spoke, "This is very important. I need to know if what you told me about Lord Ichibod is the absolute truth."

Telly gave her a dirty look and returned, "Yes, it's true. Why do you think I would lie?"

Elisa calmly explained, "I just need to be positive to decide whether a plan I am working on is necessary."

"What plan?" an excited Telly asked with widening eyes.

Elisa explained, "The plan involving all of us ruling the kingdom together. That plan, nothing nefarious."

Disappointment came over Telly's face as she said, "Oh."

Elisa looked at her moody little sister and told her, "Don't worry. You are included in these plans to rule as well. You are to be the Grand Duchess of Donegal."

Telly asked, "What even is that?"

Elisa answered, "You will oversee all the dukes and duchesses. You will make sure they are ruling their regions properly. You'll get to travel the kingdom and visit all the castles."

She hoped this would intrigue Telly, but the girl remarked, "That sounds stupid."

Elisa shook her head and replied, "I could have guessed you would say that. Would you rather muck the stables?"

Her feisty younger sister said, "No. I thought I was going to stay with you. Now you're saying you want to send me all over the kingdom. Sounds like you are trying to get rid of me."

Elisa tried to explain, "No, no, not at all. You won't assume that role until you turn eighteen so you will be with me until then if not longer. I'll join you on some of these trips too. A queen must visit her own realm."

The cheerful statement didn't dispel Telly's crankiness. Elisa became serious as some men started to walk by. She asked Telly, "So every little detail you told me is the truth, correct?"

Telly became annoyed again and haughtily said, "I already told you it was the truth. How many times are you going to call me a liar?"

Elisa scolded her, "Lower your voice immediately. I never called you a liar, not once. Much thought and *so* much more goes into my decisions and I need to make certain all information is verified. By no means am I calling you a liar. Now let's get back to the coach."

Telly disagreed, "No, I'm not riding with the Ellsworths. They always whisper around me and I hate it. I'm riding with Sir Brehan."

Elisa promptly said, "No, you are not. I really don't like you spending so much time with him."

An agitated Telly told her older sister, "So what? So you want him to ride all by himself in that creaky old wagon? He's lonely and needs someone to talk to. He did risk his life for you when you should have been killed and now you won't even talk to him. He's supposed to be your friend. We argue a lot because all he does is talk about how great you are and I just don't agree."

Telly's statement shattered Elisa's heart of ice into a thousand pieces. She knew that she had been avoiding Brehan since the duel, but she kept justifying not seeing him to herself for various reasons like being too busy with her queenly responsibilities. She assumed that some of the men would talk to him but understood that they might avoid him as he had killed their champion as an accused criminal in the duel.

She told Telly, "Alright, you can ride with him. And tell him I want to talk to him but the circumstances are…they are confusing."

Telly finally looked happy and said, "I just know that he really wants to talk to you. Don't forget he did risk his own life for you, you know."

Elisa responded, "I know, I know, you can stop reminding me now, thank you. I feel awful enough already. I'll see him soon, you can tell him, but a queen cannot ride in that wagon. I am going to catch flak for letting you ride in it."

"Thanks," Telly yelled as she ran over to Brehan's wagon and jumped on just as it was starting to pull away.

Elisa smiled and waved but she was crying on the inside. She stared at the man she had been responsible for disfiguring and waited until he left her sight to stop waving. The thought that hurt Elisa most was the fact that she knew he would do anything for her and she couldn't say the same. She tried to think about something more pleasant but paranoia about the Ellsworths' plan to dispatch her crept in. She got into the coach and looked at Lady Victoriah and still didn't want to believe she could be part of the devious plan as she put her veil back on.

Whom can I trust? This is a queer game I've involved myself in. With Jon Colbert usurping without claim, Lord Ichibod doesn't really need me. My king husband is dead, nullifying any true claim to the throne. Why are they still pressing on with me as their queen? I could be joining my dead husband if I don't figure this out soon. Whom can I trust? An idea shot into her head as the coach dipped into a ravine.

Later that night, after everyone had gone to sleep, Elisa went to see Brehan. She had to wake him up but the groggy man was excited to see his love. Even in total darkness, his grotesque face made Elisa want to vomit. She had hoped that nightfall would improve his looks but he was just as hideous.

"Sorry to wake you," she whispered.

He rolled his eyes and said, "Don't be silly, is something the matter?"

Elisa answered, "Nothing, really, however, my sister brought to my attention that I haven't been around to see you as much as I should have, so I've set out to remedy the situation."

She thought Brehan smiled, but couldn't be sure with his new face, and he said, "I like the sound of that."

Elisa explained, "Yes, well, I would endlessly apologize, but the duties of a queen seem to be endless."

Brehan reminded her, "It's what you've always wanted."

She said, "We."

Brehan asked, "Excuse me?"

She looked into his eyes and said, "This is what we've always wanted. I've lost track of who means the most to me. I've taken you for granted with all the other happenings."

"I know, but I realize that circumstances have changed and I've come to understand that," Brehan told her.

Should I do this? Does this make me an awful person?

She said, "Perhaps I was a bit hasty in our previous conversations. There may just be a way to make everything work for us. But I guess it won't matter if what Telly told me is true."

Brehan asked, "If what's true?"

Elisa quietly responded, "Oh, it could end up being nothing. Just between the two of us, it may seem that I'm in some trouble with Lord Ichibod."

He bluntly asked, "Why?"

Elisa looked around before she spoke, "Well, my sister overheard him saying that he was going to dispose of me once we captured the castle."

"I'll kill him," an angered Brehan stated.

Elisa told him to lower his voice. *I've got you. Now that's how a real man acts.*

"No, no, no…at least not yet," Elisa said as she thought about what she needed to do. *I really don't want to do this but it will guarantee that Brehan will kill Lord Ichibod or anyone else who stands in my way.*

"I've missed you so much," said Elisa as she touched the side of his face.

It felt jagged and scabby. She wanted nothing more than to snatch her hand away but she kept it on his cheek. She tentatively leaned in to kiss him but stopped short. Brehan moved forward to avoid the awkward moment and the lovers' lips met once again. The kiss felt disgusting to Elisa. How could the man she had once loved with all her heart now repulse her? She fought off the gagging sensation as he shoved his tongue into her mouth, and kept kissing him back. She drew away and stopped for a moment. She pulled down Brehan's britches and pulled up her fur-lined silk nightgown. She mounted her lover and was relieved to find that he hadn't suffered any terrible injuries to that region of his body. The sex felt the same physically, but not mentally. She had to keep her eyes shut and fight off the urge to retch. She couldn't look at Brehan's face and closed her eyes again. *Now that I fully have Brehan, I need to make a foolproof plan to eliminate Lord Ichibod.*

A-BREHAN

Brehan lay back and basked in the afterglow of being with Elisa. The stars looked more luminous as he felt complete for the first time in a long while. The sex felt perfect to Brehan, just the way it should be. His entire body tingled with the pleasure of having his lover back.

My first, my last, forever my only. I thought I was being punished by the Gods for my sinful actions during my pirateer days. I assumed they would smite me by chasing Elisa from my heart forever, but she's back, she's finally back. The fact that I survived the Royal Road ambush, the pirateer battles, the duel with the Grizzly Bear and Lord Nanbert's ambush shows that we are meant to be together forever.

The brisk autumn night didn't bother Brehan, who had pushed the heavy blanket off to the side. Love kept him warm as his fiery blood surged throughout his body.

TERSEN

Tersen lay face down on the stone ground, not moving. Kryen grabbed him by the hair and pulled his head back. Tersen's eyes shot open and he gasped heavily for air. His blue face turned red, then albino white again.

"Kill me," screamed Tersen as he started sobbing. "Why don't you just kill me already?"

The torturers' favorite game for the past week had been to see how close they could take Tersen to death's door before yanking him back to life.

Kryen kicked him and warned, "No crying. You know what Lord Harolg is going to do if he sees you crying."

The sounds of boot bottoms skipping down the steps cut through the musty air as a breathless Harolg appeared at the bottom of the stairs.

As he tried to catch his breath, he managed to get out, "Don't kill him, don't let him die." The lord of the castle went down to a knee and took a few moments to steady his breathing. Harolg looked at Kryen and spoke, "We've received a very generous offer to free our former king. Yes, as it should seem, a family member has paid for your release."

Tersen tried to think of who would love him enough to risk their life for him. Only one vision materialized as he cried out, "Alvyra, I knew she loved me."

Lord Harolg laughed and told him, "She may have loved you, I couldn't readily say, but she didn't pay."

One other person stuck out to Tersen and he said, "Neron. I knew I could count on my son."

Harolg looked at him and shook his head. He responded, "You aren't very good at guessing, are you? No, last I heard about your son was that he was rotting in the castle dungeons on the charge of buggery. He'll be lucky to see the light of day again, let alone pay for your release."

Tersen guessed, "Ali-Pari?"

Harolg seemed to be enjoying this and said, "Wrong again. Just stop guessing because you are terrible at this. The family member requested that their identity remain a surprise. So what to do now? We will clean you up, throw some clothes on you, and Ali-Tersen Wamhoff will be on his way again. But for now, put him back on the stretcher." Harolg released a demonic laugh and left with Kryen as the third torturer stayed and started to strap him up.

Tersen tried to decide if they were telling the truth or moving to mental torture now. *They can't kill me so they are going to try to destroy my mind. Nobody is coming to rescue me. They made that up to have their fun with me. I am nothing more than a disposable jester to them. What has become of me? I am nothing short of pitiful now.*

Tersen bawled for the next hour and starved in the dungeon level of the castle. He felt the tightness attack his chest and a heavy layer of sweat immediately coated his body. He started to see streaks of light and swirling colors until he passed out. A cold bucket of urine woke the former king up. He faded in and out of consciousness as three men took him down from the stretcher. Tersen didn't know if he was dreaming when the torturers sat him down at a table with a plate of food in front of him. The plate contained large chunks of roasted meats. The usual feed was rotten carrot peels and brown lettuce that once was green. The torturers had made him eat an uncooked rat one day and seemed to take great pleasure in watching the starving albino struggle to eat the animal. The sweet taste of charred swine pleased the former king's palate.

After the hearty meal, two roundsmen who looked more like boys scrubbed Tersen with wet rags, then toweled him clean. The two boys helped the weakened prisoner get into a tunic and hooded red cloak, made with thick material and sweeping to the ground. He started to feel like a king again as a serving man handed him a glass of red wine. He took a small sip and couldn't remember a wine tasting so good before. *Who is coming to my rescue? Who could it be? That's a great shame about Neron, but I warned the boy about those disgusting activities. I guess not everyone is as understanding as I am. It's time to recapture my lost crowns. Harolg and Kryen will be the first to die.*

Harolg entered the room and said, "My, my, you look like a different man, or as much of a man that remains of you."

Tersen asked, "Where is the person who is paying my way?"

Harolg smiled and responded, "I am so glad you asked. Said person waits outside the castle and can't wait for you to be released."

The young lord led Tersen to the main entrance of Castle Cuthbart. Tersen could hear the front gate starting to open. The sounds of straining ropes brought a slight smile to the former king's face.

Tersen didn't see anyone except armored guards on either side of the narrow path that led out of the castle. He expected someone to jump out from behind the ivy-covered columns but nobody surprised him. He approached the seven-foot-high gargoyles made of gray stone, which signified the end of the bridge. He slowly walked away from the castle and toward the dirt road surrounded by a dull fall forest. The chilly air bothered Tersen, but not as much as the mystery family member not being present.

It has to be Ali-Pari and she couldn't make it up to the castle. As he neared the woods, the sounds of animals disturbed his ears and wreaked havoc on his nerves. He heard an arrow sizzle by his head and stick into a small birch tree nearby. The albino became terrified and ran into the woods for cover. He dove to the ground and crawled into a thick shrub that he hoped would mask his bright red cloak. His heart pounded with terror. Another arrow flew by and buried itself into the thick trunk of an oak tree. Tersen looked at the arrow and saw a scroll hanging from the arrow shaft.

A voice echoed through the woods, "Go retrieve the letter. I promise not to kill you while you do it."

Tersen wanted to go get the scroll but his fear-gripped body wouldn't budge. Another arrow landed in the dirt, only inches from Tersen. The voice rang out again, "I could kill you right now if I wished it to be. Go read the letter."

Tersen rose slowly to his shaking feet and hurried over to the arrow. He snapped the shaft and pulled the letter away. He ran back to his bush and unrolled the letter and read:

You are somewhat free, this much is true,
Beware you must of what you do,
The arrow flies, its flight so right,
Hard and true, now feel the might,
And so begins a great new hunt,
You cast away your little runt,
For he's returned, with hate and gold,
To be sure you'll never grow old,
Now run around until I choose,
When your life, you shall lose,
The hunt is on, now find some rocks,
I'll have my fun with the albino fox.

Who could this be? This couldn't be any family member of mine, that much I know. Nobody from my family would want to hunt me, would they? No. It couldn't be him. He said he left. It can't be Ali-Ster, the voice sounded so different. I don't recognize the voice. Wait, my little runt I cast away. It couldn't be Daerus. He went straight into slavery and is probably dead by now. Could it be?

LEIMUR

Leimur Leluc couldn't shake her anxious feelings because the correspondence from her reserve army had come to a sudden halt. She had finally persuaded most of the men to stay but the line of communication had broken down in the past few days. The remaining troops were growing more restless by the moment and threatened to leave at any time. Her stomach writhed in pain as she thought about her lover and brothers. She paced back and forth in full armor, waiting for some piece of good news to arrive. The sunrays shot down and made the ruby eyes sparkle on the golden tiger face carved into her cuirass.

She had been receiving regular messages from the oncoming force and then, suddenly, everything had just stopped. She worried that her backup men had been surrounded and captured. She had instructed them to take the same route that she had taken, but perhaps the circumstances were different. Leimur wondered if King Colbert had restored order in Burkeville and lured her men into a trap. That proposition scared her the most. She would have little to no chance of survival if the King had them surrounded.

They waited at the bottom of a slight hill, if it could even be called that. The King's forces were straight ahead, assembled just outside the second retaining wall surrounding the Capitol. The new construction didn't worry her because the goal was to capture the King of Donegal. Her scouts counted almost twice as many men on the Donegal side, so all the Queen could do was wait and hope. She continued to pace around the camp and listen to the grumblings of the unhappy warriors. She didn't even interrupt the arguments about whether to leave or stay. She just walked right by and thought about other matters. Little by little, some men started to trickle away to the west, off to return to their homeland. She thought about what to do if the supplemental army didn't show up. She wouldn't return as a Warrior Queen and she might not be able to return at all. Leimur tried to figure out how she could get out of Donegal if she needed to use that option.

A few snowflakes slipped lazily from the sky and disintegrated as they landed on the torn-up yellow grass. The Queen's belly ran cold again and pulled at the rest of her midsection. The sharp pains had persisted for about the past week. She hardly ate anymore as all food made her want to vomit. Her goal to conquer the Kingdom of Donegal was extremely important so she could use the influence to find her loved ones. She had already deployed all the resources within her power to find the missing group, but ruling the kingdom would open all doors of possibility.

Yet another problem still lingered. Her reports had indicated that Jon Colbert had gone east to the other end of Falconhurst. She couldn't capture a King if he wasn't going to be on the battlefield. The confused Queen went to sleep that night debating why she should stay and fight. Another plan leapt into her head about going back to Goldenfield and returning with an enormous army for a full-fledged invasion.

She woke up the next day and went back and forth on the decision to stay or go. She finally ate some sugar-cured boar belly with runny-yolk eggs and dipping bread. Because of the large number of departing soldiers, supplies weren't a problem anymore and the remaining few were fed rather well. Everyone ate like officers even though they had been thrown around enemy territory. Leimur instructed Tolaya to call a meeting with the remaining council members. She planned to tell them it was time to go home. She finished her meal and stood up feeling great. Without realizing it, Leimur had finally eaten a full breakfast without feeling nauseous. Across the campground, she watched Tolaya speak to Captain Salina. A loud, uniform thumping from behind scared the Queen and she jerked around to see a very young man approaching rapidly on horseback.

The messenger raced up to Leimur, yanked back on the reins, and announced, "We've arrived, your highness."

The teenager pointed to the bottom of the incline across an open muddy field of chewed up grass and scattered golden leaves. Appearing along the horizon were countless cavalry members, with huge flags and banners leading the way. Her favorite sight, a purple tiger's face on a black background emerged through the snowfall to wave in the wind. As the cavalry neared, an endless mass of infantry followed close behind the mounted men.

Another messenger ran up to the Queen and shouted, "Your grace, for you."

He handed her a rolled parchment and she hastily opened the seal and unrolled the crusty paper. The letter stated that King Colbert and his golden bull helm had been spotted among the enemy. Leimur excitedly ran around and ordered everyone to get ready for the upcoming battle. A sense of elation surged around the camp and the excitement became contagious as the men started screaming and smacking each other to prepare for the fight. She knew she had to act quickly because she would only outnumber the enemy for so long.

A-RUXIN

"Oh great, another letter from my father," said Ruxin as he rolled his eyes.

Torvald wondered, "What could it be now?"

Ruxin moved his lips as he read and reported, "Same as the last. He's telling us to stay behind the wall that we are already behind." The Prince winked at everyone surrounding him as he continued, "We aren't going to hide with the common guards. Nothing is going to happen anyhow. We occupy the highland, not by much, but we do."

The King's men lingered outside the newly built double wall and tried to stay warm. Ruxin and the soldiers from Bottomfoot stood around a fire, close to the wall. They remained at the very back of the pack in the rare event that action should break out. Reports had been arriving about more Goldenfield men leaving every day. He knew they had the enemy overmatched and they held the better ground. Suddenly, he heard a loud rumble from the bottom of the slope, which he assumed to be thunder.

Ruxin looked at the cooks getting dinner ready. They worked with stacks of meat on the portable tables. A young novice rubbed the primal cuts with salt while the butcher stood by making sure he wasn't missing any spots. The Prince thought about taking off his armor because they had been there over a week and a battle seemed extremely unlikely. He didn't have any trouble staying warm with his ermine cloak absorbing the falling snow and bone chilling wind bursts. However, his armor always made his upper body sore.

He noticed that Chopkins was finally starting to loosen up and talk again.

The young man had been scared out of his wits when they had first arrived. The other men seemed both confident and angry that they had been ordered to stay away from the action. Ruxin liked that attitude and everyone had quickly agreed that they weren't going to stay behind the wall.

Another crash of thunder sent a chill up the Prince's spine and wouldn't go away as it was tickling his entire back now. A loud roar of the earth followed and a horde of oncoming cavalry galloped up the slight incline. The surprised men quickly sprang into action and found their respective horses. Ruxin vaulted up on his black destrier and raced for the front. He heeled his horse and as he got closer to the front, he found that they were greatly outnumbered. He kept flying ahead and pulled back on the reins so he could grab a fourteen-foot lance from one of the squires up front. He turned around and saw the Bottomfoot men following suit. They all charged ahead, along with the gathered cavalry, and sped down the small hill to meet the enemy. Ruxin didn't have much jousting experience and he tucked the lance under his elbow to steady the bouncing piece of pointed wood. He crouched on his mount and peered straight ahead at the thundering herd of mounted horses with chunks of earth scattering from their hooves and a wall of steamy breath shooting from their snarling noses. His attention was diverted to the task of avoiding the tip of an enemy lance.

The enemy closed in rapidly and Ruxin rode alongside the first line of men as the earth-jostling crash of two huge masses of horses and humans rocked his balance. Most of the collision was glancing as ravenous screaming horsemen invaded the infantry line of the enemy. Ruxin saw the line of pikemen and moved his lance point even lower. He smashed into the front of the enemy and his lance penetrated past the pikes and exploded after striking his opponent in the chest. He threw down the useless weapon and drew his long sword. He ran down a whole row of pikemen from behind. He circled around a small area and ended the lives of more than a dozen men. He fought for a few more minutes on his mount until the fighting became more intense. He knew if someone cut down his horse, he would soon follow, so he jumped down to engage in hand-to-hand combat. Ruxin shook his head and couldn't believe that on a white destrier, only a short distance from where he stood, was the Queen of Goldenfield in her suit of golden tiger themed armor. He ran over and sliced into the front calf of her horse.

Leimur Leluc tucked her head and did a front somersault as she was thrown from her ride. She jumped up grabbing her left shoulder but managed to get both war axes out before a man jumped in front of Ruxin to engage her in battle. Ruxin spun around and used a quick high-low attack to kill an approaching soldier and looked to his right to see J. Everson and the Queen locked in a furious battle. Ruxin expected J. Everson to be slow and methodical like his general demeanor, but the young man impressed him. The Queen ducked and spun in the same motion and used her whirling axes to cut straight across J. Everson's knees. He fell down and she swiftly kicked off his unsecured helm. The thud as her unforgiving axe buried itself in his new friend's head made Ruxin want to throw up right there. He had always liked J. Everson, a man of very few words.

Sir Bastion jumped in to avenge the death of his friend and Ruxin kept peeking over as he fought away and killed more men. He kept getting pressed backward and more Goldenfield soldiers kept appearing out of nowhere. Leimur used an attack unlike any Ruxin had ever seen before to overpower the stout knight of Bottomfoot. She effortlessly cut his throat after magically dancing behind him and confusing the skilled warrior. For the first time, Ruxin was scared on the battlefield.

However, his youthful exuberance kicked in to squash the fear and his arrogance got the better of him. He rushed the Queen of Goldenfield and used one of his better attack sequences. The female warrior used both axes to meet Ruxin's green-tinted blade every time. Bluish-purple sparks flew from the curved silver blades of Leimur's weapons but Ruxin couldn't break through her defense. He had never been opposed by someone with two smaller war axes. He had brief experience against a longer, two handed axe, but when the Queen went on the offensive, he struggled to keep up with the constant flashes of cold silver steel coming at him. The attacks came so fast that Ruxin could only defend himself with his right hand and even that was becoming hard as he fought to keep his wrist high enough for proper defense. Leimur used different combinations of high and low attacks, the likes of which Ruxin had never seen before. He noticed someone behind the Queen moving in quickly with a pike and jabbing her in the small of the back. It was Chopkins Haddock, who stood still with a look of intense fear on to his red face. The Queen cried out in pain and turned around. Ruxin could have ended her life at this moment, but it wouldn't be clean. He needed to kill his enemy face-to-face. She swatted Chopkins across the mouth with the flat of her axe. The joker fell down and quickly scrambled away crying in agony as the Queen focused back on Ruxin.

He would have never dreamed that a female fighter could be so strong. She seemed angry and determined as she took rapid strides forward toward Ruxin. He tried to backpedal but slipped in a patch of mud. He had to put both hands down to brace his falling momentum and the Queen landed her axe into the Prince's helm. The world disappeared and Ruxin Colbert fell flat on his face with the axe still sticking out of the helm. Miraculously, the blade stopped only the width of a rabbit's hair from the Prince of Donegal's skull. It took Leimur several moments to pull the weapon loose and this seemed to anger her even more. The Queen used the back end and flat sides of the weapon to strike Ruxin repeatedly in the head. She kept going with both axes and showed no mercy. Twenty, thirty, forty times.

She jumped up and yelled, "Now, where's that little pork chop. I want his blood." She took off after Chopkins.

Ruxin's body started to be trampled as the King's men started getting pressed back into the wall. People were being crushed to death against each other's bodies as the enemy strategically pinned them in. Torvald reached down and tried to pick Ruxin up, but the heavy teenager weighed too much.

Torvald screamed with passion, "Save your Prince. Help me save your Prince."

Several bloody hands reached down and picked up the still body of Ruxin Colbert. Torvald helped push the Prince on top of the dying men and they started to move him along. Suddenly, Torvald was thrown up on top of the pile of dead and dying men. He followed Ruxin as a wave of hands and heads helped push the men to the outside of the danger area. Torvald seemingly wept tears of joy at the dedication of the men below to carry out their duty to the realm even in their dying moments. They were guided to a zone near the outside of the fighting and Ruxin was plopped down on the earth. Torvald started to drag Ruxin to safety but a small group of enemy fighters surrounded them.

One man screamed through the chaos, "Hurry up. We need to take these prisoners away, fast."

B-JON

King Jon entered his castle. He was supposed to be on the west end of the Capitol but he needed to talk to his wife. He had a huge argument with her just before leaving and couldn't stand to leave unresolved matters behind. The castellan, Omar Regent, greeted the King with a confused look on his face.

Jon clarified, "I just need to talk to my wife."

Omar responded, "I believe she and Mariah are in the Castle Square, busy at needlepoint, your majesty."

Jon quickly said, "Thank you, good man." As he walked toward the Square, a bunch of guards came running at him.

Bryan Caughleigh shouted, "Sorry highness, but she's at it again."

Jon asked, "Who?"

Bryan answered, "Queen of Goldenfield. She's replenished her forces somehow and hit us with another sneak attack. I've already sent all the men currently stationed at every northern guard post and sent word south."

Jon ran and got his battle helm and jumped back on his horse. He headed west and hoped Ruxin had listened to him and stayed out of the action. He saw a steady stream of mounted men ahead of and behind him as he blended in. He only hoped they wouldn't arrive too late.

Damn it all. I knew I should have stationed more men over there. Why did I convince myself she would just go home and Ichibod Ellsworth would be the true threat? She's just as young and unpredictable as Ruxin. I should have known better.

259

The long ride seemed to take even longer today as Jon urged his horse along. He made it through the first wall and speeded toward the second. Jon finally made it to the second wall and came upon a scene of mass confusion. All the mounted men were trying to squeeze through one small opening.

Jon screamed to Bryan, "Take some men south. About a half mile down there is another door. Come up and hit their flank and rear. And hurry."

Bryan Caughleigh shouted orders and men started to follow him south. Jon looked around for his son, knowing Ruxin wouldn't stay out of the action. The division of forces gave Jon enough room to plough his way to the front and worm through the open gate. He saw the utter carnage as his men were smashed against each other and into the wall, the wall he had ordered to be built to save his men. Some of the stacked up bodies close to the structure almost neared the top of the fourteen-foot high wall. The mass destruction was the worst sight Jon had ever seen and he realized his regal responsibility for the deaths. The men had died in the name of King Jon Colbert. Most of the original fighting force had already died as Jon drew his sword. The King smashed into the northern flank. They couldn't save the pinned-in men from being crushed, but they did start to overpower the enemy. Jon thought about his son as he rode down an opponent who couldn't have been a day older than Ruxin.

C-LEIMUR

The Queen of Goldenfield didn't know what to do. She stopped chasing after the short, fat squire who had poked her in the small of the back and searched the chaotic field of battle for the King of Donegal. She jumped into the air to get a better view of the battlefield and saw heavy enemy cavalry storming the northern flank of her forward attack. She looked to the south and saw the same disastrous sight. Her men stopped pressing forward and started to run north and south to stave off the King's refreshed forces. Leimur tried to scream at the confused men to try to put together an organized attack but disarray reigned on the battlefield.

Leimur knew her men could taste impending death and even the bravest of men become unpredictable when their time seems near. *I hope we already have the King because this is about to be every man for himself if more of the enemy keeps showing up. How can I get out of here alive? I love you, Ali-Tiste. I love you, Huber and Romer. We need the King to get my family back. I really hope we have him.*

She fought through a swarm of oncoming enemy swords and made her way to the outer edge of the heavy action. She saw the gates of the wall and a steady flow of wild warriors funneling out of the opening. She turned around and her remaining fighters were surrounded on all sides. The wall that had been extremely beneficial in crushing the initial stock of Donegal soldiers now became her army's worst enemy. They were trapped and the Queen understood she needed to escape. An unmounted horse trotted by and Leimur lunged to grab the leather reins. She held on but the scared animal bolted, trying to get away from the Queen. The black beast dragged her through the hardening mud but she maintained her grip and the horse came to a halt.

The snow had stopped but the chill remained as Leimur got up, steadied herself and hopped up on the horse. She rode northwest by herself and spotted Captain Salina ahead. She spurred the horse with her muddy heels and more earth erupted off the pounding horseshoes.

She caught up with the Captain, who said, "Right up over here. There is a reserve of escaped men, I've been told."

She entered the thick woods and a new chill ran over her body. They moved down a hill and Leimur looked to a clearing ahead. There were a good number of her men and prisoners. She didn't see the King of Donegal. Leimur Leluc debated whether to join her defeated soldiers or leave on her own for Goldenfield.

D-MARIAH

"So what exactly did he say again?" Mariah pestered the castellan with the same question.

Omar Regent spoke in his soft, soothing voice, "Same as I told you the past seven times, my Princess. I understand that you're worried; we all are. Perhaps this calls for a prayer."

Behind the castellan, a bloody and battered Chopkins Haddock stumbled through the door. Mariah ran over and hugged the distraught young man.

She asked, "Where are the others?"

She pulled away but still held his arms. The Princess looked behind Chopkins, but didn't see any other men entering the Princess Hall.

With a spooked and shameful look on his face, Chopkins said, "She killed them." He stopped and just looked at the ground.

Mariah shook him and frantically asked, "All of them? Whom did she kill? Tell me."

Chopkins' lips quivered as he spoke, "J. Everson and Sir Bastion at least. She killed both of them. She was going to kill your brother before I spiked her in the back. She might have killed him and Torvald for all I know. The Queen did this to my face and I ran away. I could've stayed, but I ran away."

Mariah's head spun out of control as she needed to know, "What about Torvald and my brother and my father?"

Chopkins shook his head and said, "I don't know about any of them. I think Torvald and Ruxin were crushed against that wall. I can't see how they could have escaped. Your father, I never saw him out there, not even on my ride back. I should've gone back and helped them but what did I do? I ran like a coward. I've been called that and a craven my whole life and I always had some witty comeback every time. But they were right. All the insults were spot on about me. I'm everything they've always said I was and more."

Mariah didn't have time to deal with his shattered confidence and told him, "Stop, Chopkins. You aren't a coward. So did you see Ruxin and Torvald die?"

He looked up to a bull banner fluttering from the ceiling and spoke, "I saw two of my best friends in the world, Sir Bastion and J. Everson gasp for the elusive breath of life, only to come up short. Have you ever watched someone die, let alone a friend? They were like brothers and I stood five feet away and watched it all."

Mariah was becoming restless and asked, "What about Torvald and my brother?"

His gaze was still on the banner up above as he answered, "I didn't see their dead bodies but they were right in the middle of the mess. I don't see how they could have escaped in any direction. Maybe I could have helped get them out if I had only stayed."

Mariah decided to appeal to his favorite vice and said, "Come now, Chopkins, let's get you a drink."

They walked through the Princess Hall where family and friends had gathered in hopes of a happy return. News had already arrived that Donegal had won the battle but none of the men except Chopkins had returned. Another hour went by as the castle bell rang again and Mariah really started to feel ill. As the sun slowly retreated for the day, a haggard crew of battle participants lumbered into the room. She didn't see her brother, father or husband. More men kept filing in and finally Jon Colbert appeared behind a screen of guards. She ran over and hugged him.

She asked, "Where's Torvald and Ruxin?"

Jon looked into Mariah's desperate eyes, lowered his head and slowly shook it from side to side.

She pounded her fists on her father's chest and screamed hysterically,

"Why did you make him go? I know you and Ruxin made him go. WWHHYY? WWHHYY?"

Her knuckles bled from the rough armor but she kept punching and slapping until Jon powerfully pulled her in for a hug.

He whispered in her ear, "We didn't find them, which could be a very good sign. They might still be out there or be captured, in which case, we will have them home in no time. I promise."

Mariah pushed him away and said, "Sure, the same as you've done everything possible to get Krys home…except you haven't done anything. Krys isn't here, Ruxin isn't here, and now my husband isn't here and it's all thanks to you, your majesty."

She backed a few feet away and noticed the bedraggled White Raven walking over from her left. His normal battered look gave the impression that he too had been involved in the mayhem.

He commented, "Sorry to see this ugly sight."

Jon looked at him with unwelcoming eyes and asked coldly, "What do you want?"

The old man answered, "I often see the rigors of war. Firsthand abuse and the unintended damage that it causes, both carry destructive qualities nonetheless. I see that not even the royal family seems safe as I can feel the worry in the room."

Jon responded, "If you stopped by for a philosophical chat, your timing is terribly off."

The High Holy Leader had a slight smirk on his face as he said, "I have come to ask for a small team of horses so my brothers and I may go to the battle site. We will administer last rites to the living who have little hope and deliver posthumous prayers to the unfortunate souls who can no longer do it for themselves. From seeing the destruction, I fear this may take several days and we will be blessing the fallen enemy too. How many of the Gods' beautiful creatures did you strike down in the name of Donegal?"

A crazed look came over her father's face and he moved closer to stand almost face-to-face with the High Raven.

Jon said with a scratchy voice, "Never bring that kind of talk in front of my daughter. I did what I had to do to protect you too, but you're too foolish to realize it. The stable master will take care of your request. Please leave right now."

The King went over to his wife, who wouldn't talk to her husband. Mariah watched as Camelle kept turning her back on Jon until he became so irritated, he stormed out of the room.

The White Raven looked at Mariah and said, "I can sense the great sadness but I never provide inspirational words to a wounded creature unless they should happen to seek me out. I shall always be around if you should want."

Mariah took two steps over to the old man and hugged him with all of her strength resulting from her pent-up anxiety. His kirtle was shredded in spots and scratched her still sore and bleeding hands but she didn't care. She needed someone to hug other than her father and she seemed to have a holy connection with the High Raven. His fierce body odor usually bothered her, but she didn't notice it now.

She softly pleaded, "Please tell me everything is going to be alright. Can you please do that?"

She waited for an answer from the holy leader, but instead she heard a voice from behind, "My brother, all is arranged and we are only awaiting your arrival at the stable to perform our duty to the Gods."

The White Raven pulled back and told her, "I'm sorry, but I must go now."

Mariah interrupted, "Can I go with you?"

The old man had a look of pain on his face and he quickly shook his head as he warned, "You may not want to see these horrors up close and personal just yet. It might be best to start by blessing a few of the dead at one time, not thousands. You can never unsee man's destruction of each other. It becomes branded into your memory, never to escape or disappear."

Mariah wanted to try to find her husband and Ruxin and didn't care how many bodies she had to sort through. She needed proof one way or the other.

She told the older man, "I need to go. The Gods are telling me to go with you. They want me to do this."

The White Raven shrugged his shoulders and exclaimed, "Then so shall it be done."

THE MAN WITH THE GOLDEN SWORD

"So we've reset all the water wells and it looks like we've flushed the poison out, your highness," Tucker reported.

The Man still didn't trust the supply and had been drinking wine since the incident. He stared at a pewter ewer as Tucker poured himself a cup of clean water.

"We will leave as soon as I win this duel," The Man announced.

Gamelda warned, "I say we should leave before this fight. I see dark clouds forming and there is no avoiding this storm. We should definitely leave before the fight."

The Crippler argued, "And that is precisely the reason you shouldn't be permitted to talk in these meetings. We'll be slaughtered if we make a run to the mountains like you've suggested."

Gamelda glared back at him and said, "Put your hand on the table and prick your finger, good man. Show your king that your blood runs true."

The Crippler immediately retorted, "I've already proved my loyalty to my king, and I've always called him a king, long before you ever showed up."

"ENOUGH," screamed The Man as he slammed his hand on the birch table. He continued in a more relaxed tone, "Gamelda, go wait in my quarters. I shall return shortly. I can't have this bickering in these meetings."

Gamelda stood up and said, "What about him?" She pushed the chair back under the table. The woman waited a few moments as she glared at the Crippler before turning to leave. The men remained quiet until she left the room.

The Crippler broke the silence, "I don't know how you put up with her…"

The Man interrupted him, "Not another word on the subject or you will be sent away too. She's barely gone and you want to talk about her. Now, have all the men ready to leave immediately after the duel."

The Crippler asked, "Are we taking Ali-Pari Wamhoff with us?"

The Man answered, "They've rejected every trade offer we've made for Krys Colbert and the Wamhoffs won't even pay a decent ransom for her. She has no value anymore. Stop wasting food on her."

The Crippler asked, "So we should kill her?"

The Man rolled his eyes and replied, "Yes, that is what I meant."

The Crippler lowered his head and said, "Just wanted clarification, my king."

They talked for another twenty minutes but the plan had remained the same for months. Everyone knew exactly what needed to be done before the Wamhoffs had washed ashore and thrown off their plans. The Man thought about Benroy's burial again. He showed little emotion on the outside, but Benroy's death tugged at his heartstrings. He felt responsible for his friend's demise and to a lesser extent, for approximately three thousand soldiers who had met their death from the tainted water. When he was a soldier, he only had to fight alongside the other men and follow the General. Now, the men fought for him and the responsibility weighed on him.

After the meeting, The Man, Tucker and Terry went to check on the newest soldiers. The trio arrived at the training yard and The Man was impressed. The current hiatus had allowed the inexperienced men to practice day and night. The Man noticed a drastic improvement as he watched a series of different drills being executed flawlessly. He noticed that they didn't need Terry to direct them as some veterans had been helping out when the Training Master had to attend the meetings. The men hadn't been exposed to the true rigors of war yet, but they weren't completely green anymore.

The Man stayed for a few more unit marches and headed back to the castle with Tucker. He looked down at three tree stumps. He remembered when he and Benroy had sat there and he had named his friend as the Falconer of Donegal. In honor of Benroy the Builder, The Man didn't plan to name a new Falconer until they had won the crown. He returned to his quarters and heard shouting coming from the door, which was slightly ajar. The Man slowly pushed it completely open and peered inside to see Gamelda shouting at the Crippler. The Crippler had his back to the door and faced Gamelda who didn't even notice that The Man had entered the room. Her rage focused on the Crippler.

"I'm looking out for his best interests, too," screamed the diminutive man.

Gamelda yelled back, "Then why does he mutter phrases in his sleep about serving you and the demons. You tried to steal his mind."

The Crippler retorted, "Stop making things up to cast a dark light on me."

Gamelda came back at him. "You might have everyone else fooled but I see who you are. You are the black shadow hanging over him. You are the reason this journey is cursed."

"Me, ha, everything was running smoothly until you were dragged in here, completely bound by shackles," the Crippler responded.

The Man readied himself to stop the verbal fight until the Crippler suddenly extended his arms and a continuous stream of lightning rays shot out of his hands and crashed into Gamelda. The force pushed his lover back several feet but she stayed on her feet. She started to redirect the sparkling rays back at the Crippler. The force pushed his mentor closer to him. The king put his shaking hand on his sword grip and intently watched the supernatural brawl in awe. He didn't know what to do. His mentor and lover continued the lightning fight as The Man slowly drew his weapon. The buzzing sounds filling the room hurt The Man's ears and the smell of burning flesh offended his nose but he watched as the Crippler started to overpower Gamelda and push her backwards. The sorceress fell to her knee and appeared to be running out of strength.

The Man stood, frozen in place, torn about what to do. He looked back and forth at each person and debated whom he should kill, if necessary. Smoke started to shoot out of Gamelda's ears like steam from a tea kettle, and tears formed in The Man's eyes. He shook like a leaf, sword in hand, as he watched the woman he loved dying slowly. Tears cascaded down The Man's scarred face and he couldn't stand by idly any longer.

"AAAHHHH," screamed The Man as he delivered an overhand stroke by which the golden blade ripped into the Crippler's right shoulder and ran down to the small of his back. The dead man collapsed to the ground and turned into a black puddle. The pool of demon blood moved around the room and looked for a spot to sink into but couldn't find any cracks in the stone floor. The ebony liquid ebbed across the floor, up the wall and flowed out an open window before drizzling down into the grass and retreating into the earth. The Man ran over to Gamelda. He hugged her smoking body and could feel the intense heat. He quickly wiped away the tears as his disoriented paramour regained her wits and sat up.

"Are you alright, my love?" he asked as the dulled green emerald on Gamelda's forehead returned to its normal brilliance.

She answered in a whisper of a voice, "I will be. I'm sorry you had to kill your friend. I know he meant a lot to you."

The Man told her, "Forget that, you were right. He was a demon. He tried to kill you. No one will ever kill the woman I love." He didn't even realize that he was admitting his love for her. He wouldn't admit it to her, but the situation bothered him greatly. *How could I have never known the man was a demon? Maybe I'm not fit to be king?*

"He was strong, but full of demonic energy. I think we found your black cloud. Maybe now we will see better visions," Gamelda said with a smile that appeared to cause her pain.

The Man carried her over to the soft bed and set her down gently. She started to shake and her body turned cold. The Man used every blanket in the room to cover his lover and the twitching finally stopped. Gamelda quickly slipped into sleep and The Man paced around the room. After this incident, The Man had no clue as to whom he could really trust.

Two days later, he sat at the table in his quarters with Gamelda.

"Are you still broken up over the Crippler?" she asked.

He tried to sound tough as he answered, "I'm much more upset over the death of Benroy than that demon. Benroy was like a…a…a really good friend."

Gamelda hinted, "Like a brother?"

The Man shrugged his shoulders and said, "I wouldn't know precisely, but from what I've heard, yes, something like that. A lot of men respect and look up to me like a father. The Crippler tried to be like a father to me so I guess Benroy was my brother. I don't know, maybe it's just because I never had any real friends until he came along. I used to look out for that little guy. He wasn't the best swordsman, but I made sure he never died on the battlefield. I saved his life a countless number of times, and for what? To watch him die because I couldn't protect our water?"

Gamelda suggested, "Maybe we should choose another man to fight the duel considering your current mental state. Mad Dog would represent you well in a duel. Let him have the chance."

The Man laughed snidely and said, "No way. I want to kill Ali-Samuel myself. Revenge will set my head straight and motivate me plenty."

Gamelda informed him, "I haven't seen you fighting a red-headed man in the duel, only you saw that. You are fighting a massive man with long black braids and an unorthodox fighting style."

The Man shook his head and couldn't believe her as he responded, "There's no chance Ali-Samuel would let another man fight his battles."

She rubbed his blond whiskered chin and said, "You lose to the foreign man in the visions."

"What?" The Man asked sharply as he pulled his face away.

She peered into his eyes. "You heard what I said. You die. Don't do this. You saved my life and I am trying to return the favor. Head for the mountains and they won't catch you. They hardly have a cavalry unit. Don't fight. And if you will stay, let Mad Dog fight, please."

The Man laughed through his nose and said, "I am going to fight. You probably saw those visions because of the Crippler's bad aura being too close to me."

She shook her head and replied, "No, I just saw them this morning."

The Man knew he would never be able to face his men if he backed out. He said, "That's a great shame that you think you saw me lose, but I am fighting for my kingdom. I am fine to fight; in fact, I can't wait to kill that barbarian. Get ready to see him die in real life, not with some flames in some stupid skull. We leave in one hour." The Man got up and left the room to be fitted into his dueling armor.

The lighter suit consisted of overlapping plates of thin ovals of gilded metal and allowed more movement than his full battle gear. Tucker handed him the golden battle helm after the squire helped slide the gauntlets on both of The Man's hands. He went to meet Gamelda at the stables. She waited for him on a tan palfrey with white spots and he jumped onto his barded destrier. The war horse snorted and reared back before The Man could get his left foot in the stirrup. He almost fell, but secured his footing and sat firmly on the horse. Gamelda looked at him and shook her head but he tried to ignore it. He knew she would try to make it seem like a reason to back out of the duel.

The destrier calmed down enough to trot slowly out of the stable and head south as they started toward the Gates of Elkridge. They rode in silence up to a full gallop and tasted the breezy autumn air.

There's no way I can lose this fight, not to Ali-Samuel or some savage from Histomanji. But I'd rather kill Ali-Samuel.

The two arrived at the designated fighting location in the late afternoon and his guard, Lennix, approached.

The tall, thin man said, "There's about two or three hundred of them out there saying they want to come in for the duel."

The Man contemplated for a moment and answered, "Let's head for the gates and give the message ourselves."

He stared at Gamelda's green eyes as he heeled his horse and rode toward the Southern Gates.

A-EMILIA

"The king said fifty of you can come in. The only person who is allowed to be armed is your champion. Everyone else must leave their weapons outside these walls. King's orders," shouted a stout man from about fifteen feet away.

Emilia looked at the huge wall of Elkridge, and Ali-Samuel commented to the guard as they passed, "Don't worry about our weapons. We aren't cowards who loose blazing arrows at women and children."

The stout man replied, "No, your side only poisons water so everyone can die. By everyone, I mean true citizens of Donegal, not a bunch of barbarians invading our kingdom."

Ali-Steven sorted out who would go in, and they walked up to the main gate. A huge wooden door with rusted brass overlay creaked as several men helped push it open. One of the guards noticed Cobra's wood and chain weapon and his short curved sword.

The toothless man chided, "He's allowed to wear armor, you know. Once he gets in, there's no running out to get more protection. Don't want to hear no complaining if he loses like that."

Ali-Steven said, "Just open the gate. I'm quite certain your primary task isn't to give your unqualified opinion."

The door stopped opening and they entered the city of Elkridge. Emilia sensed a trap as armed guards lined their walking path to the dueling area. A small patch of flat, green grass had been designated as the fighting grounds. She followed a small group that was escorted up front with Cobra. Emilia looked at the gold tinted armor of the opponent and began to worry that her champion only wore a loincloth.

She could see the residents snickering and chuckling at the strange-looking foreigner. The enemy's horned helm looked more intimidating than the tattoos and scars on Cobra. The Wamhoff men walked to the center with Cobra and Emilia instinctually followed right behind. The Man ripped off his helm and his blond hair became exposed.

He looked directly at Ali-Samuel and spoke, "I didn't think it could be true. A man is not a man if he doesn't fight his own battles. This is between you and me. Let's finish it right here, like real men."

Ali-Samuel calmly responded, "Perhaps had I been able to bring in my sword, we would have the option to fight. Do you think you have enough guards around?"

The Man with the Golden Sword smiled and said, "You'd be wise to swallow that tongue of yours. Look around, you are at my mercy. Don't be stupid. I am a man of honor. I will fight your champion. I will kill him and then your party shall leave in disgrace…again."

Emilia looked behind The Man at a mysterious looking woman in a glowing purple dress. She disappeared as everyone retreated to their respective sides except for The Man and Cobra. Emilia still worried about the armor which not only acted as protection but also reflected the sun's rays and was nearly blinding. The Man was a tall thick warrior but her champion towered over him. Cobra held his scimitar in his right hand and whirled his chain and wood around in his left, whistling through the air. The Histoman leader stopped as he and The Man stood face to face.

The Man backed away and pulled his golden sword. *He definitely has the better-looking armor and weapon. This could end badly.*

A bugle tore through the afternoon air, silencing the buzz of onlookers but neither man rushed the other. They both slowly maneuvered around in circles to counter each other. The Man unleashed the first attack, but Cobra easily fended off the advances. Cobra used his whirling shaft of wood to pepper The Man's armor, but the wood only rang like a drum stick as it struck The Man over and over. The man in gold tried to counter after Cobra went low with his weapon but the nimble foreigner dodged the lunging attempt. The two men continued to parry attacks back and forth as neither man could gain an advantage. Cobra returned with a quick move and used his flying rod of wood to smack The Man on both earholes. The Man ducked to avoid the attack and staggered back, almost falling, but held his ground. Cobra moved in close and struck the dazed man with an uppercut punch that knocked his golden helm to the ground. Cobra thrust a barefoot into The Man's midsection and knocked him back. The Man lost his sword and Cobra quickly wound up the scimitar and stroked down at The Man who put his gloved hands up in defense. The curved blade sliced through the soft leather underside of the gauntlets and into the palms of the enemy. Cobra relentlessly kept slashing downward onto the arms of The Man with the Golden Sword. The protection seemed to help at first but Emilia noticed the blood spurting out of the armor on The Man's arms as her champion continued.

Cobra kicked The Man in the face and blood spurted out of his nose as he fell onto his back. Cobra closed in to deliver the death blow. He raised his short sword high above his head. *Finish him off already. What are you waiting for? Wait, what is going on? There's that woman in the purple dress again.*

Cobra remained as still as a well-crafted statue. It seemed as if some magical spirit held Cobra's body frozen in place. He didn't even blink. Emilia started to panic as the discombobulated opponent began to stir and got to his knees. The Man finally regained his energy and rushed over to his sword. He grabbed the grip with his red hands and grimaced. With blood running down his mangled arm protection and dripping from his wrists, The Man with the Golden Sword delivered a cross-stroke with just enough strength to separate Cobra in two at the midsection. The loser's insides spilled all over the feet of the victor who quickly rushed behind a horde of his guards. The forty-nine remaining supporters were irate with the shady circumstances of the fight.

They marched toward The Man, and Ali-Samuel shouted, "What was that? I don't know what you did, but you cheated."

The Man screamed back from behind his wall of guards, "I did not cheat. The Gods obviously don't want a barbarian to win a duel in Donegal."

His nose still bled and he gasped to catch his breath. Emilia noticed the woman in the shimmering dress running away. *I had heard the rumors that he had taken a sorceress as his lover, perhaps that's her. She must have cast that spell on Cobra to stop all his movement.*

The venomous yelling back and forth continued until Ali-Steven bellowed over everyone, "Stop this now."

To Emilia's surprise, everyone quieted down to listen.

He said, "I don't know what just happened here, I really don't, but I know our champion lost somehow. Now we leave, just as promised."

The Histoman grabbed both pieces of Cobra and walked back out the southern door. They met with the rest of their party for what Emilia had hoped would be a victory parade. The dejected group began the long walk to their desolate campsite.

Ali-Samuel asked his father, "We're not really leaving Donegal, are we?"

Ali-Steven answered, "Yes. I don't agree with that black magic or witchcraft we just witnessed, but we gave our word. A man is only as good as his word. We leave, yet we shall return to Donegal once again under a better circumstance. As for the two of you," he pointed at Emilia and Ali-Samuel, and said, "Because of your size, you will be instrumental in our plan to get to the Capitol once and for all."

Emilia could tell Ali-Samuel was steaming mad about the decision to leave and refused to try to engage him in conversation. He had a horrible temper that seemed to rear its ugly head more and more often recently.

They made it back to the beach by sundown and word started to spread about the evacuation. The Histoman were very happy to be going home. Emilia didn't want to break the news that they would probably be landing just down the coastline for another attack. Everyone started to pack away their few remaining belongings and got ready to hit the sea again. Ali-Steven decided they would leave at sunrise so they would have one last night on firm ground.

"Why are they putting riches back inside that wooden fox?" asked Ali-Samuel as he pointed at the activity.

Ali-Steven said, "Because we are returning all that treasure back to them."

An incredulous look came over Ali-Samuel's face as he asked, "And why would that be?"

His father answered, "We need to give it back. We have much more gold that we pulled out of the mountainside. We may need allies at some point in time."

Ali-Samuel shook his head and said, "We will *never* ally with a cheat like that."

Ali-Steven tried to calm his son down and said, "Trust me with this. Do you think I would let all of this occur if I didn't have a sound plan? Would I be this calm after seeing that atrocity of a duel back there? I'm not worried at all; in fact, I think this may help our cause. He likes to use tricks. I guess we need to use some tricks of our own. We will use them to get right back into Donegal again. I know what to do and how to do it, so worry not, my son."

SUNNY

Sunny wiped the sweat from his bright orange brow with a roughened palm. Winter was setting in for most of the world, but Gama Traka remained warm and sunny all year round. Seven other students had joined Sunny in the expedition to find Riceros Colbert. For several days, they had been trudging blindly through the sand and Sunny was getting demoralized. He also wanted to find Kazu because he couldn't believe that his mentor, who had graciously accepted him into the School, could be an evil man.

Kazu has been acting strange for the past few weeks. He had me beaten and ordered me to stay away from Ollor. I still can't believe that he kidnapped Riceros. I think both of them are in trouble. They have to be. However, they both have special powers that would make it nearly impossible for them to be captured. Dolpho did warn me about a dark spirit in the School. Could it be the golden boy and not Kazu?

They combed the surrounding areas, looking for buried entrances and cave openings in the hills. There were thousands of little cracks in the mountains that would take years to search. The people who had disappeared were tiny and it seemed unlikely that they would be found in the sand pit of pink and gray pebbles or the burnt orange and beige mountains. Even the cacti were few and far between in this drab landscape. Sunny had a sinking feeling that the missing men had gone up to the Sea of Green and boarded a boat that could have gone anywhere in the world. He knew if that had happened, they would never see the two again. Sunny didn't actually believe that they needed

Riceros to defeat the demons, but Dragon-Eyes made everyone feel that it would be a lost cause without the little boy. Sunny hadn't been very impressed with the half-man either. He could barely even walk at a normal speed and thought the Imp would only get in the way during a real brawl. He even thought the wizard could be the dark spirit.

They searched for the rest of the morn until a shadow appeared on the horizon, a great distance away. The sounds of marching were muffled by the deep sand, but it was evident that an army was coming straight at them. Every one of the students pulled their weapons in vain and Sunny smelled fear in the air. Hundreds of men were walking directly at Sunny and his friends. As they got close enough to identify, Sunny told his schoolmates not to be scared and that they should put away their weapons before they made the approaching men angry. Ali-Ster Wamhoff led the Noble Army of Undead Kings right up to the students before they came to a uniform stop.

The former King of Donegal looked at Sunny as he spoke, "The time has come. The fleet of demons has broken through the circular pool created by the water dragons. They will soon be back on track to land on the northern shores. The water dragons will continue to slow their progress but Damian Doome and all the rest should be landing in the next ten days, if not much sooner. What are you doing out here?"

Sunny hesitated for a moment before answering, "We have a slight problem. The Riceros boy has disappeared."

Ali-Ster's eyes opened wider and he asked, "Whaaaat? Disappeared, did you say?"

Sunny swallowed the lump in his throat and replied in a meek tone, "Yes. He left the School to go outside for a bit and never returned."

Ali-Ster looked disturbed and shook his head as he asked, "Why? Why would you let him leave the School?"

"He asked to leave by himself. I wasn't going to stop him." Sunny tried to defend his actions but Ali-Ster was still shaking his head and said, "Well, you should have. Is that what this is here? A desperate, hopeless search for a boy who is vital to the cause?"

Sunny said, "Don't worry, we'll find him. These are some of the best students from the School." *What is wrong with Ali-Ster? He sounds just like Dragon-Eyes.*

Ali-Ster looked around at the small group of students and his eyes came back to Sunny as he said, "Best of luck, little brother. I'm sure you'll find the boy in no time at all."

Sunny nearly forgot in all the commotion that he was looking his sibling in the face. He still had mixed feelings about his birth and wasn't sure he believed all the stories that the Imp Wizard had told him. Hearing the words 'little brother' added some legitimacy to the dwarf's story. However, Sunny hoped he would live much longer than his dead eighteen-year-old brother.

"How did the meeting with the Triumvirate go?" Sunny asked.

Ali-Ster put his head down and replied, "I never got to see them. I did talk to a chancellor who seemed to take the message to heart but I didn't get a guarantee that they would provide any men. I am going back later today to try again. As for the students, you need to bury the northern entrance to the School. The demons are too close and if they can get to that entrance, there will be nowhere to hide if needed. Use only the southern entrance but the demons know about that one too. Hide that one as much as you can too. They seem to have an inside source in your School."

Sunny immediately thought of Kazu and didn't want to believe that the old man could be in cahoots with the demons.

Ali-Ster looked Sunny in the eyes and said, "Be safe, little brother."

He and the Army turned and marched away. Sunny called off the search and they went to the northern entrance of the School. It took two days and most of the students' help to completely bury the northern entrance of the School in more than ten feet of sand.

They inspected more cave openings hoping to find Riceros but didn't have success. The group made it back to the other entrance just before the sun went to bed for another day. Sunny walked along the straight corridor wearing a look of defeat. He looked in the library and caught the Imp Wizard sporting a look of anticipation. Sunny walked in with his head lowered and didn't need to say anything. The wizard's face went from hopeful to dejected within moments.

A-RUSSELL

Russell's confidence soared as he bit into a wrinkled, dried apricot and looked at Lizeria. He wasn't sure why he'd involved her in this, but it had felt right at the time to bring her. He looked around the vast sand pit bounded with hills and mountains to the east and west. An occasional cactus broke the pattern of pink and gray sand but Russell thought everything looked exactly the same. He didn't have a specific plan but Shireez' motivational talk had made him feel invincible. The Imp Wizard had tried to talk him out of going with only Lizeria even as Russell closed the door to the main entrance. He didn't like the sultry weather of the Pearl Islands or Gama Traka. He dealt with the frosty cold much better. Lizeria seemed to be the exact opposite as her dark skin absorbed the sun well and she was barely bothered by the sweltering conditions. Russell thought she must be part dragon to not be affected by the heat. Russell knew she didn't understand what they were doing, but the young girl would follow him anywhere. They didn't talk very much and he tried to concentrate on figuring out the best places to find Riceros.

He assumed the help of the spirits would be vital and hoped they had made the trek from the Pearl Islands to join him here. They finished a meager lunch and searched the vast desert for several more hours. Impending darkness forced Russell to end the day of fruitless results. Russell pulled two thin sheets from his shoulder sack and laid one out for Lizeria. He rolled the other one up to use as a pillow and leaned back to look at a bright half-moon.

The longer this carries on, the lower our expectations should drop. I was confident when I left the School, but today we barely covered much ground with Lizeria lagging behind. Maybe I shouldn't have brought her? Maybe I'm not going to find the Pearl after all?

He smashed his eyelids together and tried to force sleep but a thumping heart and thoughts of failure dancing in his head prevented any chance of slumber. The next two days yielded nothing promising and Russell started to get depressed. He decided he wouldn't go back to the School as a failure and thought about how he could get Lizeria to safety.

B-RICEROS

A fluttering candle lit up the dark, dreary cave and magnified the floating dirt and dust particles. Riceros leaned back against the wall and tried to loosen the silk cords that had been expertly looped around his wrists and ankles. He had been forced to bend down with his hands on his feet and both had been tied together to keep him balled up. He couldn't sleep being curled up like this and his back felt like it carried the collective pain of all the people in the world. He looked at Kazu and didn't see the old man with tattoos on his neck. Instead, he viewed a lanky man with deep purple skin, yellow eyes, three ears and a distinct tail. Kazu had transformed into a demon as soon as they got inside the cave.

He spoke to Riceros in the common tongue, "I still cannot believe you are the one. The chosen one is smaller than the human version of me. All these years, everyone thought you needed a Pearl to summon the dragons when all you need is this."

The demon threw the gleaming golden whistle that would summon the Noble Dragons into the air. It captured most of the light the dim flame could provide before landing in his left palm. He tossed it slowly back and forth as he spoke, "The plan is perfect now. I blow a little flute and your dragons come to save you and the humans. However, the trap will be set by Damian and the demon dragons. All your dragons will be killed and that should all but assure victory for the coldomores. Have you ever smelled the sweet scent of burning dragon flesh, I must ask you?"

Riceros shook his head.

"Unfortunate, because it smells delicious, I tell you. When I took over this body almost one hundred years ago, I never realized it would climax here, in a dark cave. The Pearl of Wisdom landed in my hands. How could you be so careless? Leaving the School alone was so foolish. I assumed you were setting me up. I've been at that School for nearly a century, waiting and waiting for the right moment. I had to first let Kazu control his own thoughts and actions as I sat inside his body and observed his actions until I learned enough so as not to sound or look strange. Then I took full control and wallowed in the weeds, waiting."

"So you can just transpose from demon to human and vice versa?" Riceros asked.

The demon said, "Yes, you are a wise little boy. I am going to especially enjoy drinking your blood. I bet it makes me smarter as soon as I sip that delectable nectar. I'd love to always look like a demon but duty prevailed and I've been in the uncomfortable skin of a human for far too long. The special kids, Muriel and Sunny, they almost walked into my quarters when I looked like this. I dove behind a desk and never forgot to lock my doors after that episode. To my surprise, no one else even suspected the slightest problem."

Riceros interrupted, "So you've been sabotaging the School for hundreds of years now?"

The demon stopped tossing the whistle back and forth and said, "No, in fact, quite the opposite. That School has progressed past the point of anyone's highest expectations. But I know the force of coldomores and Damian Doome's crossbreeds and nothing short of a miracle will stop them. This was your only hope, you stupid human."

He waved the flute in the air and Riceros asked, "Why do the demons hate the humans so much?"

The demon let out a laugh and said, "Why? Ha, why, he asks. Why do the poor citizens hate the nobility? We've cowered in caves in the ground for far too long. You humans have lived in castles, palaces and the like. You can frolic in the sun whenever your heart desires. We've had to hide because of lies perpetrated by Esogenus. We never resorted to cannibalism first. We learned that from people like you. I'd love nothing more than to end your life right here, yes I would, but you will be a grand gift to Damian Doome. I hope he grants me a meeting with the Plades for this. Yes, I wonder what he will do with you? Feed you to the dragons? Perhaps, but only if you are lucky. He'll probably rip off all your finger- and toe-nails and make you eat them before moving on to some real torture. Personally, and this is just me, but I hope he stabs you one thousand times and slowly drains out all that blood for us to drink."

Riceros interrupted again, "I thought you weren't cannibals."

The demon responded in an angry voice, "We have been persecuted for thousands of years for the offense. We might as well do it."

A noise came from outside the cave and the demon closed his eyes. He transformed back into the human body of Kazu. He ran over to the small opening and stuck his head out. Riceros struggled with the bonds but couldn't loosen any of them. He twisted his aching body around, desperately trying anything to get free. He stopped when Kazu pulled his body back in and changed back into demon form. He thought about how Brehan had escaped from the Fox Chapel farmers. Brehan had never revealed how he had gotten free and Riceros could have used any insight right now. He started to think about the Colbert family and wondered if he would ever see any of them again. Riceros lost consciousness and fell onto his left side.

He woke up in even more pain. More than anything in life, he would have loved to stretch out. Instead, Kazu propped him back up and fed him some mysterious meat from his hand. Riceros didn't want to eat it but needed the sustenance to survive. He closed his eyes and chewed on the tough stringy meat that he hoped was ostrich. The hunger and exhaustion started to play with Riceros' mind.

I'm going to die. I'm going to die at the hands of a demon. I need to make this demon kill me before Damian Doome can parade me around like a prize. I came all this way to die like a fool. Why didn't I take Dioneer when I went to see the dragons? Why did the dragons tell me to come alone? This doesn't add up at all. Why did Ikeros tell me to come alone? Is he in cahoots with Damian Doome to help rid the earth of humans? Is this all a giant ruse or a dream? But why me? Why am I involved in all this?

ELISA

"What do you mean, he defeated the Goldenfield army with ease?" Elisa asked in an angry tone.

Her new Master of Defense, Lord Paler Remeby, responded, "Precisely that, your highness. He suffered substantial losses early on but a second unit of cavalry arrived to attack both flanks of Queen Leimur's advance. They caused enough chaos and disarray to send Goldenfield running back to their homeland. The Queen had launched a surprise attack with almost twice as many men, but the King's side wouldn't break. It would appear he's staved off another stiff assault. Impervious, so far he is."

Elisa said, "That's quite a lovely endorsement for our King, but what do you propose we do?"

Lord Ichibod spoke up, "Siege. A siege is our only option. We can run a supply line to Lightview. I'm not sure King Colbert has the complete backing of Fox Chapel yet."

Lady Victoriah responded from behind her veil, "He certainly had the backing of Lord Nanbert without even asking for it. I think you might overestimate our reach amongst Fox Chapel. Every moment he remains king further solidifies his support in Fox Chapel. We need to get to the Capitol posthaste."

The Master of Defense asked, "Do you really think we can cut off their supply line from Mattingly?"

Lord Ichibod unconfidently nodded and replied, "It shall be a struggle for the storybooks, but we can starve them out. We have the upper hand in this matter, trust me."

The sun beat down on the weather-beaten coach's peeling red and gold paint. Small flakes started to fall in front of Elisa's eyes and she could feel the stiff breeze even inside the luxury coach. As autumn wound down and winter threatened, everyone bundled up in various forms of complete fur layers or fur lining.

The overcrowded coach didn't even have an open spot for a small brazier as the lady asked, "Do we have any options other than camping outside during winter to execute a siege on the King's warm Castle?"

Ichibod answered, "Unless you can come up with another, better plan, for right now, that's our best option."

The coach came to a sudden halt and Elisa became nervous about another ambush. She strained her ears for the sounds of fighting from a distance but couldn't hear anything. Every passenger tentatively got out to investigate the situation. Two messengers raced up on light brown chargers.

One man shouted to Lord Ichibod, "My lord, we've run into a stone wall. It's like a double wall in fact, and must be fifteen feet high at the least. Stretches north and south far as the eye can see."

Lord Ichibod looked stunned and responded in a monotone, "Are we talking about the Falconhurst city wall or are you simply speaking metaphorically? Please tell me you're speaking metaphorically."

The messenger said, "I don't know what that means, my lord, but I've seen them city walls before. These is different, it's like a double wall. Two stacked stone walls with some space between 'em."

Ichibod ordered, "Bring us riding horses. We need to figure out this conundrum. He couldn't have already built a wall around the city wall. That would make it nearly impossible to get through both."

Elisa followed Ichibod east with the rest of the Ellsworths. She rode up and stared at the menacing gray wall. Huge rectangular stones, one stacked on top of the next, reached high into the air. It looked higher than fifteen feet to Elisa. *How did he build a wall like this already? He's only been king for about one month. Can I really defeat a man who is so organized?*

"Send men north and south. Let's find out how far this extends. There's no way the wall can surround the entire Capitol," Sir Anderley instructed and several men sprang into action.

Lord Ichibod spoke in a whiny voice, "The first wall around the Capitol took seventeen years to complete. I know he has heavy resources and manpower, but can a king build a secure wall in this short a time? There must be one or two cracks of penetrability in this wall. This should only be a minor setback."

Another delay! Maybe this is a sign to give up? They're fully expecting us now. Even if we get around this wall somehow, the loss of life would be extreme. Then we have to get past the most heavily guarded area of the kingdom to even get close to the Castle. I'm not sure the men will keep lining up to die for their queen. A few honorable men will, but most won't.

They set up camp for the night and awaited news about the length of the wall. Elisa bit into a slow roasted pig shoulder and noticed the food wasn't as good as castle food, but she had been hardly suffering the rigors of war. The Ellsworths had brought the most talented cooks from the castle kitchen and they did quite well given the limited resources. Most of the fare consisted of various forms of fire-roasted meat, some slow roasted or fully cooked and the rest was charred black on the outside and red and raw in the middle.

The table setting for the queen and the Ellsworths housed numerous spices and salts. The silver spoons and knives twinkled in the afternoon sunlight. Wiping linens had been folded into the shape of a bird and placed in front of every hickory chair. The dark red tablecloth made her think about the blood of her soldiers. She hadn't liked that shade of red when the Wamhoffs had forced her to wear it and she especially avoided deep crimson now. Elisa had also started to tire of always wearing black as per Lady Victoriah's advice. She planned to forge her own style once she became the officially recognized Queen of Donegal.

I just need the real crown on my head and the power paradigm shifts in my favor. I still have that one problem to take care of.

She glared at Lord Ichibod as he bit into a burnt black chop of spotted mountain lamb. Elisa knew he preferred the young animal to mutton because every single time they had lamb he made sure to tell everyone how much he hated the tough texture and off flavor of the older animal. The queen couldn't believe how small the animals were when she had witnessed her first slaughter. Lord Ichibod whispered something into Lady Victoriah's ear and Elisa's mind began to race. The lady looked over and Elisa quickly turned her head away after making brief eye contact.

I think I have my answer. That was the look of pure guilt. You shouldn't have taken your veil off to eat. I can see through your empty act now. I need to move quickly. My value is starting to lessen by the day.

Later that night, Elisa sneaked away to see Brehan. She had to wake him up again and they took some blankets over to an empty field and had sex. This time felt more comfortable than the last, but still not totally right. The two lay on their backs and looked at the glowing stars.

Alright, if I am going to sleep with this beast, I need him to take care of something for me. It's only reasonable. Now it's time to plant the seed.

She said, "This could very well be the last time this ever happens, so savor the moment."

Brehan turned on his side to face her and asked, "What? Have you changed your mind again?"

She smiled on the inside and responded, "No, that will never happen again. My mind isn't clouded any longer but I've heard that our good lord's plot against me has been accelerated. I don't have a proper claim any longer. It should seem he has no use for me anymore."

Brehan leaned in and gave her a kiss on the cheek as she continued to look skyward. He whispered, "We can take care of this problem. Don't fret."

She asked, "But how?"

Brehan rolled onto his back again and grabbed Elisa's hand. He kissed her cold fingers and said, "I don't think you want to know the details involved."

Elisa told him, "I need to know. You said *we* can take care of this problem. You've saved my life. I want to at least help you in the planning. I know things that might be valuable to know."

Brehan spoke gently, "Obviously, the only way to prevent a person from offing you is to get to them first. We won't directly say what needs to happen, but we both know."

Elisa suggested, "Perhaps he drinks a liquid that turns his face purple and black?"

Brehan looked over and shook his head. He paused for a moment and said, "I can't do that. That's the device of a coward. I need to find out when he isn't being guarded, which is probably only when he sleeps."

Elisa warned, "No, he is heavily guarded in his sleeping pavilion. However, he dismisses all guards when he relieves himself during the night, I've noticed. He always walks off into the woods by himself. But those areas are still being watched by general guards."

Brehan kissed her hand again and said, "I'll just have to stealthily lure him away somehow."

He smiled at her and even in the dim moonlight and starlight, she saw a hideous beast. She tried desperately to see the man she had always loved. She tried with all of her icy heart, but she only saw an ugly bastard from the Pearl Islands. She saw a man she could manipulate. *Has my heart run this cold? He doesn't have the duties that come with being a queen. I've had every responsibility thrown on my aching shoulders. Anyone would change. Everyone would change.*

Elisa had tried to validate this line of thinking but never truly convinced herself. Brehan broke the brief silence and asked, "What does the man hate?"

Elisa immediately answered, "He hates the Wamhoffs, enthusiasm and anything that resembles a fun time."

She smirked at Brehan and listened as he said, "That gives me something to work with, I suppose. Remember the night, our first night, when…"

Elisa butted in, "Goodness, I've lost myself here with you. I must return to my pavilion or suspicion will be raised."

She put her nightdress back on and Brehan got dressed and grabbed the blankets. She gave him a quick kiss and rushed away before he could say anything except goodbye.

She entered her pavilion and heard Telly snoring lightly. Her heart raced from the secret encounter and she dove into her bed. She didn't want Brehan getting too sentimental and decided to end the affair before it became too emotional for her. She felt like she had to use Brehan to survive, but she had no plans for a grand reunion. She didn't want to think about the loving memories of the past. She validated her actions by convincing herself that she would be expelled from the kingdom for marrying a foreign bastard.

She had lied to Brehan, telling him that they would rule together, but she had no intentions of carrying out that plan. She intended to use her lover to take care of a few matters before she eventually revealed her true intentions. The Ellsworths had turned her into a cold, vindictive creature who remained perpetually paranoid. Most of her nervousness stemmed from the evil reputation Lord Ichibod carried. She had felt empowered after standing up to him several times, but now she understood how that could make him resent her. With the knowledge of his vast sanctioning of killing for silly reasons and Telly's eavesdropping report, she remained constantly on edge. She didn't sleep very well anymore because she knew it would be easiest to kill a still object. She also felt a responsibility to protect her younger sister and knew Ichibod didn't seem to have a problem killing females.

The queen slept terribly again and rose with hopes of hearing some good reports about the wall. She left her pavilion shortly after the pink sun rose above the blue-lined gray clouds. Lord Ichibod and Lady Victoriah were already seated around a small fire, warming their black-gloved hands. Winter couldn't wait to arrive and Elisa saw her breath in the air as it shot from her nose like steam from an angry bull's nostrils.

She asked the Ellsworths, "Any word from the scouts yet?"

Lord Ichibod looked at her with a face full of madness and said, "No cracks. Not one damn crack. The men rode as far as they could, north and south, and then they followed the wall to the west. There isn't one compromised spot to exploit. He built a wall around a damn wall. They can trap an army of men in between and then let the slaughter ensue."

Elisa debated not speaking because of Ichibod's mental state but went ahead and asked, "What if we go through the wall?"

Ichibod rapidly shook his head and said dismissively, "I don't believe we can craft a ram to bust through that thick a wall. Did you see the size of those stones?"

Elisa suggested, "Do you think the elephants could bust through, if we could get them to work together?"

This seemed to brighten Lord Ichibod's mood momentarily until he blurted, "I…I'm not sure. I'm going to the war council meeting to see if we can come up with a solution." The lord stormed off like a spoiled child.

Elisa turned to the lady and asked, "Shouldn't we be in the meeting? I just came up with the only viable option up to this point."

Lady Victoriah said, "You'll have to excuse my husband. Patience, they say, is a grand virtue; however, it has never graced our good lord. This wall has him obviously agitated. I know it's impossible to believe, but he was such a happy man, not too long ago either. Oh maybe it has been a little while."

Elisa took off her veil and said, "I can easily believe that. I used to be that way too, until you taught me to throw away all emotions."

The lady removed her veil. Her bright blue eyes had dulled and Elisa could see wrinkles that she had never noticed before.

Victoriah said, "Yes, well lately, I'm not so sure if that is sound advice. My, how times have changed. Do you know that Lord Ichibod risked being ousted from his family to marry me?"

A confused look came over Elisa's face and she asked, "I thought you were from a proud and noble family?"

The lady looked old in the unforgiving sunlight that unmercifully highlighted all of her blemishes. She said, "That's what everyone was ordered to believe. My father was a swineherd, my mother, a tavern wench. Lucky for me she was a beautiful tavern wench and passed on her looks to me. I don't fool myself. I know he picked me because of my looks and only my looks. I knew I could provide so much more but that wouldn't come until later. Once he took rule after his father's death, anyone who talked about my true upbringing had his or her tongue cut out. He said that I was his princess and people should mind their own affairs."

Elisa sported a fake smile as she said, "It's a murderous way, but a nice gesture nonetheless."

The lady told her, "He's performed very nice gestures for you as well."

Elisa looked confused and asked, "And how is that?"

Lady Victoriah looked around to make sure nobody would hear as she said softly, "Early on, his main advisors told him not to include you in the plan for the crown. They all told him to usurp the crown for himself. He said no. He said you held the claim for a reason. The Gods meant it to be. Lord Ichibod told his advisors that he would only serve as Falconer and advise Queen Elisa."

Elisa shook her head and said, "I'm not sure I can believe that."

Lady Victoriah looked at her with a smirk and responded, "I only believe it because I heard it with my own ears, my queen."

Elisa wanted to believe the story, but couldn't tell if Lady Victoriah had made it up to obtain sympathy for her husband. Elisa's head was going crazy with all these games.

You barely supported any of his decisions back at the castle and now you blindly follow his every move and cheer him on all the while. You scarcely call me your queen either. Don't think I would miss a slip like that. You never pander to anyone, especially not me.

As the week moved on and the party stood still, bad news kept arriving. The double wall seemed endless in all directions.

That day all the queen could do is worry. Nothing seemed to be working out and she felt her time was running out. Elisa's head hurt when she lay down to sleep later that night. Flashes of good memories of Lord Ichibod flew into her head. She remembered the falconing, feasting and puppet shows.

What if he did stand up for me? What if Telly didn't hear him correctly? What if Brehan should fail? It will be obvious who put him up to it. Maybe I should call off the entire thing. What have I gotten myself involved in? All this is becoming too much to handle.

Her mind shifted back and forth a thousand times before she got out of bed and went to tell Brehan to call off the plan. The cold night tested her triple layered nightgown and fur-lined cloak. She shivered as she made it to Brehan's tiny tent. She pulled the flap open but nobody was visible. The small area was empty.

A-BREHAN

Brehan lurked along the tree line, just inside the woods, near the Ellsworths' Pavilions. He hadn't noticed any movement, and rubbed his palms together to warm them up. He exhaled into a rag to conceal his visible breath from being detected by the wrong person. The former knight of Mattingly finally had the love of his life back and everything seemed so right.

If this man thinks he is going to intimidate my queen, I'll gladly perform this task. I didn't risk my life many times over to let some cranky old man kill my life's dream. Elisa and Brehan will be together in the end.

He had been scouting out this area for several nights and noticed the lord's pattern. The guards protected the front side of the Ellsworth pavilion, but Lord Ichibod went around back and into the woods to relieve himself.

Brehan's body had almost healed from the latest near-death experience. His heart stood divided as he marched on his father figure, Jon. He often agonized over the change in circumstances that had caused him to oppose Jon Colbert. He tried to avoid thinking about the entire Colbert family, but that always proved impossible. Brehan didn't even know if he could attack Jon or Ruxin Colbert on the field of battle. He had failed in his task of protecting the family and now they stood as his enemy. He waited nearly another hour before he heard some movement.

Lord Ichibod appeared in his heavy night robe and walked down the hill toward the woods. Brehan ran over to two horses and untied their reins from a tree. He leapt up on the one horse and lightly heeled the animal while also holding the reins for the other. Brehan slowly approached Lord Ichibod as he was coming back out of the woods.

The knight said, "Lord Ichibod, many apologies for disturbing you here, but you must know that they've found Tersen Wamhoff."

This seemed to excite the lord, who said, "Who found him?"

Brehan pointed behind Lord Ichibod and said, "Some of your men. They were arguing over who would get to kill him before you could show up."

"I deserve the right to kill that albino," said an annoyed Ichibod.

Brehan told him, "That's what I said, but they told me they would never listen to a criminal. If we hurry, we can stop them before they kill him."

Lord Ichibod looked around quickly and spoke, "Yes, well, I should go get my cloak."

Brehan warned him, "There's no time. I'll give you my spare cloak when we get there. We can't waste any more time. I have a horse ready to go."

The lord agreed, "Alright, alright, let's go."

The two men rode away from the camps and Brehan kept looking around to make sure no one had spotted them. They quickly reached the outskirts of the soldiers' campgrounds and Brehan kept riding on.

They reached an open plain and he acted confused and said, "They were all right here." He could see the lord shivering. Brehan said, "Over there, maybe they took him over there."

Lord Ichibod took off and Brehan followed just behind. The knight reached under his cloak and slowly pulled out Dragon-Bite. He tried to create fake coughing sounds to cover the sounds of the green steel scraping the scabbard.

"Oh wait, here he is," cried Brehan.

As Lord Ichibod turned his horse around, Brehan delivered a swift stroke of the sword with his right hand. The emerald blade mingled with the crimson blood as it sliced through Lord Ichibod's neck. The head hit the ground but the body slumped forward and remained on the horse. Brehan moved in to knock the body down, but the horse bolted with the dead lord still on its back. The animal headed straight toward the soldier camps. Brehan heeled his horse and rode north as fast as he could. He looped around to the campgrounds and nothing seemed amiss. He tied up the horse and walked back to his tent. His heart felt like it would swallow his chest. He heard a commotion beginning and shut his eyes and pretended to be asleep. He knew that neither horse had any markings that could implicate him, but he still had trouble breathing as he heard the murmurings of the death of Lord Ichibod outside his tent.

LEIMUR

The still-reigning Queen warmed her hands over a fire as she wondered if her short rule would continue when they arrived in Goldenfield. Everyone had been extremely understanding about the defeat and that scared her. Leimur expected and wanted someone to scream at her and blame her for the loss. She didn't really care about life as word about her loved ones still hadn't arrived. Visions of a bloody massacre of her brothers and Ali-Tiste kept playing through her head. She could only believe the worst had occurred and hoped with an empty heart that news of the defeat would magically reach Ali-Tiste and they would rendezvous on the way home. The Queen couldn't convince herself that her family was safe and every letter carrying raven they had dispatched had either got lost or been intercepted. She had gone back to not eating and her stomach tightened with hunger pains and the cold feeling settled in, sending chills throughout her body.

She listened to the men hammering away on the tent posts to set up camp for the night. They had started well before nightfall to get everything erected by full twilight. Her mind shifted back to the worry about a mutiny. She believed her fellow officers would never betray her but she also needed the support of the entire royal army. She knew that she had taken the kingdom from her parents so easily because she had secured the backing of the King's force. Her grip on the soldiers' loyalty had been slipping and she knew if they banded together, she would have no chance. The mental tension tugged at her exhausted body and centered in her lower back where the pike had found a small chink in her armor.

She had only really talked to Captain Salina since the battle and didn't know what to say to anyone else in a one-on-one situation. The Warrior Queen had lost her identity. The victory parade she had envisioned only months ago would have to be put on hold. There wasn't going to be a third attack to capture Donegal. In her mind, she should have already secured Harbor Valley and Donegal by now. She hadn't seen her tigers in a few weeks and wondered if they had finally returned to the Animal Kingdom. The cold weather didn't suit the animals and took away some of their ferocity. She didn't dare talk to Captain Tetine or General Rigby who had both suffered wounds in the failed attack. The reports of King Jon being in attendance turned out to be false, but they had captured the Prince of Donegal, Ruxin Colbert. Leimur thought she had smashed his head into oblivion and killed the young man. She looked at the long pen containing the Prince and about twenty other prisoners. One of the locked-up men tried to grab at a war horse that was tied close to the pen. The destrier snapped at the man and he jerked his hand back inside the mobile cell.

Her thoughts went right back to Ali-Tiste and her princes. She reminisced about their time at the palace and wondered why she hadn't brought all of them with her from the beginning. Her head became flooded with a series of images featuring her failed attempts to breach the castle, and the utter mayhem of the last open field battle washed the sweet memories away. Her brain kept twisting and stressing over the separation from Ali-Tiste Wamhoff. She had never been in love before the red-headed vixen had arrived in her meeting room out of the blue. Since then, she couldn't stand to not be around her lover. Her hands were finally toasty as the crunching sounds of leaves being crushed by boots resonated from behind her. She turned and saw more than twenty armored guards moving in with their weapons drawn.

Laruse Cornwell announced, "Queen Leimur, you have been summoned to the strategy tent and we are here to escort you."

She replied sarcastically, "I thank you all greatly for your passion to make sure your Queen makes it to her meeting tent safely. I would thank all of you individually but I don't have the time." She stood up and said, "You better hope my tigers don't show up as they are known to do. They have defeated more men than you have here and those were real men, much more skilled than anyone here. It took no time at all, and those men weren't even cowards if you can believe it."

All the men enjoyed a hearty laugh at the Queen's expense and she promised herself that she would take all of their heads at some point in time. Laruse shoved the resistant Leimur to get her moving and as they neared the tent, she looked in horror to her right at a pile of six dead tigers. The men kept pushing the Queen of Goldenfield along and she saw another pile of tigers to her left. Leimur could only assume that her council had been killed and a low ranking soldier had claimed power. She knew her chance of escaping alive was extremely bleak. One last shove heaved Leimur into the sizable strategy tent.

She was shocked to see Captain Tetine, General Rigby and several knights with swords drawn off to their right. She didn't see Captain Salina.

"Please sit," General Rigby said as he pointed at an isolated chair in the middle of the room. Everyone else stood up and the only thing assembled in the open area was a small trestle table behind Rigby. He said, "We have many matters to discuss and you have many questions to answer."

Leimur responded, "I can plainly see that. You brought more men than my Uncle Marcel so you can rest easy knowing you are smarter than he."

The General shook his finger at her and said, "Your cute little quips will help you no longer. You stand accused of treason."

Leimur almost jumped out of her skin and asked incredulously, "Treason?"

Captain Tetine stood silently by as Rigby said, "Yes, treason, which makes you a traitor." He walked over to the table and picked up a letter. He held it in the air. "A concerned scribe alerted us to a disturbing letter in which you offer to give our kingdom to our sworn enemy, Ali-Tiste Wamhoff. You know; the kingdom I delivered to you on an ornate platter."

A dejected Leimur said, "What difference does any of it make now? We've been defeated and she and my brothers are probably dead."

Captain Tetine finally broke his silence, "Wrong again. You seem to have a penchant for being wrong. And the people who were advising you against all these actions, like the General and I, were correct, as we have been for decades. You didn't want to listen to our advice and now your brothers and that Wamhoff bedswerver have been captured by Donegal. At least that is the story as it stands right now. We all have half a mind to think that Ali-Tiste delivered the future King of Goldenfield straight to the enemy."

Leimur immediately dismissed the thought and said, "She would never do that."

General Rigby spoke, "You talk so surely for someone who doesn't actually know her at all. I don't care how close you think you were with her, you weren't. She had been alive for more than three decades and you knew her for a few weeks of fun in the Royal Palace. Put that into perspective along with the fact that you were willing to give her our realm. Every battle you could conceive in your head, we followed like blind sheep, diligently carrying out our duty to our Queen. And now you spit in all our faces as you disrespect our blood and service in favor of our enemy, and a woman at no last."

Leimur didn't make eye contact with any of her captors and just kept looking around the pavilion with a defeated look on her face. She could hear the constant sounds of the rippling wind beating against the poorly constructed canvas wall.

Captain Tetine cleared his throat and said, "You have been given opportunity after opportunity to heed our counsel and you've smugly shoved it aside. We were willing to accept failure at the cost of noble intentions, but treason is obviously inexcusable. One of the traits I truly admired about you was your vigilance in upholding our sacred laws. It pains me to have to exercise the same characteristic against you now. The wage of treason has always been death and nothing less; however, due to your previous record of duty to Goldenfield, your life has been spared."

She cut off the Captain and asked, "What about my brothers?"

The General jumped in and told her, "If you would only allow him to finish. You will be taken prisoner until we get home, at which point you will be sent away. You will know your destination only when you arrive there. As for your brothers, they have no claim to the throne and likely share the same traitor blood with you. We are much more worried about the twelve hundred men that were taken prisoner following you into battle. Therefore, your brothers will rot in the dungeon until King Colbert realizes they are worthless and kills them. It's probably better that they are in the dungeon. If they were in Goldenfield, they would be dead already to eliminate any claim for power."

Leimur didn't say a word and stared at a piece of tightly stretched yellow linen. The heavy wind barely moved that wall of the tent.

General Rigby continued, "And just so you know, we are all hoping with a passion that Ali-Tiste hangs for treason. Now we know why you two got on so well."

The Queen said rhetorically, "I suppose I don't need to venture a guess at who is going to rule Goldenfield."

The General let a little smile sneak out as he responded, "No need for guesses. It shall be the same man who should have started ruling months ago, instead of you. The royal guard has spoken and they want me to end the age of ruling family dynasties. I have been chosen to restore our realm. I only propped you up to the top because I thought the people wouldn't respect anyone without a true blood claim. King Colbert has shown that a family name can always be crushed if there is no true power behind the name. You had your chance time and again and have no one to blame other than yourself. Do you have anything to say in your defense?"

She still looked around the room as she spoke, "It certainly appears that your minds are made on this matter, but I could stand to point out a few thoughts. Will you enjoy that stocked treasury, filled with gold, courtesy of Huber Leluc?"

The General nodded his head and replied, "We will. Same as you, when you emptied the rest of your parents' reserve and every other ruler has done in the past. A person can have many great deeds canceled out by treason."

Leimur pleaded, "It was hardly any reserve but that isn't important now. My brothers aren't accused of treason, I am. Save my brothers with a small portion of the vast sum left for your new kingdom and let them leave with me. A queen's last request."

Captain Tetine said, "Their asking price is for the Prince of Donegal, a real, recognized prince. We aren't giving up a Prince for two boys who have no value. Remember, you are the one who is killing your brothers. Your actions have caused these consequences. If we pay any ransom to get your brothers back it will only be to kill them and eliminate any attempt to reclaim the throne."

Leimur knew what she had to do.

She sat up quickly with her eyes wide open and looked terrified. She pointed to the group of lined-up guards to the side with her left index finger. "What is he doing?" she asked, shaking in her chair.

Everyone turned to look at the guards and she pulled out her war axe with her right hand. She sprang to her right and sliced a diagonal hole in the tightest wall. In the same motion, the Queen of Goldenfield dove headfirst through the seam and landed on the frozen tundra outside the tent. She hopped up and chopped through the thick rope tied to a metal spike. She ran around the tent and cut three more ropes and the entire structure collapsed before anyone could get out. The people on the inside wrestled with the linen as the stunned guards outside finally started to chase Leimur. The guards' armor was much heavier than hers, so she ran fast up a slight hill. She looked off to the left and saw the scribe who had betrayed her. To the right was the prisoners' pen, made of oak. Tied to a post next to the pen was a black destrier.

She sprinted for the horse and saw the wooden lock on the door of the mobile prison. In a final act of rebellion, she swung down with her axe and shattered the wood and the prisoners started to rush out. She jumped up into the saddle that felt designed for a large man and grabbed the long reins. She took another swing of the axe right next to the horse's face to cut the leather straps loose. A huge commotion started close behind her with guards screaming and yelling to get horses to capture the queen. She heeled the horse and took off north. She rode and rode until she felt safe. After galloping for at least twenty minutes, she turned around and the emptiness of the forest had never looked so sweet. The early dusk had helped to hide her in the drab and dark woods. She had little idea about where she was, but she found a stream for her horse to rest and drink. She got down and held the shortened reins as she tried to figure out exactly where to go. She hoped the civil unrest in Burkeville hadn't been settled and she could hide out there to devise a plan. She heard a rustling of leaves behind her and jerked her head around. Nothing appeared.

The dull forest, full of shades of brown highlighted by the pearly moon's glow, was completely still. Leimur wasn't worried about eating but knew she would have to feed the horse at some point. She checked the saddlebags, but they were all empty. She heard more rustling at the top of the hill but when she looked closely, there was nothing. Suddenly, a horse's face broke over the horizon and Leimur panicked. She put her left foot in the stirrup and swung her right over the saddle and heeled the horse before even sitting down.

She heard a familiar voice cry out, "My Queen, my Queen. I come in peace, my Queen."

She looked back to see Captain Salina slowly moving downhill on horseback. The Queen pulled back on the reins for a moment and turned around.

Could this be a trap? She wasn't in the meeting. Was there a reason? Leimur waited as the Captain moved leisurely across the forest to meet her at the stream. The Queen kept expecting a heavy onslaught of cavalry to come thundering down the hill and looked back and forth as she listened to the Captain, "I couldn't take part in it. My loyalty still lies with you."

The former queen was touched and responded, "Thank you. I believe you are the only one. Do you know where we are?"

Her trusted knight answered, "I do, your highness. We have two choices. We can go northwest and try to escape back to Goldenfield where you can rally support to your cause. Another direction we can go is south to try to free your brothers from the dungeons of the King's Castle. Either way we are two women versus two kingdoms that both want us dead. I believe we would be safest in Goldenfield."

Leimur Leluc looked at Captain Salina with a slight smile and said, "You're absolutely right, heading to Goldenfield is our safest option. Which way is south?"

JON

Jon and Camelle paced back and forth in their bedroom as the argument continued.

She said, "Maybe your father's prophecy won't come true. Maybe you will live to watch your father and all your sons die. How could you even live like that?"

Jon exhaled audibly before he said, "Do you really think I am alive right now? I have a shattered heart and while some of it is coming back together, I'll never be the same unless our entire family returns. We will get Ruxin back soon enough and Krys will come right behind him."

Camelle wouldn't accept his promise and berated her husband. "Krys should already be here and Ruxin should have never been in harm's way. I knew everything was too good to be true when we were basically given this castle. Why wouldn't someone defend their own castle, I asked myself."

Jon didn't waste his breath trying to explain to her that he had ordered Ruxin to stay behind the protectionary wall several times. He knew she wouldn't believe him. His daughter still blamed him too, and he realized being king didn't carry the glamor of all the old stories. He had anticipated some rainy days but a constant hailstorm since the coronation was getting tiresome.

Jon tried to quell his wife's fears. "We were separated once and we came back together, remember?"

Camelle stared at him with fire in her eyes and replied, "Ah, I do remember.

I remember lying in our bed in Riverfront and you said, 'I will never let our family be torn apart again' and here we are, again." She screamed, "Here we are again."

The noise startled the baby and he started crying on the bed. The King walked over and picked up his son. He cupped his hand around the back of the baby's head and pulled him close to his chest. Jon felt a smile coming on until Camelle pointed to a window and interrupted her husband.

She said sarcastically, "Are you sure you don't want to throw him out that window? Just get it over with now before we become attached to the boy."

Jon's anger didn't have time to develop as a heavy rap shook the door. Jon handed the baby to Camelle, checked for his sword and walked over to the source of the loud thuds.

"Who goes there?" Jon asked without opening the looking slot.

"Lord Bryan Caughleigh, your highness. There are pressing matters that require your attention. The council has requested your presence before you go back out to battle. They are in the meeting chamber, your highness."

Jon yelled, "Be right there."

He put the mid-morning argument on hold and followed the guards to his meeting room. The entire council sat around the circular oak table. They stood and bowed to the King as Jon walked in.

A serious tenor made Jon nervous as his Falconer led by reporting, "My King, Queen Leimur has been overthrown."

Jon was somewhat stunned. "Really, that didn't take very long. Perhaps I picked the wrong time to be a monarch? This isn't good at all. Now the two Princes of Goldenfield have no value. That was going to be the trade to get my son back. Well, that isn't going to happen now. Even twelve hundred prisoners won't equal a Prince. What…what happened?"

Kelvyn Harros said, "Lost the support of her army. General Laslo Rigby will now serve as king. The new regime has already stated that the crown will not be passed down a family line, yet rest upon the head of the strongest person in the realm. So yes, it would appear that they have no need to get the Princes back unless to kill them."

Jon shook his head. "My son is as good as dead. We need to get in contact with this new King and see what it will take to get Ruxin and Torvald back."

Lord Hydell opined, "I'm rather certain we have other resources of interest and great value to them. We will be able to strike a deal to facilitate the return of Ruxin."

The Falconer told everyone, "Apparently, when they informed the former Queen of Goldenfield that she had been relieved, she crafted a daring escape and her whereabouts are currently unknown. Best thing she could do is run back to Goldenfield. She'd be quite stupid to stay in Donegal with no support."

Jon said, "I don't care about her and neither should you. She's as much a threat to us now as Tersen Wamhoff is. They have my sons. That should be our only focus. We will find the former queen at some point, I can assure you that."

Lord Enric said, "I want to let you know that we have sent King Rigby letters to gauge his interest in coin or weapons. We felt appealing to a former general with a few new weapons was a wise move. Word should arrive back in a few days. A few other matters have come to light, your highness. High Lord Ichibod Ellsworth has been killed."

Jon asked, "How did that happen?"

Count Silzeus responded as he twisted his long mustache. "Word came in that he went for a midnight ride in his sleeping attire and returned without his head. I thought this may discourage his family and urge them to turn around and go back to Lightview but they still camp right outside our new wall. They have elephants stomping around and everything."

Jon replied, "I think I have a plan to make sure they never get past that wall. I suppose they are hanging onto Elisa Burke Wamhoff or whatever name she goes by now and her stretch of a claim. Ali-Varis is dead and King Ali-Stanley is well removed from the line. It seems like they are too stupid and stubborn to realize their best action is to leave. They aren't going to make it past the double wall, and even if they get lucky somehow, we'll have them trapped between both walls. They cannot win and hopefully they will come to that reality and just submit. I never fought alongside Ichibod, but I heard he was a good leader. Who will take charge now, Brehan?"

Lord Rance Perry said, "It appears as though his son from the King's Guard, Anderley, will lead their attack. Noted as a fine swordsman but he's never led an army into battle during winter. Best of heavenly luck with that."

Errol Swansmore laughed as he talked and had to stop several times to collect himself. "I hope they don't have silly thoughts of a siege, hah, that's laughable just to say out loud. We've got a better chance of eating so much that our bellies blow out before we would ever starve. The weather will start to drop and after they haven't felt their toes in a fortnight, every last one of them will go crawling back to that shitty piece of land that should be pushed out to sea."

Lord Enric Plast talked in a somber tone, "We also have word from up north, your majesty. The Wamhoffs have upped and left Elkridge. There were reports of a duel involving a barbarian from Histomanji and The Man with the Golden Sword that ended with the foreigner leaving in two pieces. The Wamhoffs accused the bastard of cheating and using magic or witchcraft but they ultimately packed up and left. Krys got on one of the boats. Our spy said he watched them sail away and disappear out to sea."

Jon immediately insinuated, "Who's to say they won't try to invade Fox Chapel?"

Lord Errol answered, "They could try and I hope they would. They might even make it ashore but we would finally stomp out the Wamhoff threat once and for all and bring Krys home. We've been told their fleet only totals twenty-four ships now. If they couldn't come through an unoccupied Elkridge, they have no chance making it through Fox Chapel. It's time all these upstarts come to understand they simply cannot win. Look at what happened with Goldenfield. Nobody is going to take this kingdom from you, my King."

The threats to upend the King were shrinking, but so were the hopes of seeing both of his sons alive again. He planned to avoid Camelle because he didn't want to tell her about these proceedings. He needed to get back out east. He didn't hesitate about a King's responsibility to be present on the field of battle. That duty would always be upheld by Jon Colbert. He hated to leave on a bad note with his wife, but he was avoiding a gigantic fight that would only make him feel worse than he already did.

He thought about his life one year ago. The entire family had seemed blissful as he envisioned a big supper with everyone. He remembered how he and Camelle had never really fought until they reached the Capitol and now that's all they ever did.

Maybe Camelle was right. Maybe I should have stayed in Mattingly and been content being a duke. Now, it's one malady after another. I can't think of one good thing except for Mariah's wedding which was interrupted by a near defeat at the hands of the Warrior Queen. Now, all I do is fight with my wife until my baby starts to cry. I thought all the problems would melt away once that crown hit my head but they've only intensified.

His mind drifted as the meeting carried on and he wondered about his sons again. He wanted to give in to Camelle's demands and abandon the kingdom to get back his sons.

A-MARIAH

Mariah sat in the rectory and prayed for Torvald and her brothers. Her mother, Haley, Lucille and Deydranna sat on the bench with her. The stained glass windows appeared dull today as the pale sunrays barely poked through the thick clouds outside. Nothing looked as bright as it should anymore to Mariah. Again, she found herself arguing with the Gods as to why they would help her find a perfect mate and take him away so soon. Mariah knew that here had been reports that Torvald and Ruxin were alive as prisoners of Goldenfield but she wasn't going to hold out hope for a safe return. In her mind, Jon had been making excuses about getting her brothers and husband home. Even the story concerning Krys' return seemed to change on a daily basis. She tried to prepare herself emotionally for the harsh reality that she might never see her husband or brothers again.

Mariah questioned the motives of the Gods and her soul was lost without Torvald. When all else had crumbled and disappeared, Torvald was everything to her. *He saved my life and I brought him here to be killed. We should have just stayed in Riverfront. We would still be together if my father hadn't got so greedy. He had to be king.*

Her desperate mind kept swirling around with incomplete thoughts jumping in and out. Mariah opened her eyes to see the other crying women looking at her.

"Should we get back to the Princess Hall now?" Haley asked, sobbing.

Mariah nodded and remembered the phrase that time healed all wounds, but the shared pain among the ladies seemed to intensify as the days passed. The news that the men weren't dead only momentarily buoyed their spirits before they went back to worrying. They had received news of Queen Leimur's overthrow, which muddied the once-clean waters. The only constant that remained was crying and blaming her father for everything.

The ladies got up and moved into the warmer Princess Hall with most of the Colbert family filling the seats and benches. The somber tone in the room matched the mood of the arriving ladies who sat at a round table. The women could sit in silence for hours. All words of encouragement or hope had already been exhausted and they mostly tended to pray in silence. Dinner would be served soon and Mariah's stomach told her that she wouldn't be eating again today. Ever since she had gone with Orian to bless the men on the battlefield, food had become vile to her. Every bite made her flash back to the gruesome bodies and turning over dead men in fear that one might be Torvald or Ruxin. The White Raven had warned her that she might want to stay away, but Mariah had insisted she attend. The sights and smells made her resent her father even more and blame him further for everything. She hadn't spoken to him since she had yelled at him after the battle.

Mariah tended to lash out at others when she felt hurt and angry and right now her father bore the brunt of the abuse. Mariah saw Deydranna get up and scurry out of the room. About a minute later, the hand maid came rushing back across the hall toward the Princess.

She approached the ladies and could barely contain herself as she said, "Princess Mariah, your highness and ladies, follow me, please."

Mariah didn't know what to expect as she followed the pregnant servant up two floors and down a hall to a huge window. She pointed to two people near the front entrance of the main castle. One man pushed another along the frost-tipped green grass. She looked closer and saw her husband and brother, bruised and battered. The ladies hustled down to the main gate to greet the men. Her heart bounced up and down in her chest as they descended another stairwell. Her mind couldn't focus on a single thought and excitement coursed through her entire body. She looked over at Lucille, who sported a wide grin, and tried to keep up with the determined pace of the

Duchess. The men stumbled through the rising portcullis and Mariah ran up and wrapped her arms around her husband. She lost herself in his body and looked over at Ruxin.

Her brother's head looked misshapen and lumpy with clotted, dried blood clumping his hair together and staining his ears. His face was filthy with having been ground in dirt and his wide-open eyes stared blankly at the chandelier.

The look scared Mariah, and Torvald whispered in her ear, "There is a problem with your brother."

She pulled back and saw Haley try to hug Ruxin but he just stood there with his arms at his sides, emotionless. The Colbert boy was being barraged with questions from Camelle and Haley, but he just looked around the room in a daze. He looked completely lost inside his own home. He acted as if he couldn't hear anyone's words.

Count Sproul moved in and said, "Perhaps Count Silzeus and I should take a look at the boy."

Camelle responded, "Thank you, yes. Please bring back my son."

Camelle and Haley followed the counts and Ruxin as Mariah turned to Torvald and asked, "What happened?"

Torvald took a deep breath and said, "It was bad. We almost didn't make it out alive. I thought she'd killed your brother."

Mariah interjected, "She?"

He continued, "Yes, the Queen of Goldenfield. I thought she had bashed his skull straight in with those war axes of hers. She did kill J. Everson, Sir Bastion and perhaps, Chopkins."

Mariah shook her head quickly and said, "No. Chopkins returned soon after the fight."

A look of slight relief came over her husband's face, and he said, "Good for him. He should have never been in the middle of that mess. I told him to stay behind the wall. After almost being crushed to death, we were captured by a unit of Goldenfield soldiers. They marched us back to their camp and locked us in a wooden pen. They were going to take us back to Goldenfield to ransom us back to you until that one day."

Mariah cut in again, "What day?"

Torvald smiled and continued, "Just a day that seemed like any other. Sun in the sky with the clouds, but this day started to feel different around mid-morning. The commotion broke out sometime in the afternoon. I saw the Queen of Goldenfield running from her guards. She was coming straight toward our pen."

Mariah burst in again, "Oh, I wish you had killed her." It was unlike Mariah to be so vengeful.

Torvald went on with the story. "She is actually the one who busted open the lock on the wooden pen. After every last guard chased after her, the rest of us prisoners ran out of the open door and scattered in different directions. I grabbed your brother and dragged him back here. He didn't say a single word the entire time."

Mariah hugged her husband again and whispered in his ear, "Thank you so much for saving my brother and bringing him back. I hope he will be alright. Oh Gods, I love you so much."

She got up on her toes and kissed his dirty lips that still felt perfect to her. She smiled for the first time in weeks and said, "We should probably get you cleaned up."

As they turned in the foyer of the castle, Lucille appeared a few feet in front of the couple. Torvald stepped away from his bride to give his mother an emotional hug.

Mariah overheard him ask about his father and Lucille replied, "He is still out east. He couldn't accept that you were gone and now he doesn't have to."

The two held the embrace as they slowly spun around. Mariah saw the relief in Lucille's smile; her sparkling eyes were filled with tears of joy and as they spun around again, a strange sight caught her vision. She saw liquid coming from her husband's eyes. She had never seen him cry before and even after they stopped rotating, Torvald held his mother tight for several minutes and told her that he loved her several times. Mariah could easily overhear him and her tears started to flow again. After they separated, Torvald quickly wiped off his cheeks and looked at Mariah with a genuine smile. Lucille and Mariah escorted Torvald back to his quarters so he could be scrubbed clean.

As the ladies left, one of his room servants passed by with the soap and Mariah smelled orange blossoms.

Lucille lightly patted her on the back as they walked and exclaimed, "What a wonderful day this is turning into."

Mariah replied, "I couldn't agree more but it would be much better if the counts could help Ruxin. Should we go check on my brother now?"

Lucille answered, "Of course. I hope they are able to fix the young man."

Mariah said, "I only know what I saw earlier was very scary and that wasn't my real brother."

They entered Count Silzeus' room and saw Ruxin, Camelle, Haley and the two counts.

Count Sproul asked, "Can you write your name, Ruxin?"

The count dipped a quill in some ink and extended it to Ruxin who sat at a small table with parchment laid down in front of him. Ruxin grabbed the quill and kept licking the tip before Haley could wrestle the pheasant feather from his strong hand.

Count Silzeus looked at his contemporary and said, "I've never seen anything like this before. It's almost as if he's a deaf mute."

Count Sproul added, "I've seen some cases that have had a similarity or two but never all these factors at one time."

A distraught Camelle asked, "So that's it? There's nothing you can do?"

Count Silzeus looked at the Queen and said, "Your highness, this is just an assessment. We will need to convene for several days to decide what course of treatment is best for the lad."

Camelle needed to know, "How can you decide upon treatment if you both just agreed that you've never seen anything like this?"

Count Sproul interjected, "My Queen, I've cured ailments that had never been seen before several times during my tenure in your castle. Have faith in the Seven and put your son in all your prayers."

Camelle scoffed, "That's it, huh? Put my faith and hopes into more empty prayers. Look where all the prayers have gotten me."

Mariah rushed over to her mother as Camelle went on, "My family has been destroyed and yet I pray and pray and pray. For what, more destruction?"

Mariah squeezed her mother from behind and softly spoke into her ear, "These men are going to do everything they can to help Ruxin return to normal. Many matters concerning our family could have gone much, much worse. The Gods returned me back to you. They will bring Ruxin back eventually."

Count Sproul recommended, "Let's get the boy cleaned up and into some of his clothes. Perhaps that will spur some memories and trigger some words to flow from his mouth."

Everyone went their separate ways and Mariah went back to her quarters. She passed Torvald's room servant again as he was leaving. She went inside and shut the door behind her. She looked across the expansive room at her husband in a long linen robe with wet hair. He was hugging a sobbing Chopkins Haddock and neither man noticed Mariah entered the room.

The portly young man spoke through his tears, "I'm so sorry. I should have come back instead of running away. I'm such a coward."

Torvald slapped him on the back as he spoke, "Are you kidding me? Chopkins, look at me." The shorter man used his long sleeve to wipe away the moisture from around his eyes as he peered up at Torvald. Her husband said, "You saved Ruxin's life. He'd be dead and probably so would I if you hadn't hit the Queen with that pike. You are a hero and you would have died if you had stayed and tried to fight her, just like J. Everson and Sir Bastion. You were extremely brave on the field of battle and you should be proud of yourself. We are all proud of you and your actions." He stepped back and patted Chopkins' moist, chubby cheek with his right hand and Mariah started to get emotional. *I have the perfect husband.*

Two days later, Ruxin's condition still hadn't improved and Mariah went to see the High Holy Leader. She left the castle and crossed the bridge to get to the Walk of Kings. She continued down the cobbled path and to her left, men standing on platforms were whitewashing the outside of the House of Eternal Light. They had almost completely covered the elaborate paintings of the Gods. Mariah walked inside and noticed most of the interior decorations had been stripped. Only a simple oak altar remained in the humbly furnished open room. The dimly lit area needed more torches to increase visibility in

Mariah's opinion. She found the White Raven sitting on the floor with poor citizens all around him. He noticed Mariah and excused himself from the parishioners.

She went and helped pull Orian to his feet as he said, "I thank you greatly. I just don't have the same jump as I did twenty years ago." The old man laughed. This was the first time she had heard him even chuckle.

Mariah said, "I think it is I who needs to thank you. I appreciate how understanding you were in my time of need."

She caught The Raven of Light staring at two women in light, nearly see-through robes. He broke the concentrated look by shaking his head and whipping his left shoulder.

He said, "Sin needs purged." He looked at her again and told her, "I help people who are in need. I generally focus on the poor and desolate, this is known. However, I seek out anyone who may require my efforts. I was just about to go to the cells and pray for our prisoners if you would like to join?"

Mariah replied, "Certainly."

She helped the older man as he struggled to get down the stairs and he squeezed her forearm harder with each descending step. They got to the bottom and he released his death grip as they walked slowly down the narrow hall toward the prisoner cells. Mariah recognized a young man in the cell to her left.

She pointed at the man in the cell and said to Orian, "What is Neron Wamhoff doing here? He was cleared of his charges in agreement that he would leave the kingdom."

The White Raven calmly retorted, "It appears he had no intention of leaving the kingdom. We detained him right here in our Capitol."

Neron apparently overheard the conversation and screamed in a hoarse voice, "I didn't have a chance to leave. They apprehended me the day I was released from the dungeons. I told you I needed some guards to help me get out of the realm."

Orian spoke softly, "Unfortunately, this one has a long reputation of willful sin repetition. Accused by one or two, we raise our brow. Accused by more, that's a field to plough. He is set to stand trial unless he first admits to his crimes against the Gods. The Seven will save him if he is innocent."

Mariah demanded to know, "Who is overseeing the trial?"

Orian Vangor licked his lips with a white-spotted tongue and said, "The brothers and sisters of the Faith will carry out the will of the Gods."

Mariah argued, "So the same people that have accused him, will now decide his guilt? Hasn't the verdict already been decided?"

The White Raven responded, "I'm not sure you understand the wide range of accusations levied against this devious young man. Several dozen eyewitness accounts are no coincidence. He always reserves the option to carry out the truth and admit to his plethora of sins."

Mariah asked, "And what happens if he does admit to those accusations?"

The new leader of the Faith casually answered, "He will be put to death with a clean soul and conscience to enter the tests of heaven."

Mariah posed the question, "And if he is found guilty in a trial?"

The High Holy Leader informed her, "He will die with a dirty soul and likely plunge down into the depths of the hells."

Mariah was flabbergasted and wondered, "Well then why don't you just kill him right here? Do you even hear how ridiculous you sound right now? He's already paid for his sins and wrongdoings. He's been pardoned by the King."

Orian's dull eyes lit up in the swaying torchlight as he said, "That is terrific for him, but the King has granted me supreme authority to punish those who denounce the Words of the Gods and knowingly commit sin time and again when we know it to be wrong. He has a long record of charges and he must come to understand that the Gods see everything. Everything."

Mariah shook her head in disgust and disbelief. She said, "I believe I need to talk to my father about this. Why should I grant people mercy if you are going to punish them cruelly for the same crimes?"

The old man looked at her with a wry smile and spoke in almost a laugh, "I hope you aren't trying to threaten me with your father. I answer to a higher calling than our King. If I am to be struck down as we stand here now, I will die with a clean soul, so death doesn't scare me in the least. Now a princess is viewed as the highest station in the eyes of the citizens of the realm. But she will always be of lower status than a sworn brother or sister in the eyes of the

Gods. Only they have the true authority to excuse sin in our people."

Mariah thought for a few moments before she said, "Then maybe I need to be sworn in as a Sister of the Faith."

Orian warned her with a smile, "You would first have to denounce your title of Princess of Donegal as all of the Gods' creatures are equal. A sister of the Faith also carries the responsibility to travel and spread the word of the Gods."

She gave a sharp grin back and replied, "Yes, well, perhaps we can revisit the conversation of touring Fox Chapel to lift the spirit of our realm."

THE MAN WITH THE GOLDEN SWORD

The Man sat at his oak table and struggled to flip the page of a book with the back of his hand. He had lost two fingers and his palms had been shredded by Cobra during the duel.

Gamelda sat across from him and counseled, "We need to leave now."

The Man looked embarrassed as he spoke, "I can't hold the reins of a horse to ride. I'm a king. I can't ride in a coach or wagon. A true leader rides with his men. Why don't you have your spirit friends heal my hands?"

She looked at him with sympathy. "I don't have any friends that do that, I'm afraid. You could walk for the first few days, if you must, until your hands heal. You cannot stay here or it's the end of days for you."

He gave her a sharp look and asked, "For us, don't you mean?"

Gamelda shook her head and said, "It can only be us if you take my advice. I don't warn someone endlessly only to walk directly into a fire with them. My advice has been given. Use it, ignore it, do what you wish."

He responded, "I can't even walk among my men now, thanks to you. The men know their leader couldn't even beat a barbarian in single combat. Everyone knows what you did back there."

Gamelda told him, "I didn't do anything. That man was smitten by the Gods."

The Man looked down and shook his head, "Even I know that's a lie. I couldn't beat a barbarian in battle. How can I be a king?"

Gamelda tried to make him feel better by saying, "I told you he used queer weapons and had a fighting style you had never seen before. Now that you've seen his attack, you will never lose to a Histoman warrior again."

The Man understood that Gamelda had saved his life in the duel, but now his men knew that Gamelda dabbled in the spirit world. The Man knew that the inevitable rumors had been going around about Gamelda's powers. Most men didn't understand magic and felt it was an instrument of the demons. People called it black or dark magic. The Man had become extremely depressed since the duel. The fact that he had needed help from an outside source really irked him. He had never come close to losing a one-on-one battle, but his opponent had almost defeated him easily. The respect of his men was of utmost importance to him. He could barely look anyone in the eyes anymore. The Man had never been embarrassed about his skills before and had trouble dealing with the emotion. Closing the heavy book caused sharp pain to shoot up his hands all the way to his shoulders. He got up and went to a meeting with his war council without saying goodbye to Gamelda.

There weren't any real matters to discuss and everyone was antsy to leave. A small group of veteran warriors had forged ahead to blaze the trail for the rest of the men. The majority of the remaining men were stationed near the northern gates, waiting to leave.

Tucker announced, "My king, I have some good news and bad news. I'll start with the bad. All the riches we had stored in the mountain tunnel are gone. We assume the Wamhoffs found and stole the gold. Interestingly enough though, they returned the wooden fox and we checked the inside and the riches were still stuffed in there. It was sitting right outside the southern gates, so I had the men bring it inside and we will empty the fox deep into the night to avoid drawing unnecessary attention."

The Man wondered aloud, "Why would they return that gold? They would need it too."

Tucker said, "Maybe they couldn't fit it all on their decimated fleet of floating timber. They picked the mountain tunnel clean without leaving a single gold round."

The Man's mind raced as he said, "That gold might not have been essential for victory, but the path becomes more difficult with less resources."

Terry spoke up, "With all the men up north, we shouldn't have any trouble unloading that wooden fox. Then we can bring the coin back and burn that ugly fox." Terry laughed but no one joined him.

The meeting ended and The Man asked Terry and Tucker to stay and invited Mad Dog, who was standing guard, to have a seat with them.

The Man still only drank wine out of fear of the tainted water and poured goblets for the other men. He said, "We are going to leave tomorrow, men. I don't care if my hands are raw meat by the time we reach the Capitol. We leave tomorrow. There will be much madness along the way and things will get rather hectic. I just want you to know I won't forget all of you in the end. You will be taken care of as promised. And who knows, if the Gods have any mercy on their bastards, we'll all make it to the King's Castle no worse for wear."

Terry looked at The Man with a smile and said, "They haven't had much mercy up to now, but maybe the tides will turn."

A-EMILIA

The former queen felt like she was going to pass out again. The warm, thick air made it difficult to breathe. She had been sitting on top of the jewels inside the wooden fox for days. They had crafted hidden doors to stuff her in. She could only communicate in whispers with Ali-Samuel, who had been packed into the treasure fox too. He had instructed her to keep quiet or they were sure to be caught. Emilia could only see the faint glimmer of the precious jewels. She had been crammed into the fox two days ago and had already grown tired of the dwindling store of assorted dried meats and fruits. The thought of relieving herself hadn't occurred until nature called and she realized that she could barely move. Her pants had absorbed most of the urine and she prayed it wouldn't drip down through the money and expose them. The awful smells had become intensified in the stale air. She had thrown up several times already and felt the dreaded feeling again. She sipped on a skin of wine and impatiently waited to get out of this uncomfortable work of carpentry.

She hadn't heard any sounds outside for several hours. With winter rapidly approaching, there weren't any buzzing bugs and the silence was spooky. Emilia hadn't been able to sleep even though she lay flat out on top of the treasure. She would nod off occasionally but the rank smell and heavy air always woke her up. She had lost consciousness several times and thought she was about to die. The air holes that the carpenters had carved didn't do much to help her.

"Sam," she called. No one answered. She said, "Sam, you awake?" Silence answered her.

Why won't he answer me? I know I never call him Sam, but I need to keep the words to a minimum. I know he can't sleep in this thing either. He won't even tell me to mind my tongue this time. I hope he hasn't fallen short of air. If so, I am as good as dead.

She didn't hear anything until the creaking of wood sounded behind her, indicating someone was opening the exterior door of the fox. She could barely breathe in anticipation of who was waiting on the outside. Someone grabbed her feet and pulled the petite woman out of the fox. *This better be Ali-Samuel or both of us are dead.*

She glided over the gold and jewels trying to make the least amount of sound possible. She felt hands on her hips, then ribs as the former queen landed on Elkridge soil. She staggered around to secure her footing and saw Ali-Samuel signaling to her to be quiet. He pulled his sword from a secret compartment on the wooden fox and pushed Emilia down. She crouched down and he hovered over her and surveyed the guard situation. The wooden fox sat about one hundred feet inside the main southern gate. The couple had to get to the southern gate, unhinge the latch and let the Histoman inside.

Emilia couldn't see anyone, but Ali-Samuel gripped her really hard above the elbow and dragged her toward the gate. She only saw three men at the main gate and they all had their backs turned. Ali-Samuel increased the speed and they arrived behind the guards quickly. One man didn't even have a chance to unsheathe his sword. The guards only wore layers of boiled leather, which proved no match for Ali-Samuel's sword. He had little trouble defeating the other two men and ran for the lock.

Emilia scurried behind as she saw Ali-Samuel struggling to get the latch high enough to unlock the gates. He shoved his shoulder under the lock and pushed up on the huge wooded latch but his height prevented his shoulder from getting it high enough. She heard yelling coming from behind them and turned to see thirty guards approaching from the top of the hill. She realized they didn't have much time and even up on his toes, Ali-Samuel couldn't unlock the door. The former queen knew they were about to die.

She ran over and dove on the ground in front of Ali-Samuel. She wedged herself under his feet and he pushed down on the right side of her back, giving him the necessary height to push the lock up. She felt something crack and immense pain followed as Ali-Samuel quickly jumped off of her, grabbed her by the shoulder and pulled her up to avoid being stomped on. The massive doors swung open and an entire army of screaming Histoman warriors began to pour in. They met a small amount of resistance on the way in and Emilia was caught right in the middle of everything.

Ali-Samuel shoved her into Sir Ralph's hands, who pushed through the oncoming horde to guide Emilia to one of the guard towers. They rushed up the steps of the abandoned tower and took refuge on the top level. There were several cutout squares for archers but Sir Ralph instructed her to stay away from them to avoid the unlikely chance of an arrow coming in. This was the first battle she had experienced. The grunting sounds of men in battle mixed with the sullen songs of hard metal and her ears stung as she heard the resulting screams of desperate, dying men.

Sir Ralph moved to an opening and quickly turned and peeked out. Emilia saw a slight smile form on his profile. She decided to peer out for just a moment, and looked over Sir Ralph's shoulder. Emilia stared at the Histoman army destroying the enemy. Numerous large fires raged to show that her side heavily outnumbered the opponents. More Histoman were still pouring through the open gates and Emilia became confident of victory. She looked to the left and found Ali-Samuel and Ali-Steven fighting back to back. To their right, the Histoman warrior, Broken Leaf, was methodically killing over a dozen men who kept rushed up to him in a steady stream only to meet their doom. The sounds played havoc on her ears and the malodor started to affect her stomach, so she ducked back down to safety. She was also experiencing great pain and having trouble breathing. She lightly poked her ribs to gauge the severity of the injury.

B-THE MAN

A thumping shook the door of The Man's quarters. He shouted, "Go away or I will kill you."

Thunder cracked just as the person tried to speak and The Man hoped that would make them go away. Another powerful pounding of wood precipitated The Man out of bed.

He walked briskly to the door, muttering to himself, "We leave tomorrow, but it looks like someone wants to die today." He swung open the heavy door and Tucker stood outside.

Before The Man could say anything, Tucker spoke rapidly, "Southern gates, southern gates have been breached. We need your help. I need to tell everyone." Tucker ran away and The Man went back inside, cussing under his breath.

Suddenly, he realized that there was an opportunity to prove himself to the men. This would be the perfect situation.

Gamelda casually said to him, "That is your call to death. I don't want to know the fool who answers that call."

He returned, "This is more than likely just a small uprising that needs the boot of a king to squash it. This isn't even a battle, I'm sure."

The Man with the Golden Sword wasn't going to take the time to get fitted in armor so he put on a tight long sleeved leather vest and matching sparring pants.

Gamelda warned him, "You should just fall on your sword right now, right here. Blind death will be just for a man who refuses to see."

The Man stopped for a moment and asked, "What does that even mean?"

Gamelda shook her head and said, "You damn fool. I can see the future. You cannot. If you ignore my counsel, I will not save you again."

Lightning lit up the windows and an increasing rain battered the outside of the castle.

"Come now, let's go get our horses," said The Man.

She looked at him fondly and said pleadingly, "I'm not coming with you the same as I am not going to commit suicide. I cannot save you again. Save yourself. If this is just a small uprising, then stay here. Let your men take care of the small problem."

The Man knew he had to prove to himself that he was still worth a damn. He said, "The men need to see their leader in battle to keep the morale high. This is more for show than substance. Some hooligans probably snuck inside the gates and we need to go break some skulls. If you want to stay, fine, I'll return shortly."

"Well, my king, it certainly was nice knowing you," Gamelda said as she started to gather her belongings.

The Man shook his head and yelled, "Stop with all this. Typical woman being dramatic, that's all this is."

Gamelda stopped stuffing a shoulder bag and stared at him. "Typical stupid man. Going off to die in a silly battle."

The Man needed to leave but he asked his lover, "And where do you think you are going?"

She smiled and said, "Wherever I please. I am a free woman with many friends in many places."

The Man tried to mock her, "What, your spirit friends?"

She shook her head and responded, "No, my human friends. Intelligent ones that heed my advice."

The Man said, "This is pointless. You better be here when I get back." He walked over and kissed her.

Gamelda gazed at The Man with the Golden Sword as he left the room. His horse was waiting for him just outside the castle, and the stable boy handed him the reins. He jumped on and raced toward the southern gates despite the intense, throbbing pain in his hands. *Who could have breached the gates? The Hosavarts are the only family that could pose a threat down there. We should be able to crush this in less than an hour.*

As The Man drew closer to the action, he realized the situation was much worse than he had anticipated. He arrived with about five hundred men and more behind them, but he knew this would be a tough battle. His overmatched fighters were being butchered by near naked barbarians. The Histoman were using their curved swords to carve up his honorable warriors. The Man started to circle around on his horse and stroke his long sword down on the unprotected Histoman. He kept looking for enemy cavalry as he sliced through the unsuspecting enemy. He could barely hold onto his sword and reins but he pressed on. The fires and flashes of lightning helped illuminate the scattered battlefield and The Man barely noticed that the rain had picked up. He tried to ignore the intense pain in the palms of his hands as the wounds reopened and soaked his gloves in blood.

The Man eliminated about twenty-five opponents as he worked his way into the thicker part of the battle and toward the open southern gates. A sword blade dug into his horse's front leg and The Man flew down onto his left shoulder. He dropped his sword, but a huge flash of lightning helped The Man locate his glinting golden sword immediately. He snatched it up by the grip and raised his head to a defendable level on the field. Throbbing agony now concentrated in his left shoulder as his arm hung listlessly at his side.

A much older man in an open helm with a scar running across his whole face came at The Man and nicked his injured shoulder with the point of his blade. The Man countered with a stroke across the older man's stomach and watched a spray of blood start from the right side and continue across his belly. A wide silver blade crashed into his golden resistance as someone jumped in to save the old man's life. He looked up to see the person he had been waiting for. Ali-Samuel Wamhoff.

Of course he gets me when I'm severely injured. Two furious swords tangled in the Elkridge night, a final telling of one man's life; the other deemed right in the eyes of the Gods. The Man had forgotten how skilled Ali-Samuel was. His biggest advantages should have been his power and stamina, but both were nullified by his weakened state. Thunder cracked as the two men unleashed their best respective attacks only to accomplish nothing. The Man with the Golden Sword attempted a combination of sword strokes from low to high. Ali-Samuel parried the quick attack and went on the offensive. The Man liked to fight with both hands, but his left one was basically dead. As a result, his right arm had already gone numb. He pressed on as he felt like his sword could be knocked out of his aching hand at any moment. Each of the two men continued a supreme exhibition of swordsmanship without breaking the other's defense. The Man could sense that Ali-Samuel was getting tired as his strokes weren't delivering the same impact as earlier. The Man started to regather his strength as he looked around the battlefield.

He always knew when the opponent was fighting an unwinnable battle. He knew that he was on the wrong side this time. He knew victory was unattainable. Now, he just wanted to get his revenge kill against Ali-Samuel Wamhoff, a former Battle Brother. He noticed that when one Histoman fell dead, two more ran up to take his place. Instead of winning the entire battle, he planned to kill Ali-Samuel and cut his way out through the southern gate. He thought about Gamelda and more power started to surge through his body. The Man relentlessly went after Ali-Samuel with a flurry of overhand strokes. He kept driving his opponent back until the Wamhoff man was on his knees. He kept up with the overhand strikes and planned two more swings and then a reversal of his wrists to sneak his blade in under his opponent's sword.

He went to flip his wrists when a sharp pain shot down his back and he dropped to both knees. He turned around and the old man with the facial scar stood there with a bloody blade and a rotten smile. He felt another driving pain in his chest and heard the distinct laugh of Ali-Samuel Wamhoff. He couldn't see his former battle ally but he remembered that guffaw from when they had slaughtered the men of Goldenfield together. The Man's collapsed face down in the cold mud.

I was going to be the King of Donegal. What about all the prophesies? Gamelda. Why didn't I listen to Gamelda? Why didn't she come and save me? Her bastard king. I was going to be the first bastard king. I was supposed to be king. Ali-Samuel was supposed to leave. Now my brother in arms stabs me when my head is turned. There is no honor anymore.

The last words he heard were, "It's quite a shame when someone cheats in single combat, is it not?"

He heard the laugh again as the cold blade entered again and the world disappeared for The Man with the Golden Sword. His attempt to usurp the throne of Donegal had ended with a final beat of the heart. Ali-Samuel pulled his blade out of King Ali-Stanley Wamhoff's only remaining bastard son and rolled the body into a big fire. The body still clutched the golden sword with a blood dripping hand. The flames swirled around the cold gold blade until the angry fire cracked and a glowing pile of orange embers devoured the weapon and Torryn Beakman, who will be remembered as The Man with the Golden Sword.

C-EMILIA

The former queen looked over at the southern gates for a few moments and the Histoman were still pouring in. She looked back at Ali-Samuel and The Man with the Golden Sword. The Man had fallen on his face and she turned away as Ali-Samuel drove his mostly silver sword blade into the enemy and pulled it out, drenched in crimson. *I knew he could defeat him in single combat. Now their leader is dead. That should end this slaughter.*

Her up-close view of the battle had been exhilarating. The killing became much more bearable as she realized her side was destined to win. More Histoman warriors kept filing in, screaming for some bloody action. She looked up to the stormy sky and saw a bright purple streak rush through the clouds. As she looked back down, she saw that the Histoman had the disorganized opposition surrounded from the north and the south. A smile crossed her face as the enemy started to drop to a knee and surrender.

"I think ith thafe now. We can go down," Sir Ralph told her.

He led the former queen down to ground level. The smells intensified and disturbed Emilia's nose and she felt ready to throw up. Her side rounded up all the prisoners and started to march north. She found Ali-Samuel and his father but her smile quickly faded as she neared the men. She noticed Ali-Steven holding two blood-soaked hands over his abdomen. He had refused to wear armor or mail and only two thin layers of boiled leather couldn't weather the storm of The Man's golden blade. His off-white surcoat had run red and he appeared to be holding the bottom part of the wound in place.

Emilia couldn't stand to see it for another moment. She ran for the southern gates. She got outside and looked around in a panic. She found a few counts and dragged them over to Ali-Steven. She waited nervously as the men checked out the future king. The faces of the attending counts told her that the situation was dire. They needed to get to the Duke's Castle immediately to get proper supplies to sew up the wound. Ali-Samuel flagged down a wagon and in an amazing feat of strength, he carried his much larger father over to the wagon.

Lightning looked like tree roots in the sky Ali-Samuel and the two counts used the added illumination to help the elder Wamhoff into the wagon. Emilia shook the rain off her face and jumped onto a white pony. Everyone surrendered as they moved north. As soon as she started to bounce up and down on the horse, her chest ran short of air again and she felt like someone was constantly squeezing her.

This is exactly how the plan is supposed to go. We pick up more soldiers as we go along. However, if we lose Ali-Steven, I don't know that the Histoman will carry on. I can't believe they would follow Ali-Samuel or me. They hate us. Seven Hells, I don't even know if I want to follow Ali-Samuel anymore. This helps our effort but it's still meaningless if Ali-Steven should die.

Ali-Steven had hatched the plan to stuff her and his son into the wooden fox to open the southern gates. The fleet had sailed away only to return several hours later. They stealthily killed their way to the southern gates. A single blow of a bull horn had signaled to Ali-Samuel that the Histoman were ready outside the gates. She arrived at the castle and waited for the wounded Wamhoff to get there.

The castle workers were all on their knees, begging for mercy. Emilia wanted to calm their fears and tell them that they would be safe, but she couldn't be sure of what Ali-Samuel would do. She hadn't been able to control his streaks of cruelty and only hoped they would stop at some point. Ali-Samuel started to explore the castle and Emilia followed. She tried to ignore the pain but just breathing hurt.

They found a giant bedroom and Ali-Samuel pulled her in and said, "We almost have our dreams in hand now. The Man with the Golden Sword is gone, my father is terribly injured and he probably won't make it. We shall rule as king and queen before too long, my sweet."

Emilia said, "Your father is dying and you are dancing on his grave?"

He stared at Emilia with a look of excitement that faded quickly. "No, I just said he was terribly injured."

She couldn't understand and said, "You don't seem very broken up over the possible death of your father."

Ali-Samuel turned away and responded, "My father has lived much longer than he ever should have. He should have died forty years ago when he was slashed across the face. The man has been a warrior his entire life. Most warriors don't make it close to my father's age. He had his chance and came up just short. Now it's our turn. I feel sorry for the man, but unless I can work miracles, his time might be up. The counts will have their work cut out for them on this one."

For some reason, Emilia was still surprised at his callousness and disregard for sympathy. They went back downstairs as Ali-Steven was being carried in by some of the bigger guards. Four guards took coordinated steps to hustle their leader to a room on the ground floor. Emilia cleared off the wooden table and they laid down Ali-Steven. He finally moved his hands and Emilia gagged and looked away. She wanted to stay in the room for support but her stomach wouldn't allow it. She paced around the outside of the room and cringed as she heard the shrieks of pain coming from one of the strongest men she had ever known.

The counts used an extremely thin metal wire to sew his stomach shut like they were doing needlepoint. After about an hour, the screaming stopped and the counts started to talk to Ali-Samuel.

She went back in as a count said, "I've never done anything like this before, but the procedure seems to have gone well. I cannot say with great certainty that this will heal properly but we have done all we can. He needs rest and lots of it."

Ali-Samuel told the counts, "He will have plenty of rest in the back of a cushioned coach when we leave tomorrow."

One of the counts immediately objected, "No, no, no. He cannot travel until the large gash heals. The constant movement will pull the wound apart again. He must remain stationary."

Ali-Samuel looked to Emilia and commented, "Then he can stay here while we leave and try to catch up later."

Emilia said, "Let's discuss this elsewhere. Gentlemen, thank you so much for your service, it's genuinely appreciated."

The conquerors started flooding into the castle, and were in awe of the construction and furnishings. The Histoman had never seen anything like the statues and paintings that lined the hallways.

Emilia and Ali-Samuel went back to the big bedroom. *Feels good to be back in a castle, even if I can barely breathe and I am in extreme pain. Enough of the tents and pavilions already. Too bad we leave tomorrow if Ali-Samuel should have his say. I'm not sure the Histoman will follow him without Ali-Steven, good luck with that.*

She jumped into the bed in her soiled clothes and planned to relax for a few moments. She fell fast asleep and didn't wake up until sunrise. Ali-Samuel was nowhere to be found and she went downstairs to see Pariah and Princess. Pariah had been crying since Ali-Steven's injury and Emilia tried to comfort her, but nothing seemed to work. They went for a walk around the castle and Princess came along. Winter seemed in a hurry to arrive as a light flurry of flakes fell from the cloudy sky and Princess tried to catch them. The mud beneath hadn't frozen yet and Emilia slipped on some moist leaves. Pariah grabbed and held up her smaller friend. Emilia noticed a plant on the side of the path that still had bright yellow flower buds. She couldn't believe that the petals hadn't fallen from the plant.

"Is poison," Pariah warned her and Princess nodded in agreement even though she didn't understand the common tongue. Pariah added, "Take and make dry and make powder to eat and die."

Hmmm. Who knows when I might have the need for something like this?

She ripped two buds from the dull green stem and shoved them into her carrying pouch. They went back to the castle and heard that Ali-Samuel had reluctantly agreed to wait an extra day before leaving.

DAMIAN

The leader of the demons watched from above as the final three ships broke through the circular tide and moved south. The anomaly had caused him to lose several ships with valuable coldomores, weapons and animals. Copulon flapped his wings slowly as Damian held onto his neck and looked down at his iron fleet. They were finally back on track to reach Gama Traka but the ships would still take several days to arrive.

"Back to Venom Island," screamed Damian and the dragon started to move his wings faster. They reached the ashy isle and Copulon landed with a thud.

Damian carefully got down and went to talk to the highest-ranking coldomores.

With a devious grin, he announced, "We've finally broken the trap. In less than a week we should be crashing the shores of Gama Traka." The mood of the demons spiked as Damian stared at his dragons. He looked around as he spoke to everyone, "We will send a dragon or two out to track the progress of our ships. When they get close to land, we will mount our dragons and unite with our ground force. If we can get our feet on firm land, there will be no defense for the humans."

Most of the demons went to take a brief rest and only Ephesi remained. Damian looked at the man who was like a brother to him and said, "Our time is close. I know your meeting with Travibero was cancelled but when all this is finished, I am going to recommend you be appointed as a Plade."

Ephesi cocked his long, narrow head to the side and asked, "What? Are you certain? I am thoroughly honored but I don't know if I deserve the reward."

Damian put his bony hand on his friend's shoulder and said, "You've been right by my side for hundreds of years. My name is always mentioned when credit is thrown around for building this army but it couldn't have been assembled without your dedicated service. I sent you on dangerous missions to overtake a human's body to gain secret information. I sent you because I didn't want to go myself. I didn't know the after-effects it would cause but I still sent you away. I should have been more concerned with your safety but I thwarted caution to benefit the greater cause, but it was I who sent you away. At the time, I took your dedication and value for granted, but now it is all so clear. I could never defeat the humans on my own, but WE can and will. The information you've obtained over the years has been instrumental in making this moment possible. You were the first to invade the body of the leader of the School of the Learned Warrior and lay the foundation for Hellgan to permanently infest Kazu. That information alone is the only reason we have the confidence to launch this attack. I will not overlook your tasks any longer. I know I shouldn't even think this but if you were to die in this war, I will fight for you to become a Plade. Now if you live, as I plan to do, I will talk to Travibero to make sure the ultimate honor will be waiting when your time comes."

Ephesi stared at his leader and said, "I can do nothing but continue to praise you."

Damian looked at his best friend and reminded him, "You don't have to do anything. You've already done plenty."

Five days later, Damian paced back and forth near the southern end of Venom Island. The coldomores were gathered in a cluster by the dragons. Everybody was restless and ready to attack. Copulon appeared in the sky and the normal wind bursts from the dragon pushed Damian's head back as the winged creature landed close to them.

Copulon bellowed, "Tis time, tis time. The ships are close."

Damian ran over and addressed his followers, "We've been planning this assault for five hundred years. We all know what needs to be done. The earth shall be ours once again."

A unified scream came from the warriors as they got up on their dragons. The dragons waved their wings and prepared to leave. Damian was almost thrown from Copulon's back so he sank his hands under the dragon's scales and into the soft neck flesh. The dragons ascended and moved south. Nervous excitement coursed through Damian's body as he wondered what the humans had constructed as a defense. He assumed he would be able to get an overhead view and understand the humans' plans before they could take effect. Several hours passed and the excitement reached a fever pitch as he spotted the shining fleet from a distance. They appeared to be close to the shoreline, but their progress was being impeded by something. The ships appeared to be at a standstill. He got closer and swooped down for a better view. He noticed several huge objects, just below the emerald waves, pushing his fleet back out to sea.

He rose back up and whispered something to the dragon. Copulon turned around and swooped down toward the ships. Damian held on for dear life as he had never flown at this speed before. They zoomed right next to the ships and dove into the water, feet first. Damian felt the chilly liquid as his dragon wildly flailed his wings. Damian was thrashed around until his dragon started to rise slowly out of the water. Copulon struggled but emerged from the Sea of Green, clutching a green water dragon in his sharp talons. The captured dragon flopped around so mightily it almost threw Damian from his mount. Copulon steadied himself and sank his claws deeper into the bleeding green dragon. They started to reach the streaming clouds and Damian smiled as Copulon released his grip. The green dragon fell like a boulder until a red and a black dragon moved in and simultaneously shot fire from their noses and mouths, completely engulfing the water dragon in flames. The burning body fluttered helplessly through the air before crashing into the sea. The water extinguished the fire, but the dead, charred dragon sank to the bottom of the briny deep. Damian's dragons started to pluck more water dragons from their home and repeat the process of setting them on fire. Damian started to get hungry from the smell of burning dragon flesh and licked his dry lips.

The rest of the water dragons disappeared and the blockade was lifted. His fleet charged ahead, with nothing to stop them from hitting dry land soon.

Damian flew higher in the sky and looked ahead at a sight so sweet he would have blushed if he had the ability. Damian inspected the entire northern shore and couldn't find a single human waiting to defend the earth.

A-SUNNY

The Wamhoff boy was preparing to make another reconnaissance mission as he secured his sword belt. He slid the shining steel blade into the sheath and walked toward the southern door. A group of about thirty students, along with Dioneer and Dragon-Eyes, had assembled to join Sunny and Muriel. He watched Shireez finally pull herself away from her dwarf lover. She slowly backed away and stopped. She looked at Muriel and said, "I suppose you will be staying here with me?"

Muriel looked down at Shireez and just laughed. The six-year-old said, "If the other little girl can go on a rescue mission, I'm pretty confident I can too."

Muriel grabbed the ivory handle of her knife and pulled it from the holder, exposing the blade serration and clipped point design. She inspected the object and ran a finger down the spine and up the belly, stopping just short of the serration.

He looked at the Imp Wizard and wondered if he was truly a wizard. The dwarf had the fiery eyes of a dragon, sure, but Sunny also knew the craft of magic and spirit lending. He wasn't sure he believed all the stories about Dragon-Eyes or even the ones he had told him about his birth. Sunny worried that if magic was his only defense, the little man could be in trouble. How could the spirits be borrowed by two people at the same time? He couldn't imagine magic being useful in a huge battle as he glared at the little man.

Dragon-Eyes gently asked, "Why the disgusted look, friend?"

Sunny was brutally honest and said, "I'm just not sure how much help you can be in this effort."

The dwarf raised his eyebrows and spoke, "Oh really. Shall we put it to task? Why don't you try to attack me?"

Sunny replied calmly, "No, I would never do something like that."

Without warning, he clenched his fist, raised it and went to swing down and stop just short enough to scare the smaller man. However, Sunny was frozen, still as a stone castle, with his right fist raised above his head. He could still form thoughts and hear everyone around him but his body wouldn't move.

The Imp Wizard looked at him with a smug smile and asked, "What seems to be the problem? Why, you are much stronger than I am. You should be able to pulverize me with ease, but for some reason, you cannot." He became more serious and continued, "The spirits, they are stronger in some preferred souls."

Sunny tried to invoke the spirits with mental summoning. He called for strength, invisibility, speed and even tried to reverse the ability to overpower another person. He frantically chanted the words that had always activated the help before.

Nothing worked and he remained frozen in place as the Imp gloated, "I've been underestimated my entire life, so I can understand the reasoning behind such thoughts. The belittling has helped form me into the man you see now. Please move over here for a moment." Dragon-Eyes motioned to a group of students next to Sunny.

Everyone jumped back as Dragon-Eyes filled the vacated space with a flash of flame. The fire stopped and Dragon-Eyes looked back to Sunny and said, "Imagine if you had been standing just a few steps to your left. Oh, the horror it could have caused. Never underestimate someone you don't know. Would you underestimate Muriel? Not me, and I feel sorry for the bloody fools who do because they shall be just that, bloody and foolish."

Muriel blurted out, "I won't feel sorry for those fools." She finished with an awkward chuckle and looked down at the ground.

Dragon-Eyes continued, "Alright now, I am going to release my grip but remember the spirits are stronger within some, and never assume victory will be easy because of the size of your opponent."

The dwarf closed his eyes and his big lips started to move. He didn't say a word but suddenly Sunny stumbled forward. Sunny appreciated the lesson but was embarrassed that it had to happen in front of his fellow students. He jumped back as a loud hammer-like pounding came from behind. He whipped around and saw the door bending inward as the deafening knocks continued.

This could be the demons. We would be trapped with the other exit buried.

Dragon-Eyes carefully moved closer to the door and shouted, "Who goes there?"

A deep dark voice that Sunny recognized sliced through the door, "It's the Army of Undead Kings."

The Imp Wizard looked around and rhetorically asked, "The what of undead who?"

Sunny told the dwarf, "I know them. You will too."

Sunny opened the door and hoped it wasn't a trap by the demons even though it would have been already too late. The sun blazed in and all the students pulled their weapons. After Sunny's eyes had readjusted to the glare, Ali-Ster Wamhoff came into focus.

The former king said, "They're here."

Sunny turned quickly to Muriel and said, "Go ring the bell seven times. Hurry."

The little girl scurried off and the nearby students started to move out the opening. Sunny started pushing students outside as the bell rang for a final time.

Dragon-Eyes walked up to the former King of Donegal and said, "Is that Ali-Ster Wamhoff I see? Looks like you've seen some better days, my king."

The tall man looked down on the dwarf and responded, "Yes, well, I plan to make these my best days, regardless of appearance."

Dioneer went by and out the door as Sunny fought through the outgoing mass to stay inside. A nervous feeling started to form as he wondered how his little sister would handle the situation. She had always acted tough but Sunny already felt the magnitude of the moment. His stomach started to churn until he saw Muriel. She had a wide grin on her face. She didn't look the least bit scared, causing Sunny to relax and focus on the battle at hand.

He turned and followed her outside to be greeted by the sun, high in the sky. The Noble Army of Undead Kings had assembled the instructors and students from the other parts of the School of the Learned Warrior and everyone began to march up to the beach. Sunny noticed a force of Gama Trakans that weren't members of the School and knew Ali-Ster must've convinced the Triumvirate to spare some soldiers. The native citizens led the group with the students of the School just behind, and the former kings brought up the rear. All the units trudged through the sand and Sunny and Muriel tried to catch up with their classmates. As he went to pass his older brother, a cold, blue forearm stopped his progress.

The dead king warned him, "Don't go all the way to the front. Stay near the back until we see what kind of force the demons will bring. You wouldn't listen to the little dwarf but you better listen to your older brother. Don't run out like a foolish hero destined to be feed for the blackbirds."

Sunny moved up a bit despite the warning as they started to get close to the northern beaches. Ali-Ster moved up closer and walked alongside Sunny.

He looked up at Ali-Ster, who said, "Remember what I just said. Stay near the back."

Sunny said, "I know. I understand." When he looked to his left, Muriel had disappeared. He looked at her racing ahead with reckless abandon. Sunny chased after his sister and screamed, "Muriel. Get back here. Stop right now."

He kept following her as she reached the students. He shouted, "Muriel. I know you can hear me, so just stop right now."

She continued weaving in and out of the bigger warriors and moved up to the Gama Trakans. By the time he looked ahead to see the ominous shining steel boats beached along the coast, he was walking on the front line.

If we can get to them as they land, we could cut them down before they even have a chance to set foot on this sand.

He peered at the boats as the bright sunny sky became dark. Sunny's eardrums were almost broken by the most awful series of shrieking sounds he had ever heard. A forceful, uneven wind-blast almost knocked Muriel down as Sunny grabbed the tiny girl and held her up. A sky full of red, purple and black dragons burst through some streaming clouds and descended toward the coastline.

They're going to burn our entire army before they even land. Then the demons can jump down from their boats with ease. We're all going to die.

Sunny looked frantically out at the water and reflected on his short life as he wondered if he would reunite with Ollor. A huge blue dragon's head poked through the water and ran ashore. A long tongue rolled out and stopped right in front of Sunny. He pulled Muriel onto the tongue and held her tight until they were inside the mouth of Dolpho. Several minutes later, the dragon's mouth opened and the tongue came out with the kids. They walked out into the secret lair of the water dragons.

The dragons were weeping and wailing, which sounded just as terrifying as the earlier shrieking. The dragons were consoling each other.

Dolpho informed them, "We lost more than half of our family today. We've been preparing for hundreds of years for this sacrifice, but the events of today are a wound that will take some time to heal."

Muriel sympathized, "I'm sorry."

Dolpho returned, "Yes, well it seems you both still need to learn to listen much better to survive this mess. I am going to take you back and place you slightly down shore from the fighting. Don't try to fight the demons or you will lose your lives. Retreat to fight another day. Your side isn't properly prepared right now."

As the kids were getting back into Dolpho's mouth, one of the other dragons said, "Be careful, lady. We are nothing without you."

The blue dragon nodded her head and pulled the children into her mouth. They soon reached the surface and walked out onto the moist sand and heard another awful screech from above. Sunny and Muriel started to run inland as a black dragon tracked after them from above. They tried to run in a zigzag pattern but the dragon wasn't fooled as it closed in.

Sunny heard a horrible hissing sound from behind and realized it was coming from Dolpho. He looked back at the sky and the black dragon had changed course and was going for the blue water dragon.

"NO! NO!" screamed Muriel.

Sunny yelled as loud as he could, "Go back under. Go back under."

Dolpho remained still with her head above water. The female dragon couldn't smile but Sunny saw the most gentle and friendliest look a fearsome dragon could possibly carry.

"Run," Dolpho said calmly as a huge shadow formed around her head and the flying dragon made a final stoop to pick up tremendous speed before sinking its talons into Sunny and Muriel's friend. Sunny grabbed his sister so she couldn't watch. They turned and ran, but even the sounds were almost too much to handle as they desperately sprinted back toward the School.

B-RUSSELL

Russell peered into another crack in the mountainside and found nothing but darkness again. He and Lizeria moved on to the next one. They had checked all the openings on this side of the mountain with no luck whatsoever. Russell decided he wasn't going to return to the School of the Learned Warrior without the Pearl. He tried to prepare mentally for the fact that he might die of hunger, far from his original birthplace. He felt sorry for Lizeria and chastised himself constantly for dragging her out here.

If things don't work out, I basically killed her. She would have been fine back at the School. What made me think that she could come on an adventure like this? Riceros is probably gone. He's probably back on Venom Island right now, waiting to have his blood sucked out by a coldomore. I can't return to Dragon-Eyes as a failure again. I just can't do it. I won't do it.

Lizeria tugged at his dirty, brown shirt. Russell looked down at the little girl. She was pointing to a faint light coming from one of the crevasses in the mountain. The dying day helped to expose the tiny fire inside, and Russell and Lizeria instinctively moved toward it. He carefully worked up the side of the hill while simultaneously looking around for any activity. They got about fifteen feet from the crack and stopped. He noticed the opening was too small for him and wondered if Lizeria could fit through the small crack. He wasn't going to try to stuff the little girl in the cave, and sat down behind a cactus to figure out a plan. She plopped down beside Russell and he tried to remain alert in case anything sprang from the hole. An idea struck Russell and he closed his eyes to concentrate.

Mother may I see what I cannot,
A hidden vision now needs to be sought,
Eyes I need to see wrong from right,
And rectify the smallest slight,
Mother grant me the power to see,
If you can pour your pity on me,

His eyes remained closed as his mental vision moved closer to the cave. He could now see inside the hole. A bound Riceros Colbert sat against the back wall of a dusty cave. To the boy's left stood a hideous misshapen man with legs too long, three ears and purple skin. The demon's lips were moving but Russell couldn't hear anything. He had summoned multiple spirits by name before but never from two different chants, so he just blurted out the name, Jahondo.

He could now hear the deep, gnarly voice of the whispering demon. "I can sense it. The demons are close. Without your dragons, we shall secure a quick victory and move inland. I can almost envision those lovely dragons swooping in to take you straight to Damian Doome."

Russell had heard enough and opened his eyes, shook his head around and tried to return to normal. He needed to devise a plan but the only thing that ran through his head was pain from using the magic. He thought about how the spirits could help in a grand battle. The two weary travelers fell asleep behind the cactus on the clay-like ground.

Russell woke up to bright sunlight and panicked because he hadn't planned to fall asleep and worried if they had been spotted. His stomach growled like a starving bear as he tried to focus on a plan. Russell had a thought and whispered to Lizeria about what her role in the plot was. He closed his eyes and concentrated.

Dear mother, can you take away this pain?
Dear mother, can you break this awful chain?
Sweet angel, help make me invisible and plain.
Lend your spirit and the air I'll surely gain.

Russell walked around the cactus and took a few steps toward the hole. He stopped and looked back at Lizeria, who shook her head back and forth to indicate she couldn't see him. He still saw himself but took another few steps and looked back again. Lizeria was still shaking her head. Russell moved slowly up to the opening and pushed his head into the crack. He tried to go inside but his shoulders hit both sides of the crevasse. He hadn't realized that he had an invisible frame over his entire body. He walked back over to the cactus and collapsed in frustration and physical pain. His body ran cold from using the spirits two days in a row and his head started to ache.

Lizeria seemed to be getting restless sitting in one place and started running around the cactus. Russell whispered, "No, Lizeria, we must be quiet and stay back here."

He sat up and Lizeria looked into his eyes and said, "I do."

The little girl took two steps back and turned and ran for the opening. Russell scrambled to his feet and rushed over. The brave girl stuck her tiny head in the cave and said something Russell couldn't identify. She pulled her head out and moved to the left of the crack. He drew his sword and continued running at full speed. He saw something coming from the hole that wasn't Riceros Colbert. He dove and stroked down with his sword as he glided through the air. He couldn't stop as he recognized Kazu too late and the unforgiving blade went right through the old man's head. A black liquid puddled on the ground and a golden whistle fell at Russell's feet. The ebony blood seeped into the clay and he picked up the flute. Lizeria snatched it away from his hand and gazed intently at the beautiful object.

She broke her stare and a strange look came over the girl's face as she pointed behind him. Russell turned to be greeted by a group of spirits levitating off the slanted ground.

Judithe spoke, "We will take care of Lizeria and move that stone to free the one they call Riceros. You need go now, before it's too late."

Suddenly Russell was lifted off the ground. He pointed to the cactus and told Lizeria, "Riceros' bow and quiver are in my shoulder sack. Make sure he gets it."

An invisible force wouldn't let him finish and whisked him through the air and started pushing him north at an amazing speed. He saw a force of men running toward him as he slowed down and came to a complete stop. Leading the evacuation was Dioneer with Dragon-Eyes in his arms.

The Cyclops was screaming, "Go back, we have to go back."

C-RICEROS

Kazu suddenly disappeared from the front of the cave. Riceros rolled over and over and clumsily worked his way to the tiny crack and saw Lizeria's face outside. The golden flute was in her mouth and she was blowing audibly into it, but no beautiful sounds came from the object. Just behind Lizeria, he saw what appeared to be floating ghosts. They looked like glowing white shadows forming the body shape of a man or woman. They were hollow and see-through. As Riceros gazed at them, the tight cords around his wrists and ankles started to magically loosen themselves. He heard a cracking sound as the huge rock started to break up and create a large opening for him to get out. He shook away the silk ties and dove out the hole and into bright sunlight and a cloudy sky.

He fought off the pain, got to his feet and grabbed the flute from Lizeria. He blew lightly into the musical instrument and created an eruption of sounds. The tiny whistle sent rippling waves of energy into the sky. Riceros got nervous when a few moments went by and he didn't see any of the dragons. A sudden gust of wind knocked Riceros and Lizeria down and caused the spirits to evacuate. An enormous collective shadow hung overhead as a bevy of descending noble dragons covered the sky. Riceros extracted the Pearl from his back and saw Lizeria's eyes look like they were going to pop out of her head again when he spread the golden wings out fully.

He wanted to fly up to meet the dragons but didn't want to leave Lizeria by herself.

He heard a voice announce, "We will take care of the girl. Perform your duty to mankind."

Riceros looked around and still didn't see anyone but started flapping his wings anyway and rose off the ground. He quickly flew up and saw Ikeros.

The dragon screamed, "The demons haveth landed. We needeth engage them so the humans can get away. We can't win but we will be slaughtered if we don't help."

They flew up to the northern shore and saw most of the human soldiers running inland. A huge force of coldomores was chasing after them, but their rigid movements allowed the humans to escape. He looked closer at the Sea of Green and saw a charred wasteland of dragon bodies, blacker than the dark of night. Red, black and purple dragons emerged from the sky above the Sea of Green and closed in quickly. The immense heat rippled off Riceros' body and he realized he was about to witness a dragon fight up close. Mind-shattering shrieks of agony pounded his ears as he drew an arrow. He steadied the nock on the bowstring and the tip burst into flames. He noticed Bobular and an enemy dragon circling each other and spitting orange flames back and forth. He studied the movement of the black dragon, drew back on the bowstring and waited. In a flash, the arrow sped through the air and found the hole in the dragon's ear. The injured beast wailed in pain and shook wildly, expelling the demon rider in the process. The dragon twisted around until its head exploded in fire and the wounded animal fell into the water, creating a tidal splash.

Riceros navigated around the chaotic aerial scene and saw Artemise surrounded by two enemy dragons. He tried to get an arrow ready to help but both dragons spit fire in unison and the wild blaze captured the target. His friend, Artemise, tried to fight against death only to crash down into the emerald waters now streaked with ruby. He looked over to see a ship of snarling animals, foaming at the mouth to get in on the action. Out of the corner of his eye, Ikeros glided down and burned the boat of penned up animals. Riceros had heard the sounds of dying men and the Brama Bull on his journey to get to Gama Traka, but there was no comparison to the sounds of the dragons and animals and a full-fledged battle.

The shoreline became the prime battle ground for the flying dragons, good and bad. The blazing brawl between the thousand-year-old beasts made the bright sky light up even more. Riceros' body and wings threatened to quit on him and he noticed that the coldomores had stopped chasing the humans.

Suddenly, Damian Doome's dragons flew back out to sea. Riceros flew back inland and surveyed the mass carnage below. Dragon bodies were scattered about the giant graveyard.

Ikeros flew by and said, "The demons were better prepared this time. Much better prepared than the humans. Don't let this happen again."

Within moments, Riceros was the only object in the sky and he flew back to the southern entrance of the School. He saw the students flooding in the door. He landed and retracted his wings. Riceros walked into the School and down the straight hallway. He looked in the library and noticed Dioneer, Lizeria, Sunny, Muriel, Dragon-Eyes and Shireez huddled around a small bookshelf. A look of relief washed over them when they looked at Riceros but it only lasted a moment.

The Imp Wizard said, "We are going to need more men. Did you see how many ships landed? They only unloaded a few and still chased us away."

Sunny said, "They did use their dragons to gain an unfair advantage. We would have put up a better fight if they hadn't cleared the shoreline like that."

Riceros thought he would be inundated with questions about the kidnapping, but realized everyone's minds had already shifted to the next plan.

Riceros spoke, "At least we found out one thing."

Dragon-Eyes looked skeptically at him and asked, "And what would that be?"

Riceros answered, "We need to develop a new plan to defeat Damian Doome and his army of dragons, wild beasts and coldomores."

Epilogue

So two contenders perished and one was overthrown as Queen, that much we know, but a few mysteries still persist. Who killed King Ali-Stanley? Will his twin brother, Ali-Steven, survive his ghastly injury? Will any of it matter if Damian Doome claims the earth for the demons? Three seasons turned an entire kingdom on its ear. Four kings had already taken turns ruling until they were dead or run out of the King's Castle and the year wasn't even close to being over. What does winter have in store? I know of one thing, that's for sure. Wings, sweet children, dragon wings."

Telly told her stories to the riveted crowd but Mim had trouble paying attention because she kept thinking about the illuminated pages of her book. Her aunt finished and Mim headed back toward her room. She saw the workers already bringing in items for the Spring Tournament. She knew this would continue and only get more hectic as they got closer to the date. She couldn't wait to get a chance to talk to many of the people from her books. People were coming in from all over the kingdom and Mim planned to check a few stories for factual integrity and who better than the first-hand sources. She also wanted to find out what the people from her books had been doing for the past thirty years. Mim wanted to make an addendum to her books with the information she gathered at the Tournament. She walked around for a bit to check out a few more deliveries that had piqued her interest and went back to her room. When she arrived, Telly, Paul and a handmaiden were waiting outside her door. The young woman announced, "Lady Mim, I present Queen Telly and Prince Paul." She curtsied and left.

The Queen of Donegal looked at Mim and said, "There is a serious matter that we need to discuss."

I hope you've enjoyed the journey so far and if you want to receive author updates and special offers from Jason Paul Rice, sign up here: http://jasonpaulricebooks.com/

That's three books down and one left to go in The Pearl of Wisdom Saga. Thanks for making it this far and if you have a minute to spare, I would love if you could leave a quick review for the book on Amazon. I will leave links and would be honored to hear your thoughts on the book. Thank you.

Amazon US- https://www.amazon.com/dp/B01MRGZ6GH/

Amazon UK- https://www.amazon.co.uk/dp/B01MRGZ6GH/

Amazon CA- https://www.amazon.ca/dp/B01MRGZ6GH/

Amazon AU- https://www.amazon.com.au/d/B01MRGZ6GH/

www.ingramcontent.com/pod-product-compliance
Lightning Source LLC
Chambersburg PA
CBHW061318170626
46817CB00001B/221